St. Martin's Paperbacks Titles
by David Poyer

THE MED

THE GULF

THE GULF

DAVID POYER

ST. MARTIN'S PAPERBACKS

ACKNOWLEDGMENTS

Ex nihilo nihil fit. For this work of fiction I owe much to James Allen, Park Balevre, Eric Berryman, Jean-Philippe Cadoret, Daniel Flynn, Kelly Fisher, Wayne Fuller, Vince Goodrich, John Gorton, Frank and Amy Green, Paul Golubovs, Lenore Hart, Robert Kelly, Chuck Key, Carl Kilhoffer, Sid Perryman, Art Riccio, Ervin Tate, Tim Taylor, William and Fran Schubert, Jim Sullivan, Nemat Tokmachi, C. T. Walters, George Witte, and many others who gave generously of their time to contribute or criticize. All errors and deficiencies are my own.

On the far side of the earth
You were our walls, steel and flesh,
Against the barbarisms of our century.
Yours was a strange war, a half-war, shadowy and
constrained.
This novel is dedicated to all those who serve in what we
call peace—though it isn't.
But especially for the officers, men, and families of U.S.S.
Stark and U.S.S. Samuel B. Roberts,
For the other sailors, marines, and support personnel of
the Middle East Force and the Indian Ocean Battle Group,
And for all those who made the last
sacrifice for what they believed was right.

Shake off this fever of ignorance. Stop hoping for worldly rewards. . . . Be free from the sense of ego. Dedicate all your actions to Me. Then go forward and fight.

—The Bhagavad Gita, III

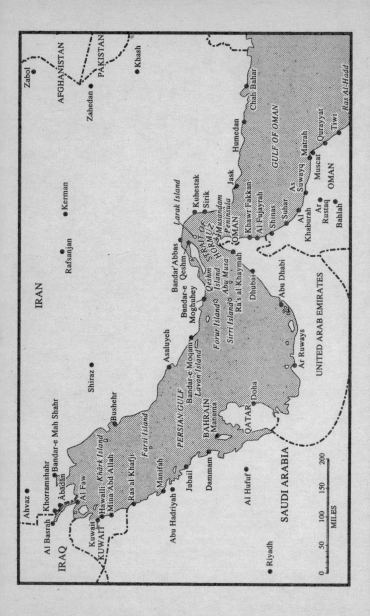

Prologue

The Persian Gulf:
U.S.S. *Louis Strong,* FF-1099

THE forward lookout, a twenty-year-old seaman from Chula Vista, was lighting his fifteenth Winston of the morning when he saw the incoming missile.

He had been straining his eyes against the sand-colored sky for hours since dawn and at first he did not recognize it. It was only a far-off wisp of smoke, not unlike the smoke from the flareoff towers that dotted this upper part of the Gulf between Kuwait and the Iranian-declared Exclusion Zone.

A moment later, he lifted his head from his cupped hands, frowning back at that same chunk of horizon. The moving haze was already noticeably nearer, and over the tan sea, stirred by the faint hot breath of a dying *shamal,* he could make out something dark inside it.

He forgot the cigarette. The lighter clattered on the deck as he jammed down the button on his phones and shouted, "Missile! Incoming! Bearing one-two-zero!"

"Say again, Butt Kit," said a bored voice in his ear. "An' make it in English this time, okay?"

"Jesus Christ, listen up! I said there is a fucking mee-sel comin' at us, you dipshit!"

At that moment, two decks above, the destroyer's captain—thirty-eight years old, from Kansas City—was reading the morning's radio traffic. Perched in his chair on the bridge wing, where it was slightly cooler than the oven the pilothouse became at twenty-eight degrees latitude, he was not so absorbed that he missed the sudden frantic gesture of the man on the bow. His glance followed the pointed arm.

"Oh, no," he whispered. Then, instantly and in the same breath, shouted through the open door, "OOD! Cruise missile incoming, starboard! Come right, notify CIC, fire chaff. Sound general quarters!"

As the alarm began, the officer of the deck, a lieutenant from St. Cloud, Minnesota, shouted rapidly, "Right hard rudder, ahead flank emergency. Fire the chaff. Fire it now, God damn it!"

He turned and put his glasses on the incoming weapon. In the twin circles of the 7X50s he could see it clearly. It was nose-on to him. It gleamed in the sun ahead of a twisting haze of exhaust. It was very low, no more than a hundred feet off the chop.

"Rudder hard right, sir!" The scared voice of the seaman apprentice behind the helm.

The captain shouted over his shoulder, "Steady up short, keep the launcher unmasked."

"Aye, sir. Steady zero-eight-zero."

Crump. Crump. Crump. Behind them, dulled by the steel doors the bo's'n had just slammed and dogged, they heard the chaff mortars fire. Given ten seconds, their bloom of thousands of foil shreds would present the missile's radar with six or eight false *Strongs.* Given twelve, their flares would ignite, pinpoint sources of intense heat to decoy away an infrared homer.

Through the glasses, the lieutenant could make out stubby fins.

There might not be twelve seconds.

In the Combat Information Center, aft and below the bridge, six men were already at radarscopes and weapons consoles. Sliding back into the chair he'd left to use the head, the electronic-warfare petty officer, a twenty-five-year-old from Sheboygan, froze as he recognized the pattern on his screen. Then he began punching buttons. He had twelve Soviet-bloc threat profiles in the computer. What he saw matched none of them.

"Cruise missile, unknown type!" he shouted, bracing with one hand against the sudden heel. "I-band altimeter, H-band seeker, radar homer, bearing one-one-five, threat close!"

"Jam it!" shouted the captain, appearing at the bottom of the ladder from the bridge. "Rossetti! Sea Sparrow, two-round engagement, now!"

"Point defense, locked on!" shouted a chief.

The tactical-action officer lifted a red cover and stabbed the button beneath it. Through the muffled whine of turbines climbing to full power came a sudden, deafening roar. "Missile away," shouted the chief. Two seconds later, another roar shuddered the plates and dwindled away.

The captain said rapidly, "Mitch, do a three-sixty search. Look for the launching platform. Get me a range and bearing."

He reached for a handset and began barking at the gunnery officer. On the radar, a first-class OS from Baltimore leaned to watch two pulses of light move away from the center of the screen, so rapidly they jumped outward with each sweep.

The lead one reached the incoming missile.

"CIC, Bridge: Warhead detonation to starboard, looked close. Wait a second—no, he just came out of the smoke. Target's still incoming."

The TAO reached instantly for the REFIRE button, but before his hand reached it, the chief said: "Six thousand yards, sir. It's inside minimum range."

"Second round intercepts—*now.*"

The GQ bell stopped ringing. The metallic voice of the announcing system said, all over the ship, "General quarters, general quarters. No drill. Missile incoming, starboard side."

"Terminal seeker, locked on," said the twenty-five-year-old, his eyes blasted wide as he stared into the green flicker on his screen. He turned up the speaker and the high-pitched whine of the lock-on jerked everyone's head toward it.

"CIC, Bridge," said the suddenly empty voice of the lieutenant, above them. "Our second round went right by it. Still boosting. Couldn't have been twenty feet apart. But no burst. It's coming right down our throat."

The captain barked into the phone, "What's the problem with the fucking five-inch?"

"We've got ammo at the transfer tray now—maybe fifteen, twenty more seconds, sir—"

The captain stopped thinking. He put out his hand to the bulkhead and bent his knees slightly. There was nothing else left to do.

The thirteen-foot-long missile's starboard wing root had been punctured by the expanding-rod warhead of the first antiaircraft round. This slowed it from .89 to .80 Mach, but the guidance computer trimmed to correct for the off-center drag, and it steadied again.

Now, in the last seconds of its flight, its discrimination circuits evaluated and then disregarded the still-expanding chaff clouds. It had picked up the ship's radar and homed on it for four seconds, but now it ignored that, too, and for the last mile locked on the plume of heat blasting out of the frigate's stack.

It tilted its rear fins slightly, arched up and over in a graceful snap dive, and hit the still-turning ship on the main deck, starboard side, frame 103.

This was the boat deck, and the missile, traveling at six hundred miles an hour, passed beneath the motor whaleboat and squarely between two steel davits. They sheared off its stub wings. The warhead and fuselage, with several hundred pounds of fuel remaining, penetrated the quarter-inch aluminum skin of the superstructure at a thirty-degree down angle.

The outer plating hardly slowed the airframe, but it sliced dozens of rents in the fuselage. Fire leapt from the still-burning engine.

The first set of compartments it entered were the starboard potable-water station, a firemain jumper station, and the executive officer's stateroom. The executive officer and a damage controlman died instantly. Continuing downward and to port, the missile entered the main-deck passageway, shedding parts. So far, a fiftieth of a second had passed since impact.

The steel main deck separated the airframe and the warhead. The fuselage rebounded from it and split apart. Its fragments scythed through the waist of the ship: staterooms, fan rooms, wardroom, and sick bay. Its sustainer disintegrated, scattering chunks of the solid fuel, burning at 3,200 degrees and containing its own oxygen, behind the flying metal.

The steel-cased warhead had been designed to penetrate the armor of a Soviet *Kynda*-class cruiser. It continued through the main deck into the engineering spaces. In main control, a chief warrant and two enginemen were blown into the electrical control panel as the warhead passed through. It continued out the port bulkhead and entered the main machinery space. It passed over the number-two boiler, shearing steam and feedwater lines, penetrated another deck, went through five feet of beef in a chill-storage locker, and detonated ten feet below the waterline in shaft alley number one.

The officer of the deck was looking aft when the missile hit. He saw no flash, no explosion, felt only a quiver beneath his feet and then the *wham* of a solid hit. Black smoke burst out of the uptakes, followed by fire and pieces of burning insulation. A low rumble came from aft.

There was a sudden eerie whir, descending the scale. The intake blowers, gyros, ventilators, all wound downward into a silence more disquieting than sound. Suddenly, he could hear the lazy slap of flags, could hear yelling and the pounding of feet aft. The frigate, losing way through the water, leaned gently to port.

"Captain's on the bridge!"

The lieutenant spun to face him. "We've lost power, sir," he said. "Lost propulsion, radio—"

"Still got sound-powered comms?"

"Yessir," said the phone talker.

"Call main control."

"They don't answer, sir, DC central's been calling them."

"Okay. Keep the lookouts alert. If you see another one coming in, use the manual toggle to fire the rest of the chaff." The CO pressed the intercom lever, but it was dead. "I'm going aft, see what we got."

"Yes, sir."

"Get one of the battery-powered radios going. See if you can raise somebody, get the word out we've been hit. Give them our position and ask them to pass it to MIDEASTFOR on three-oh-two point five. Keep your head, think slow, do what needs doing. I'll get us out of this."

"Yes, sir," said the lieutenant again, looking after him.

The 250 pounds of explosive in the warhead had blown a chunk of the ship's hull plating outward, below the waterline. Now the warm Gulf poured in. In the engine room, just above, super-heated steam had displaced the air. Main Control no longer existed. No one was alive there.

In engineering berthing, four men had been changing linens and waxing the decks. They had all gone through a blindfolded escape drill the week before. This was all that saved them when the lights went out and the compartment suddenly filled with flying flame.

The location of the hit, midships angling down, providentially missed most of the areas where the crew concentrated during general quarters. But some men had lingered for a few seconds, over bug juice on the mess decks, over coffee in the chiefs' quarters, over doughnuts in the wardroom or at their desks over paperwork. These men died or now lay unconscious, their lungs filling with smoke.

The others, belowdecks in the feeble glow of battle lanterns, squatted or stood awaiting orders. In every man's mind, the desire to bolt for open air struggled with his training and the duty to stay at his station.

A few bolted. Most stayed. Gradually, over sound-powered circuits and by word of mouth, it filtered through the ship. They'd been hit amidships, the engine room was knocked out, and they had a fire to fight—a big fire.

The men in the damage-control lockers had been dressing out when the missile struck. Repair Two was twenty feet aft of the explosion and their door was jammed shut by buckled steel. They cooked to death over the next fifteen minutes. The two other teams simply continued their routine, though now their hearts speeded up. They rolled down their sleeves, pulled their socks over their pants legs, and buttoned the collars of their dungaree shirts. They struggled into OBAs, clumsy rubber-and-metal breathing devices, slapped green cans into them, and pulled tabs to light off the oxygen candles. They buckled on steel helmets, then grabbed their tools and lines and lights and began groping toward the growing roar of the fire.

Behind them, other men unrolled hoses and spun brass caps off the ship's firemain. A little water spurted out, then stopped. The fire pumps were driven by steam and the single firemain was ruptured in three places. The team leaders hesitated. One grabbed a CO_2 canister and tried it on a burning cord of solid fuel. The propellant dimmed for a moment, then blazed up again when the extinguisher hissed empty.

Above them, on the flight deck, other men worked desperately to prime and start gasoline-powered pumps. In a few minutes, they began to buzz, like lawn mowers on a suburban Saturday morning.

Meanwhile the fire gathered strength. Fuel tanks, paint storerooms, helicopter fuel, lubricants, wooden shoring, vinyl tile on decks, insulation, the very paint on the bulkheads, all ignited. Above the main deck, the frigate's structure was aluminum, not steel, and it began to soften, like chocolate on a hot day. Furniture, bunks, carpets, cabinets full of paper reached flash point and burst suddenly into flame. And above that, as the overheads sagged and split apart, the heat licked upward toward the torpedo room and the helicopter hangar on the 01 level.

In DC central, eighty feet forward of the hit and the fire, the damage-control officer, an ensign from Lubbock, Texas, looked at the first reports from his investigators. He had to deal with both fire and flooding. He knew it was impossible to extinguish the burning propellant, as he would a normal fire. He now decided to try to slow its lateral spread by venting heat upward. Holes at frames 100 and 125 might channel the fire around the torpedo room. For a while, at least. Control of the flooding would have to wait. He scribbled notes and handed them to grimy, scared-looking messengers.

Deep in the ship, the hoses went rigid at last, fed by the portable pumps. The nozzlemen from Repair Five began shuffling forward, walking under a blast of water mist from applicators held by the number-two men.

They walked into a white hell. Through the eyepieces of their masks, they could see the flame-outlined sag of cables drooping from the overheads, ready to snag them. The overheads were on fire. The tile decks were on fire, and though they quenched when water hit them, they reignited as soon as it boiled off. The air was impenetrable with smoke and steam.

The team leader, advancing with his men, screamed as the heat penetrated his dungarees. The cotton did not flame or melt. The nylon jockey shorts beneath did, shriveling, fusing to his skin. The nozzleman ran with him. The second man on the hose did not. He moved up, pulled the bail back to release a blast of water, and began edging forward again, into the smoke and growing heat.

They came to a watertight door, closed and dogged when the ship went to general quarters. The number-two man smashed a porthole to get it open. Fire leapt out, melted his mask, and burned his hair and his face off. The number-three man stepped up and ripped his breathing bags open on a whetted shard of steel. He staggered back, sucking hot smoke instead of oxygen. The number-four man took his place and played the hose over the door, the stream spitting and boiling, then stuck it through the porthole. He left it there for a minute, then banged the dogs free and yanked the door open. The applicator man and the hose man followed him in.

The furnace beyond had been the crew's mess. Now the vinyl chairs and Formica tables glowed yellow deep in the smoke. Pieces of the missile engine were still burning like white flares. The rails of the serving line glowed a soft neon red. Above their heads, liquid copper dripped from cable runs. On the deck, bodies burned with the smoky orange of grease fires. The flames roared hollowly all around them. The three men felt their clothes catch fire. The rubber of their OBAs began to smoke. The nozzleman hesitated. Something heavy crashed through the overhead to his left.

He began backing out. But when they tried to retreat, they found an aluminum ladder had melted over the hatchway.

No one had anticipated the need to cut through the deck. The men ordered to do it hoped the special tools for getting pilots out of burning helicopters would work, but they bounced off. At last, the biggest began swinging fire axes. Each blow made only a dent, but gradually they hewed out foot-wide gaps. Like small volcanoes, each hole vented a jet of mingled flame and smoke straight up into the air.

In the helo hangar, three of the aircrewmen struggled with their machine. The tires had melted and it wouldn't roll. At last they abandoned it, and ran aft as the explosive charges on the sonobuoys began popping, sending metal pinging and whirring after them.

Just forward of them, the torpedomen, exercising their own initiative, had begun jettisoning their Mark 46s as soon as they realized the fire was gnawing its way up below them. They had enough compressed air in ready flasks to fire them over the side, but it was a slow process. They first had to move each weapon to the tube with chain hoists and dollies, by hand, without power. They had five torpedoes left when the paint on the deck ignited and they had to clear the compartment. They ran, screaming as the deck by the vent holes burned through the soles of their boots.

The captain stood on the flight deck. Between him and the bridge was a smoking mass of superstructure with flame spewing out of the 02 level. The pumps whined at full speed around him.

One of the torpedomen pounded by him. The captain caught him by the arm and asked him an urgent question. The man's face was blistered. He shook his head violently, held up five fingers.

The captain looked around, at the sea.

The ship lay sagging to port in the center of a blue emptiness. Some distance off to the east was the purple cloud of a small island. Beyond that was Iran. To starboard, the water was oily and speckled with floating debris. He thought he saw a body, but it could have been something else. The ship, still with way on, moved slowly past it. More debris took its place. The oil gentled the waves. Beyond that was empty sea, but he knew that farther off, maybe fifty miles, was the coast of Saudi Arabia.

The captain wanted to go forward. He wanted to regain his bridge, and he wanted to go to damage-control central, where the battle against fire and flooding was being coordinated. It didn't look like he could make it on the main deck, though. Below, it would be even worse.

"Chief."

"Sir."

"Take one of these pumps forward. Get water on those torpedoes."

Both of them knew what this order meant. The chief nodded and turned away. He shouted to two men to grab pump and hoses and follow him.

At last the captain took a deep breath and sprinted down the starboard side. The heat staggered him and he blundered through the blazing remains of the whaleboat with his hands over his face. For a moment, he thought he would die. Then he was in clear air again, slapping at his uniform pants. They were a new polyester the Navy had approved in place of cotton. They were sharp-looking, permanent press, but now they shriveled and burst into flame. He got them off, pulling off flesh with the burning fabric, and climbed back to the bridge.

The officer of the deck looked glad to see him. "Were you able to raise anybody?" the captain asked him.

"Got a Belgian freighter. She's putting out a Mayday for us. Sir, we have high-temp alarms in the hangar, torpedo stowage, main control—"

"I know."

The ship groaned and clattered under their feet, settling farther to port. The captain pulled out a phone and talked briefly with the damage-control officer, then put it back. "The engine spaces are flooding," he said softly, as if to himself. "The fire's right over them. I can't get portable pumps down there. The bilge pumps are electric. And I can't run the submersibles without power or the eductors without firemain pressure."

"We can dewater with P-250s."

"Not fast enough. I think we've got a big hole down there." He looked to port. "This class won't stay afloat with the engine spaces flooded. How deep is it here?"

"Six hundred feet, sir," said the quartermaster.

"I hope they saved a fucking lot of money on this ship," said the captain softly.

"DC central reports: team from Repair Five has been forced back by fire."

The first torpedo cooked off then, mowing down the pump crews on the flight deck. The secondary conning station made a somersault in the air and plunged down on the burning gig. The captain rose from an instinctive crouch, looking aft. The flames occupied the entire midships now. The frigate gave a lurch and slid farther over to port. It was now listing perhaps forty degrees and was noticeably lower in the water aft.

"All this from one missile," said the lieutenant.

"One missile," said the captain.

"Whose was it? What kind was it? Soviet?"

"No," said the captain. "It was a Harpoon. One of ours."

He took a last deep breath, then picked up the phone again.
"DC central, Bridge. This is Captain Shaker. Bring your people
out on deck. Yes. Get them all up from below." To the lieutenant, he said, "How far away you figure this freighter is?"

"About twenty miles, coming north, toward us."

"Call them back. Ask them to render assistance."

"We're not going to leave her, sir?"

"I may have to," said the captain. He looked back along the
length of the ship again. A second torpedo went off, blowing
shattered Plexiglas past him; he ducked back just in time. A
huge mushroom of inky smoke stuffed with red fire rose above
the listing destroyer.

That made up his mind. He said, "Okay, we've done our best.
Let's get as many off alive as we can. Tell Radio to commence
crypto destruction. Abandon with life rafts and jackets, off the
starboard side, and keep them clear of the oil."

When the lieutenant and the others left, the captain re-
mained, standing in the center of his bridge. Looking down at
his burning, sinking ship, then out at the emptiness of the Gulf.
He touched the flaking gray paint of the binnacle, then closed
his eyes for a moment, shuddering with emotion he only now
had begun to feel. From aft, now, he could hear the screams
over the growing roar of flame.

They surprised me, Benjamin Shaker thought. We weren't
ready for this. They told me it couldn't happen.

But next time we'll be ready.

And next time, I'll make them pay.

I

THE CALM

1

Mina' Salman, Bahrain

THE thin officer in dress whites dragged a sleeve over his forehead, then tucked his thumbs back under his sword belt. The August morning was hot and airless as the inside of an oil drum—and smelled like it. Only the shade of a canvas awning made being in the open bearable at all.

Lieutenant-Commander Daniel V. Lenson, U.S. Navy, turned from the shore. His narrowed glance found his watch, then flicked critically around at the ranked chairs, the newly painted deck, the lectern. He watched two boatswain's mates sweating the belly out of the awning. His eyes lingered on a mahogany stand holding the motionless flags of the United States, Bahrain, and the U.S. Navy, then swung outward again, searching the pier and beyond it the low line of land.

U.S.S. *Turner Van Zandt*, FFG-91, lay starboard side to alongside a concrete quay half a mile long. She was the only Navy ship there, compact, gray, and deadly looking amid a hodgepodge of tankers, freighters, and one patrol boat of the Bahraini Defense Force.

Lenson squinted into sun glare dazzling as a welder's arc. The harbor had the flat, oily gleam of dead calm. Eastward, between it and the open Gulf, the shallows of the Khawr al Qualay'ah glowed like murky turquoise under a sky the color of sandpaper. At the foot of the pier, straight as a gunshot, was the shorefront town of Mina' Salman, and beyond it Manama, the capital of this island sheikhdom. From here, all he could see of it were the needles of minarets and a green water tank. The waterfront was prefabricated warehouses, concrete silos, the gallows shapes of Japanese-made container cranes. The earth was the color of sand. The air smelled of hot tar and dust. And it was unbearably humid—as usual.

It wasn't much of a place for a change of command. But then,

Dan thought, it was better than Sitra anchorage, where American warships usually spent their liberty. Manama was the closest thing to a friendly port the Gulf offered these days. But that didn't mean it was fun.

"Awning's rigged, XO. If the *shamal* comes up, it'll flap, but it'll hold."

Dan straightened from his musing. Lieutenant (junior grade) Steve Charaler, *Van Zandt*'s perpetually harassed first lieutenant, looked out of place in service dress white, combination cap, white gloves. The redheaded deck officer spent most of his time in scuffed combat boots and khakis that looked as if they'd been bought secondhand from Mister Goodwrench.

"Button your collar, Steve."

"Aw, just till—"

"Your lip, too." Dan glanced at the canvas. "You've got Irish pennants on the quarter. And coil down the rigging lines. Get it squared away; there's a sedan on the pier."

"Yessir." Charaler headed off, yanking at his collar and shouting for BM2 Stanko. Dan adjusted the gold braid sword knot, Naval Academy issue that came already tied, thank God, and took a last turn round the ceremonial area. He stepped to the lectern, tapped the mike, and said, "One, two, three." His voice boomed out satisfactorily. On three sides, ranked along the deck edge, the crew fidgeted and sweated at ease.

The guests began arriving. Bob Ekdahl, the officer of the deck, came back from the quarterdeck with the telescope under his arm. He was leading a dark man with a mustache. Lenson greeted him warmly. Achmed Turani, the husbanding agent, decided how fast their water and garbage would be taken care of. The Arab was followed by the American consul, two liaison officers, the commanding officer of the Bahraini gunboat, and two of his men. *Van Zandt*'s junior officers ushered them to seats. There were no women. It was a remarkable thing even to see a woman in the streets of Manama.

He hadn't figured on a heavy attendance. Stateside, a change of command was an occasion. The families and friends of the oncoming and offgoing captains were invited. There would be press people, maybe even a TV crew if you were in your home port.

Things were different in the Gulf. He glanced up. At the frigate's masthead, a radar antenna rotated tirelessly. There were men on watch in CIC, and directly above him, atop the helo hangar, the six barrels of the Phalanx gun poked out aggressively.

Iranian waters were fifty miles distant. Alongside a pier or not, they were in a war zone.

Van Zandt was part of the recent beef-up of U.S. forces in the Gulf. She'd arrived two months before, and had four to go before she returned to the States. Under the operational control of Commander, Middle East Force, she was assigned at the moment to a surveillance and escort operation called "Earnest Will," convoying American and Kuwaiti tankers between the Arabian Sea and their onload points in the north.

Dan rocked on the balls of his feet, glancing shoreward again. The front row of chairs was still empty. After coming aboard briefly yesterday, the new commanding officer had spent the night ashore. No ship was big enough for two captains. But where was he now?

Ekdahl, beside him, said, "Admiral's here."

As they left the shade, the sun hit hard. Visible waves of heat shuddered off the steel deck. Dan got to the quarterdeck just as the boatswain's pipe began shrilling. He nudged one of the sideboys into alignment, ran an eye over the area—just swept, good—and took his place by the brow. He nodded to Ekdahl. A moment later, six slow bells trembled in the heated air.

"Commander, Middle East Force, arriving."

The pipe shrilled again. The sideboys saluted, Dan with them, as Rear Admiral Stansfield Hart, USN, loped up the gangway, followed by two aides. He returned the salute. The sideboys held it, then the call ended; their hands snapped down.

"Good morning, Admiral."

"Morning. Where's . . . Oh. You're the executive officer? Lenson?"

"Yes, sir."

"Good to meet you."

"Nice to meet you, Admiral."

Dan led the party aft and got them seated. The aides took chairs in back. He winked at one of them, Jack Byrne, Hart's intelligence officer. Byrne winked slowly behind dark glasses. The other staffie was the chaplain. He glanced at the crew; Charaler had already put them at parade rest.

"Sit down a minute, Mr. Lenson," Hart muttered. "How's Charlie holding up?"

"I think he'll be all right for the turnover, sir. After that . . . I don't know."

"I told him he shouldn't have waited. Not with cancer. He's gambling with his life. But"—the admiral squinted up at the awning—"I might have done the same . . . anyway. I imagine you've been carrying a lot of the load for him."

Lenson hesitated. Hart saw it. "I know, I know, you don't want to say. I thought about you, by the way, when they told me Bell had to be replaced."

"About me?"

"About fleeting you up instead of ordering in somebody new. Don't tell me you hadn't considered that possibility." Hart grinned suddenly. "But you're still a little too junior, and you'd need your command quals. It wasn't anything personal."

Dan nodded. It didn't happen often, going from XO to CO on the same ship, but then commanding officers didn't get medically relieved that often, either. And he'd finished his command qualification. But this didn't seem like the time to bring it up. The decision had been made. Meanwhile, Hart was looking around. "Hell, where *is* Shaker? You might get it yet, if he doesn't show up pretty soon."

At that moment Dan saw a set of trop whites and commander's stripes swing out of a taxi and jog up the gangway, tossing a salute toward the ensign. "He's coming aboard now, sir."

"Okay, good. How long are you going to be pierside? Aren't you on this next convoy?"

"Yes, sir. We'll be heading south day after tomorrow."

"Let's get the show on the road, then."

The trop whites slid into a seat in the back. Lenson got up. He looked searchingly around one last time. The crew waited, quieted by the gold braid in the front row. Beyond them, the harbor glittered and the shore burned silently in the sun. He could hear the whir of the motors in the gun above them, the hum of the blowers forward, the gentle slap of sea against the hull. He adjusted his sword, squared his shoulders, and walked to the podium.

"Ship's company: A-ten *hut!*"

The lines of sailors clicked into rigidity. Lenson cleared his throat. With the amplifier on, it sounded awful.

"Good morning, Admiral, Consul, honored guests, officers and men. This is the change of command ceremony for the relief of Captain Charles Bell, U.S. Navy, commanding U.S.S. *Turner Van Zandt,* by Commander Benjamin Shaker, USN. Chaplain Grace will read the invocation."

He stood to the side, head bent, for the prayer. He glanced at Turani, thinking only then of the Moslem. But Grace made it general and short, mentioning "our heavenly Father" only once and leaving Jesus out entirely. When the crew said "Amen," Dan nodded to Ekdahl, who was watching him from the quarterdeck.

"The Star-Spangled Banner" played scratchily over the ship's announcing system, interrupted by an electronic whine each time the radar went around. Lenson watched the crew; as he'd drilled them, they waited till Hart started to salute and then tried to beat his hand up. For a working crew, tired of the bone after refresher training, a long transit, and months of escort duty, he thought they looked damn sharp.

The Bahraini anthem was next. When it hissed to a stop, Dan stepped to the lectern again. He said loudly, "Captain Charles Bell."

The crews' eyes swung toward the helo hangar. From its shadow, a thin figure came slowly out into the light.

Captain Bell did not look far from death. The flesh of his face had baked away, and the body beneath the starched whites was angular. He moved slowly, holding himself erect with visible strain. Rick Guerra, the engineering officer, kept pace a step behind. Dan gripped the lectern, praying him on.

Would I do that? he wondered. Stay with my ship when I knew what he knows?

"Parade rest," murmured the captain. His thin, trembling fingers went white on the wood and Dan stood aside, melting into the line of officers along the quarter.

"Good morning," said Bell. "I believe . . . I believe you all know me. Hello, Stan. Hello, back there, Ben. Glad you could make it."

The crew laughed a little. Hart smiled. It looked as if it took an effort. Bell flexed his fingers, then regripped the lectern.

"I know this is a little early to leave. But you know how it is with us old guys. We just can't take these heavy liberties all the time." His strained, gaunt face cracked into a grin and the crew laughed again, this time with a tone of unease.

Bell's voice gathered strength. "Seriously, though. I've been aboard *Van Zandt* for a little over a year, and I feel I know you about as well as I've ever known a crew. I wanted to tell you, by the way, that I was looking at *The International Herald Tribune* international edition this morning, and we made the front page again. The people back home know what we're doing out here, and they appreciate it.

"Our job out here is very simple: to keep the sea lanes open, to our friends and to neutral nations alike, and to defend the right of free passage as laid down in the United Nations Char-

ter and the International Law of the Sea. This has been the
Navy's mission since Bainbridge and Truxtun fought pirates
not far from here."

He turned aside for a moment. The coughs tore out from deep
in his chest. Dan was about to step forward, but Bell recovered.
He lowered his handkerchief and glared out at the silent ranks
before him.

"Your efforts over the last months have made me very proud.
From the enginemen to the signalmen, the ops specialists,
who've spent so much time at the scopes . . . the supply personnel, who keep us fed . . . and my wardroom, all fine officers. I
believe this is the proudest ship in the Navy, and at this moment, I am the proudest man in the world."

Lenson looked at him. Yes. There were tears in the Old Man's
eyes. He made as if to help, but Bell stopped him with a short,
angry chop of his hand. "That's all right, XO. I'm almost done.

"I have not been an emotional man. The service does not
entrust its ships to such. But here at the end of our association,
I find myself growing emotional. So be it! I'm going home now.
Perhaps I stayed too long. I thought it was my duty. That is my
only excuse.

"My only regret is that I couldn't finish this cruise with you,
and stand on the bridge as the first lines go over, and we see
our families waiting on the pier. But I have not been given that.
So I will say to you now, trust Captain Shaker as you have
trusted me. Take care of yourselves. And all of you—go with
God."

He stepped back shakily. Guerra, behind him, extended an
arm. Bell leaned on it, closing his eyes, as the short man in solid
gold shoulderboards stood. Dan recovered himself and bent to
the mike. "Rear Admiral Stansfield Hart, Commander, Middle
East Force."

Hart began with a review of *Van Zandt*'s record. A 3.9 out
of 4.0 in the last operational propulsion plant examination. Administrative inspection, outstanding. Second highest re-enlist-
ment rate in the squadron. Battle *E*'s for excellence in
weapons, operations, and engineering, and the squadron *E* the
second year in a row. Dan stood impassively at parade rest, but
he felt proud.

"This ship has prepared itself to go in harm's way," Hart
rumbled, looking directly at the enlisted. "You men have
worked hard and done well. You're standard setters, and as my
staff knows, I've mentioned you perhaps too often to less outstanding units. *Van Zandt* is the kind of ship, and you're the

kind of crew, I'd like with me when I go into battle. I have to
compliment Charlie for a job well done.

"But it's only half-done. You're taking a solid hit losing him.
But I know you'll pull together and continue your performance
during the remainder of your deployment. I expect it, the Navy
expects it, and I know Charlie, too, expects it. We'll all be sorry
to see him go, but I for one am sure he'll be back with us in not
too long a time."

Hart stepped back, and Dan moved up again. Bending
slightly—the mike had been set for Hart—he said, "Commander Benjamin Shaker."

As the oncoming captain stood for a moment, looking down
at his notes, Lenson examined his profile. He knew without
looking that every other man in the crew was doing the
same thing. They all knew about the loss of the *Strong.* The
knowledge was a shadow in their faces. They had no wish to
. . . no, forget that, Dan told himself. He forced himself to
pay attention. The relieving officer's speech was traditionally
short.

"Good morning, Admiral, officers of the staff, honored
guests, wardroom and crew of *Van Zandt.*

"I know this is an occasion of mixed feelings. You're losing
a fine man. I've known Charlie Bell and his lovely wife, Glynda,
since we served together on the old 'Smoky Joe,' DDG-16.

"I'll wait till later to tell you about myself and about my
plans. I only hope that I can do half as well here in the Gulf,
can establish half as good a record, as he has. I give you my
word, Admiral—and to you men, too—I'll try my best.

"I will now read my orders.

"From: Bureau of Naval Personnel. To: Commander Benjamin Shaker, USN. Upon receipt of these orders, you will detach
as administrative officer, Commander, Surface Forces Atlantic,
and proceed to the port where U.S.S. *Turner Van Zandt* may
be. Report to Commander, Middle East Force, to relieve the
present commanding officer. Travel arrangements—" He
stopped. "I won't read that," he said, and the crew laughed a
little.

Shaker faced Bell then. His hand snapped up. "I relieve you,
sir."

"I stand relieved," whispered Commander Bell. Dan bit his
lip. For just a moment, he'd seen through the iron self-disci-
pline. The look of a dying man, relieved of a load grown too
heavy to bear.

He'd fought to the end, fought the final adversary, to keep

his ship. But now she and all who sailed in her belonged to
another.

From the 02 level, half an hour later, Lenson looked aft along
the pier. First Division was squaring away the ratguards. Two
men from M division were swapping out a shore power plug.
The admiral's sedan was gone. The taxi to Bahrain airport was
gone, too. His hand still felt strange from that last handshake.
Usually, in the service, you said so long, not goodbye. Almost
always, you'd run into a shipmate again.

But he knew he'd never see Charles Bell again.

There was a low whine above him and a burst of white smoke
shot from the stack. As the whine increased to a dull roar, it
turned brownish, then became an invisible stream of heat in the
already-hot air.

Leaning out over the lifelines, he ran his eyes from stem to
stern.

Van Zandt was a guided-missile frigate, smaller than a destroyer or cruiser, but tamped tight with nearly the same weapons and electronics. She displaced 3,700 tons, half again that of
a World War II destroyer, but was about the same length. Two
20,000-horsepower gas turbines drove her at thirty knots, almost thirty-five miles an hour.

Forward on the forecastle was a dual-purpose missile
launcher, and below it, inside the hull, a rotary magazine of
antiship and antiaircraft missiles. On her port and starboard
beams were triple torpedo tubes. One deck above him were the
guns, an automatic three-inch Oto Melara and the twenty-milli-
meter Phalanx. Aft was the hangar and flight deck. The *Perry*-
class frigates had been designed to hunt submarines, but their
weapons and electronics made them matches for aircraft and
larger ships. They carried a complement of two hundred, half
that of the destroyers of 1945, thanks to automation and re-
duced-maintenance design.

She was well armed and well trained. But her effectiveness
depended on one man. Her commanding officer alone bore the
responsibility for training her, steaming her, and for the ulti-
mate test of a warship, her performance in battle.

Dan put his regret for Bell behind him, as he had for so many.
That was one of the lessons of the Navy. You sailed, not with
your friends, nor with those you knew were good, nor those
you'd sailed with last cruise. You had to sail with the men on
your muster.

In his stateroom, he showered quickly and changed into fresh khakis. Five minutes later he was in the wardroom, pulling out a chair. The air-conditioned chill made his sinuses ache after the 110-degree heat outside. As the last officers filed in, he examined the man who sat smoking a Camel at the head of the table.

Benjamin Shaker was six even, built with a large chest and short legs. His head was large and his black hair was shaggy in back. It gleamed wet where he'd taken off his cap. His face looked pale among the deep tans of the others. His eyes, narrowed against the eddying smoke, were a startling blue, creased with sun wrinkles. Like all Navy men now he was clean-shaven. His silver oak leaves were rather dull. Unlike the others in the wardroom, he wore a long-sleeved shirt. Rolled neatly above his elbows, it revealed muscular forearms covered with black hair. The steward, Crockett, set a cup of coffee beside him.

"This everybody, XO?" Shaker said.

Dan glanced around. The lieutenants, the department heads, were seated. The ensigns and jg's leaned against bulkheads or perched on the couch. "Yessir, Cap'n."

"That'll be all, thanks," Shaker said to the steward. When the enlisted man was gone, he stubbed out his cigarette, blinking, and looked around the table.

"Okay. I'll be talking to you all individually later, but this might be a good time to get a few things out of the way. I'm talking about *Strong.*"

They waited.

"You all know I was her CO when the Iranians hit her with a Harpoon. You probably also know that the Board of Inquiry exonerated me. The ship was fought well considering we had no warning. The AWACs didn't pick up the F-14 that fired it because he was in the mountain clutter. Our radar didn't catch it because they programmed the flight path behind an island; it popped up just before it hit us.

"We picked it up visually in time to get two Sparrows off. NAVSEA calculates a point-six probability-of-hit on a Harpoon with one AIM-7E round and a point-eight for a two-round engagement. We happened to fall in that out-of-luck two-tenths. The first one missed and the second intercepted just inside arming range. The gun was at Condition Three and we couldn't get rounds out in time. So we got clobbered. But you also know that Admiral Gyland was relieved for ordering a non-Phalanx, non-NTDS ship to a picket station that close to Iran.

"I'm telling you this, not to say I'm happy with what happened. We lost the ship and forty-two guys. We lost them because we didn't expect anyone to attack us. I blame myself. I will never, never allow that to happen again."

He waited, apparently for some response, but the wardroom was dead quiet.

"I happened to see Charlie's medical report when it came in and I asked for this job. They didn't have anybody else qualified in frigates on short notice, so I got it. So far, looking around the ship, I like what I see. At the same time, there are going to be some changes. I'll be talking with the XO about that."

Shaker glanced at Dan. "Now. Who usually takes her out?"

"I've been doing the close conning for the last two months, sir."

"I'll take her tomorrow. Later I want the department heads to do it."

Dan nodded. It was standard operating procedure. He'd only done it when the captain—the *former* captain—was unable to. "Yessir. That'll be day after tomorrow, not tomorrow."

"I want to move underway time up twenty-four hours," said Shaker. "Give us time to shake down before we pick up the convoy. Department heads, any problems with that? Can we fuel, onload supplies, finish any repairs today and tonight, and get under way a day early?"

Dan saw Guerra wince, and Ron Brocket, the supply officer, suddenly dive for his wheel book. The engineer said, "Uh, we're testing PLA on Number One right now."

"What's the problem?"

"Fuel-oil control valve's been leaking."

Shaker said, "That shouldn't take you long. Any other hitches? Okay, let's plan on oh-six-hundred." He turned to Dan. "That'll be okay for tide, won't it?"

On *Van Zandt*, the XO was also the navigator. "Yes sir. I'll get with ops and work out the details with the harbormaster."

"Okay," said Shaker. "I'll be over at the compound most of the afternoon; they want to see me with the convoy op order. Are there any questions now?"

Nobody had any questions. He looked around the room once again, then got up. The officers jumped to their feet. He nodded, his face expressionless, and went out.

When he was gone, Dan kept the department heads for a few minutes, discussing what they had to finish to get under way early. When they were gone, he drew himself a glass of iced tea and stood by the porthole, reviewing his first impressions.

Shaker seemed confident. He didn't waste any time taking over. Well, he ought to know what he was doing; he'd had a frigate before in these waters, though an earlier class.

Of course, there would be changes. Every captain ran his ship differently, according to his inheritance of the trade and his own ideas of leadership. Some were book men, while others didn't worry over regulations as long as the ship met her commitments. Some were sticklers for etiquette, others relished an earthy style; some were operators, others spent their time in the engine room, greasy as any machinist's mate; some ruled with an iron hand, others left the reins loose. He remembered those he'd served under. Packer. Sundstrom. Leighty. Fish. Some had been masters at the craft of command. Others were disasters. It was far too early to hazard any judgment about Benjamin Shaker.

There was one thing different about this situation, though. He'd never served under a captain who'd lost a ship. No matter what a board concluded, it was remarkable Shaker had gotten another command. And he'd know that—know that his margin for error, always slim, was now nonexistent.

There was another question, too. What would it do to a man's psyche, his mind, his emotions?

It occurred to Dan then that if Shaker screwed up, he might succeed to command of *Van Zandt*. An instant later he dismissed the thought, angry at himself. He had his job as exec, and that was to support the skipper. Anything else would be poor leadership, dishonorable, and possibly, nose to nose with the enemy as they were, dangerous as well.

He decided to hope for the best. Gulping the last of the tea, he grabbed his cap and headed for the bridge.

2

Stonefield, Vermont

THE dawn light was like golden wires strung through the Green Mountains. It came through the barn door glittering with dust, painted the age-darkened planks red-gold, glowed yellow off a stainless vat. The air smelled of sweet hay and bitter silage, leather and disinfectant, sour milk and manure. It smelled of cow sweat and man sweat.

John Gordon leaned on a wooden scraper, ankle-deep in the nitrogenous excreta of forty Improved Holstein milkers. He was a narrow man whose slight stoop and Lincolnesque angularity made him seem taller than he was. His hair was long and spiky, black brushed with gray, and his face was made of knobs and awkward planes like some nineteenth-century invention. He was wearing coveralls, a sleeveless T-shirt, and old knee-high rubber boots. Stout-bodied blueflies whined around him in short, angry half circles.

Gordon had been up since four. His milking schedule was 5 A.M. and 4 P.M. It took only a few minutes to rinse out each stainless DeLaval milker, attach it, and turn it on. Then on to the next stall, the next fidgety stanchion-hemmed cow, her rump shifting like a fat woman waiting for a bus.

Now he was almost done. Spread fresh sawdust, hose down the milk house, then it'd be time for breakfast and the paper. He wondered what was happening with the Boston markets. And the town meeting was coming on; he'd entered his name as selectman; it was time he tried for a seat.

He drew the crisp air slowly through his lungs and looked around the barn. Its tenants were outside now, straggled up along a polywired section of the hill with the imperfect randomness of creatures governed by simple wills and simple loves. Four were heifers yet. One should freshen this month. His eyes lingered on a corner stall. He'd just sold Galatea. Twelve years

old and with more heifers to her credit than he could remember.
The dealer had come yesterday and he'd stood with his hat in
his hand watching the closed truck pull out and away down the
hill.

Now the barn filled with the smell of maple as he scattered
and leveled fresh sawdust. He propped the scraper against an
oak beam covered arm's-reach high with carved hearts and
gouged initials, pulled a coil of hose off a rack, and went next
door. A moment later, water leaped forth in a curved, clear
cylinder and broke spattering under the bulk tank and around
the sink.

Cleaning, feeding, milking, breeding: That was how a dairyman spent his day. The first was the most time-consuming.
Cows were delicate animals. This almost ritual renewal of the
floor, for example; without it, there'd be hoof problems before
winter. Mastitis was another plague. There was a flare-up every
so often, no matter how careful he was.

He opened a cupboard and tipped disinfectant into a bucket.
The chlorine fumes watered his eyes. He sloshed it onto the
floor and it ran in little steaming streams here and there, following invisible channels in the concrete. He scrubbed for a while
with a long-handled brush, his lips formed around a whistle that
was never born, and then picked up the hose again.

"John."

He turned, the water spattering across the floor. In an oblong
of blue-green brilliance stood a human figure. He looked toward
it for a moment, not speaking, as if listening to the golden light,
or the random drone of flies. Then, moving deliberately, he
twisted the nozzle closed and coiled the grass-green snake back
into its wonted place. He passed his hand over his hair, bending
forward, hesitating a little. Then the rubber boots went squish,
squash across the concrete.

The woman held the yellow envelope against her apron. Her
eyes were not so much self-contained or self-assured as past all
need for containment or assurance; like the eyes of an oak, if
an oak had eyes, or of a waterfall. But to someone who did not
know her they might have seemed unexpressive, almost dumb.
Faded blue, like her denim skirt. Her heavy, shining hair, the
color of clover honey, was braided tightly and pinned up under
a figured kerchief.

"What is it, Ola?"

"Telegram."

Their hands met briefly, her clay-dried fingers to his leather
gloves. She looked at him closely, her lips parted. But he was

studying the address; had not yet made a move to open it. So
she turned, and began making her way back through the yard
to a white house, double-porched, toward a clapboard shed in
back of it. Its door was all but blocked by a waist-high heap of
shattered crockery.

Gordon glanced around absently. His eyes found the straggling, slow-moving line of ruminating beasts. The distant blue-
green, like deep water, of the hills over which Ethan Allen had
fought. And above it all, the molten glow of the rising sun.

A moment later, the envelope fluttered to the cow-tracked
ground.

FROM: COMMANDER, US NAVY RESERVE FORCES
TO: SENIOR CHIEF GUNNERS MATE (DIVER) JOHN W. GORDON, USNR

1. IN ACCORDANCE WITH PROVISIONS OF US CODE 673 (B), NAVAL
RESERVE EXPLOSIVE ORDNANCE DISPOSAL DETACHMENT 20 HAS
BEEN NOMINATED BY THE PRESIDENT FOR EMERGENCY ACTIVE
SERVICE. THIS CONSTITUTES TWENTY-FOUR-HOUR NOTIFICATION
OF YOUR CALL-UP. CONTACT YOUR RESERVE CENTER IMMEDIATELY
TO PICK UP ORDERS AND AIR TICKETS.

2. FOLLOWING MINE CLEARANCE REFRESHER TRAINING, YOU
WILL DEPLOY TO USS AUDACITY, MSO-442, FOR ACTIVE SERVICE IN
THE ARABIAN GULF AREA.

3. ADVISE IMMEDIATLEY IF FOR ANY REASON YOU ARE UNABLE
TO RESPOND TO THIS ACTIVATION ORDER.

He stood motionless in the growing daylight, looking at the
words. When he had them nearly by heart, he folded the paper
slowly in two, then creased it with his thumbnail. It hung down
by his side, in his long, awkward arm.

He lifted his eyes to the hills.

They rose to four thousand feet, rocky and rounded, domi-
nated by the distant blue of Mount Mansfield. He'd opened his
eyes to life to see them brooding above him, as if someday they
might slide forward over the small dairying towns on their way
to Champlain. Closer to him, the land gentled, and gradually
became grazeable. Crevecoeur Farm was three hundred acres
of those foothills, rolling meadow, and orchard ten miles out
from Stonefield.

Gordon's maternal grandfather had share-farmed on the
other side of town. His father, a quarryman, had died young in
a fall from a granite terrace. So he'd milked for his grandfather
until his country needed him—as wittier people than he had said

at the time—to travel to distant countries, meet exotic people, and kill them. He'd spent ten years in the service, then left it for a woman and a farm. But he had had to do something else to make ends meet. So a few years later, he'd gone back, in a way, affiliating with a Reserve unit in Burlington.

At last he moved toward the house. Just before he got there, he changed his direction, for the smaller building.

His wife was standing with her back to him, bent over a brick kiln. Steam hissed up out of it, and a sulfurous stink. As the door creaked, she straightened from a peephole and inserted a plug. She tapped a gauge, then turned. She looked at him for a long time before her eyes followed his arm down to the paper.

"What was it?"

Wordless, he extended it. It hung between them for a moment, then passed, gloved hand to gloved hand. After a moment, her lips went white, sucked against her teeth.

"What is it? A rehearsal?"

"No. It's real."

"Are you going?"

"I'm thinkin' on it."

She looked at the kiln, touched it lightly with the tips of her fingers. Then she looked away, out a square of wavy old glass filmed with powdered clay. "There's Mike. Breakfast's ready."

Gordon bent at the back door to pull off his boots. In damp stocking feet, he padded on into the kitchen. The boy was standing at the stove. He was twelve, tall for his age, with an abstracted, introspective look. His light hair sprang up in a cowlick. He was wearing jeans and boots and a Poison T-shirt under a flannel shirt. When he saw them, he smiled shyly and said, "Hi, Mom, Dad. Y'want some eggs?"

It had taken two years after he married Ola for the boy to call him that. It sounded good to him. "Yeah, thanks, Mike. You sleep good, pal?"

"Uh-huh."

Gordon sat heavily, then caught his wife's eye and got up again. When he came back, wiping his hands, his plate was steaming with hot eggs and fluffy buttermilk cakes oozing sweet butter and homemade maple syrup.

"How's Wanda doing, Dad?"

"The antibiotic cream's working," said Gordon. He ate for a while, then added, "Teats don't seem to pain her much as they did yesterday. It's more expensive than that sulfur ointment, though."

"Mike, what are you doing today?" his mother asked him.

"We're gonna meet down at the church and fly some airplanes. Jimmy said I can fly his P-51."

Gordon cleared his throat. "Michael."

"What?"

"I might have to go away for a while. If I do, you think you
can help Mom run the farm here?"

The boy had been smiling, and it lingered yet forgotten on his
face as the eyes receded, sinking away like flat rocks dropped
into a glacial lake. "What do you mean?" he said.

"I mean, going back to active duty. In the Navy."

"For a weekend? For how long?"

"I don't know how long."

"Where are you going?"

"I think maybe a good piece off."

The boy sat looking at his plate, but he didn't move to eat. He
murmured, "You said you wouldn't leave us. That you'd stay
here."

"It wouldn't be because I wanted to," said Gordon. "You
understand that, son? But I gave them my word, y'see. There
are things, if a man's promised to do them, he ought to no
matter what. I promised to go back if they needed me. They say
they do."

The boy glanced up. His eyes were still distant, but a kind of
desperate longing filled them now. "You mean, for a war?"

After a moment, Gordon said, "Not exactly."

The boy cried out then, something inarticulate and savage,
and his voice was twisted and high. Part of it was: "You liar.
You fucking liar! And I'm not your *son!*" The plate hit the floor
with a pottery crack. They heard his footsteps rapid on the stair
and then, just as the door slammed, a sob.

His mother bent to pick up the pieces. She ran her finger
cautiously over a fractured edge. They looked at each other
across the table. "He's right," she said. Her eyes were quiet
and sad. "You told him you wouldn't leave. Like his father did.
The counselor said that was important to him."

Gordon stared at his stocking feet. Finally he said, "I know."

"It wouldn't be easy, the two of us, with the haying and
all—"

"I know," he said again. He tried to eat another mouthful of
eggs, but he couldn't.

The bedroom was cramped and dim. He bent, tugged a beat-up
olive-drab box from under Ola's old bedstead, and snapped open
the padlock. In it were uniforms, faded but clean, blue paper
banding their starched rectilinearity. He took out a khaki shirt

and trousers and laid them out on the star quilting; found a web belt and threaded it thoughtfully through a Marine Corps-style buckle, flipped open a cigar box.

He laid them on the bed and looked at them for a moment. The silver helmet of a first-class diver. The silver-and-gold fouled-anchor-and-star of a senior chief. A parkerized combat-modified nine-millimeter Browning. And the bomb-and-lightning of a master explosive-ordnance-disposal technician.

From upstairs came rock music, played louder than it was allowed to be played.

Gordon sighed, closed the box, put it back in the trunk. Though the world ended, a dairyman had to feed, had to clean, had to milk.

Leaning forward over the quilt, he closed his eyes.

Two sweat-darkened backs ahead of him in a close, hot world of green. No sky overhead, only green, close and silent, as if this doomed country had been bagged and tagged and left to rot.

"There it is," said the squad leader, stopping. He pointed down with the muzzle of his rifle at the piece of bamboo. Broken at right angles, the apex pointing ahead along the trail. "Good thing you guys come along. Can you check it out for us?"

Gordon nodded. He turned to the man behind him. "Beaner, see that? That's another one of their signs, like the three rocks, or the broken branch hanging down."

"Right."

"Better move your troops back, Sarge. Beaner, come on up with me."

The third class nodded. He was new, just out of EOD school. This was his first time in the field. Gordon went ahead cautiously, looking at the ground for nails or depressions, to the side for launching pits, at the air for the faint glint of monofilament. He needed to shit bad. He'd had the runs for a week.

To someone who didn't know how to look, the device would have been invisible. Hanging in a tree at head level, with still-living branches lashed around it for camouflage. About the size, Gordon thought, of one of the Chinese-supplied pineapple mines. He put out his hand and stopped Beaner. He examined the surface of the ground very closely for perhaps five minutes, then moved off to the right, pulling out his knife. He scored lightly across the surface of the ground, digging a quarter of an inch deeper each time.

"There. See it? The wire?"

"Yeah."

"Cut it one strand at a time. Use your nonconductive cutters. Don't cut them both at once or you'll complete the circuit."

Snip, snip, and he straightened. Ripped up the wire, up through leaf mold and dirt, until the homemade split-bamboo detonator and two PX-brand flashlight batteries came into sight.

"Do you want to blow it?" Beaner whispered.

"I'd like to take it back. If it's Chinese, the intel people will want a look at it."

"Is it safe? Can I take it down now?"

Of course it wasn't, Gordon thought. Nothing was ever really "safe" in explosive disposal. Sometimes you had to accept a risk. But Beaner should know that. He'd had the training. "Should be," he said. "Go ahead."

He'd been squatting with his pants down twenty feet away when the flat crack of high explosive sent fragments whipping through the leaves and scything down the bamboo above him. Beaner screamed for a long time before he died.

Ola was still sitting in the kitchen, her plate untouched. The broken halves of the boy's dish lay atop the trash. Her hands were curled around a mug in the shape of a bull's head. She'd made and fired it herself. She made many things that way— things so beautiful he had no words to praise them or her—and sold them at field days in Addison and Franklin counties and all over the state. Now she watched him as he went to the stove and poured another cup of coffee.

"John. I'm not sure I understand. Do you absolutely have to go to this—wherever they want you to go?"

"No. I don't absolutely have to."

"And you haven't decided yet."

He didn't answer.

"I don't want you to."

"I know." He took a deep breath and looked out the window, toward the sun, now a pale disk, cool and remote.

"And Michael. The school counselor said he was doing better. Starting to trust you, the way he never could trust Louis."

"I'm sorry," said Gordon. "I don't want to leave you. Or him. Believe me. But I took the obligation. I took the pay all these years, Ola."

He waited for a minute, but she didn't say anything else. So he went out.

The muddy, hoof-cratered yard was growing bright now. The

sky was red to the east, with only a few high, golden clouds.
The wind was losing the chill of early morning, going mild in
that brief New England summer mildness, warm yet with a hint
of steel, that is like no other weather on earth. The smells of
the warming earth, animal smells, breathed up from the ground
and mingled with the forest scent of the wind.

He stood in the yard, watching the stock on the near hill.
They were due to rotate into the next square Monday. He had
to remember to go over the ground one last time, make sure
there were no thistles, no buttercups to bitter the milk. Then he
remembered: He'd be gone by then.

Well, if he had to leave, now was as good a time as any. Ola
and Mike could keep up with milking. The herd was in good
condition. Their feet were sound and their teats were holding
up. He had second-cut hay coming up, not needing much attention till harvest, and he'd just bought fourteen tons of sixteen-
percent grain from Bourdeau Brothers.

If he wasn't gone too long, it would put them money ahead.
Active-duty pay, plus diving pay, maybe hazardous-duty pay—
that looked pretty good next to a dairy farmer's income.

But they'd miss his labor. And Ola wasn't any too good on the
computer, keeping up with the payments and things.

He looked at the mountains for a long time. At last, he went
inside the barn again, and a moment later water spattered anew
on concrete, and on the hill the tails swung lazily, and in the sky
the sun rose, and rose, and rose.

3

Karachi, Pakistan

THE parrot merchant hung on Phelan like a grinning tick, explaining how rare the birds were, how valuable, how easy they were to take care of. "He is perfect pet for ship," he said over and over, washing him from inches away with breath like the garbage littering the alleys off Paradise Street.

Phelan evaded his eyes, hoping he'd give up. Passersby pushed past, women in dark clothes dangling enough gold to doom them in any American city, short men with glittering eyes that saw and understood everything instantly: American sailor, cornered by street merchant.

But then those eyes would freeze on his face.

The merchant reclaimed his attention by tugging on his arm. "Hey, I just don't want the fucking thing, man," he said. His voice was so soft it was almost lost in the racket of unmuffled exhaust.

"But you want the women, yes? The women, they love birds. How beautiful he is. Look, just look at him."

He found himself nose to beak with one of the parrots. He had to admit it'd give the guys on the Bitch a shit fit. Green and gold, its mascaraed eyes like inlaid disks of polished obsidian. But still it was just a bird in a cage. It smelled bad. The man had eight of them hanging over his back. A bicycle jostled him and they all screamed, a hoarse, terrible chorus of rage and vengeance that sliced through his Benadryl tranquillity like a honed straight razor.

"How much you askin'?" Phelan said in that same shy voice.

"Fifty dollars, U.S."

"Forget it." But at the mention of money his hand had gone to his back pocket, and the merchant's eyes had followed.

At last Bernard shook him off. He was fifteen minutes off *Long Beach* and had forty-eight hours of liberty ahead. He had things to do, places to be. And though he wasn't sure yet where they were, he didn't plan to look for them with a parrot on his back.

He'd looked forward to Karachi for weeks. Long weeks, out on the Be No Station. That was what they called it. Be No Booze, Be No Broads, Be No Liberty. Pakistan looked like a hellhole, but everyone said it was the best liberty in the Indian Ocean. The place was made for sailors. You could get anything there, they said in the gray passageways. Anything you wanted. Just make sure you took the bucks.

He slicked back sweat-wet hair and torched a Marlboro. The street was wide for the Middle East, lined with carpet shops and jewelers and Pakistanis selling shoes and leather and rugs. It reminded him of that place in New York City he'd gone once, couldn't remember the name, but it was crowded with street people like this. Lot of Paks there, too, Ethiopians, Russians, just about anything you could name.

Now that he thought about it, though, he'd never seen another American Indian the whole time he'd been in Manhattan. That was a kick. His people had kept their land. Thrown the Spanish out, killed the priests, then holed up on Sacred Mesa and dared the conquistadors to fuck with them. And made it stick, too.

Hospitalman Bernard Phelan, USN, hurried through the throng, and his reflection followed him in the storefronts: a lithe little man with a roll to his walk, broad cheekbones, a drooping mustache, and black eyes that never looked directly at anything. His bare shoulders were pale with old knife scars. His face was so smooth and expressionless no one could have guessed his age or his emotions. He had on Levis, Dingo boots, and a tooled leather belt with a hammered silver buckle. He'd had to wear a shirt across the quarterdeck, but now it was stuffed into the camera bag tossed over one shoulder. His sleeveless tank top said I'M STUPID.

For a moment, glancing back, he thought he saw a face looking his way. Then it turned away, looking into a window crammed with cameras. The lenses looked like birds' eyes. He stood rigid, anxiety struggling against the haze in his brain. Then he made himself relax. No problem, he reassured himself. They just never seen a Zuni before.

A few blocks on, he stopped before a curb full of cutlery. The vendor, a toothless old guy with something growing on his nose, immediately handed him a four-inch folding blade with a brass hilt decorated with rosewood. Bernard tried it on the sparse hair of his forearm. It was sharp, all right.

A little bargaining, meanwhile trying not to stare at the guy's nose, and he tucked the knife into his jeans with the money. Four hundred bucks. His paycheck, plus a nice chunk of change from coming in second in the anchor pool. He'd decided to plow it into the business.

He squatted back to the old man's level. The nose aimed left and right, then bent forward.

Phelan held out a five-dollar bill and asked him where he could buy some hash. The old man, grinning, told him to go to the sari market.

He figured it wouldn't be hard to find.

Phelan was Bernard Newekwe's second name. His *Melikan* name, his white name. He didn't care for it, but circumstances had forced him to use it for the Navy enlistment. He'd used his Zuni name the first time he'd joined up, at seventeen, in the Army.

From time to time, he wondered whether they were still looking for him.

Bernard was twenty-two now. He'd grown up in western New Mexico, one of six whose mother had been neither pretty nor sober enough to hold a man long enough for the formalities. At four, lousy and potbellied, he'd been taken away by white women in long dresses and placed with a family in Gallup. At seven, he'd been placed with a second family; at ten, a third. These people received money for taking care of children. There weren't enough of them and standards were low. He grew used to men's fists and women's tears. At thirteen, he'd gone to an aunt in Grants, then back to the pueblo with her when she'd lost her job making Indian fried bread for the tourists.

He learned from the older boys there how to fight, steal, and use a knife. Unemployment on the reservation was eighty percent, and he saw no point in wasting time in school. At sixteen, drunk, he'd tried to enlist at Fort Wingate, but they'd turned him down. At seventeen, he'd convinced his aunt to sign the papers for an underage admission.

For perhaps half an hour, waiting for the bus on Route 66, he'd thought his life was about to change.

At Fort Jackson he'd taken all the Basic shit, the Sitting Bull jokes and the pugil-stick poundings. Then on his first pass, he'd met a woman from Leesville who'd never screwed an Indian. She also needed help smoking ten ounces of prime grass. After nine days with her, it was gone and he decided he didn't feel like going to cooks' school—let alone the stockade time the Army would want first.

He'd hitchhiked home from South Carolina, making up a story about a medical discharge, and stayed there with his aunt and then two or three other women, Denise being the last. Till he'd carved a five-inch groove in Donicio Kawayoka's chest.

He couldn't remember now whether it'd been over money, jealousy, or an envelope of speed. Late that night, however, two of the elders from the Muhewa, his mother's clan, had come by to visit him. They'd pointed out in a friendly way that he wasn't really one of the Corn People. He'd taken no initiation, and no sacred animal had revealed itself to him. He didn't even speak the Shi Wi tongue. They admitted there wasn't much future in the pueblo for a young man like him. Perhaps life would offer him more somewhere else, far away.

Bernard took this advice seriously. The elders looked harmless and feeble, but people who ignored them tended to get run over by pickup trucks on dark nights. He'd headed for Santa Fe the next day. Far away? He decided to join the Navy.

His destination, when he found his way to it through the mazy streets, wasn't what he'd expected. It was surrounded by alleyways so narrow the light reached no inch of them directly—the typical souk layout. The air was crowded with spices, sweat, perfumes, and wailing Arab music. The last man he asked about the "sorry market" pointed to a huge concrete-block building.

He stood outside for a few minutes, peering in uncertainly. Was this it? The people going in and out the glass doors were all women.

The Benadryl he'd sneaked on the ship was wearing off and he stuck his hands in his jeans to stop their shaking. This was the part of town they told you not to go into without your buddies. But he had no buddies—or none he could take with him on this piece of work.

Twice in the half hour since he'd bought the knife, he'd thought he saw the face behind him. It was hard to tell. They all looked the same, short and dark with big mustaches. But this guy had on a pink shirt.

Now he couldn't decide whether to go in or not. The sense of doom increased till he could hardly breathe.

At last, he crossed the street, sweating and dizzy, and had a slow drink and a slower smoke, watching from a café. The guy didn't show again, so he paid and went out. He stood for a moment blinking and mumbling to himself in the sudden heat, waiting for a donkey cart to go by.

It was like bingo night on the reservation. The fluorescents were nearly all burned out once you got past the entrance, and the interior was thronged with about a million women, all of them yelling at the tops of their voices. He swallowed nausea as he looked down flickering blue corridors roofed with the spinning disks of electric fans. Each booth was lit with a bulb in the back, where the samples hung, more colors and embroidery than he'd ever seen in his life, and women sat in folding chairs drinking coffee out of doll-size cups and picking flies off sticky pastries.

This wasn't what he was looking for. He came to a smoky space of air and found himself at a cooked-meat stand. The smell made him suddenly ravenous. He bought a shish kebab. The flesh was unfamiliar, strong, but it was good and he ate it all. Then he rubbed his greasy fingers on his jeans and was back in it again, the noise, the heat, the flies, the musky perfume so thick he wanted to hawk it out like phlegm. On impulse, he asked the meat man, "Hey, you know where I can buy some drugs?"

The guy didn't speak English, and Phelan drifted off again.

Eventually he came to the back. This was lit even worse than the main area, and there were no women. Just stalls, most of them dark, and men sitting in the shadows, smoking or talking in low voices. Phelan saw a brass telescope in one of the stalls. There was other junk, too, old lamps, used radios, that kind of stuff.

He suddenly felt it again, very strong now, that irrational, doomed fear that grabbed him more and more often the last few months. He stood trembling in front of the stall, looking around again for the guy in the pink shirt, or for cops.

The light clicked on. Someone was in there. He unslung the camera bag and went in.

The bearded Pak bought the big Navy binoculars for thirty dollars. Phelan insisted on being paid in American money. The bills were grimy and faded, as if they'd been lying in the cash box since World War II, but they looked spendable.

Bernard asked him where he could buy drugs. The man examined him for a few seconds, his smile unaltered. Then turned to the shadows and called out.

The Paks with the dope were kids, fourteen or fifteen. There were two of them. They had drip, hashish, in several forms. They had it in paste, in what they called brown sugar, and in what looked like chewing tobacco. Phelan didn't like the looks of the tobacco. Or rather, it looked too much like tobacco. He'd been burned on buys before. The paste looked like shoe polish

and tasted like marijuana. "You got anything else?" he said.
"That rubbed Kashmir, or hash oil?"

"We have some opium," said the one who spoke English.
"Real qual-i-ty."

"Let's see it."

The opium came in plugs the size of his little finger. It was
wrapped in aluminum foil. Phelan unwrapped one and sniffed.
It smelled like it looked, dark brown, sweetish, burnt honey and
incense. "How much of this is a hit?" he asked the kid.

"That's a hit."

"What do you people do with it? Smoke it?"

"You can smoke it or eat it. Smoking it is better."

"How much is it? For a hit?"

The kid wanted twenty dollars. Phelan thought that was
high, but he wanted some. Now. He said, "You got more of
this?"

"You want a brick," said the Pak. "Do you want a brick? It's
cheaper. Enough for a long time."

The other kid showed him the brick. It was easily the size of
three regular Hersheys. There had to be enough for a month
at sea. Phelan wanted to try some right there. But at the same
time he was afraid. Like he always was at a buy. The kids didn't
seem worried, though, even when someone walked by. They
must have their protection behind them. He let his fingers
brush the knife.

"How much is the brick?" he asked the kid.

They only wanted three hundred for it. Phelan felt he'd stumbled onto good luck at last.

Once the money was in their hands, it seemed as if the trans-
action was over. They turned instantly and walked away. He
decided to imitate them. He jammed the opium down into his
jeans and went back very fast through the chattering women,
under the drone of the fans. When he hit sunlight again, he felt
safer. He grinned, anticipating the high he was going to feel in
a few minutes. No more cough syrup stolen from the ship's
pharmacy. No more Tylenol with codeine. Not for a long time.

Then he realized he was lost.

He'd come out a different exit and he didn't know which one.
The souk was all around him. This seemed to be the shoe department. The stalls were filled with boots, sandals, sneakers. He
started walking, his fingers clamped inside his pocket. What a
deal. He'd chew some first. He'd heard you shouldn't do that;
they rendered it with rat fat and you could get hepatitis. But
just then, sweating and trembling, he didn't care.

There were no windows in the shoe stalls, but as he passed

one he saw a mirror. An old man was looking at a pair of wing tips in it. They looked out of place under his baggy white pants and embroidered vest. Behind him in the mirror was Phelan, looking foreshortened and pinheaded, and behind him was a pink shirt.

He halted, pretending to examine a pair of women's pumps. In the mirror he saw two men now. One short, one tall. The short one was wearing the pink. He hadn't seen the tall one before.

Now he was happy there were people around. He had to get back to Paradise Street. From there, he could take a taxi, shake them, or if he had to, just go back to the ship. They couldn't follow him aboard. On the other hand, he'd have to ditch or hide the opium then. He rubbed sweat off his forehead. He waved off the shoe vendor, who came out after him, and walked briskly around two corners and into a dead-end alley lined with wrecked cars piled four deep on either side.

When he turned around, they were standing between him and the souk. There was no one else in sight, though he could hear the distant words of Madonna, "I'm a Material Girl," from a cassette player somewhere.

You or them, he thought, almost like hearing it. You or them.

"What do you want?" he said.

"We are police," said the tall Pak. He wasn't really tall, but he was taller than Phelan. "We saw you buy the hashish. Give it to us."

"It ain't hash," said Phelan in his soft, almost shy voice. "I mean, I didn't buy nothing."

He knew they weren't police. Then he wondered how many other American sailors had bought the brick in his pocket. Hell with this, he thought, fear and need turning into a murky, desperate rage. He wasn't going to give it to them, that was all.

He glanced around, making sure they were alone, and drew the blade.

The short man took a gun out from underneath the loose shirt.

Before he had it free, Phelan cut him across the belly. The Chinese knife was sharp enough that it didn't hang up in the cloth. He shoved him into the taller Pak and got his boot on the dropped gun. The little Pak started screaming. The tall one had his knife out by then, a real pigsticker, a foot long and curved like a sickle. But he didn't come in. Phelan thought about picking up the gun, but he didn't know guns. He hadn't done well with the .45 at boot camp. The blade felt good in his hand and he decided to stay with it.

"You want some, too?" he asked the tall Pak softly. The man was still hesitating, holding the short one up. The smaller man was screaming louder now, his hands trying to hold his belly together.

He didn't want any. Phelan picked up the dust-covered pistol and stuck it in his belt. He backed out of the alley, holding their eyes, then turned quickly and made several sharp turns through the bazaar. He hit concrete block again and went back into the market.

The man who had bought the binoculars gave him forty dollars for the gun.

The room was two dollars and two flights up, a stinking hole without a lock on the door. There was a pallet on the floor. Phelan decided not to check it for bugs. He liked the room. No one else off the ship would come here.

He tied the latchstring, put the paper bag on the floor, and began taking things out of it. Four quarts of Coke, so cold his fingers left prints in the condensation. He'd have preferred beer, but he couldn't find any for sale. Six packs of Marlboros. A sack of the flat, doughy Arab bread. A bag of what he hoped were pretzels or chips, though it was opaque and the label was in the funny Pak squiggles.

He was still scared, still angry, and to calm himself he took a deep swallow of the pop. Then another. At last he felt calm enough to proceed. He sat down on the pallet and flattened out the grocery bag for a work surface.

The brick was warm from his pocket. He peeled a slice off it with the knife, noticing as he did so that there was still blood where the blade folded. He wiped it quickly on the pallet and kept peeling, making the slices thin and curling, with plenty of air. He could smell it, thick and sweet and heavy. His fingers shook and he gulped more Coke till they steadied down.

When he had enough, he slit open some of the cigarettes and shook out the tobacco. He mixed this with the opium and glued the paper back together lengthwise with spittle.

When he had five fat joints, he lined them up on the windowsill. He put the open knife beside them. He looked down at the street, at the passing taxis and dark-haired heads. No one looked up. There was a shade and he pulled it. The room went dark.

Fuck them, he thought. Fuck the fucking Paks. Fuck the fucking Navy. Fuck the Indian, fuck the white man, fuck the world. This is where it's at.

He picked up the first joint, smiled shyly at it, and pulled fire out of a match with his thumbnail.

Turning his head, Bernard Newekwe slowly and solemnly blew sweet smoke to the four corners of the room, then up, then down. Then he drew it in, to the seventh corner of the world, to writhe and curl and purify his own turbid and troubled soul.

4

Manama, Bahrain

THE heat, Blair Titus thought; that was what blindsided her every time she did the Middle East. Certainly Washington, twelve hours before, had been grim in the dread dog days of August. Paris, that morning, had been hot but not uncomfortable beneath a gentle rain.

But Bahrain was like a junket into Hell. Her lightest traveling suit had soaked through just coming in from the airport. She pushed her hair back, annoyed at its clingy dampness, and scratched at a prickle under her armpit.

"When's Admiral Hart due back?" she asked the aide. It came out more sharply than she'd intended. Blame it on the heat.

Trudell started; she noted with a flash of annoyance that he was staring at her chest again. "Uh, he must have been delayed, ma'am. He wanted to attend a change of command down at the pier. But he knows you're here. He knows about the brief."

"Can we start without him? I'd like to make the five o'clock to Riyadh."

The lieutenant was so horrified his eyes lost their fix on her bust. He began giving her the reasons they couldn't start without the admiral. Blair tuned him out. She scratched again and strolled to the window. She looked out, absently flipping the collar of her blouse.

The Middle East again. Last time it had been Israel, the Purchasing Commission trip. The ridges and blasted flats of the Sinai, the crump and flare of shells against the hush-hush explosive armor of the new Merkava tank. This time, it was the outskirts of a city. In the distance, vibrating like a wine hangover, she could make out white buildings and spires. Beyond that was a clear and tremulous blue. She stared out at it, won-

dering whether she absolutely had to spend the afternoon on
the second floor of the local Navy headquarters. She'd brought
the new swimsuit, just on the off chance . . .

Then she curbed her mind. She was here on business. A
whirlwind tour, Bankey had said. Check it out and tell me what
to do about this mess. Be back next week. No, that didn't sound
as if she had time for the beach.

"There he is," squeaked the lieutenant, sounding relieved.
She dropped her eyes. A dusty-looking military sedan was edging through the concrete barriers at the gate. As she watched,
Marines surrounded it, rifles at the ready. One circled it, inspecting the chassis with a mirror. They'd done that to Trudell's
car, too. Then they fell back, snapping up their hands in salute
as the Reliant rolled into the compound, the blue starred flags
stirring flaccidly in the hot, still air.

A few minutes later, Hart was pressing her hand. He smelled
of sweat and oil. "Good afternoon, Ms. Titus, and welcome.
Sorry I'm late. Did you have a good flight?"

"Yes."

"How's Bankey? I met him two years ago when I was at the
Joint Chiefs. Fine man, very impressive grasp of naval matters."

Said with the proper condescension of a military man toward
a politician, Blair thought. "The Senator's well," she said.

"His health holding up? You know what you hear—"

"I wouldn't know what you hear, Admiral," she said. She
never discussed Talmadge's drinking, nor did she stay around
when it got out of hand. "He's busy, as usual, but doing well."

"How long have you been with him?"

"Three years."

"Well, again, sorry I was delayed . . . damn, we have got to
get this air conditioning fixed. Jim, you should have taken her
down to the exchange. You know we have a perfume shop right
here in the building? There's a company in town makes concentrated perfumes, essences they call them, smells like any brand
you want—"

"Admiral Hart."

"Yes?"

"I'm not here to shop," she said coldly. "My time is limited
and there's a great deal I have to see. Could we start the brief,
please?"

Hart looked blank for just a moment, then turned to the
lieutenant. "Get the guys in here. Top staff only. Let's get
moving; Ms. Titus doesn't have much time."

* * *

The briefing officer was a dark-complexioned colonel—no, Navy
ranks, she corrected herself, captain—in beautifully tailored
khakis. When the last of the staff were in the room, he asked
for a closed door. The blinds came down, and Blair settled in in
front. She crossed her legs, smoothed her skirt, and took a Sony
out of her briefcase. A woman with a notebook equaled a ste-
nographer. And a recorder allowed her to give full attention to
what was being said—or, usually more important, was being
left out.

"Good afternoon, Miss Titus, Admiral Hart, gentlemen. I'm
Captain Jack Byrne. This will be a high-level brief on the situation in the Gulf today. Its classification is secret." He looked at
the recorder, and at Hart; the admiral winked. Byrne cleared
his throat and asked for the first slide.

"Sixty percent of the world's oil reserves lie on the shores of
the Persian Gulf—or, as we call it now, the Arabian Gulf. Very
little is consumed here. Most of it goes out by tanker through
the Strait of Hormuz to the U.S., Western Europe, and Japan.
Our naval and air forces in the area, under the control of Commander, Middle Eastern Force, are deployed to guarantee freedom of navigation and to protect our allies in a region essential
to our interests.

"Recent events in this part of the world—the Iranian revolution, the Iran-Iraq War—have reminded us that we live in a
time of challenge to the West. The loss of *Strong* year before
last underlined this. But this is not a new commitment. The
Navy has maintained a presence here since 1949, and our
buildup signals our willingness to continue defending our interests in the area.

"As the Secretary of Defense said recently, 'Our ships operate in the Persian Gulf to represent, immediately and directly,
America's commitment to stability in the region and our deep
concern over—' "

She held up her hand. Byrne stopped. "Yes, ma'am," he said.

"I understand why you're here, Captain. Could we skip the
basics, please?"

"Uh, Admiral . . . ?"

"This update is for the Senator's senior defense staffer, Jack.
Let's give her what she wants."

"Yes, sir." Byrne fiddled with the pointer, then skipped the
next two slides. "The next item, then, will be strength and
dispositions.

"We currently have fifteen U.S. cruisers, destroyers, and

frigates in the Gulf op area. Other assets we can call on include a carrier battle group in the Arabian Sea. Some time ago, we requested an augment to the minesweeping forces, and four MSOs are arriving from the States.

"Associated forces. We can call on backup units from several of the Gulf states. They have modest navies or coast guards, mainly high-speed small craft, but these are useful in patrol and interdiction. Finally, several Allied navies are also operating here, not under our command, but cooperating at a multinational level. France, Great Britain, Belgium, Italy, and the Netherlands currently have escort or minesweeping units in the Gulf. The French also have *Foch* off Socotra. The total complement of friendly forces is about sixty ships."

Blair said, "What's the basing, logistics structure?"

"Fuel and consumables are bought out of locally available stocks. Parts and ammunition are Navy Supply."

"I mean, where?"

"We don't have any fixed bases. Bahrain is the closest thing we have to a shore establishment. Overhaul, major repairs, it's either Diego Garcia, Subic, or back to the States."

"Exactly what kind of cooperation are you getting from the GCC states, Admiral? Oman, Bahrain, the Saudis, the emirates?"

"Excellent," said Byrne.

Looking down as he packed a pipe, Hart said, "We have mooring privileges in Oman, Bahrain, and Kuwait. The other Gulf states limit us to one-day stays."

She didn't ask for elaboration. After a moment, Byrne went on.

"Our most recent initiative has been the escorting program, operation Earnest Will. This assigns two to four small boys—sorry, destroyer-type ships—to U.S./Kuwaiti tanker convoys. So far, we've completed three convoys with no loss or damage. We're starting to get neutrals asking to tag along. Three times in the last month, though, we've had to put missiles on rails or take other defensive measures against approaching aircraft. In two cases, the aircraft were Iraqi. The third was Iranian jets out of Bushehr. On radar illumination and warning, they broke off and left the area."

"What is your estimate of Iranian intentions?"

"Uh, maybe the Admiral would—"

"Yes, I'll take that, Jack." Hart shifted in his chair to face her. "At the moment, Blair—may I call you Blair?"

"Sure, Stan."

Hart blinked. She could see it happening behind his pupils. Twenty-seven-year-old female civilian calling him by his first name in front of his staff. Then the counterbalance. This wasn't just any woman. She was the primary defense adviser to the Chairman of the Armed Services Committee, the legendary Bankey Talmadge, confidant and gadfly of five administrations. And through whose committee passed, not only all defense appropriations, but all promotions within the flag ranks of the services.

"Fair enough." Hart smiled broadly, turning it into a joke. The other officers giggled.

"Blair, my feeling for the situation is that their navy's about shot its wad. Malekzadegan's never been trusted by the Ayatollah's people; there were too many Shah-era officers left. Since the war began, the army's gotten the attention and funding. Their air and surface activity is at a low level. And my pilots report that when their air does come out, they're docile, very docile. They catch our radar and they turn back into their own airspace."

"That's excellent," she said. "What you're saying, then, is that we can begin reducing the U.S. presence here."

Hart began a nod, then caught himself. "Well, now, not so fast. It's more complicated than that. The other side of the coin is that the Pasdaran, that's their revolutionary guard, has been stepping up their activity. They harass shipping, lay mines, and raid oil platforms. We're developing countermeasures against this type of attack. What worries me is what they might do if they get some real resources to operate with."

Byrne, beside him, bent and whispered. Hart listened, then shook his head slightly, glancing at Blair. "Shall we continue the briefing?" he said.

"By all means."

The swarthy captain reviewed the Iranian order of battle, the rules of engagement, talked about weather, and discussed rotation of escort units in and out of the Gulf. Then he stopped. "I guess that's about it. Admiral, Miss Titus, thank you. Are there any questions?"

"You're finished?" she said. Byrne nodded. He collapsed the pointer down to a nub and clipped it to his shirt.

"Thanks, Jack," said Hart. He lit his pipe, puffing out clouds of vanilla smell, and looked at her evaluatingly over it. "Well. In as few words as possible, I'd say we have the situation under control. Congress and the administration have given us the resources we need and we're out here putting 'em to work. Our allies are with us, the Gulf states are happy we're here, and the Iranians are blowing smoke as usual. Is that your understanding of it, Blair? Is that what you wanted to know?"

"No."

"No?"

She found a tissue in her purse and blotted her forehead carefully with it. "No. It's not my understanding of it, it's not under control, and the brief was unsatisfactory."

"Excuse me?" said Byrne.

"I said it was unsatisfactory! This is what you call high-level briefing? This is the sort of thing you put out to the press pool."

"I don't understand," said Hart, his forehead meshing into wrinkles. "Of course, we didn't get down into beans and bullets and comm plans. Didn't think you wanted that. I asked Jack to keep it light, give you an introduction to the situation—"

She crossed her legs the other way, instantly annoyed at the way their eyes fastened to them. They were all staring at her now. Her voice went flat, the tone she'd learned in the Special Prosecutor's office. "You don't understand. In that case, let me bring up a few points for your consideration, gentlemen. Things you might think about now and then while you're moving your little gray toys around."

She considered, organizing her thoughts the way she did before sitting down with Bankey.

"The first point is that this entire operation is too expensive. Our defense budget is now three hundred billion. That's more than we spent at the height of Vietnam. Godwin's resigned, Weinberger's own procurement chief, because Defense has no noticeable commitment to controlling spending.

"Now, you tell me you have fifteen ships in the Gulf. That's horseshit. My count is twenty-five, with the *Forrestal* battle group, and if you include everything, minesweeps, auxiliaries, survey ships—thirty-eight. I estimate our effort here is running almost a million dollars a day in above-normal costs. That doesn't include losses. Maintaining a carrier in the Indian Ocean is straining our entire defense posture. It's showing in retention, upkeep, and manning. And all at a time when Congress is desperate to cut expenses. I'm sure you've heard of Gramm-Rudman, Admiral?"

Hart said in a fatherly tone, "These forces pay for themselves. If the Iranians were ever able to close the Straits—"

"Please let me continue. Point two. Several people in the Association for a Rational Defense have told me the Gulf proves we've built the wrong kind of navy. We're top-heavy in carriers and expensive cruisers, leading-edge technology, but when we had to sweep mines, you came to us hat in hand and said you had to mobilize the reserves. That made people very angry on the Hill, Admiral. We mean to modify the Defense Five-Year Plan to reflect this sort of oversight."

Hart was turning red now. He tried to interrupt again, but she kept on, her voice calm but insistent, hammering fact after fact into the smoky air. "Point three. The Western Europeans are increasingly concerned about what you're doing out here. The recent defense ministers' meeting at the Hague—well, I'm sure you read your press summary. They don't understand why we have such large forces here when, as you say, the opponents are fanatics in speedboats. They're afraid we're going to engage Iran for reasons of our own. They're supporting us so far, but every new incident makes them more nervous. The French and the Dutch are especially wary. They're not beyond pulling out their forces and letting us go it alone.

"Point four. The Gulf states aren't 'happy,' they're desperate. They all have large Shi'ite minorities and any hint of crusading encourages revolt. They have to live here after we've gone home. They're worried about trading relationships, about the attacks on their oil platforms, and they wonder every day whether Hormuz is going to be closed.

"Now let's get to what concerns me, gentlemen. That's what the Iranians are going to do. The war's stalemated in the north. It has to be settled, but without Khomeini's having to tell millions of bereaved families their sons died for nothing.

"His strategy may be to expand the war southward, into the Gulf. If it succeeds there, Iran's a geopolitical winner. If it fails, if the major powers step in and force peace, it can be presented as a dictated armistice, a stab in the back by the Great Satan. The way the Pasdaran are being used is consistent with this. They're perceived as out of control, but the chaos they cause plays right into Iran's long-range plans.

"Now, the last point I want to make. And probably the most important." She got up, drawing their eyes with her, feeling now their hostility, and crossed to the far wall. It held a huge map of Southwest Asia. Her finger swept past the blue writhe of the Gulf, inland, to the northeast.

"You act as if Iran were our enemy. That's the short view, gentlemen. Beyond Shi'a fundamentalism is still the Soviet Union.

"There are twenty-five divisions in the Transcaucasus and Turkestan military districts. Twelve of them are armored or

mechanized. They're seven hundred miles from the Gulf. There
are four more, battle-hardened and highly mobile, in Afghani-
stan. The Soviets can drive across Iran anytime they like in two
weeks. They can airlift a division and take the choke points in
two days. All we have to stop them is a couple of antique
ship-based nuclear weapons.

"What could we do about it? I've discussed it with your boss,
General Cannon. The Shah-era strategy, theater nuclear
strikes, is out of the question now. The Soviets have us out-
gunned four-to-one in medium-range missiles, and they can
reinforce faster. Cannon's plan is to put six light divisions into
the Zagros Mountains. Once they're dug in, they might stop an
invasion. But it would take five weeks for them to get there.
The limiter is heavy lift, because no one in this part of the world
will let us base equipment in advance.

"So really we *can't* stop them. The Russians know that as
well as we do. So we just can't let Iran destabilize. Even
Khomeini's government is better than that.

"Our strategy doesn't have anything to do with 'freedom of
the seas.' We have to keep either side from winning and bring
them both to the table. Over time, we can then reestablish a
relationship with Iran, which is the key to the whole Gulf area.
And that, gentlemen, is why you're here. Not to fight a war. To
end one."

"This is all very enlightening," said Hart. He had leaned
forward to look at the map. "But what's it got to do with us?
Broad-brush strategy belongs to the Joint Chiefs. I appreciate
congressional interest, and I understand your concerns. Par-
ticularly the budgetary question. But as far as I'm concerned,
I have my orders, I have sufficient forces, and I know how
best to use them. Give me credit for that. Therefore, and let
me put this as gently as possible, I'm still not sure why you're
here."

"Admiral, you're in charge of our forces in the Gulf. That's
fine, but we're not sure you have the long-range interests of the
country in mind. This buildup is forcing us into a no-win situation. The Navy's strong enough here to start a war, but not
strong enough to win it. Unfortunately, we can't afford a war
in Southwest Asia. And the more we weaken Iran, the more
inviting we make it for the U.S.S.R. to intervene.

"Now, as you know, we, not the Executive, are responsible
under the Constitution for final oversight of foreign and military policy. The Chairman has decided it's time to reexamine
that policy, and decide whether to pull the plug on it. And that

means the War Powers Act. Sixty days, after we invoke it—and you people are out of here."

After a long silence, broken only by the hum of the defective air conditioning, Byrne said, "You wouldn't do that."

"I assure you, we would, and that's exactly what Senator Talmadge is considering."

Finally, Hart cleared his throat. He knocked out the pipe in an ashtray, the blows hammer-loud, and got up. "I believe that lays your concerns out adequately," he said dryly. "And gives us—right, Jack?—some idea of the basis for your being here. I personally think invoking the Act would be a disaster for the West. But as you say, it's the law.

"I'll support your fact-finding mission, Ms. Titus, on that basis. Shall we go up to my office? We should look at the ship schedules, discuss your itinerary. That is, if you have time."

She nodded and crossed the room. But Trudell already had her briefcase, recorder, and purse. He held the door for her, too. She said "Thank you" coldly as she brushed by him.

The corridors were dim, 1960s style, lined with cork boards, yellowing notices, and tables of rank of various nations. They climbed a flight of worn stairs and Trudell held the door again, this time for them both. The other officers lingered in the hall. Hart went immediately to a coffee maker, turned, raised his eyebrows; she nodded. He took his in a Styrofoam cup and gave her china.

"So, what did you want to see?"

"As much as possible. The aspects of the problem that concern me most are force strength and ally support. I'll also be talking to some people who can tell me what's going on inside Iran."

"I wish I knew that," said Hart. He'd regained his composure, but she felt distance now. Well, it was better than the patronizing attitude he'd started with. "Sugar? Cream?"

"No, thank you. . . . I'll be going up to Riyadh this evening. There are State people waiting to brief me, and some host-country contacts I want to check out. The Saudis, of course, are the most important from our point of view."

"I'd say that's accurate."

"Then Abu Dhabi, then back here. I'll want to see, if you'll pardon the cliché, the Navy in action. Can you arrange that?"

"I hope not in *action*, but we can fix you up. What kind of units do you want to visit?"

"A sample. Say a frigate, a cruiser—perhaps one of the convoys. Can you arrange that?"

"I'll put Jack on it. I don't see any problem, as long as you don't want to stay overnight." Hart grinned as if his shoes hurt. "You people have put some restrictions on what I can do with women aboard ship."

That wasn't the way she understood it. At the last hearings, the admirals had fought increasing female recruitment tooth and nail. But she'd argue that with him some other time. "What about the convoy?"

"We'll have number four making up in three or four days. If you're back by then, we'll fly you out."

"I'll be here."

"On your travels—they sound extensive—one thing I might suggest." Hart grimaced. "I'd like to loan you a man. Say, Trudell. Don't take it wrong, I'm just thinking of the impression you'll make on Arabs."

"Thank you, but I prefer to travel without a chaperon."

Blair gave him a beat, but he didn't say anything more. So she looked at her watch. "I should be going—"

"Lieutenant!"

"Sir."

"Take Ms. Titus to the airport. Use my sedan. Then come right back; I'll need it later."

"Aye aye, sir."

Hart put out his hand. "This has been an interesting meeting for me, Blair."

"For me, too."

"Look, I'm not used to you young, bright Capitol Hill types. Forgive me if I sounded . . . chauvinistic?"

"I'm used to it. But it's nice of you to apologize."

"There are some great restaurants in town. Maybe when you come back, we can take an evening off."

Like hell we will, she thought. But she smiled, shook his hand politely, and followed Trudell out.

When she was gone, the staff officers in the corridor regarded one another with frank astonishment. "That kike dyke. Who'd she have to blow to get that job?" said one.

"Watch the language, fella," said Byrne mildly. "She's on our side. I think."

"Bullshit, Jack! You heard her in there! They want to close us down! Leave the Gulf to the fucking Ayatollah!"

"Captain Byrne." Hart, angry, from the next office. "Jack! Get in here, goddamn it."

The captain turned away, heading toward the voice, but said quietly over his shoulder, "A lot can happen to change her mind."

* * *

Trudell turned the Reliant's AC on full blast and she leaned back, suddenly freezing and grateful for it. He slowed at the gate, returning the guard's salute, then accelerated out toward the city.

She smiled grimly, remembering Hart's feeble apology. She was sick of dealing with brass. A politician or a businessman learned to deal with all kinds of people. Everyone had power of some type, even if it was only a few dollars, or the vote he earned by being warm.

The military mind didn't work that way. If you weren't one of them, you were the enemy. Since she had to deal with them, she'd evolved Titus's Law, to wit: It was better to be perceived as a powerful adversary than as a weak friend. She had no illusions about what they'd be saying about her now, back there. She'd done enough history to know how the American military felt about civilian rule. In every war, it was the same. The bit had to draw blood before they understood it was there.

It didn't make her popular. She knew that. But she didn't want to be popular. She didn't have time for it. Or for a lot of other things. Like a family, time off, a personal life.

That was the price you paid in Washington, for being the best at what you did.

"Which terminal?" said Trudell a few minutes later. She started, coming back from her thoughts, and told him to go to British Airways.

She had to stop thinking about herself.

It was time to think about how to prevent a war.

5

U.S.S. *Turner Van Zandt*

THE hangar was cave-dim, oven-hot, crammed solid with
noise and the heavy stink of kerosene. The two officers
stopped just inside. One stood six feet in his dress whites; the
other was shorter and much broader. One was black, the other
white. For a few seconds, they looked up at the aircraft. Then
the heavyset one tugged open his collar. He blew out, then
raised his voice above the clattering howl of a grinder. "Chief.
Hey, goddamnit, *Chief!*"

A sweat-slick face appeared over an open cowling fifteen feet
up. "The Good Humor man! I'll have two scoops a rum raisin,
on a sugar cone."

The heavyset pilot scowled. His name was Claude Schweinberg, but he was better known in Helicopter Antisubmarine
Squadron (Light) 52, the Killer Angels, as "Chunky," "Chunk
Style," or "No-Neck." He was twenty-five and a native of Jack-
sonville, Florida. The taller officer was Virgil "Bucky" Hayes,
from Montana.

"Cut the comics, Mattocks. When you gonna have this whis-
tlin' shitcan ready to fly?"

"Working on it, sir. But you flyboys can dick 'em up a lot
faster than us workin' men can fix 'em."

The two pilots were only half-listening. They circled the aircraft, their eyes flicking from nose section to cockpit, hydraulics bay, transmission. . . .

The "shitcan" was an SH-60, side number 421: ten tons of
magnesium, Kevlar, fiberglass, and aluminum, painted a flat,
low-visibility gray. On the flight deck, it stretched sixty-five feet
nose to tail cone. Now, with tail pylon, stabilator, and rotors
folded to fit *Van Zandt*'s minimal hangar, it looked like a praying mantis in a matchbox. It was built to carry sonobuoys,
radar, torpedoes, and other gear to find and kill submarines. It

cost $19 million a copy. Usually, *Van Zandt* carried two, but 403 had been craned off in Sicily because of tail misalignment.

"What was that chip light for, Chief?" Hayes shouted, pushing back his cap.

"We didn't find no chip, sir. The fuzz burn must of took care of it. Who had the stick?"

"Me," said Schweinberg.

"Well, you must of did something right for a change, sir."

"I got somethin' else down here for you to lubricate, Mattocks."

"Somethin' that size, you want you a watchmaker, sir, not a aviation machinist." The crew chief looked into the open engine. "Yessir, if you'd had a real chip, it'd tear this friggin' gearbox up like a hand grenade. But I'll check it out. Should have her back together around midnight, or anyway before we get under way."

The whine of the grinder died. "Under way?" screamed Schweinberg into the sudden silence.

"We're shovin' off a day early, sir. Didn't you hear?"

"Who told you that?"

"Come straight from Mr. Woolton. He was in some kind of meeting with the new captain. Says we're pullin' chocks for Hormuz tomorrow, sharp in the A.M."

Schweinberg kicked one of the tires.

"Take it easy, Chunky."

"Easy, hell! I thought we had two more days. That means"— the Floridian jerked his hands out of his pockets, dropping to a linebacker's crouch—"we got some serious drinking to get through tonight."

"Ain't no liberty tonight, Lieutenant," called one of the mechanics, his teeth brilliant in a greasy mask. "Not for nobody. That's from Commander Lenson."

At the mention of *Van Zandt*'s exec, Schweinberg's face went sullen and crafty. "We'll see about that," he muttered, half to himself, half to the tire. He wound up and kicked it again, so hard the strut rattled.

"You're gonna ruin them pretty white shoes, sir."

"Fuck 'em. Come on, Bucky," said Schweinberg, his heavy lids falling till they were almost closed. "We got an exec to see."

Neither its members nor *Van Zandt*'s crew considered the aviation detachment part of the ship. They were based ashore, with seagoing assignments at most six months long. HSL 52,

Det 2 consisted at the moment of 421, sixteen pallets of spares and tools, and thirteen men. Four were officers and pilots. The rest were enlisted, mainly maintenance ratings. The senior aviator, Lieutenant Woolton ("Woolie"), reported to *Van Zandt*'s commanding officer for aircraft operations, and to the XO for admin, housekeeping, and personnel matters.

"Aren't you going to change first?" said Hayes, bottom man on the ladder to the 01 level.

"Hell, no, the shoes like these monkey suits." Schweinberg glanced back. His eye lingered on Hayes's gleaming aviator's wings, then on the dark face, still beaded with sweat.

What do you get, something in his mind asked, when you cross a nigger with a nugget?

"Okay, here's the plan. I don't know what's biting him, but Lenson was wound tight this morning. So we're just going to hover in his face till he gives us the wave-off."

"Okay."

"I'll do the talkin'. You just keep your mouth shut, and nod when I say something."

"Okay," said Hayes again.

The lieutenant knocked. "Come in," came a voice from inside.

Chunky stepped in; Buck lingered in the doorway. Schweinberg looked around, taking in the racks of books on the bulkhead, the built-in file cabinet, the desk with its bolted-down in/out baskets. Lenson sat half-turned from it, his flat and businesslike look bent on the stocky flier.

"Ah, the Bobbsey Twins. Mr. Schweinberg. What are you doing awake?"

"Sir, I thought I'd stop by, see if you had anything for me before I head on ashore."

"No liberty tonight. We're getting under way early."

"Liberty?" Schweinberg opened his eyes wide. "XO, this isn't for liberty. I'm detachment operations, see, and I got to get some charts over at the met office." He glanced over his shoulder, and remembering his cue, Hayes nodded.

"You've had two months here to get charts, Schweinberg. I know we've got all the DMA series of the Gulf."

"Yessir, but they don't show the stuff that's been going on, the bombing, the wrecks . . ." He glanced at Hayes again, but found the brown eyes turned full on Lenson. "Anyway, I met a guy who said to come over before we shoved off and he'd give us something the Bahrainis use. If they're what I think, they could be a real ass-saver if we have to do a combat search and rescue."

Dan closed his eyes. Why did they put him in this position? He glanced at his watch as Schweinberg droned on, then said abruptly, "Well, why are you coming to me about it? What does Lieutenant Woolton say?"

"I didn't want to wake him up, sir."

Dan sighed. "How long's it going to take?"

Schweinberg drawled, looking out the porthole at the beach, "Oh, I don't know, sir, that depends on a lot of things. See, I got to find this specific guy—"

"You just got to get ashore one last time, don't you, Chunky?"

"Like I said, sir, it's not for me, it's—"

"I know, I know, the charts." Lenson glanced past Schweinberg at Hayes. Buck caught the tired irony in his eyes, knew suddenly that the XO understood he was being conned. "Okay, *enough*. Go ashore, if it's that important to you. But I want you back before dark."

"Yessir."

"Thank you, sir," said Hayes, giving the XO a half salute, though he had no cap on. Lenson fixed him with a gimlet eye, but all he said was "Keep an eye on him, Buck."

Back in their stateroom, Schweinberg grinned and banged a fist into his shoulder. "How you like them apples? Told you Papa Chunky fix!"

"One of these days you're going to step on your crank with him, Claude, and you'll walk out with it nailed to your boots."

Schweinberg's voice was muffled by his soaked skivvy shirt. "I never fly higher than I'm prepared to fall. Shower for me, then I'm off to the local Hooter's. You comin'?"

Buck considered it. He tended to regret nights out with his roommate. Then again, this might be their last time ashore in a while.

"Well?"

And after a moment, Hayes said, grinning, "Sure."

Virgil was one of the western Montana Hayeses. His family had raised sheep near Kalispell since 1888. He'd grown up there, and his dad and mom still ranched on the South Fork. But he'd wanted to see what the world held. The same impulse that had pulled his great-grandfather west in the Seventh Cavalry pulled him east, first to the University of Iowa for aeronautical engineering, and then into the Navy.

Pensacola, the sweltering sea-level Gulf Coast, had been a revelation. And not only in climate. Living among whites, he'd

never consciously differentiated himself from them. How
wrong he was, he'd found out one night in a waterfront bar.
He'd nearly lost an eye, and graduated flight school six months
behind his class.

Now Bucky Hayes was a married man, with two kids and
coming up on his five-year decision point. In his locker, he had
a letter from ATI, Advanced Technology Instrumentation. It
was a job offer, developing night-vision displays for helicopters.
He'd have to answer it pretty soon.

Now, his half-minute shower over, he pulled on boxer shorts
and paused before the mirror. Well-defined pecs, triceps coming
up; he turned, tensing deltoids to show smooth muscle. Next
time someone swung at him, the outcome would be different.

Behind him, in the other stall, Schweinberg was bellowing a
fight song under the steady roar. Hayes thought of saying
something—fresh water was always scarce—but then decided
it wasn't his place. And he had to bunk with the guy. It was
better to have him clean.

Schweinberg. He remembered the time he'd visited him at
home. Schweinberg's uncle, a construction contractor in Or-
tega, had hired him to knock down a wall. Schweinberg had
strapped himself into an old Fury and crashed it into the building at forty-five, with Hayes getting it all on the VCR.

Back in their room, he pulled on jeans and a rugby shirt he'd
picked up in Gibraltar. Bahrain was friendly territory, but only
a fool went on liberty in uniform in the Gulf.

By the time they emerged onto the quarterdeck, the sun was
turning the desert to the west gold and scarlet. They nodded to
the flag, then ran down the rattling gangway.

The quay was just oil-stained concrete, hot and still. "Take
you, foot of the pier," Hayes said, starting to jog.

"It's too fucking hot for that shit," said Schweinberg, and
then, as Hayes slowed, lunged past him in a linebacker's sprint.
He stayed ahead for a hundred yards before Hayes caught him,
but he was fifty yards behind when their feet thudded on the
dusty soil of Bahrain.

At the gate a dented yellow Land Rover coughed into life and
ground toward them. The driver was at least seventy, with a
beard like a goat's and sandblasted eyes under a dirty burnoose. "Hello," he said, his withered hand gripping and releasing the wheel as if that was all that kept him upright. "My name
is James. You gentlemen require a ride?"

"James, huh?" said Schweinberg. "We needum go Manama
Airport, lickety-split. Can do?"

"Manama airport, sure. Get in."

Hayes held him back. "Wait a minute, Chunky. How much you want to stick with us all night?" he asked the driver.

"Yeah, good idea. . . . You understand, buddy? All night?" Schweinberg traced an arc on his watch. The old man stared at him for a while, then said, "Sixty bucks."

They winced, protested, but he wouldn't drop a nickel. At last, they got in. Hayes slammed the back door fruitlessly twice before noticing a twisted hook of coat hanger.

They sat there for almost a minute, then realized he was waiting to be paid. "Later, later," said Hayes, but the truck wouldn't go into gear till they each passed up ten dollars earnest money. When he had it carefully put away, the old man bent to the snapped-off shift column. Too late to do any good, Hayes saw that the one hand was all the old Arab had. His left arm ended in a neat surgical stump.

They left the jitney at the service wing of the air terminal, cautioning the old man again to wait, and wandered down a corridor with signs in Arabic and English. At last they found the meteorological officer. Short and fair and flushed, he was sipping from a teacup when Schweinberg laid his elbows on the counter and belched politely. His pale eyes slid up over the rim like two slowly rising moons. "Pilots only in here, chappies," he said.

The heavy lids flickered once. "We're pilots, Jack. How's about some maps?"

"What kind of pilots are *you?*"

"U.S. Air Force, advance party for the B-52 wing."

"I beg your . . . ?" The official's mustache seemed to have suddenly stuck to the teacup. "Did you say—"

"Didn't you get the word? Got a wing of fifty Buffs movin' in. Revetments, bunkers, shops, the works. Going to bomb the Assahollah, I mean the Ayatollah, to Kingdom Come. Now. Maps."

"Ah, what kind of maps did you need, gentlemen?"

They left with two tubes of old commercial air charts of Iran. The Land Rover was waiting where they'd left it, and James was asleep. Schweinberg shook him, then wiped his hand on his jeans. "Okay, that's enough doo-dah for the fucking XO," he grunted. "Let's get turgid."

Bahrain being officially dry, there were only a few places to foregather for beverages. They discussed their choices as they

headed back toward town. One was the Navy Administrative
Service Unit (also known as the Alcoholic Service Unit), which
had an attached bar. The beer was cheap, but they agreed it
tasted like embalming fluid.

"The Londoner Club's got fresh Guinness on tap. Besides"—
Schweinberg lowered his voice for some reason—"that's where
all the Gulf Air stewardesses go."

"There's some nice stuff at the Regency."

"Well, lemme put it this way, Buck. Who's the fucking helicopter commander here?"

Hayes said, "On the other hand, I like the Londoner, too. Why
don't we go to the Londoner?"

They left James and the Rover out front after paying him
another thirty dollars, accompanying it with careful directions
to wait till they came out no matter how late it got. The old man
grinned toothlessly and waved his nonexistent hand. Hayes
swallowed and turned away.

The Londoner was comfortingly dim and smelled of yeast
products and fish and chips. Two Saudis were playing darts.
The rest of the crowd were Americans, Brits, and Germans,
expatriates and contractors. Hayes and Schweinberg slid behind a table and ordered Guinness.

"Now, is this so bad? Why couldn't we all have had tonight
off?" Chunky asked rhetorically. "We're gonna be out there
bleeding from the eyeballs for a week. What's wrong with
Lenson, he can't give us one night to blow off steam?"

"Beer's up, gentlemen."

"Move it, nugget," said Schweinberg, leaning back. Hayes
frowned, resenting his tone, then got up. After all, he was the
junior pilot.

Suds billowed above the steins, ran like sea foam over his
fingers and spatted on the floor. Chunky fastened his to his lips
like emergency air. When he came up, he said, "What were we
talkin' about now—"

"About the XO."

"Oh, yeah. XOs! I seen some winners," said Schweinberg.
"Like off Libya, in the *Ouellet*, there was good old Commander
Horlburt. Give you an idea what we had to deal with, he used
to sleep naked except for a jockstrap and white gloves. Our det
OIC, Ski Collins, roomed with him; he saw it. Horlburt's wife
converted him, and he had these gory pictures—the Bleeding
Heart, the Virgin, all over the room. He had a high drift factor
even for a shoe." Schweinberg closed his eyes and submerged
again for a while, then resumed. "Bertie-Buns loved to do in-

spections. If you didn't do your hospital corners right, he'd pour water in your rack. You'd go out for a double bag at oh-three-hundred, eight hours in the air, then come strolling in ready to pull some serious Zs and find that waitin' . . . Finally he got in a fistfight with one of our guys."

"A fight? No shit?"

"Yeah. We were at the NATO club in Civitavecchia. Well, Ski had a kind of a gas problem. So he was standing there at the bar and just as Horlburt comes in, he lets a juicy one go. And Horlburt says, real annoyed, 'Can't you people act like gentlemen?' And Ski says, 'Sorry, sir, I meant to say "Attention on deck."'

"Well, he took that as an insult, and goddamn near landed one before we got hold of him. And it was funny, 'cause he wasn't a big guy, and we had four big pilots there. We figured, why report something like that, ruin his career, but we decided to take care of him on the side."

"What did you do?"

"Well, one of the guys found this old *Nautical Almanac* in the USO library in Palma. Nineteen fifty-eight, I think it was. We peeled the covers off it and swapped it for the one Horlburt was using. Not one of his star fixes came out for the rest of the cruise. We let the captain in on it and every day he'd ask him where his fix held him. The sonofabitch'd sit there all seized up, and finally mutter 'Ontario' or 'Java.' "

Schweinberg's eyes slid closed in bliss. "You know, black-shoes just ain't like us, Buck. The junior guys ain't so bad, but they get to be oh-fours, oh-fives, shoes get rigid. All the imagination of a bedbug—"

"Hey," said a voice. They looked up at a leather-faced man in a civilian-style flight suit. "Who are you guys? I don't see you here before."

"We're Navy," said Hayes. "Pilots."

"Yeah? Zat so?" He tipped back an oil-company cap to show a gray crew cut. Crow's feet were engraved deep around aviator's eyes. He had a cigar in his mouth and there was a scar on his neck, as if he'd been beheaded, then clumsily repaired. "Peeps Richards, ARAMCO Air Service. Put in twelve years in the Marines. Started at Chu Li, flyin' H-34s, and then 46s."

Schweinberg belched. "Did you hear why the Marine crossed the road?"

After a moment, Richards said, "What's that?"

" 'Cause his dick was in the chicken."

"Shut up, Schweinberg," said Hayes, annoyed. Sometimes

his roommate's no-class act was out of place. "I apologize for him, Colonel."

Richards studied Schweinberg for a moment, then turned to Buck. "Oh, I ain't got no rank anymore, been out for years. I'm a civilian now. Flyin' resupply, Northwest Dome."

"What're you pushing?"

"Jet Rangers. How about you?"

"SH-60s."

"Is that right? I never been in one a them yet. Hear they're candy-ass fly-by-wire airplanes."

"Can we buy you a drink?" asked Hayes.

"Oh, you don't want to buy for me. You're payin' ten a pop for those Guinnesses. Tell you what, bring your glasses over, I got some jungle juice in my flight bag."

It turned out to be Glenlivet, two fifths carefully swaddled in Richards's underwear. The sight unbent Schweinberg's attitude considerably. "Don't get me wrong," he said, looking into the pouchy eyes, "I never refuse gas, but we don't want to drink up that kind of liquor."

"Oh, don't worry about that." Peeps's crow's-feet deepened. "Least I can do for you boys, out here defending me and all. Empty those glasses. Let's see what kind of men the Navy's turning out these days."

They drank steadily as the windows turned black. Richards didn't need much urging to talk. He was well liquored already and he told them several stories about flying in the Gulf, about Lester and Larry and the whale shark, and about life in the expat community. After a few shots, Hayes asked him how much he made, and he modestly admitted to seventy-five.

"Are you ever sorry you got out?"

"I have my moments."

Before Hayes could ask what Peeps meant, Schweinberg wanted to know how he'd picked up the scar.

"Oh, that. A recon team got in trouble out near Quang Tri. Let's see, this was sixty-nine.

"They was surrounded by VC and asked us real nice if we could do a night extraction. So the squadron CO said we'd try. He took the lead bird and two of us volunteered to go in with him.

"Well, the ground fire was so heavy you could hang your flak jacket on it. My heart was jumpin' around like a mouse in a paper bag, but we followed him in. All three choppers took ground fire. My pilot caught a burst in the chest just as a B-40 exploded in the engine. We had fire lights all over the cockpit, and I could hear my gunner screaming, just before he jumped. He'd always said he'd jump before he'd burn.

"Anyway, I tried to autorotate but I misjudged the collective and used up all my turns fifty feet up. Next thing I knew, I was neck-deep in night honey and rice shoots, surrounded by guys shoutin' in Vietnamese and firing AK-47s."

"Wasn't you armed?"

"Just the thirty-eight. Still got it, too." Richards nudged his pocket, slopping prime single malt. "Always been my philosophy, if they're gonna get you anyway, take some of the fuckers along. But there was no sense drawin' attention. So I just wiggled down there between the turds and played dead all night. It was tough, 'cause it opened me up like a smoked mullet, going through the windscreen.

"But I don't want to do all the talkin' here—you need a refill there, Chuckie?"

"Chunky. Yeah, thanks."

Schweinberg told a story that Hayes had heard about six times before. He'd been flying SAR when the Air Force hit Tripoli. He described how the horizon lit up as the F-111s bolted by beneath him, three hundred feet off the water. Then Buck told one: not a war story, but about the time Admiral Augenblick hoisted his flag on the *Deyo* and three planes had been scrambled to get oatmeal for his breakfast. Then the landing lights crapped out on the destroyer and they'd had to do bombing runs with the canisters of Quaker Oats.

The bottle gurgled and Peeps switched instantly to reserve. "So, what you guys doing up here?"

"Convoyin'," said Schweinberg thickly.

"Them Iranians are getting to be a pain in the ass." Richards gazed into his glass, then granted it a quick death. "Fact, I got thumped by two of 'em a couple a weeks back."

"Thumped?" said Hayes.

"There's two F-14s out of Bushehr do a patrol down the demarcation line. Well, I was dropping off a rock-guesser in East Thirty-four when they come out of the sun." He illustrated with his hands. "I wasn't psyched to go evasive just then. They come down in a dive like bats outta hell and then broke, one left, one right. Jet wash was like hittin' a wall in the sky."

He paused to top off. "You want to watch out for those guys. I think they know us in the commercial choppers. But they might figure you for enemy. . . . Chuckie, you ready? Shit, you don't do so bad for swabbies."

"Take it easy, Claude," said Hayes. He'd lost track of how

many, but Schweinberg was staying neck and neck with the old
guy.

The Floridian waved him off. "Hit me," he said thickly, waving the mug. "Fill that fucker to a hundred percent. We're
gonna be at sea for a long, long time."

Richards left when the scotch gave out, but Schweinberg
wanted more beer. They stayed till there was no one playing
darts, no one left at all. At last, the manager threw them out.
"Airway, breathing, circulation," mumbled Hayes as they staggered forth. Schweinberg's arm was over his shoulder and his
Nike Airs squeaked as they dragged. Outside, the dark was
very dark and the quiet was very quiet. The night was cool and
the parking lot was empty.

Buck Hayes slowly became aware of a total lack of yellow
Land Rovers with one-handed ex-thieves in them. "Fo-ock," he
mumbled. He sat down on the curb. The night looked as if it had
been taken apart and put back together wrong. He had to hold
a steady left rudder to keep it out of a spin. He'd partied hearty
before with Schweinberg, but now he realized they'd made a
mistake trying to keep up with the old Marine. Also they were
miles from the pier, and the only thing moving on the whole
street was a dog, far off, eating something off the pavement.

He got up suddenly, staggered a few steps off, and stood
bent, waiting miserably for the inevitable.

Chunky Schweinberg was feeling no such anxiety. When
Hayes had let go, he'd buckled slowly at the knees, muttering,
"Death—but first, cheech." Now he lay face down, examining
a cigarette butt up close.

He was remembering the double-wide he'd grown up in. Shep
and Blackie and Bull Head out in the yard. His mother, sitting
in the car with white gloves on, looking at him and his father
with that hopeless expression on her face. He was suddenly
conscious of a tremendous sadness. "I used to have a ferret,"
he mumbled.

"Say what?"

"A ferret . . . got him when he was little, raised him by hand
. . . I really liked that fuckin' ferret."

"What was his name?" asked Hayes. Claude saw Buck's face
in the streetlight and thought with sudden piercing insight, No
wonder they call 'em shines.

"Oh, we called him Shit. 'Here, Shit.' 'Have you fed Shit yet,
Claude?' my mom use to say." His lips were smiling against the
concrete, but unshed tears were dissolving his heart. He saw

the russet and cream muzzle nuzzling the earth, heard his dad's
shovel grating . . . his mom was gone then. . . . He'd really loved
that fucking Shit, goddamn him, why did the fucking dogs have
to get him? It seemed like everything you loved passed like
that, and he would eat dirt too someday. . . .

The black nugget went away again. Chunky listened to him
tossing his grits for a long time. At last, heavy breathing
rasped above him, and then a loose-lipped mumble. "What?" he
muttered.

"Quit playin' speedbump, Chunky. We got to get back to the
ship."

"Jus' cool it, Buckwheat."

"What'd you say?"

"Huh?"

"What'd you call me, Schweinberg?"

"Bucky. Thass your name, ain't it?"

"I thought I heard somethin' else." Hayes stared at him, then
reached down. "Come *on.*"

Dragging the senior lieutenant down the empty median,
Buck Hayes felt mingled fear and hilarity. It hadn't seemed
funny while he was spraying cookies, but now it was so horrible
he wanted to laugh. Then he thought, If somebody comes out
of these alleys, it ain't going to be funny at all. He couldn't
fight, and he couldn't abandon Schweinberg, either.

"Hey, there's a car."

"It's not a taxi, though."

"I don't care what it is, flag it."

"Maybe it's cops."

"Do they got cops here? I ain't seen any yet. I hope it is a
cop."

"Don't say that." Hayes shivered, remembering the old
man's stump. He didn't even want to know the penalty for
public drunkenness in Bahrain.

The lights drew closer. The pilots separated, each taking a
lane. When the car stopped, Schweinberg, fumbling at his wallet, weaved around to the driver's side.

There were two tiny people in the Honda, a middle-aged couple. There were suitcases in the back seat. They looked pleased
at being stopped in the middle of the night. They smiled up as
Schweinberg breathed his predicament into their faces. When
he was done, the woman said something to her husband. Then
they all four just smiled at one another. "Jeez, she's pretty,"
said Chunky. "What are they, Japanese? Andrea, forgive me,
I'm in love."

Hayes said doubtfully, "Do you think they have the faintest idea who we are?"

"Do you understand me?" said Schweinberg to her, raising his voice. "American military, need to get back to ship?"

The woman bobbed her head, and after a moment the man did, too.

"See? They understand."

"Will you give us a ride?"

"There, she's nodding."

"What a smile."

"What nice teeth."

"But how we going to tell them where to go?"

"We can't," said Schweinberg. He opened the door and motioned her out. Laughing in low, nervous voices, the Japanese looked around the empty street. Then they bowed. Schweinberg bowed back, steadying himself on the hood. This seemed to reassure them, and they got in back with the suitcases.

"You better let me drive."

"No, I got it." Schweinberg seized the wheel with an expression of great concentration. He mashed the gas experimentally and the engine tried to chew its way out of the hood. There were whispers in back. Hayes beamed them his best shit-eater. "Don't worry, we're U.S. Navy," he said. "We really appresh, appre, well, this is sure great of you. Won't take us long, just down to Salman."

"Hey, Bucky."

"Yeah?"

"How do we get back to the ship?"

"Christ! Claude, don't you know?"

"Course I do. Lemme think. Lessee . . . lessee . . ." He craned upward through the windshield. "Aw right, Big Dipper's on duty! Keep it in the back window and we ought to get there."

"Oh, Christ," said Hayes again.

They went east till the water glimmered. Hayes picked up a radio tower he recognized and they steered for that. They were almost on the causeway to Sitra Island before they realized it. At Hayes's shout, Schweinberg jerked the wheel, too suddenly, and they hit the median and went airborne. The car sailed over the dry ground between lanes for what seemed like a long time, then hit with a rattling jolt that snapped their heads into the dash.

"Down and locked!" howled Schweinberg. "You still there, man?"

"Still here, you still there?"

"ATO, get me a fucking fix!"

There was an excited babble from the back seat. They ignored it. "Home plate dead ahead, range one mile," said Hayes.

They slowed for the gate guard, holding up I.D.s. When they were clear, Schweinberg accelerated again. Warehouses loomed ahead. They plunged between them into a hardstand of palleted cargo, racing down a twenty-foot-wide lane at fifty miles an hour. There was muffled whimpering from the rear now.

Looking out the right window, Hayes saw a head. This seemed odd and he blinked and tried to focus. Yep, a yellow hard hat was moving along with them on the far side of a long stack of oil drums. "Hey," he said. "Look over there."

"I can't. I'm driving," said Schweinberg. His lower lip was between his teeth and he was staring straight ahead.

"There's a guy over there."

"Is that so? He's workin' late."

"Uh-huh." Hayes closed his eyes for a moment. When he opened them again, the head was in the same relative position, but it was larger. This was interesting. When another aircraft did that, it meant you were on a collision course. "Wonder 'f he sees us," he muttered.

"What?"

"I said, wonder—"

They came to an intersection and the forklift, with the man Hayes had been watching on top of it, came out of the side aisle with the forks three feet off the pavement. Metal screamed as it tore, and Schweinberg shouted, "Shit! That sonofabitch almost hit us!"

Hayes felt wind on his feet. He looked down to see the roadway going by. "Uh, hey, he did. Hey, uh . . . do you see that water ahead?"

"Huh?"

"God damn it, Schweinberg, *stop!*"

The brakes worked great. There were thuds and cries from the back seat. The pilots unfolded themselves clumsily. Hayes took all the money he had left and leaned back inside. The Japanese were staring fixedly forward, no longer smiling. "Uh, thank you," he mumbled thickly. "We're sorry about the car. Is it a rental car? I hope so. Send us the bill if it's more than this, aw right? Thank the nice people, Chunk Style."

"Th' y'," mumbled Schweinberg. He let go of the door tentatively, grabbing handfuls of air to stay erect. Behind him, the door slammed. The Honda's little engine tapped, and torn sheet metal squeaked against the rear tire as it moved off.

They stumbled down the pier. Hayes felt as if the air had

been let out of his legs. Schweinberg didn't feel anything, no more than if he were floating toward the ship on a whiskey cloud. At last the brow slanted ahead. Grimly, like mountain climbers assaulting the summit, they hauled themselves toward the quarterdeck.

Hayes glanced around, ready for Lenson to jump out from the shadows, but there was only a sleepy, pissed-off-looking enlisted man. "Hope you *officers* had a good time ashore," he said.

"We had a *great* time," roared Schweinberg, groping forward toward the hatchway. But Hayes stood still for a moment, peering into a sudden, yawning blackness. The hangar. In the dimness he could make out the folded tail boom, the looming mass of 421.

The liberty, the snatched hour of freedom, was over. Suddenly he was aware that his shirt was soaked with sweat, that he stank of beer and vomit. He was getting too old for this. He had a family now. A family he ought to be with more, provide for better. . . .

Not knowing why, he stepped into the waiting maw. It eclipsed the distant twinkle of Manama, swallowed it in a gulf of absolute blackness. Not as if the light had never been at all, but the blacker black of a final end, of what had once been but now no longer was.

He was staring into it still when a jingle came from behind him. The faint metal kiss of pocketed keys. He turned, and made out a figure between him and the stars. "What are you doing in there?" came a sharp voice.

"Just looking at the plane. Who're you?"

"Duty officer. Who are *you?*"

"Lieutenan' Hayes. Hi, Terry."

The voice came closer. "Virgil? You all right?"

"Had a couple drinks . . . just going below."

"You sure you're all right?"

"Yeah. Yeah, I'm fine."

"Well, okay. Take care of yourself, brother."

He swallowed. "Will do," he said thickly. "You, too, brother."

He felt the light slap of a hand on his own, and made out, in the faint light from outside, the dark, somber eyes of *Van Zandt*'s weapons officer.

Schweinberg's holler, deep in the ship: "Bucky! You comin'?"

"Comin', Chunky," he said. Turning, he staggered forward, after his friend.

II

THE CONVOY

6

U.S.S. *Turner Van Zandt*

DAN leaned over the chart table, squinting into the morning sun as it fired a warning shot of heat across the flats of the Khawr al Qualay'ah and through the windows of the bridge. Senior Chief McQueen, the assistant navigator, was correcting their courses out for the tidal current. Around them was the usual morning yawning and chatter, but today it was muted, expectant, like an audience before a premiere.

It was always like that, the first time under way with a new skipper in charge.

Captain Shaker strolled in from the wing, lighting a Camel as the harbor pilot explained the channel out. Lieutenant Terry Pensker, the combat systems officer and at the moment the officer of the deck, was talking on the intercom, finishing up the underway checkoff. Dan shoved away from the chart table, catching the captain's eye.

He wanted to stay visible, ready to take over if the skipper decided on prudence over valor. *Perry*s were single-screw ships, harder to maneuver in close quarters than older destroyer classes. Today their situation would challenge any shiphandler: starboard side to, with a northerly wind setting them on the pier. And a tanker behind them and a waste barge tied up forward left no room for learning on the job.

The Bahraini was saying, "The tug will make up to you forward, Captain, so if you want to—"

"No tug," said Shaker. He didn't look at Dan. "Thanks. Terry, we ready to shove off?"

Pensker saluted. "Checkoff list complete, Captain, ready to get under way."

"Very well." Shaker raised his voice above the mechanical and human murmur. "This is the captain. I have the conn."

"Aye aye, sir." A chorus from the bridge team, helmsman,

lee helmsman, phone talkers, boatswain, quartermasters, and
Dan. Talk and yawning came to an abrupt end.

"Take in lines one, three, four, five, and six. Hard right rudder."

As talkers and helmsman repeated the orders, Dan followed
Shaker's top-heavy bulk out to the wing again. The wind
brought him the captain's smell, tobacco and sweat and a hint
of shaving cream. Below them, the lines came in, tossed off the
bollards by overalled pier crew, then hauled aboard smartly by
the deck gang. The phone talker trailed the officers, tugging his
cord behind him like a ladies' train, relaying reports as the lines
came in. When only number two still restrained them, Shaker
looked into the wind for a moment, glanced back along the ship,
then snapped, "Engines ahead one-third, indicate three knots."

Seated at the console that filled the center of the bridge, the
helmsman advanced a lever; a needle followed it upward.
"Ahead one-third, indicate three knots . . . engines answer,
ahead one-third, sir."

Dan propped his shoe on the signal-light bracket and watched
fascinated as Shaker, cap tilted back, walked the stern out,
holding the bow back from the barge with a combination of
spring line and jockeying the throttle between ahead and
astern. The Bahraini harbor pilot hovered behind him, looking
anxious. The strip of oily water slowly widened.

Shaker ordered the last line in as the stern cleared the tanker,
then slacked his rudder and increased power aback. The pier
began to move forward.

The combination of stern-walk and the wind swung *Van
Zandt* neatly onto course for the southern fairway. Shaker
ordered an ahead bell, steadied her, then looked around, grinning faintly at the relieved faces around him. "This is the skipper," he said, raising his voice again. "Lieutenant Pensker has
the conn."

"This is Lieutenant Pensker, I have the deck and the conn."

I wouldn't have done it that way, Dan thought. I'd have
walked us out with the bow thrusters, and done it a lot slower,
too. At one point, they'd been only fifty feet from the tanker.

But Shaker hadn't even deployed the thrusters. He'd done it
the hard way. And on a ship he'd never maneuvered before. It
was an amazing display, and not only of shiphandling.

McQueen muttered at his elbow. The captain was out on the
wing again, saying something funny, apparently; the high, relieved laugh of the pilot drifted in. Time to navigate. "Officer
of the deck, hold us on track," said Dan. "Recommend ten
knots; next turn, time two-nine."

"Steady as she goes," said Pensker. "Engines ahead two-thirds, indicate ten knots."

"Steady as she goes, aye; course zero-seven-two, checking zero-seven-zero."

"Ahead two-thirds, engines indicate ten knots, sir."

"Very well."

Dan muttered, "You got it, Mac." His assistant immediately said, "Officer of the deck! Turn bearing on fairway marker 'ten' will be two-seven-zero; now bears two-nine-zero; time to next turn, two minutes; next course one-zero-seven, pick up the A.S.R.Y. range markers."

Pensker was staring through his binoculars at the channel ahead. "Very well," he said again, in a tight voice.

Dan studied the weapons officer from behind. Early as it was, there were stains under his lifted arms. It was good to take conning seriously, and a new CO put everyone on his best behavior, but Pensker seemed nervous. He was a good officer, intelligent, dedicated, but sometimes he tried too hard. Maybe it had something to do with his being the only minority officer in the wardroom.

Beyond him was the blinding dazzle of morning at the latitude of the Sahara. To starboard, coral reefs drew a sapphire line beneath the crème de menthe of the bay. To port, a short chop splintered the new sun above the shallows. The fathometer clucked sleepily. Six feet under their keel. Astern, their screw would be kicking up mud, turning the wake the color of bakers' chocolate. But it would deepen past the next turn. They were headed fair.

McQueen marked the turn bearing and Pensker rapped orders to the helmsman. The steering gear hummed and the jack staff began marching right. Past the choppy line of shoal, past the low metal buildings of the repair yard, past the scorched, fragment-ripped bridge of a tanker holed by an Iraqi missile two months before. The sun shafted through the windows, painting the shadows of the bridge team across the receivers and cables on the aft bulkhead. Pensker ordered fifteen knots. They felt the acceleration almost at once; the gas turbines, marinized jet engines, responded faster than the steam plants on older ships.

Shaker came in from the wing. He studied the chart over Dan's shoulder. Exposed rock slipped down their starboard side, looking like the pumice in gas grills. A few minutes later, Sitra anchorage came into view. A dozen ships, freighters and empty, waiting tankers rode to anchor in the morning breeze, all pointing the same way, like sheep on a hillside. Service boats and water taxis skimmed among them. They moved past rusty hulls, the flaking paint of working merchantmen. A Dutch ship dipped her flag. *Van Zandt* returned the salute.

"Mr. Lenson."

"Yessir, Captain."

"What's the watch routine? What condition did Bell steam at?"

"Condition three, sir."

"How many sections?"

"Three."

"We have enough tactical action officers?"

"Yes sir, our TAOs are school-qualified and they've stood watch since we inchopped."

"Okay, good." Shaker looked closely at Dan's shirt. "That's polyester."

"Yes, sir."

"Get the word around, I don't want people wearing that under way anymore. Cotton uniforms only."

Dan nodded.

"Pilot boat approaching to port," said the phone talker. Shaker went out on the wing again. He shook hands with the Arab, then led him aft. The boat curved toward them, matching course and speed and then nuzzling closer, like a baby whale moving in to nurse.

When Shaker came back up, he stood for a time looking out. He had that same abstracted expression Dan had noted before. Finally he said, "Any more course changes?"

"We'll be on this leg for another hour, into the Gulf, Captain."

"Okay," said Shaker. He brought his watch up. Like most Navy men, he wore it on the inside of his wrist, to avoid cracking the crystal against bulkheads or ladderways. "General quarters, Bo's'n, if you please."

The bridge exploded into activity. "General quarters, general quarters," the 1MC barked in BM2 Stanko's clipped growl. "All hands man your battle stations. Set material condition zebra throughout the ship."

Dan stabbed his Seiko and snapped to McQueen, "You got it, Senior. Keep an eye out for *fashts* and fish traps."

"Right, Commander."

He slid into the combat information center, one level down, and caught a gas mask and a life jacket in the air. Snapping them on, he settled into the captain's chair and looked around. CIC was lit in dim blue, air-conditioned icy for the electronics.

The last few arrivals were flipping switches and buckling seat belts. The ESM console was lit and operating. As he looked around, thumbs came up at the surface-search radar, the air-search repeater, the plotting board, the weapons console. Beside him, Al Wise, the operations boss, plugged his headset into the TAO jack. "Sonar, manned and ready," came a shout from behind the curtains, and Dan put on his own headset, dialed the battle circuit, and said, "Bridge, CIC; manned and ready down here."

"Bridge aye."

"Engineering, manned and ready," said another voice on the line.

"Weps Control, manned and ready."

Dan asked him, "Terry, what are you missing?"

"Just DC . . . wait . . ."

"Damn it," Lenson muttered.

"Damage control, manned and ready."

"All stations, manned and ready, sir," he heard Pensker telling Shaker. Dan looked at his watch. Two minutes and thirty-two seconds.

The bridge door, locked watertight, came undogged. The captain appeared. He looked around in the darkness, then came toward Lenson. "Isn't that my chair?" he said.

"Yessir. Captain Bell wanted me here for GQ. He preferred the bridge. If you want to change that—"

"We'll discuss it. Is that as fast as we button up?"

"We're the fastest in the squadron, sir. Average is more like five or six minutes." Dan hesitated. "And if you're talking incoming ordnance, we're ready to fire in seconds with the regular watch."

"Is that so? Okay, let's stand down."

Wise passed the word up and a moment later the boatswain's pipe shrilled "Secure." Dan took off his headset, hesitated again, and said, "Captain, we'll be serving breakfast in about twenty minutes."

"Have them send it up. I'm going over the officer records in my cabin."

"Aye, sir."

"And I'd like to see you there, say about eight?"

"Yes, sir."

He left. Dan unbuckled his gear and left it with a radarman, then went back up to the bridge. McQueen was correcting the track south. Lieutenant (jg) Tad Proginelli was relieving Pensker. Dan had a word with him about navigational aids off

Qatar and warned him to be alert for small contacts, dhows and oil-rig service craft.

He stepped out on the wing and took a last look around. The land was dropping behind them, dun and gray, already blurred at five miles by the dust-laden air. Below the tan sky, below the climbing ball of sun—it would be deadly later—the Gulf shimmered ahead, blue and vast, interrupted only by the distant white superstructure of a hull-down freighter. It was headed north, to Kuwait or the Iranian oil port at Khārk Island. He stared at it, disquieted at the captain's evident dissatisfaction. This was the best ship in the Mideast; Hart had said as much.

Then he dismissed it. He was hungry, and it was time to eat.

The wardroom was empty, the twin tables waiting set with silver and plates. Then, in the corner, he heard voices, and frowned as he glanced toward them.

Two of the pilots, Schweinberg and Hayes. They had no assigned stations unless they were launching the bird. He half-listened as he studied the menu. Omelets, french toast, bacon, juice.

"Yeah, she was fat all right. Should have painted stripes on her, tell you which end to make your approach from."

"A real pizza and beer special. She was all over you, Chunky."

"Like white on rice."

"Like stink on shit, you mean."

There was a pause. Outside in the passageway the speaker announced "Breakfast for the crew. Watch reliefs and first-class petty officers to the head of the mess line."

The next voice he heard was Schweinberg's. "So, whaddya think of this new captain?"

Hayes's: "I don't know anything about him, Chunky."

"You know he lost the last ship he was on? They never fired a shot."

"Why not?"

"Just slack, just a nonperformer. They say he had the guns turned off. They say this turkey's a real—"

"Mr. Schweinberg," said Dan.

The heavy head came around the corner of the TV nook, the heavy-lidded eyes peering blearily for him. "Oh, hello, XO."

"When did the two of you get in last night?"

"Oh—not too late."

"I said *when?*"

"I didn't really notice, sir," said Hayes innocently.

"I see. Where were you at officer's call?"

Schweinberg said, "Well, sir, we sort of thought, the flight det don't need to be up and about for getting under way. That's ship-driving stuff. So we, well, we were checkin' our eyelids for light leaks."

"Those are for all officers. *All* officers."

After a pause, Hayes said, "Okay, Commander."

"And another thing. I didn't like what I just heard. First off, it's wrong. But regardless of that, you're way, *way* out of line talking like that about the CO. I don't want to hear that kind of crap aboard this ship again. Is that understood?"

He was shouting when he finished. The black flier nodded; then Schweinberg did, too. Dan, still angry, stared at them a moment longer, then turned away.

The other officers trickled in, saw him seated, and requested permission to join him. Dan nodded shortly. He had a western omelet and picked out the meat bits, shoving them to the side of his plate. The juice leaned slowly in his glass, then inclined gradually to the opposite side. The conversation was subdued. Guerra and Wise ate stolidly; Hayes and Schweinberg said nothing, ate with their eyes on their plates. Pensker still looked nervous. Dan thought about getting them talking, then decided he'd leave it up to them. He didn't have long before he had to see Shaker one on one for the first time.

For some reason, he wasn't looking forward to it.

At five minutes to eight, he was outside the captain's door. The ship's chief master at arms, Nolan, was standing there with a short man in tow. "Waiting for the Captain?" Dan asked him.

"For you, too, sir. Meet Hospitalman Bernard Phelan, sir."

Dan shook his hand. It felt cold. Phelan looked very young; Indian of some kind, at a guess. "Welcome aboard, Phelan. I got to get on the PN's tail, I missed your orders somehow."

"We weren't expecting him, sir," said Nolan.

Lenson considered that, then decided it could wait. "Chief, this isn't a good time for him. The CO wants to see me now and it'll probably take awhile. Have you got him a bunk? Sheets? Got his records?"

"I got a bunk, sir," said Phelan. "Records, though, they're still on the *Long Beach.*"

Lenson nodded and looked at the door. Then he thought, What? "What do you mean?"

"I missed the ship in Karachi, sir," said Phelan. He had a low voice, soft and timid-sounding. Dan evaluated his uniform, hair-

cut and mustache. They were borderline acceptable. Phelan
didn't meet his eyes, but that could be shyness.

"You missed movement? That's pretty serious. What happened?"

"Well, it's complicated, sir."

"Give me the short version."

"Well, we had forty-eight hours libs, sir. I was on my way
back when there was a traffic accident. I got involved taking
care of a little girl. She was messed up pretty bad. I rode with
her to the hospital. I sort of forgot about the ship, making sure
she was all right. Then when I got to the pier, it was too late."

"Then what happened?"

"Well, I didn't know what to do at first, so I got a room in
town. The next day, I figured the thing to do was turn myself
in at the leg—leg—"

"Legation?" said Nolan.

"Yessir, I mean, yes, Chief. They held me for another couple
of days and then got me on a flight to Bahrain. They said over
at headquarters I could sort of augment with you for a while."

Dan nodded. He had no way to evaluate the story. Or the
man. He'd learned long ago you couldn't tell what another
human being was like from appearances. You just couldn't
judge them that way. Not even military people. The uniform
was misleading. It said, We're all alike, we're all the same, less
complex than civilians. But under the uniforms there was just
as much variation, depth, mystery, suffering, and enlighten-
ment as anyone else possessed.

So you had to take them on faith. The kid looked sincere.
Close up, though, his eyes had an unfocused look. "You been
getting much sleep?" Dan asked him.

"No, sir. Up all night on the plane."

"Well, you got a home till we meet up with *Long Beach*. I'm
glad you're aboard; Doc's been complaining he's up to his ears
in record review. I'll drop down to sick bay tomorrow and we'll
have a talk."

"Aye, sir."

They shook hands again, Phelan saluted, and they left. Dan
glanced down, checking his own uniform. Everything was cotton now, and he'd exchanged his shiny but flammable Corfams
for leather shoes.

He knocked, and a moment later let himself in.

The captain's cabin was the size of a small bedroom. It held a
low round table, two chairs, a built-in sofa, and a porthole. Dan

noticed that Bell's print of *Channel Dash* was gone. In its place
hung a family portrait. An insulated coffee server and cups
waited on the table, along with Van Zandt's *Battle Doctrine*,
the *Organization and Regulations Manual*, and several manila jackets. He recognized two as service and medical records.
The last, the red one, was the personnel reliability folder kept
by the COs of each ship that carried what the Navy called
"special weapons."

"Be out in a minute," Shaker's voice boomed from the wash-
room. "Sit down."

He took the sofa, noticing, as he edged by the table, that the
records were his own. He noticed something else, too, something about the photo on the bulkhead. As he got closer, he saw
what it was. A woman and two boys. The woman's face had
been razored out in a neat rectangle.

Shaker came out a few minutes later, in uniform trou and
T-shirt, with a towel round his neck. His cheeks and nose were
reddened already from the sun. He looked tired. "This humidity's a killer," he said. "How we fixed for water?"

"Topped off yesterday. Both evaps are up. We allow thirty
gallons per man per day, including laundry and cooking."

"Certainly sounds adequate. Coffee?"

"Yessir, thanks."

Shaker poured himself a cup, too. "In here," he said, glancing
across at him, "what do you say, let's make it Ben and Dan."

Close up, Shaker's pale blue-gray eyes reminded him of those
Alaskan dogs, huskies, malamutes. Dan had to look away.
"Okay . . . Ben."

There was a knock at the door. It was the messenger of the
watch, a seaman apprentice named Billetts. His voice shook as
he relayed the officer of the deck's respects and requested permission to strike eight bells on time.

"Do it. Thank you," said Shaker. The seaman saluted, and
left with a look of relief. When the door was shut, he said,
"That's something we don't need to do anymore."

"Eight and noon reports?"

"Right. I know it's in *Customs and Ceremonies*, but it's a
time-waster. We'll do it in port. Not at sea."

Dan pulled out his wheel book and made a note.

"Okay," said Shaker. He shook out a Camel and proffered the
pack; Dan shook his head. The captain flicked a Zippo and inhaled. "Well. Here we are, back where sailors belong."

Dan nodded and waited.

"I don't know much about you, Dan. I looked through your

records, though. There's some funny things there. Anyway,
let's see, Naval Academy, thirty-five, divorced . . . any kids?"

"One. A girl."

"See her often?"

"Not a lot. She and her mother live out west now."

"How long since you split up?"

"About ten years."

Shaker nodded slowly. "I know how it is. I'm just coming off
a break-up myself."

Dan couldn't think of anything to say other than "I'm sorry
to hear that."

"Forget it. It was a relief getting to sea, away from FX-2 and
her fucking lawyers. At least here you got some steel between
you and the sharks . . . okay." Shaker tapped the service jacket.
"You've got a real interesting career path on you, Lieutenant-
Commander Lenson."

"I guess so."

"You were on the old *Ryan* off Ireland when she went down,
right? Spent some time in the hospital?"

"Yes. Burns."

"Those are hell. I got toasted a little myself on the *Strong*.
The legs. That still bother you?"

Dan rubbed his shoulder as he thought. Did the old destroyer's death still bother him? How could he answer that?
The nightmares he'd had for years seldom came now. No longer
did he hallucinate, even in waking, *Kennedy*'s bow towering
above him as he clung to the splinter shield, too terrified to
move. On the other hand, he'd never told the Navy doctors what
it felt like when he tried to lift his left arm over his head.

"It was a long time ago," he said at last.

"Then, let's see, you were in the Med when the Syrian thing
broke. I remember reading about that. What ever happened to
that commodore?"

"Sundstrom. He retired," said Lenson. "Right after that."

"Then the business with the Spru-boat off Cuba. The *Barrett*.
How'd you get issued that can of worms?"

"That was my department-head tour."

"Good God. What's the story on the Silver Star?"

"No story," said Dan uneasily. "It's all there in the record,
isn't it?"

"Sort of. Then this last tour, Pentagon, J-3. And then back to
sea duty again. You've pulled a hell of a lot of it, one shore tour
in fifteen years."

Dan shrugged. Shaker eyed him for a while, then flipped the
folder closed and leaned back. "Okay, talk to me."

"What do you want to know?"

"The basics. Muster, for instance."

Dan cleared his throat. The smoky haze around the table was making his eyes water. "We have a full wartime complement aboard. Hundred and sixty-eight crew, thirteen officers including you and me. No, one sixty-nine, just picked up a corpsman from *Long Beach*. We have a partial helo det, since we're carrying only one SH-60; that's thirteen men, four pilots. Total assigned, one hundred and ninety-nine. We have one man on emergency leave to the States and two in sick bay."

"What's the story on the leave?"

"One of the radiomen. His father died. He'll rejoin us after this convoy."

"The guys out sick?"

"Minor, or we'd have left them in Bahrain."

"What kind of personnel problems do you see?"

Dan considered. "We won't have much turnover till we get back home. A couple people went to captain's mast after Diego Garcia. Unauthorized absentees, disagreements with the base police, one complaint of harassment from a female P-3 mechanic. No trouble since we hit the Gulf. There's a couple det officers who tear loose sometimes in port. But nothing serious. We have a strong wardroom."

"Tear loose?" said Shaker. "You mean what by that?"

"Getting drunk, fighting, hung over. Late over liberty a couple of times."

"Shit, XO, that's what the Navy's all about. Don't you enjoy a few brews?"

"I don't drink much anymore," said Lenson.

"Oh yeah? Now, Guerra told me he got that control valve fixed, so that leaves one casualty report outstanding."

"Yes, sir, one of the satellite receivers. We can cover broadcast with the other one and go to HF in a pinch."

"Okay. How about efficiency? Fuel consumption?"

"It's better than fleet average, considering the sea temperature."

"Hart seems to think our engineering plant's in good shape."

"Yes, sir, it is. Rick's an excellent chief engineer. He was main propulsion assistant on *Paul Foster;* he knows gas turbines."

"Damage control?"

"Everyone's general DC-qualified, and our repair teams got outstanding grades at refresher training."

"What's our weapons loadout?"

"The missile mag's full. One test round, four Harpoons, the

remainder Standards. Two of them are the extended-range Mark One-Alfas with a retrofitted RIM-2 Terrier warhead."

"Yeah, I noticed that. Why are we carrying nukes?"

"I frankly don't know," said Dan. "They're the old-style anti-aircraft warheads, for breaking up big flights of bombers."

Shaker seemed to ponder this for a few seconds. Then he said, "How about the guns?"

"We have full magazines for the seventy-six millimeter and the Phalanx, and our small arms locker is full, too. We've used some up for practice, but we're well within wartime allowance."

"Torpedoes?"

"Full loadout of Mark 46s."

Shaker sat motionless for a while, staring at the circle of light that was the porthole. He lit another cigarette. At last, he said, "Dan, I'm sorry to have to say this. By Navy standards, this is an outstanding ship. But from what I've seen, she is far from ready to fight."

Dan stiffened in his chair. This wasn't the response he'd expected.

"Go ahead, say it," said Shaker.

"With all due respect, sir—Ben—I think it is. Certainly it's the best-prepared ship I've ever served on. This is the second time we've won the squadron *E*."

"It's certainly the *cleanest* ship I've ever seen in a war zone. And the admin inspection was four-oh. But I'm not sure either of those are valid indicators of battle readiness." Shaker deliberated, then stretched to pull a message from his desk. "I was reviewing last week's traffic. Since *Van Zandt*'s been in the Gulf, Iranian activity has been low. Their attention has been tied up with the offensive up in the marshes.

"Now that's come to a halt. There's a stalemate on their front, and in order to break it they may decide to heat things up again at sea. I don't think they'd try anything on our way south. We're not an attractive target alone. But on our way back with the convoy, I'm insuring my ass for all it's worth. They have the perfect weapons now in that shipment of Silkworm missiles the Chinese sold them, and they may still have a few Harpoons like they used on *Strong.*"

"I still think—"

"No, listen. I know your previous CO was a book man. And you've done well—by the book. But I don't think it goes far enough. Or in the right direction. For one thing, *Van Zandt* is a firetrap. I intend to change that. We're going to get her ready to take hits and keep fighting."

Dan nodded. It was a reasonable posture for a man who'd been through a major conflagration and sinking.

Shaker said casually, "How long have you been XO?"

"Six months, sir."

"I've looked at your last fitness report. Charlie thought a lot of you."

"Thanks."

"Don't thank me. I didn't ask for you, and at the moment I'm not impressed."

Through sudden anger, Dan said, "I know my job, Captain. It's my duty to carry out your orders. If you want changes aboard this ship, tell me what they are and I'll get to work on them. But it's unfair, I think, to hold me responsible for unspecified matters that the previous commanding officer found satisfactory."

The bridge buzzer chose this rather tense moment to go off. Shaker snatched the phone from the bulkhead and snapped, "Captain."

Dan fought for control as he listened to the one-sided conversation. The captain said, "Wait, wait. I don't want true bearings on incoming surface contacts, Mr. Proginelli. Pass that on to the other officers. Give it to me in relative, and tell me his aspect—port bow, starboard quarter, whatever. I can visualize the situation faster that way.

". . . What's the closest point of approach if you do that?"

". . . Any other contacts to the east? How far away is he? Okay, make it so. Come back to base course when he's past and opening."

Shaker hung up. He evened up the ends of the towel. "Now, what were we talkin' about?"

"This ship's battle readiness. I said that it was unfair to—"

The captain smiled and held up his hand. "Whoa! Let's backtrack. I'm not holding you responsible for anything except carrying out Charlie's agenda. You've been here six months, I've been aboard a day. These are just my initial impressions."

"Yes, sir."

"To go back to your record. In order to pick up lieutenant commander, with the things you've got in your jacket—you got to admit, it's kind of surprising. Who's your rabbi?"

"I don't have a rabbi."

"You must know somebody. Who do you know?"

"I know Vice-Admiral Niles."

"Barry Niles?" Shaker nodded slowly. "I see. Where'd you meet him?"

"During my tour on the *Barrett.*"

"He's a good man," said the captain. "I ran into him in Pearl. Hell of a character. But let's get something straight, Dan. I'm going to judge you, not by what you did before you came to *Van Zandt,* good or bad, and not by who you know. My evaluation of you will be based squarely on what you do for me."

"I expect it to be that way."

"Good. How loyal are you to your commanding officers, Dan?"

"Loyal as hell, Ben."

"I wonder. There's a note here about a letter of reprimand."

"I was an ensign then. And the letter was because I defended Captain Packer after the collision."

"Why did he need defending from an ensign?"

"He was dead."

"I see. And this business with Commodore Sundstrom. You defended him, too?"

"No. He was an incompetent fool. I disobeyed his orders to save lives. His retirement proves I was right."

"Maybe, but it's still not what I'd call a confidence builder." Shaker scratched his chest slowly under the T-shirt. "You and I have got to work together on this ship. I don't want to have to cross swords with you every time I want to do something. I need to know whether I can trust you to carry out my orders to the letter, Dan, without dragging your feet or second-guessing me because they're unorthodox. And they *will* be unorthodox. I've had time to ponder what happened on the *Strong* and I intend to put my conclusions into practice."

"I can understand that."

"Good. Like you said, that's your duty. I want to make sure we get this straight. I know you might have had some idea, before I was ordered in, that you might get this ship yourself. I could understand that. But it can't affect your performance. Because if it does, if there's going to be any jealousy or back-stabbing, let me know, right now, and I'll ask for another XO. Today. I know that won't look good for me, either, but it's important enough to me that I'll take the risk."

"I said I understood that, Ben."

"Understanding's not the same as agreeing, damn it! If I keep you, it's because you've given me your word to support me, even if what I want to do neglects the book, goes beyond the book—or even against the book."

"Yes sir," he said. "Okay, I agree. As long as it's legal, I'll do it for you."

"Good," said Shaker. He extended his hand, and Dan took it.
The captain sat silent after that for a few seconds, as if organizing his thoughts. He lit another cigarette. Then got up and looked out the porthole, his hands gripping the ends of the towel like a fighter stepping into the ring. Past his head, Dan saw the sky: a blurred tan, backed by smoke, as if the horizon were afire. Already the brimstone stink of the Northwest Dome was filtering through the ventilators. They would pass through it on their way south to Hormuz. Beyond it, on their own long trek in, were the ships they'd have to bring through.

"Okay, XO," Shaker said, "Welcome to the fighting Navy. We've got three days till we pick up our convoy. Here's what I want you to do."

7

U.S. Naval Base, Charleston, South Carolina

L IKE most Yankees, Gordon felt uneasy accepting personal service from blacks. And his driver was as black as they came. There was a language barrier too. He'd had to explain where he was going several times, and he had no idea what the man had said in response.

The wipers flailed and clacked at a desultory drizzle. He looked at the ebony nape for a while, then out again. He didn't remember Charleston well—it had been ten years—but this seemed to be the proper direction. The airport limo paralleled the flat green flow of the Cooper down Route 80, his seabag snuggled beside him like a faithful olive-drab dog.

At last they turned off, then slowed for the main gate. Gordon's long face nodded as the wheels thudded over concrete slabs. He held up his I.D. to the bullfrog gaze of a Marine without thinking about it. It had taken him only a few days to regain something unnatural for Americans, and thus suspect to them: the sense that a life of subordination, duty, uniformity, and impending violence is normal, sane, and perhaps even necessary, at least for a few.

He was in khakis now, but he and his men had spent most of the ten days since leaving Vermont in Seabee-style fatigues. Their departure had been hasty and confused. The Reserves were set up for mass mobilization, the "big one" expected daily for forty years, but the way things went when they were asked to handle five men on short notice gave him grave misgivings. Their Burlington-to-Boston tickets had been drawn on PBA, which was on strike; they had to ride a Navy bus to Boston and fly out on an Eastern redeye. There was no advance per diem, and some of the men were eating off the pocket money the staff at the center had put together.

But they'd all been through snafus like this many times during their active-duty years, and since then on annual training, and though they bitched, no one was much surprised. Once they got to Fort Story, things improved. The explosive ordnance T&E facility there had barracks reserved and had set up a special course for them. They'd worked through the weekend, classes on mine identification and triggering mechanisms, intelligence briefings by technicians from Indian Head, render-safe procedures. Then they put it into practice, diving on dummy devices in Lynnhaven Roads.

The fifteen reservists from EOD Group Two had shaken down well, losing only one man from Maine; he got disoriented on a night dive and washed out. All Gordon's guys, the Vermont det, had made it through.

And then, this morning, off to Charleston. Where, in a few minutes, he'd see the ship they'd be going to the Gulf on.

The driver turned his head. Speaking very slowly and distinctly this time, as if to a fool or a foreigner, he said, "Is you goin' to one these ships, suh?"

"That's right. Look for number four-three-three."

"Ow-dassity, right? Pier Two. Thass one them minesweeper boats, goin' over there to A-rabia."

Gordon nodded. So much for security. He pulled on his raincoat and got out. He paid the driver, hesitated, then added a quarter. Hoisting the seabag to his shoulder and carrying the B-4, he headed toward the waterfront through rain smelling of pulp mills, mud, and waste steam.

She was tied up at the pier head, where the water was shallow and muddy. The closer he got, the smaller she looked, until when he was opposite her he stopped, still balancing the seabag, and just stared.

This class had been laid down in 1952, after North Korean mines held MacArthur up at Wonsan. A lot had changed in the Navy since then, but it looked like *Audacity* had missed the updates. She seemed small, and tired, and dirty amid the new steel and aluminum hulls, the antennas and phased arrays, missiles, and helicopters of the rebuilt fleet of the late eighties. Splintered gouges showed on the wooden planking beneath shiny gray paint. A dingy awning stretched over the open bridge. The ratguards looked serious, though, tightly rigged and slathered with yellow grease.

The gangway was varnished teak, faded and cracked. Gordon scraped the mud from his shoes before he stepped up on it. The rails were wrapped with decorative marlinework saffroned by age. It led to a tiny quarterdeck bannered WELCOME TO U.S.S.

Audacity. WHERE THE FLEET GOES, WE'VE BEEN. On the other side, a sign proclaimed ON WOODEN SHIPS, IRON MEN.

Letting the seabag thump to the deck, he looked slowly around, scratching the back of his neck.

"Afternoon, there, Chief. We help you?"

The first thing he noticed were the gnarled hands, like oak roots grown deep into bagged khaki pockets. Then the gray hair sticking out from under the ancient pisscutter. Then a dangling cheroot, and last, the flat, cynical, fuck-you eyes of what had to be the oldest lieutenant in the U.S. Navy.

Gordon saluted the flag. Then he turned and tapped one off to the lieutenant. The latter half-lifted a shoulder, then seemed to think better of it. He shoved himself free of the bulkhead and came out into the drizzle. "How you," he drawled, chewing his words as if they were Skoal-flavored. "I'm Sapper Kearn, swee- pin' officer. You got to be the EOD honcho, right?"

Gordon moved his seabag to a dry patch of deck. He straight- ened and nodded.

"Got your orders?"

He nodded again and bent, began digging them out.

"You don't talk much, do you? Where's the rest of your boys?"

"They'll be along," said Gordon. He refused Kearn's offer of a cigar and handed over his orders. The officer took them inside. Gordon watched the slow drift of drizzle past the hull of a landing ship, the creeping progress of a roach coach down the pier like a funeral cortege.

Kearn came out. In the short time he'd been below, his face had darkened. He said, "What is this? What is this bullshit?"

"What bullshit is that, sir?"

"This *R* bullshit, Chief!"

"Senior Chief, Lieutenant. That's us. USNR."

"We got no time for weekend warriors. We're expectin' an explosive ordnance disposal team. See, we're leaving for the Persian Gulf tomorrow."

"That's us," said Gordon again. He prodded the seabag with the toe of his combat boot. "We're going with you. You got a man can give me a hand with this?"

"How many you got coming?"

"Four more."

"All reserves?"

Gordon nodded. Kearn stared at him for a moment, his wa- tery eyes narrowed in what looked very much like hate, then said, "You wait here. I better see Honey 'bout this one."

Burgee and Everett came aboard while he was below. Gordon had them stow their bags in the dry and stand easy. Finally, the lieutenant came back. "Come on," he grunted. "We'll talk to the captain about this."

The interior of the little ship made Gordon think of flogging, Fletcher Christian, and Horatio Hornblower. The decks were caulked oak, the bulkheads varnished plywood, the ladder steps teak with rope handholds. He had to bow to each door. Everything was undersized and the air was rank with varnish, diesel fuel, insecticide, and a mildewy smell he couldn't identify. Kern rapped at a cherry-stained door marked CAPTAIN E. HUNNICUTT, then went in without waiting.

"C'mon in," said a balding lieutenant commander perhaps twenty years younger than Kearn. He stood up so they could close the door. "Hey, Senior Chief, how y'doing. Sapper here tells me y'all are reserves, that right?"

"That's right, Captain."

During the ensuing pause, Gordon watched both Kearn and Hunnicutt examine the chest of his khakis, reading the devices and ribbons. Like most of his men, he wore only the top three, in this case the Purple Heart, Bronze Star, and Combat Action.

"What you do for a livin', Chief?" said the captain at last.

"Dairy farmer, sir. Vermont."

"Uh-huh. And your other divers . . . how about them?"

"One's a high school teacher, one of 'em's an electrical contractor, one's a paramedic, and there's a fella who runs a bank."

He caught Hunnicutt's glance at Kearn; the lieutenant's rolled eyes. The commander cleared his throat. "Well, now, don't get me wrong, but I suspect somebody's fouled up here, Senior. We're going into a hot area, we need up-to-speed people. Now, I'm goin' to call Mine Warfare Command, and—"

"I say something, sir?" said Gordon, looking around. At last, he saw a whittled hat peg and hung his cover from it.

"We're waiting," said Kearn.

"I've got twenty years in, ten of it active duty, and I'm a qualified master blaster and dive supervisor. We're all first-class divers, senior EOD techs, and jump-qualified. We pull two weeks a year active duty in Gitmo or New London. Together we got sixty years of experience and we just finished the mine-warfare update at Fort Story. You call Commodore Steadley, he'll tell you we're as good or better than any regular team's been there so far."

Hunnicutt glanced at Kearn again. "That's all very well, but this isn't going to be a pleasure cruise, Senior. For one thing,

it's going to take a heap of sweat and Geritol even getting these
old MSOs across the pond."

"I understand that, sir."

"Then think about this: about what your, ah, teachers and
bankers are going to be doing once we get to the Gulf. Minesweeping's changed. We don't just cut moorings and detonate
'em with gunfire anymore. You're going to be getting in the
water with them, figuring them out, disarming or blowing them
up on the spot. You really think you're ready for that?"

"Yessir," said Gordon.

Hunnicutt looked skeptical. Kearn leaned forward and murmured something. The captain nodded. "Take your gear
below," he said to Gordon. "I'll make a couple calls, check it out,
let you know."

"Sir, I got a truck coming today."

"I'll let you know," said Hunnicutt again.

Gordon decided to leave it at that. He followed Kearn down low,
narrow passages to the chiefs' quarters. It had the same airless
darkness he was beginning to associate with minesweepers.
His locker was doll-size, a pine drawer beneath his bunk, but he
managed to get his personal gear in it. He'd learned to travel
light in Vietnam. That meant two sets of khakis, three green
utilities, and a set of whites. Throw in underwear, razor, towel,
and a couple of copies of *Vermont Life* and he had a seabag
and a B-4.

He learned his way around the ship that afternoon, getting
his orders stamped, drawing linens, turning in his personal
firearm to the gunner's mate, and seeing the corpsman for his
medical check-in. At 1600, he got his men together around a tiny
table in the mess room.

His team, or detachment, had four divers, aside from himself
as team leader: Burgee, Everett, Terger, and Maudit. He knew
them all from active duty together and weekend drills diving in
Lake Champlain. They were older than the average Regular
diver. But he knew they were in shape—the tests and swims
assured that—and they had far more experience and, in his
opinion, intelligence, too, than any twenty-four-year-old. So he
started by saying, "You fellas all get a place to sleep?"

"You can call it that," said Terger. A barrelly, graying man
with glasses, he taught high school chemistry and made perfumes on the side. The others nodded. "Down in forward berthing. Dark, and the air ain't real good. Actually, it's a lot like a
coffin. But officially it is a bunk."

"Clint?"

Burgee, the electrician, had large tattooed biceps and a blond mustache that pushed regulations. He shrugged.

"Lem?"

Lem Everett was the oldest man in the team, forty-two, and managed a branch bank in Burlington. He was bent and reserved and wrote poetry; he had four daughters and had won a Navy Cross aboard the *Mayaguez*. Now he pushed back hair that was retreating on its own and said, "John, are you sure this thing's safe? It's an antique. The engineman chief told me two months ago they took off for a week's cruise up to New York. One engine gave out as soon as they passed Fort Sumter. Then the loran went, and finally the gyro. They hit fog off New Jersey and they were lost. They waved a fisherman over to ask where they were and managed to hit him and sink the guy. They never got to New York, but it took them two weeks to get back. Now they're going to cross the Atlantic?"

Maudit muttered something in his Vermont French.

"You might be right," said Gordon. "But that's not our problem. Our problem is to get our gear aboard and stowed, get under way tomorrow, and get ourselves up to speed to deal with mines."

"We're up to speed, John. Didn't we just blow their minds at school?"

"We have a lot more to learn, Clint. And a lot more work to do on the way over." He looked at Etienne Maudit, the paramedic. "Tony, you're checked in? Medical, bunk, pay, orders?"

"*D'ac,* Chief. By the way, I may be working with the medical department some of the time, if it goes well with you."

"As long as our training and maintenance gets done first."

"Scuse me. There a frogman chief here?" A seaman with red paint on his nose was hanging in the hatchway. Gordon lifted his chin. "Got some shit on the pier for you."

"That's our gear."

"Let's go."

A green five-ton was backed up by the brow. Gordon asked the quarterdeck watch to call away a working party, then headed over the swaying gangplank to the concrete. He was in the truck, counting boxes and checking them against the driver's manifest, when he heard his name being called by an angry voice. He looked over the gate into Kearn's narrow, reddened eyes. *"Hey!"* Did you call away a working party?"

"Yessir, we got diving gear here to get aboard."

"You load your own gear."

"I only got four men, sir—"

"You load your own fucking gear," said Kearn again. "My people are busy." He turned and went back up the brow. Gordon looked past him, to where his det stood in greens and T-shirts. They looked old beside the seamen and petty officers who stood around on the afterdeck.

Gordon consulted with the driver and the Marine escort and got the truck backed a little closer to the brow. The gate came down, his men moved into position, and boxes, crates, and gear began scraping out over it. He checked them off the invoice as they went by him to a growing stack on the fantail. Heavy green and blue tanks of gas—helium and oxygen, five sets of Mark 16 semiclosed-circuit diving gear, four canisters of chemicals, six sets of twin scuba tanks and regulators, crated personal diving gear. A safe, three wooden crates of shaped charges and satchel charges, a Bowers portable air compressor, four black bags containing inflatable boats, and two silenced 25-horse Evinrude motors. Lifting balloons, boxes of publications and tools, crates of wire and hose. Midway through the offload, the petty officer of the watch came down and told Maudit that they had to get their gear off the deck; Lieutenant Kearn wanted to lay out some sweep cable. Gordon sighed and sent two men up to pass it below to the tiny space that had served up till now as a luggage room and was now the dive locker.

Well after taps, when at last everything was inventoried, stowed, and secured, he went ashore. On the pier, the lights were a grim sodium yellow and steam hissed up in lazy, writhing clouds. A needle gun clattered like distant harassing fire, some late-night working party; aside from that and the ever-present sibilance of steam, the waterfront was quiet. The sound, the smells, the humidity brought back Saigon harbor. He stepped carefully over power cables and water lines. A row of lambent yellow and red rectangles at the head of the pier marked the phones and vending machines. The concrete was littered with spent butts and candy wrappers. Sailors in dungarees slumped or curled into the support of the receivers, murmuring cajoling love words or forcing the bland cheerfulness nineteen-year-olds use to their idiot parents. He waited for a free one and tapped in numbers.

"John? That you?"

"It's me, Ola. You asleep?"

"I was in bed."

She sounded sleepy and at the same time distant. He asked her how she was, and then the boy, and then the herd.

"It's not been easy, John." Two more milkers had mastitis and production was down. The machines were hard to handle and Stacey and Suzanne wouldn't let down for her. "I think they know you're gone," Ola said.

He wanted to ask about cleaning, had she disinfected the milk house every day, but then he thought, You know she did. So he only said, "Look, if you need a hand with the herd, call Lew Drexel. His boy's lookin' for work this summer."

"What are we going to pay him with, John? Have you sent me anything yet?"

"Ain't got anything yet."

"Well, I'm doing the best I can here. I'm working fourteen hours a day, keeping things up and cooking, too. I haven't been out to the kiln since you left. The boy's workin' hard nights after school."

"How's he taking it?"

"I'm not real sure, John."

He couldn't think of anything else to say except, "Well, hard work never hurt a boy."

"How is it there? Where are you, anyway?"

"South Carolina. Oh, good enough."

"Are you getting enough to eat?"

"Yup. But I miss that maple bread you make."

"I thought you were going overseas."

"We are."

"When are you leaving?"

"Tomorrow," he said. "It'll take us three or four weeks to get across, I figure. No phone. No mail. So you may not hear from me for a while."

She didn't answer for a time. And all she said then was "All right."

He said goodnight, waited for a response, and at last hung up. Stared toward the little ship. A curtain of steam came up and hung in the air, glowing with yellow light.

Under way tomorrow, he thought. He didn't know what they'd find on the other side. Their instructors didn't, either. The reports from the Gulf were contradictory. They'd lost one team already and no one knew why: only a sudden explosion, then mute drifting bits of wet suit and flesh. The technicians and engineers wanted him to send reports on what he found, what types of mines and fusing mechanisms, and what worked on them. And by elimination, by silence, what didn't.

He didn't like the way Ola sounded . . . she was tired, sure
. . . that was all it was. She was tired.

He wiped his feet again, unthinking, as he stepped off the
gangplank. Then he squared his shoulders, and snapped off a
salute.

8

U.S.S. *Turner Van Zandt*

STANDING on the flight deck, melting in the fireproof flight suit and fifteen-pound survival vest, Chunky Schweinberg dragged a glove across his face. His mouth felt wooden.

He hadn't expected to fly today. Or, he told himself now, I'd of kept it in the green in the Londoner. He'd felt numb at breakfast, but now he was at that stage of a hangover where it hurts when your heart beats. And the slow roll of the flight deck didn't help a bit.

But Woolton had given them the first twelve-hour shift under way, and now the new captain wanted to see them strut their stuff. Well, Claude R. Schweinberg had never said "I can't" in his life. Never in three years of high school ball, never in three with the Seminoles. You didn't play a lot when you were number three behind Paul McGowan. But he'd done all right—thirty-eight tackles and two blocked punts in three seasons. Till that deadly day when Bobby Bowden had called him into his office and shut the door.

He farted sadly and squinted into the sun. It burned furiously down at him through the dust and murk of the Gulf. He wished he'd drunk another Coke. No, that just made you want to pee. One goddamned thing after another . . . "Okay, Buck," he muttered. "Let's get this over with."

Hayes was sweating, too. Along with the Nomex suit, vest, and gloves, he was wearing thirty-eight pounds of body armor. Now he shifted his gum to his right cheek and his helmet to his left hand, and flipped open the blue NATOPS checklist. He ran his eye down the preflight, trying to ignore his headache. It was centerlined between his eyes, like an ax blade pressing outward. "Chocks," he mumbled.

"Forget that flight school stuff, Bucky-boy. I'll take right side and meet you on top."

Hayes agreed dully and the two pilots started at the nose, checking the main rotor blades, windshield, wipers, and air-temperature gauge. Schweinberg found an oil smear and called for the chief. Mattocks shouted to a mech.

Van Zandt shuddered under them, accelerating. The men on the flight deck leaned without noticing the heel. Wind rattled the plastic-coated pages in Hayes's hand. He squeezed his eyes shut for a second. Red video games played behind his retinas, but the headache backed off a bit. TACAN, ESM, data link. He yanked on a stubby antenna. It seemed to be firmly attached.

They moved slowly along. Hover lights, radar housing. Hayes peered into the pitot tubes to make sure they were clear, then leaned into the cockpit to check harness, mirrors, flight controls, and pressure gauges. A tire gave a dull thud as his flight boot impacted it.

Hoisting himself heavily by footholds in the fuselage, Schweinberg perched himself on the aircraft's back. It seemed awful high off the deck. A lot of water around them, all right. . . . He popped the cover on the hydraulics bay. Fluid levels, access covers, servos, flight controls, transmissions. He inspected the rotor-drive system carefully for forgotten tools or parts. Chief Mattocks strolled around below with his arms folded, looking out at the horizon and whistling soundlessly through his teeth.

Chunky held tight to a rotor while he wiped his face again. He'd found nothing. Not that he'd expected to, but it was his neck. He closed the access panels and banged them to make sure they were secure before he climbed down. Standing on the deck, he felt dizzy for just a moment.

Finally it went away and he continued aft. An SH-60 had 117 items to check in the preflight and Schweinberg, as he always did, made himself concentrate for every one. The most minor thing, like a loosely fastened cowling, could trick-fuck you in the air.

They met at the tail cone and agreed that the exterior looked okay. Chunky, having a previous deployment under his belt, was the HAC, or aircraft commander, and without speaking, he headed for the pilot's seat, on the right.

Hayes went around to the port side. The Navy called its H-60 copilots ATOs, airborne tactical officers. He settled into the sheepskin-covered bucket, inhaling the mingled smells of paint, fuel, hot plastic, and lubricants. His pulse accelerated as he brought up external power and the cockpit came to life. He buckled the seat belt and shoulder harness and cinched them tight, adjusted the seat for his long legs. He pulled the helmet on last. He hated the issue lids. They were hot, heavy, bulky, and flew off your head if you hit something.

But then, he thought with a sudden touch of depression, there were a lot of things not to like about flying for Uncle Sam. In some ways, it was just a job, and a dirty, hard, and not-very-well-paid one at that.

Whereas a civilian engineer . . .

Thinking vaguely about the job offer, he plugged in and adjusted the mike. Within the plane, since ambient noise was so loud, the crew communicated through an intercom system. The ICS was voice-actuated. If he wanted to radio the ship, he tapped a foot switch or pressed a trigger on the cyclic. Beside him, Schweinberg was checking the shear wires on the windows. Neither the pilots nor the crew wore parachutes. No one bailed out of a helicopter. "Pilot, ATO," Hayes said into the mike.

"Loud and clear."

"Ready when you are for prestart."

"Go."

Hayes glanced around the cockpit. He and the pilot sat side by side, separated by a central console at elbow height. Ahead of him, shielded by an overhanging dash, was the main panel. This included an airspeed indicator, radar and barometric altimeters, an artificial horizon and horizontal-situation indicator, fuel gauges, and engine RPM and rotor torque readouts. To the right was the caution panel. When he pressed the test button, seventy-five indicators flashed on and then off. Two inches above his helmet, the overhead was crusted with circuit breakers and switches.

A whine began above them as Schweinberg started the auxiliary power turbine. AW2 Kane, the SENSO, climbed into the cabin. The sensor operator sat behind the pilots, a battery of sonobuoys against his back and a radar and computer display in his lap. There was a seat for a door gunner/hoist operator, but it would be vacant for this flight, which would be a routine radar patrol.

Schweinberg unlocked the blades and pressed the radio switch. He looked to the right, into the eyes of the landing signal officer. "LSO, Killer Two One. How you doin' today?"

"Good, Chunky," crackled the voice in his phones.

"Request clearance to start and engage."

"Anytime you want, big boy."

"That's what they all say." He grinned, then winced. It even hurt to smile.

Forward of them, the hangar door was sliding down. Behind

it was the fire team in their reflective suits, helmets under their arms. He hoped if there was a fire they'd come in fast. He remembered what the old guy, Richards, had said about burning to death. . . . He moved the engine ignition switch to NORM and fuel selectors to cross-feed, then mashed the START button. Now the engines got JP-5 and spark. They fired with a double bump followed by a climbing whine and the airframe began to vibrate. Engine oil pressure, check; starter light, out.

Hayes's voice in his head. "Harnesses and doors locked. Deck clear."

"Center the cyclic, collective down." He wrapped his right glove around the cyclic. Between his knees, like a conventional stick, it accomplished much the same purpose, controlling the helicopter's attitude. The collective, a horizontal column to the left of his seat, controlled main-rotor pitch and engine fuel flow. Cyclic, collective, rudder pedals; those were the flight controls.

Kane came up on the ICS. Schweinberg rogered and went over the flight profile and lookout procedures. It wasn't complicated. In the Gulf, they seldom used the expensive antisubmarine gear. Most of the SENSO's attention would be on the radar, while the front-seaters would be eyeballing water and sky. When he was done, he hit the radio switch and made sure the guys in CIC were on the right frequency.

"Getting hot in here," he heard Hayes mutter.

"No shit." The interior was black, and in the tropical sunlight, in suit and gloves and helmet, he knew how a potato felt in a microwave oven. "Ready to engage," he added, checking pressures again.

The swept tips of the SH-60's four blades accelerated swiftly. In five seconds, they were a flicker at the top of the windscreen. He ran RPM up, watching the instruments. A caution light flickered—number one hydraulic pump—then went out. He reached up and pushed the black ball of the power control forward to FLY. The engine changed pitch and their heads nodded to a long-period airframe shudder. The collective was still horizontal, the blades whipping through the wind without biting out lift, and the throttle and torques matched on the indicators.

"Buck, you ready?"

Hayes gave him a wordless thumb. Schweinberg saw Hayes had dropped his visor, and he did, too. The glare lessened. He leaned back and glanced out. The ship was ready. He forgot his uneasy gut and the way his heart was thumping in tune with the blades. *Click.* "LSO, Two One."

"LSO, go."

"Rotors engaged, request clearance to launch."

"Stand by for clearance. Takeoff data to follow. Barometric pressure twenty-nine point thirteen. True wind zero-one-zero at seventeen, relative starboard twenty at twenty. Deck pitch negligible, roll five."

Buck gave a thumbs up as he copied. "Roger, we're ready to lift."

"Stand by . . . beams open, green deck, *lift.*"

The LSO tossed them a salute. Chunky hauled up on the collective. The turbines rose in a twinned scream. But 421 stayed glued to the deck, held down by ten tons of weight. Eight. Six. Four . . .

Suddenly the thrust of air downward exceeded the weight of airframe, engines, and crew. He went heavy in the seat. The flight deck dropped away, the ship dropped away; the cyclic described a tiny arc astern in his gloved hand. "All clear, Four Two One," crackled in his ears.

He came slightly forward on the stick again, maintaining full power. The helicopter shuddered as it transitioned to forward flight. *Van Zandt*'s masthead flashed past. The altitude needles wound upward. His eyes flicked to the horizon. It widened with every foot they gained in the familiar succession of illusion: became first a disk, then a bowl, at last a separate, gently curved world below. He brought the cyclic an inch back and to the right and gently lowered the collective. The helicopter, climbing more slowly now, banked to starboard. The coast of Oman came into view, dry, flat, tan and yellow, dancing and shimmering madly in the heated air. The sea beneath him was tan-green, the shallows shading to a blue so delicately brilliant it made his heart hurt.

"After takeoff checklist." Hayes's voice in his headphones. Schweinberg nodded, still looking out. As if shaken loose by the vibration, fragments of memory came free and drifted through his mind. "The Michigan State video shows you flinching, Schweinberg. Noles can't use linebackers who flinch. . . ."

"I don't want that animal in the house anymore, Claude. . . ."

Fuck it, he thought savagely. Fuck it all; all that was over. He didn't need to drink, but it passed the time. He didn't care that much about bodybuilding, either, though it was good to stay in shape; too many ball players let themselves go to fat. Everything else in his life was just something to do when he couldn't be where he wanted to be. Which was here. High above the sea, adrift in the sky . . .

"ATO, ATACO."

It was the voice from the ship, a petty officer in CIC. He took his orders from the TAO, theoretically welding ship and plane into a coordinated tactical whole. Before Hayes could answer, Schweinberg pressed the trigger. "Yo."

"Killer Two One, hold you too high and too far east. We need you to scout out ahead of us along our track, one-two-zero."

There was a leash in the sky, and he was on it. "Shit," he muttered.

"Two One, ATACO, say again your last."

"I say again, roger, coming right. I'll mark on top and head out on the one-two-zero, angels four."

"ATACO aye."

Leaving the channel open, Schweinberg sang tunelessly: "If I had the wings of an eagle, and the ass of a great buffalo-o-o, I'd climb to the highest church steeple, and shit on the blackshoes below." Beside him, Buck Hayes grinned. He finished the postlaunch, slammed the book closed, and stuffed it into a pocket. Then he stretched his arms, eased his chin strap, and looked down.

The chin bubble was transparent, and through it now he saw a distant point of darkness on the sea. It threw a shadow against the wrinkled Gulf, and drew behind it, like a bride's train, a widening V of wake. *Van Zandt*, far and small, a tin purgatory for two hundred men. But they, at least, could escape.

They spent the next hour floating along at four thousand feet while Kane monitored the passing traffic on the scope. After a while, the ship asked them to check out a surface contact. Schweinberg rogered and headed toward it at 140 knots. They seemed not to be moving, just hanging like a balloon above the immense curve of sea. A band of dirty brown lay just above the horizon, a thick layer of haze, smoke, and airborne sand. But it was below them, and their sky was the normal blue one seldom saw from sea level in the Gulf.

Hayes wiggled his toes. Cramps nibbled at his arches. Part of his mind was on the instruments. Part of it was wondering whether he'd be happy with a desk job, nine to five and an hour for lunch. But then he'd be home every night. Dustin and Jesse were getting to the age they needed a dad. And still a third part was back in Montana. Ghost riders in the sky . . . not one of the Rambling Hayeses, footloose though they'd been, had ever gotten this far, he thought. Then he remembered that at least one of them must have. The first one. Chained in the guts of a slaver.

"Two One, ATACO, you see him yet?" crackled the petty officer's voice.

Hayes glanced at Schweinberg; he was leaning back, staring out at the horizon. He pressed the foot switch. "No, we don't have him."

"Two One, I still hold you too high. Get down to around four hundred. Maybe you can see it then."

"Oh, fuck that," muttered Schweinberg. "I'm just gettin' cooled off."

Buck glanced at him. But the collective was easing down, as requested. He couldn't tell whether his HAC had been serious or not.

Finally, Hayes picked up the wake, a scratch on the sea, like a diamond dragged across blue glass. They edged in gradually, paralleling it. Both pilots stared out the windscreen. Hayes focused the gyrostabilized binoculars. A speedboat, white, no flag. "Not fishermen," he said.

"What are they?"

"I don't know. Looks like bales on deck."

"Druggies?"

"Could be."

They peeled off before they got inside small-arms range. Hayes called it in and asked whether they wanted a positive I.D. After a while, the ship came back and said no, unidentified smuggler was good enough, as long as they stayed clear of *Van Zandt*.

Schweinberg turned south again and gradually climbed back to radar altitude. They droned along high above earth and sea. From time to time, Kane came over the intercom with a contact, or the ship vectored them around. But for the most part they just sat and logged time. Neither man minded. It was daylight, and once they met the convoy, they'd fly mostly at night. Besides, being bored was better than most of the alternatives.

After three hours in the air, Hayes started to get sleepy. He was considering telling Schweinberg he was going to flake out for twenty when the radio crackled again. "ATO, ATACO."

"ATO, go."

"Heads up, Two One. Be advised you got two bogeys closing from the north."

"What kind of bogeys? Fast movers?"

"Affirm, look like fighters, not sure yet whose—hold on, we just got ESM. F-14s, batch one. Iranians."

Hayes felt more awake now. He said, "SENSO, check up to the north of us, ship says—"

"Yeah. I got 'em too. Range fifteen, our eight o'clock, high."

Schweinberg's grunt: "They closin'?"

"Yes, sir."

Two One rolled left. Both pilots narrowed their eyes, concentrating on sky. Hayes clicked from one block of blue to the next, watching not for shape but for movement. "Think it's Peeps's thumpers?" he muttered.

"Could be."

"Emitter tag!" shouted Kane. At the same moment, the data link said, "ATO, ESMO, fire-control radar bearing two-nine-zero from you."

"There they are. Eleven o'clock, above the horizon."

"Padlock 'em!" Schweinberg instantly pushed down collective and cyclic together. He just glimpsed them as the horizon rolled up, two flyspecks on blue immensity.

Air-combat training over Lake George came back to him. He came left and steepened his dive. Airspeed, 175. The sea filled the windscreen, the airframe shook, the wind screamed by. Eight hundred, five hundred. The altimeter unwound downward faster and faster. The vertical-speed indicator passed 3,500 feet per minute.

"Christ, Chunky, how low you going?"

"Till I run out of air." Nobody going eight hundred knots liked to point his nose into the water. "You still got 'em? What're they doing?"

"They see us. One's inbound. The other guy's hanging back, high orbit."

High orbit; waiting for the leader to complete his pass. That was good. Helicopter evasive tactics were predicated on one jet. Once they both mixed it up, though, he wasn't really sure what he'd do.

Now Chunky concentrated on the oncoming fighter. On a head-to-head pass, there were maybe three seconds when the jet pilot could see you and was in range. He had to lead you slightly to let the missile seeker lock on before he fired. So you had to keep him guessing wrong as to which way you were turning, keep him out of phase with you.

Now, watching the jet, he suddenly slammed the cyclic to the right. Yes, Christ, the left wing came down!

"Don't let him acquire!" shouted Hayes. "Passing two hundred."

Schweinberg's whole attention was on the fighter. It was

closing at an alarming rate. Its right wing came down and he
jerked the stick right. Two One skidded around as the horizon
went momentarily vertical. Normally, you banked no more than
forty-five degrees, but limits were out the window now. He was
trying to stay alive.

The airframe began shaking violently. Hayes glanced sideways, and found himself looking straight down on the waves.
His skin tried to inchworm up his neck. "Christ, Chunky! You
can't bank like this at one-seventy-five, air's hot, you're gonna
blade stall!"

"Death—but first, cheech!" howled Schweinberg. The shaking intensified till their teeth buzzed and their vision blurred,
but he kept the stick hard right.

The fighter's nose came up suddenly and it flashed over them,
so close they could hear its engines over the scream of their
own. "SENSO! Padlock left on number one, call position!"

Hayes shouted, "Number two, ten o'clock, high high!"

"Altitude, altitude!" shouted Kane. Schweinberg flinched. If
a rotor tip hit the water, they were fucked. He was startled to
see they were no more than sixty feet off the deck, so low their
tip vortices sliced into the water, leaving a path on the sea. He
pulled out of the bank and brought the cyclic back slowly,
keeping the tail rotor clear of the waves.

"Fuck me, I wish I'd took the fucking gunner along."

"He couldn't shoot down an F-14, Chunky."

"It'd improve my morale. Shit. Shit!"

"Number one's opening to starboard," reported Kane.

"Keep your eye on him," muttered Schweinberg. The drill
was that once he was past, you watched him, then turned inside
him. Jet jocks thought they were hot squat; they always figured
they could get around you onto your six. But a Seahawk could
outturn a jet all day long. If he tried to get smart and hauled
ass straight up, you skated around underneath him. Then when
he rolled in, he found himself looking past you at a water
impact—a bad position for a jet at low altitude.

Two attackers, though, made it a lot harder. The wingman
was coming in now. Kane was watching the leader. If he tried
for their tail, Schweinberg would have to break off number two.
But he couldn't face in two directions at once. Once they got
coordinated, 421 was dead meat.

Schweinberg had reasoned to this conclusion in less than a
second. Meanwhile, the second fighter had dropped and was
rapidly growing larger. Shaking his head to fling sweat out of
his eyes, he hunched at the stick like a poker player over a hot

hand. Couldn't make your play too soon or he'd outguess you, had to time it just right. . . . If the Iranian fired a missile, he'd have maybe two-tenths of a second to get a flare off and bank. The sky was big, but not big enough when your combined closing rate was a thousand miles an hour.

"Break left!" shouted Hayes. The F-14's wing dipped and Schweinberg slammed the stick to port so hard his eyes went dim.

"Hundred twenty knots, torque's too high, two hundred feet and dropping."

Was that a flash? "Flares!" he screamed. Hayes pickled the button and the fuselage jolted. The data link hummed and then they heard, "Lieutenant Schweinberg, this is Captain Shaker. Understand you are being—"

"Get off the circuit! Where you got him, where you got him?" screamed Schweinberg.

"Number two's inbound again, on our eight—"

"ATO, ATACO, we're picking up another fire-control radar, bearing two-seven-zero from you."

"I got the fucker, shut up, I'm trying to get out of this fuckin' nutcracker!"

"Number one's on our six!"

"Shit!" They were wise to him now, boxing him. In a minute, they'd come in simultaneously, from ninety degrees apart, and he'd be shit out of luck. Shaker tried to interrupt again; no one answered him. "What's two doin' now?" Schweinberg said, almost breaking his neck as he craned around the sky.

"Turning inbound, two o'clock. Hey. Chunky."

"What?"

"Oil rig." Hayes pointed off to a straddled spider five or six miles away. Schweinberg hadn't noticed it before, but took his meaning instantly. He whipped around so hard the low rotor RPM light flickered and poured on power. They roared along forty feet off the deck, flat out at 165 knots. The fighters wobbled, undecided or coordinating, then steadied.

He got to the rig just before the lead F-14 and ducked immediately behind it. His rotor arc was still visible, but he didn't care. With his maneuverability, he could keep the structure between him and them forever, and there was no way they could fire through the mass of beams and derricks.

The Iranian pilots realized it, too, and broke off. He allowed Two One to drift out from behind its makeshift shield as they joined up, dwindled to specks again, then finally disappeared to the southward.

"ATO, ATACO, hold two bogeys opening your posit."

Hayes rogered, his voice high. Schweinberg pried the fingers of his left hand off the collective and groped behind the seat. At last he grunted, "Kane, you got a canteen back there?"

"Hold on." It came forward. He uncorked it and gulped greedily, his eyes still mincing the sky. Then held it out. "Buck?"

"Yeah." Hayes took a swig. He was handing it back when he became conscious of something warm and squishy-soft on the seat under him.

"What?" muttered Schweinberg.

"What?"

"I said, what'd you say?"

"Nothing."

"Man, that hot water's gonna feel great when we get back," said Schweinberg, looking down at the sea. With a strange detachment, he saw that his hands were shaking. He peeled off his left glove and examined his sweaty, beet-red palm. "Hey, good thinkin' there, Buck, on the oil rig, I mean."

Hayes nodded, then remembered that the new CO was trying to reach them. He pressed transmit and said, "Uh, *Van Zandt*, this is ATO; sorry, we kind of had to concentrate there for a minute. Over."

"This is Shaker. I understand. Buck, did they fire on you?"

How did he know my name? Hayes thought. "No, sir. Thought for a minute they did, but it was the sun on the wings."

"But they made passes at you?"

"Yessir, no shit."

"What I need to know is, was there hostile intent? They weren't just playing around, were they?"

Beside him, Schweinberg snorted. Buck said carefully, "That's hard to say, sir. We dived away as soon as we saw 'em. I guess that might have, you know, sucked them in. Invited 'em to hotdog a little. But it looked serious to me, like they were just waiting for a good-enough setup to justify expending a missile. We never gave them one, so they didn't. But I can't say what was in their raggedy heads."

"Well . . ." Was it his imagination, or did the new captain sound disappointed? "Anyway, good flying, guys. Stay alert, and look, stick a little closer to us, all right? We could have put a missile out there if you'd been closer."

"Aye, sir." He clicked off and tried to relax. They were at two thousand and climbing. It was cooler now and the sky was turning blue again. He cracked his knuckles slowly, relishing being alive.

"Want to take it for a while?" said Schweinberg. Buck Hayes took a deep breath. Then another. The trembling in his diaphragm eased off. He set his boots on the rudder pedals, nodded, and took the stick.

9

U.S.S. *Turner Van Zandt*

B ERNARD Newekwe, aka Hospitalman Bernard Phelan, sat
curled like a stepped-on rattlesnake in the quiet of sick bay,
sniffling and gnawing on his pencil. Among many other things,
he wanted a smoke. But he couldn't. Fitch would smell it and
give him hell.

Tuh. Couldn't even smoke. . . . He closed his eyes, digging
his fingers in above his belt buckle. He wanted to howl like a
runover dog. The cramps were getting worse. Didn't dare take
more aspirin; his ears were ringing from them. And anyway,
they didn't help. He didn't feel good. Christ. *Christ . . .*

He sniped a yearning glance toward a gray steel safe, but it
stopped at the CLOSED placard. He sucked shuddering air
through locked teeth. He wanted to get up, rattle it again, but
he'd done that a dozen times already. *Shit.*

He was alone in the frigate's little sick bay. Little, compared
to the medical spaces on *Long Beach.* It gleamed soullessly
antiseptic from waxed tiling to freshly painted overhead. Gray
filing cabinets were squeezed among a sparkling stainless
scrub sink, two empty bunks—tucked and smoothed with inhu-
man neatness—and a folding operating table. It was down now
and covered with medical records and the shadow tracings of
X rays. Below a battery of operating lights, an oxygen bottle
was lashed to the bulkhead, valve polished to a mirror finish.
The closed-in air stank of alcohol and Betadine, a medicinal
smell, like the ghostly smoke of piñon and juniper that hung
over the pueblo in the calm, cold nights of February, under the
steady stare of the desert stars. . . .

Phelan bit hard on the yielding wood, trying to blot his need
from his mind by thinking about something else. About the
setup here, for instance. You had to know the setup if you
wanted to get anywhere in the Navy. Had to figure who to

impress, who really counted. Same as in the pueblo. He
wouldn't be surprised if it was the same everywhere.

Van Zandt was short of corpsmen, all right. They'd had
seven on *Long Beach* when she deployed. This ship had one
rated man and one striker. The leading HM was a first-class
named Fitch. He was forty, bent, balding, obsequious toward
the officers and a pint-size tyrant within the ten-by-ten confines
of sick bay. Medically, he seemed competent, though all Phelan
had seen him deal with so far was seasickness, hammered
thumbs, and one case of clap.

The striker's name was Golden. He was a seaman, same as
Phelan, but since Bernard had his rate, he was senior. He could
see this pissed Golden off. The guy watched him out of the
corners of his eyes. He hadn't said anything, but Phelan knew
it was coming. Golden made him nervous. He was weird, a
creepy, pale, know-it-all.

A jarring clatter began from the deck above. He closed his
eyes. What the hell was going on? It sounded as if they were
tearing the ship apart. It felt like the chipping hammers were
taking the top off his skull.

He had to make some connections. He'd drifted around the
decks after dark the night before, nostrils flared for the autum-
nal aroma of marijuana. But he hadn't whiffed any, and hadn't
seen anyone who looked stoned. He couldn't believe no one
aboard got high. If they didn't, this was the first drug-free ship
he'd ever seen. He'd tried sitting with the dudes at their tables,
figuring that was the best way to find out what was going
down. They let him sit there, but he didn't feel they trusted him.
Shit, he was no white! Finally, he'd asked one of them, Jackson,
what he did to feel good, and he'd just laughed and said he got
blowjobs off Indians.

There'd been five of them and Phelan couldn't take him then.
He would, though, he'd fix their fucking little trains. Nobody
fucked with him. Jackson. *Wa na ni;* remember the name; he'd
get his.

For about the thousandth time that day, he thought about his
brick. How could he've been so stupid. Enough there for a
month if he'd taken it easy. Rationed it. He still couldn't understand how he'd smoked it all in four days. It must have been
weak, cut with something, that was all he could figure.

Four days . . . he shuddered, reliving the horror of waking
that last morning and realizing his stash was gone, his money
was gone, and the ship was gone, too, and he was in trouble
unless he came through with something fast. Staggering out

into the sunlight, already dog-sick, reeling and puking and knowing it was going to be worse. Much worse. He'd sold his belt and buckle, knife, watch, boots, wallet, and I.D. card (he'd known that was stupid, but he was beyond stupidity) for two more hits. He'd decided to save one, but in the end he ate them both as he shuffled through the streets of Karachi in his socks, cursing and wondering what in hell he was going to do.

Finally, something had occurred to him. He walked in front of a taxi, not a fast-moving one, and got himself taken to the American legation with a story about being robbed and beaten. They'd bought it, got him a doc and a week's prescription for pain pills. Nothing he recognized, Pak stuff, but there was codeine or Dilaudid in it.

And, God, he'd managed it. Instead of wolfing them, he'd taken just enough to keep him upright. It hurt like hell, but gradually he'd reduced the dose, come down easy. No real addict could have done that.

Only the last of that was gone now, too, and he hurt again.

He shivered. Christ, it was cold in here. Icy cold. He had his jacket on over the dungaree shirt, but it didn't cut it, not even with the knit watch cap. He wanted to feel good again but couldn't think of a way to. Maybe he should have stayed in Karachi. Lots of stuff there. No, that was impossible.

The pencil snapped in his teeth, bringing him suddenly back to his job. He hunched shivering over the folder, trying to focus on immunization dates. Tetanus toxoid, series of three; typhoid, PPD . . . Who the hell cared. He scrawled something in the block for medical review and threw it back on the pile.

Someone knocked on the door. He started guiltily, then shouted, "Yeah, get in here."

It was a seaman recruit off the deck gang, nursing a splinter. Phelan got up, glad for something to do. He tried to keep his fingers steady while he washed the guy's hand, needled the sliver out, disinfected the wound, and carefully placed a Band-Aid.

Fitch came in. He hung his ball cap on the oxygen tank and glanced at them. "Problem?"

"Splinter. Almost done."

"How those records coming?"

"Almost finished."

"Anybody past their reimmunization dates?"

"Uh, not yet."

The seaman recruit thanked Phelan and left. Fitch jingled his keys. He looked carefully around the space, then bent to peep under the sink. Looking for dust, Phelan supposed. Fitch was a suckass, a crawler. He hunched there suffering, hating him and every other white and black face on this floating prison.

Fitch jingled his keys again, humming under his breath, and at last squatted. He flipped the placard on the safe from CLOSED to OPEN. He spun the dial left, left, right, left. The door clicked, then swung noiselessly out.

Phelan's eyes stopped, unable to move from the rows of bottles and boxes suddenly visible over the first-class's shoulder. There was the hard stuff, the morphine Syrettes and more morphine in blocks, pure and potent. Along with softer pharmaceuticals, Valium and Percodan, cough syrups, Seconal, amyl nitrate, pain pills and sleeping pills, grain alcohol and medicinal brandy. Stocked for two hundred men for six months in a battle zone. And all of it two steps away from him, with only the back of Fitch's balding head between.

His lips were suddenly dry. "Hey," he said.

"Hey what?"

"A guy was in here with a headache. Bad one. I wanted to give him something for it, but all there was out was aspirin."

"Aspirin's good for headaches."

"He had a bad one, I said."

"You should have passed the word for me. Could have given him something stronger. Who was it?"

"I forget his name. Look, Albert, I ought to have the combo to that safe. Like then when I'm on duty, I can take care of things without bothering you."

"I'm thinking about it," said Fitch, maddeningly noncommittal. "Okay, this afternoon we got to set up for urinalysis."

"For what?" said Phelan. He felt a premonitory shiver.

"Get the bottles out. It's Operation Golden Flow. We do a random piss test on twenty people, twice a month. Got a new kit; we can test right here on the ship."

The cramp hit him sudden, like a knife sliding in just below the navel. He bit down on a gasp. Was Fitch watching him? Was the bastard *smiling?* Finally, he got up and fumbled about in a locker, trying not to groan. "Behind the condoms," the senior corpsman supplied.

"Here they are."

"And here's the list."

Phelan's shaking fingers dropped it. It drifted to the floor and he looked down at it, helpless, unable to bend over the slowly twisting blade. "What do you want me to do with it?"

"Didn't you do these on *Long Beach?* Take it down to ship's office. Get 'em to type the names on sticky labels." Fitch's rabbit eyes gloated down at him. "Yeah, your name's on there, Big Chief. And guess what? I'm gonna be watching while you fill that bottle. See if you've been smoking any of them magic mushrooms."

There was nothing more ignorant than a *melikan*. You didn't smoke peyote. It was a cactus, not a mushroom. And anyway, that was Navaho or Apache medicine. In something not far from panic, Phelan pulled his wandering mind back to the freezing, empty sick bay of U.S.S. *Van Zandt*. "What do you mean, man? They don't come no cleaner than me."

"I mean, I don't know you, Phelan. And you don't look good to me. You ain't looked good since the day you came aboard."

"I told you, I got the flu or something. And I get seasick, cooped up down here."

"We'll see. Go get those labels typed." The first class turned his back on him.

Phelan slowly bent for the list. He was on it, all right, written on at the bottom. In pen. He cast a glance of pure hatred at Fitch's back. He wished he had his knife. He'd cut this son of a bitch here and now. Get the combination, too. He'd make him tell.

Watching mind movies of Fitch bleeding, whimpering for mercy, looking down where his balls used to be, Bernard went back to ship's office and waited till the personnelman was busy. He got the labels and hitched himself cautiously behind the typewriter. He couldn't type fast, but he got them done eventually.

Fitch was still in sick bay, grinning like a dog in garbage. "Okay, Hiawatha," he said. "Ready for those shining waters? Let's see 'em—good. Paste 'em on and meet me down in Ops Berthing. I'll pass the word and we'll do it in the head there."

Phelan went forward, carrying the tray of bottles like some kind of waiter, he thought. The men he passed made jokes. He didn't look at them.

As he entered the head, he heard the names being read over the 1MC. He arranged the bottles on the counter, wiping his nose with the back of his hand, trying to do his job despite it all.

Suddenly he was filled with a desperate pity for himself. Nobody had wanted him since he was born. Not the Corn People, not the white man, not his so-called friends, who'd wanted only what he sold. He'd grown up poor and hungry and now he was sick. They shouldn't make a sick man work. It was all so *fucking* unfair! He needed medicine. Just for a little while longer, till he got clean. Even a drink would help. One of the chiefs ought to have a bottle stashed. How could he get to it?

Fitch came down a few minutes later, and with him the day's lottery winners. They stood around watching and joking as each one peed into his container. Urine burned bitter in the air. Some of the men bitched; one couldn't produce a drop in front of the others. Fitch let him slide shamefaced into a stall, but left the door open and watched him from the back.

At last, it was his turn. The first-class handed him his bottle personally. Phelan kept his face expressionless, though he wanted to throw the collected samples into the grinning, triumphant face. Prick, he said to himself, and added a Zuni obscenity as he nursed a shaky trickle into the plastic.

When it was done, the last man milked and checked off, Fitch nodded to the box of bottles, now a fluid honeycomb of a score of shades of yellow, saffron, red, and purple (the man being treated for gonorrhea). "Sick bay," he said, and left.

Phelan looked around; he was alone. It was the work of a moment to peel the labels off two of the vials, revealing beneath two identical, already-typed stickers with different names. He put the curling slips into his mouth, picked up the tray, and tinkled after the first-class out into the passageway and up the ladder. On the way he chewed, chewed, swallowed. The gummed paper was sweet. Take that, you sonofabitch, he thought, glaring at Fitch's narrow-shouldered back. Take that, lifer asshole, fucking *belagana* prick.

Though he was still hurting, for a moment he almost felt good.

Later that night, he was sitting on the mess decks, smoking a Marlboro and eating his third bowl of ice cream and strawberry jam, when he caught Fitch eyeing him through the latticework that screened the tables. The first-class hesitated, then drew a mug of joe and sat down across from him. Phelan kept his eyes on the bowl.

"Hi, Bernard."

"What you want, Fitch?"

"I got an apology to make."

A tiny hope flared up in him.

"About that piss test today. I thought . . . well, never mind what I thought." Fitch looked at the bowl. "You're seasick, I wouldn't eat no dairy products."

"I'm hungry."

"I guess you just can't tell who's using and who isn't. I'd've bet my ass old Jackson wouldn't have been on that shit. But I ran the sample through twice. I don't know why he's conscious, it's the highest opiate reading I've ever seen. Anyway, he's in deep kimchee now."

"That so," said Phelan. He tried not to smile.

"Anyway, I wanted to give you this." The square of paste-board clicked as Fitch snapped it on Formica and stood up. "Give it back to me after you memorize it. We'll stand one in three underway, you, me, and Golden. He's up there now. Can you take the twenty to midnight?"

"Sure," said Phelan. He dragged his widened gaze from the combination. He looked at his wrist, then remembered: no watch. "What time you got?"

"Seven-thirty."

"Sure," he said again. His spoon clattered against the bowl. He wanted to run to sick bay, relieve Golden early and himself, too. But he controlled it. Fitch had sat down again.

"What else you want?"

"Just to talk. You got a minute?"

"What about?" He was unable to keep the quaver out of his voice. Jesus, he thought, there's all kinds of shit in that safe. The card gleamed a foot away. He slid his hand over it casually, afraid Fitch would change his mind. Only when it was buttoned into his shirt pocket did he relax a little.

"Take it easy. Just about you. Get acquainted; we ain't really talked yet. You married? Got any kids?"

"Yeah. One kid. Little boy."

"How old is he?"

"Three."

Fitch took out his wallet and showed him pictures of his kids. Phelan's wallet was gone and his picture of Denise and Little Coyote, as they called the kid, gone with it. He wished now he'd kept it, but he hadn't been thinking about pictures at the time.

He told Fitch about the robbery, laying on the detail. By now, he could see it all clearly. The first-class clucked his tongue and offered to loan him ten bucks for cigarettes till his pay caught up with him. Phelan took it.

At last, Fitch stretched and got up again. "Well, just thought we'd get acquainted. You know, we got a billet for a permanent HM3. I was figuring Goldie for it, but . . . You might think about staying with us, 'stead of transferring back to that cruiser. You get a lot more responsibility on a ship this size."

"I might put in for that," said Phelan, making his voice sincere, as he had with the XO. "I'd sure like to make third. What do you think, would you help me out with that?"

"I can order the test if you want. Are you studying?"

"Oh yeah, I'm reading that manual every night."

"It ain't a hard test to pass, but there's lots pass ain't advanced. Well, we'll see."

Finally Fitch left. As soon as he was out of sight, Phelan jumped up, leaving the bowl for somebody else to clean up, and went directly to sick bay. Golden was reading a Conan the Barbarian comic book and was glad to get off a few minutes early. Phelan closed and locked the door behind him.

He was squatting down in front of the safe, the card in his hand, when he realized he'd screwed up. He'd told Fitch he was robbed, which was the story he'd used at the legation. But he'd told the exec, Lenson, that he'd saved a little girl. If they got to talking about him, they might compare stories. They might get suspicious.

But they wouldn't. He was getting crazy, that was all. Paranoid, yeah. But they were so fucking stupid, Fitch, the officers. He was safe here. He was reaching for the dial again when something inside his head stopped his hand in mid-movement.

What if he didn't open it; didn't use? Just rode it the rest of the way out. Cold turkeyed it. And really got clean.

Phelan squatted there, undecided and a little angry, scared, that the idea insisted on his considering it.

So he did. Thought about not using. Even though he could.

Then he thought, Hell, I can do that anytime. Relief flooded him at the decision. He could do it tomorrow. All he needed right now was something to calm himself down. Come down easy, that was the trick. In a couple days, he'd be clean and then he wouldn't have to touch any of it again. He'd only use a little. One cap, that was all he needed. They owed it to him. After all he'd been through.

His body twitched with hunger. The dial clicked into the final number, and the gates to paradise came open deep within the guts of a gray ship.

10

U.S.S. *Turner Van Zandt*

THE staccato clatter of chipping hammers filled the passageway outside Radio Central, varied with ripping noises, thumps, and yells. Beneath Dan's boondockers, where the deflooring party had passed, was naked steel, still bearing the circular scars of shipyard grinders.

RM1 Wolfe pulled off a stencil, revealing a gleaming red arrow six inches from the bottom of a door. "Uh, can I ask a question, XO?"

"Sure."

"Why down here? What's wrong with eye level, where they're supposed to be?"

Dan straightened, looking down the passageway at the stack of torn-up tile. How many thousands of man-hours had been lavished on it, buffed daily for XO's inspection, stripped and waxed every week till it shone like a calm green sea. Now it was flammable trash, ready to go over the side.

"If we have a major fire, this passageway's going to be full of smoke. And you'll be on your belly, crawling for the weather decks. Get the picture?"

"Oh," said the petty officer. "Who thought of that? That makes *sense.*"

Two hull techs banged their tools down, conferred over a sketch, then began sawing a hole in the skin of the ship. Behind them, electronic technicians were popping lids off cans, laying a coat of deck gray mixed with sand.

Dan decided to get out of the way and let them work. He pulled out his wheel book and drew a line through 01 LEVEL DECK.

As he headed aft, the whole ship clanged, clattered, and whined. *Van Zandt*'s crew was stripping ship. Ridding her of every piece of tile, wood, or plastic, every nonessential that could shatter, break, burn, or explode—as well as modifying quite a few things in ways not strictly in accordance with the *NAVSHIPS Technical Manual*.

"Where they're *supposed* to be." He'd sidestepped the petty officer's real question. Because no one had approved what they were doing. No one had been asked to. Not one message had gone to Washington about it. Not one dollar had been spent on research and development, environmental-impact studies, leading-edge engineering, or comparative testing. Shaker had simply given the orders. And Dan had decided, despite some misgivings, to carry them out.

The midships passageway, eight feet wide and half the frigate's length, was crowded with boxes and garbage bags. A narrow walkway threaded between couches and rolled-up carpets from the wardroom and chief's mess. Against the bulkheads were stacked cruise boxes filled with civvies, dress uniforms, Corfam shoes, and everything made of the deadly polyester Shaker called "walking napalm." One box was Dan's. There were bundles of surplus charts from the quartermasters' shack. Lengths of wooden shoring. Souvenirs: pseudo-Persian carpets, djellabas, sheik outfits. Bunk curtains and shower curtains. The oiled walnut cabinet that had held the flag and silver of the old *Turner Van Zandt*, lost at Savo Island taking on two Japanese cruisers.

"How's it going, Chief Dorgan?"

The harried-looking storekeeper, neck trickling perspiration, was directing four petty officers bagging armloads of pubs and records. "Getting it done, sor. But I never realizing this fooking tub carry so much paper. What'm I gonna do, I need to look up a regulation?"

"Same as you always do, Chief. Make one up."

Dan had briefed the senior enlisted after he'd left Shaker's cabin the day before. Not without some doubt. The officers could issue all the orders they liked, but it was the chiefs who either made things happen or let them fall by the wayside. To his surprise, there'd hardly been a grumble, hardly a hint of their usual response to anything out of the ordinary, which was not-very-muted bitching and moaning.

The varnished gratings from the bridge bobbed by him on the shoulders of two signalmen, followed by their cherished collection of foreign flags. The ship's library lay stacked on deck, along with chair covers, plaques from the captain's cabin, and boxes of videotapes, mostly kung fu, mercenary, and porn. Two disbursing clerks were packaging everything frangible: glass covers, shaving mirrors, the sneeze shields from the serving line, and the trick Greek painting from the chiefs' quarters, an ample nude that became an innocent landscape when turned upside down.

The air on the fantail was like a hot, wet sponge. Squeezing a reluctant breath out of it, he looked around.

It, too, was the scene of hectic activity. Between him and the slowly heaving horizon was a small mountain range of cleaning fluid, furniture polish, paint remover, drums of extra oil and grease the gunners and snipes had been packratting away since commissioning day. Brocket and Jimson, the supply officers, were bustling about getting it inventoried and strapped onto pallets. To port came a sudden cough and buzz; Ensign Loamer was testing the portable pumps. A petty officer aimed a nozzle, and a cone of mist split the oppressive sun into a rainbow. Dan let the wind of *Van Zandt*'s passage blow it over him, lifting his face gratefully to the cool fog, tasting the sting of brine.

"Hey, Percy."

"Sir." Loamer ran toward him, tripping on a hose.

"How are those flash hoods coming?"

"We're still cutting up the fantail awning, sir. Going to start the stitching pretty soon."

"When's the last time somebody looked at our gas masks?"

"Well, I don't know, sir, I've only been aboard since—"

"I know, I know. Pull them all, all over the ship. Check them for airtightness and replace the filters. Today."

"Yessir, but we got the pumps to test, and the—"

"I understand that, Percy, and now you got gas masks to do, too. So don't waste time arguing, all right?"

"Aye aye, sir."

"Start your repair-team leaders going through the lockers. Make out a requisition for a hundred and fifty more OBA canisters. Write it down, Mr. Loamer! If you need new gaskets, strainers, hoses, order them, too. Make sure we have the right fittings on the eductors. Let me know what you need by sixteen-hundred and I'll get a message off to *San Jose.*"

When the ensign rushed off, Dan stood by the lifeline, looking out over an oily, windless, gently heaving sea toward a far-off line of ocher.

In their tortuous passage through the southern Gulf, doglegging to avoid Iranian waters, oil rigs, and offshore loading points, they'd steamed 350 miles to make the straight-line distance of 200 from Bahrain. Now, re-creating the chart in his mind, Dan guessed he was looking at Dhubai. Guessed; this southern coast was low; sand, desert, or saltwater marsh. It sloped so gradually upward from sea level, the radar showed only ghosts. Here, close to land, dust fogged the air, making the shore look more distant than it was.

His squint caught something off the bow, dark and inchoate, shimmering and weaving in the sun-tortured air. Why, he wondered, was everything in the Gulf so hard to see as it really was . . . then just for a moment the mirages steadied into cliffs. Abrupt masses of rock, fissured and gullied by erosion or earthquake. The Musandam Peninsula. The United Arab Emirates on this side, Oman on the other. The bluffs reminded him of Nevada, when he'd gone out there to see his daughter.

And between *Van Zandt* and the distant land stood a procession of ships, tankers, freighters, coasters, set out like chess pieces across the oily sea. Most were beam to him, proceeding into or out of Dhubai for repair, refueling, and offload. There must be eighty of them in sight. And this was only the beginning. Traffic would be even heavier in the approaches to the Strait.

The Strait of Hormuz: the busiest maritime channel in the world. Through that thirty-mile-wide gap between the Omani peninsula and the coast of Iran passed 19,000 ships a year, and sixty percent of the world's supply of oil.

He looked aft, where the frigate's bow wave, marching away from the wake, disappeared into the blurry melding of atmosphere and sea. Dropping astern now was a nest of dhows, slowly circling as they laid or hauled their nets. They'd caused him anxious hours in the past two months. Milling around on no fixed course, following the schools below them, occasionally they'd aim themselves across *Van Zandt*'s bow as if intent on snaring frigates rather than fish. He'd be sleeping light tonight.

Then, with a stab almost as of pain, he remembered: She wasn't his anymore. Now the OOD would call Shaker if he was confused by lights, or wondered which way to turn.

He couldn't decide whether to feel relieved or regretful.

Tim Jimson came up with a question about pay for the new corpsman. When that was settled, Dan fingered his wheel book. So much more to do . . . but he lingered still, looking off to port. Toward the Mubarek oil field. Its black derricks poked over the curve of the sea, writhing in the shimmer like black flames. Above several flickered yellow points. The sky was stained with smoke and dust. And farther off, so far he could only just make it out, a huge inky pall streamed endlessly upward: a British-owned separation platform. The target of a Pasdaran attack, it had been burning since before *Van Zandt* arrived in the Gulf.

Beyond it was Abu Musa, Iranian-held, a base for the revolutionary guards—the Pasdaran, fanatical vanguard of Khomeini's fundamentalist revolution.

"Commander Lenson: Bridge."

Jerked from reverie, he went into the hangar. Shaker answered the bogen. "Dan? Where are you?"

"Fantail, sir. Been making the rounds."

"How's strip ship progressing?"

Dan gave him a rundown. Halfway through it, Shaker interrupted, "When are the passageways going to be done?"

"I'd say four, five more hours, sir. By the way, Doc Fitch asked me about sick bay. He wanted to keep his tile, said it'd be more sanitary. I said he could."

"I guess that's okay, but I want metal everyplace else."

"Yessir, it's being done."

Shaker hung up. Dan looked at his book again, then went into the port hangar.

It was dark in there, and almost cool. The insectile bulk of the helicopter filled it like a butterfly in a tight pupa. In the minimal space left over, three crewmen had rigged a scaffold and were working, bent over hinged-out aluminum like Saturday mechanics under the hoods of their pickups. Dan looked around; a CO_2 extinguisher stood near to hand; only one thing missing. . . . He called up to their oblivious backs, "Hey! Chief Mattocks up there?"

"Yeah! Who wants him?"

"Me. Where're your pilots?"

The chief emerged for a moment; his face was smeared with blue grease. "Dunno, sir. You check their stateroom?"

"Maybe I will."

As he turned away, he heard a mutter from one of the other crewmen; it was just loud enough to make out: "Don't knock too loud, you might wake 'em up."

Late that afternoon, as soon as strip ship was complete, Shaker called a surprise general quarters. Lenson was in the ship's office, proofing a hastily revised conflagration plan. As he sprinted through the mess decks, the crew jumped up from full trays, cursing heartily. The ladders were thronged, but only for a moment; the clamor of feet came loud through the overhead. He reached CIC, to find Shaker calmly examining his watch. "You take TAO," said the captain. "We'll say I'm dead."

Dan snatched the headset out of Wise's hand. He glanced

swiftly around, barked, "CIC, manned and ready," and focused his attention on the surface repeater.

The two-foot-diameter horizontal display was a madhouse of ships and low fliers. To the east was the dull green glow of land, freckled with mountain. To the west—they'd left Dhubai behind—was a scatter of fishermen. To the north, in the shipping lanes, were two solid, clearly outlined columns of ships, so many the course-and-speed circuits had been overwhelmed.

He swiveled, his hands still occupied with his life vest. The air picture was not quite as crowded. Its operator had managed to keep up, identifying aircraft through the automated link with the AWACS, the Saudi-owned, U.S. Air Force-manned radar bird that orbited over the Gulf twenty-four hours a day. West of them were two helicopters, probably servicing the oil field they'd just passed. To the south, dozens of aircraft, commercial airliners, were stacked up over Dhubai. In the upper Gulf, the prime worry was Iraqi aircraft, Exocet-armed Mirages and Styx-carrying Badgers. They lay in wait for ships enroute to and from Khārk Island, the main Iranian oil terminal. Here the danger lay to the north. Near the coast of Iran, pulsating electronically to stand out from the land clutter, were the symbols for hostile aircraft. Two of them, over Larak Island, not far from the Iranian Navy base at Bandar ‘Abbās.

The intercom said, in Pensker's taut voice, "This is a drill. ESM contact, bearing two-six-oh true, snoop scan radar."

"ESM identify," shouted Lenson across the compartment.

"ESM identifies: Soviet radar: associated with Styx missile."

Dan passed it to the bridge and put the weapons console on standby. The next thing he heard was, "I-band homer, bearing two-six-five degrees true."

"Styx missile, bearing two-six-five true"—he thought for a fraction of a second—"Weps control! Fire chaff, port battery, activate Phalanx automatic mode. Mark 92, search and acquire; assign to Mount 31." He snapped a switch beside his chair. "Bridge, TAO: come left, steady up two-nine-oh. Gun control, TAO: Your target bears two-two-five relative. Air target, low flier, incoming. Load with mixed infrared and proximity fuze. Commence fire when locked on."

The captain reappeared and crossed the room to stand beside the ECM operator. A moment later, the sailor cried out, "New contact! Surface radar, frequency twelve megahertz, pulse repetition rate three point two. Corresponds—"

"Classify friendly," shouted Lenson. "That's a Bahraini."

"Correction. PRR four point seven."

"Iranian, *Combattante*-class gunboat. Classify hostile! Weps control, TAO: Load one Harpoon, set search mode two, range unknown, fire on command, next round search mode one. ECM, get me a bearing!"

"H-band homer! Missile incoming, starboard side!"

"XO, you're out of action," said the captain. Dan stopped in mid-order and handed the headset to Wise. The operations officer took over instantly, ordering more chaff and telling Pensker to shift his rudder. The captain looked displeased, and he altered it hastily to maintain present course.

"You were right the first time, Al. Missile hit forward, frame twenty," said Shaker.

Wise told the bridge. A moment later the 1MC said, "Missile hit forward, frame twenty, Repair Two provide."

"Let's go," said Shaker. Dan ran after him down ladders and passageways till they reached Repair Two. The team was already dressed out and moving, laying hose and comm wire behind them. The captain reached up and with a piece of chalk Dan hadn't seen made an *X* on a pipe. To one of the men, he said, "Fragment hit, main firemain."

The team instantly divided, most continuing forward as the team leader yanked a valve to isolate the broken main, two dropping axes to break open a pipe-patching kit. Shaker paused at a bogen. A moment later the lights went out and ventilation died.

An eerie silence fell, broken only by the muffled panting of the men. Battle lanterns came on, yellow beams groping through sudden darkness. The air grew hot. Shaker was chalking every other man, declaring them casualties. Loamer came out of a side passageway and the captain *X*'d him on the chest, chewing him out meanwhile for leaving DC central.

They reached frame twenty. Bodies lay strewn about the deck. The char of third-degree burns blackened their bare chests. Dan stepped on a hand, lying some distance from the nearest body, and nearly slipped in a pool of "blood." The moulages looked realistic. "Forget about him!" shouted the captain at a man who bent. "Report the casualties, then concentrate on saving the ship!"

After watching them fight the "fire" for ten minutes, Shaker left. Shortly thereafter, the 1MC said, "Prepare to abandon ship. Nearest land bears one-two-zero magnetic, distance twenty miles."

The interior of the ship, dark as a mine disaster, filled again with running men, this time rushing for their assigned life rafts and a hasty muster. Dan matched names on the bridge, sweating. He found two missing and passed the word for them, hoping they were the ones Shaker had told not to report. *Van Zandt* quaked under his feet as the engines went full astern; below them, Guerra was running his own series of casualty drills.

After that, they remanned battle stations and fired Phalanx and small arms for an hour. Shaker wanted to shoot the 76mm as well, but Wise looked up the Omani regulations and nixed it; nothing larger than 20mm without prior notice. The captain nodded quietly and thanked him. From surface firing, he exercised them in Rules of Engagement interpretation, anti-Silkworm tactics, and vectoring of attack aircraft.

They finally secured just after midnight. Dan found himself standing on the starboard wing, trembling, his clothes wringing wet.

He stared out on a scene of apocalyptic grandeur.

Ahead of him, the sky was burning. Close in the torches were visible, vibrating bands of fire that waved slowly in the wind. They lit the water like lines of gaslights in a London fog. Farther away, they were cut off by the horizon, but still their light trembled in the sky like an infernal aurora. Not a star was visible, though there were no clouds; dust, smoke, and ambient light blockaded their feeble glitter from the Gulf.

In the glowing night, row on row, outgoing ships stood eastward in a line that stretched beyond sight. Deep-laden, swollen with oil like honey ants, their palely glowing superstructures seemed to plow through the sea without benefit of hulls beneath. Like some giant, primitive invertebrate, the Gulf's narrow mouth and anus were the same. This was its only entrance, and for two hundred miles the traffic divided, left and right, a great highway on the sea. Behind him, over the bridge-to-bridge circuit, came the gabble of hundreds of voices as the Omani authorities tried to maintain order.

He became aware then of someone beside him. He turned his head and made out Shaker. The weird sky glow was bright enough to see dark heeltaps under his eyes. The captain bent, instinctively masking a flame behind the splinter shield. Then straightened, his cigarette glowing like a dying sun.

"It's like fucking Fifth Avenue out here," he muttered. "What are you doing still up, XO? We got a long day tomorrow. Rendezvous with the battle group, do the refuel, then find our convoy."

"I don't know." Lenson looked out at the ships. "Just taking a breather. I'll go below in a little while."

He glanced toward the chart table. But as if he'd read his mind, Shaker murmured, "We're on track, half an hour ahead of intended movement. Your senior QM, he's sharp."

"I've known Mac since I was a jaygee. He's about the best there is." Dan paused. "This whole crew's good, Ben."

"They're shaping up," said the captain, his voice noncommittal. "We still got a few slackers. But they'll come around quick. Or they won't be here long."

"Slackers?"

"Or let's say, people I'm not sure about yet." The captain's voice trailed off as he looked aft. "Lieutenant Pensker, for one. What do you know about him?"

"About Terry . . . let's see—"

"Where's he from? Where'd he go to school?"

"He's from Indiana. OCS. Graduated from Ball State, I think, with a masters in electrical engineering." Dan searched his memory for more. "He's married, but I've only met his wife once. A pool party at Glynda Bell's. Lena's a nice girl. Quiet. No kids yet."

"Kind of car's he drive?"

"Car? Uh, Japanese. One of the sporty ones. Toyota or Datsun, I think."

"What's your impression of him? Good guy? Bad guy? Strong or weak?"

Dan considered this, uneasily wondering whether the fact that Pensker was black had anything to do with Shaker's questions. It wasn't a pleasant thought. The Navy discouraged and punished discrimination—there were black COs and even admirals now—but it still existed. "He's sharp, Captain. He rewrote our Combat Systems Doctrine, and the Fleet Training Center inspectors, when we went to Gitmo for refresher training, they wanted a copy, said it was going to be Fleet standard for *Perry* class as far as they were concerned. Leadership, he's good there too. Takes care of his men. He's taking this deployment seriously. All he needs is seasoning."

Shaker asked nothing more. Dan glanced at the bulky silhouette. The captain had perched himself on the wing chair, and looked like he was settling in.

Then he thought, That's exactly what he's doing. With the Strait transit tonight, hundreds of ships on the scope, this man planned even less rest for himself than he allowed his overworked crew.

He hoped he was wrong about the racial business. Aside from his momentary suspicion on that angle, so far he couldn't, if he was honest, fault Shaker in anything he'd done. *Van Zandt* had been a standout ship, a measure for excellence by the Navy's book. Shaker wanted to make it even more of one—but by some only gradually revealed Scripture of his own. He was driving the crew, the officers, as if at any moment the sky might open to a plunging missile.

But it could! Dan had wondered himself about Bell's preoccupation with cleanliness, preservation, administrative correspondence, lectures on safe driving and sexual harassment, sometimes ahead of combat training.

So what was it about Benjamin Shaker that however obscurely bothered him? Because something did. Something he couldn't quantify, but felt nonetheless.

He decided now that his instincts were wrong. Two days into command, Shaker had already changed the ship beyond recognition. Dan thought of the chiefs, how they'd carried their cherished sofa out of their lounge with their own hands. Remembered the men on the mess decks, leaping up from loaded trays with curses, yes, but also with alacrity, with something not far from eagerness, exhausted as they were.

Shaker was a leader. And he was right. *Van Zandt* was a warship in a war zone, and anything could happen. And the crew knew that. In liberties to come, early in the evening they would piss and moan about him. But later they would defend their captain and their ship with their fists as something that had almost disappeared from the fleet: a fighting ship, a grimly honed instrument of war. What they sweated for, what they sacrificed and bled for, there they would find their pride.

Till now, he'd supported the captain because it was his duty. Now, looking at the lights of the distant tankers, glittering and dancing on the undulating mirror of the sea, Dan thought, I'm wrong. He's what this ship needs. Maybe what the whole Navy needs. No polish. All business. Shaker was no peacetime sailor, no advancement-obsessed careerist like Ike Sundstrom had been. He was a man of war.

"Good night, captain," he said, and gave him a short salute.

Shaker's voice came muzzy; he was dozing in his chair, ten feet from the officer of the deck. " 'Night, XO."

He stopped at the chart table, studying their course in the dim red light. He extended the DR trace to noon the next day. It ended at Point Orange, the rendezvous. He checked it again, signed a movement report McQueen had left for release, and set his watch for 0400. As Shaker had said, it would be a long day.

Lying in his rack a few minutes later, Dan smiled. For the first time in two months, he felt safe.

11

Riyadh, Saudi Arabia

THE car from the palace turned out to be a Silver Shadow. Blair leaned back into brushed leather and the scents of oiled walnut, cowhide, and a memory of perfume. The door clicked closed and, separated from them by soundproof glass, the chauffeur slid behind the wheel.

"These people don't go tourist class, do they?" she murmured.

Beside her, Harrison L. Shaw III, U.S. Ambassador to Saudi Arabia, chuckled as he tilted a mirror, ran his fingers through his hair, tweaked his tie. He was career Foreign Service, an immaculate man who looked like a young George Bush. He didn't answer her right away. He never did, as if somewhere behind his washed-out blue eyes a rather slow computer was iterating down to a possible response, judging its suitability, then translating it into Yale English.

At last he said, "No. Not in anything. Like the new Specialist's Hospital. Fahd threw out the first plan; he thought it was too conservative. He wanted the best hospital in the Middle East. The highways are planned for a city with three times the population Riyadh has today."

"Of course, they can afford it."

"Of course."

"Will the king be there, do you think?"

"Tonight? I doubt it. But Ismail's the man you want to see. Governor of the Eastern Province, overseer of the Defense Ministry, Fahd's favorite nephew—he's the one you want, all right."

"Thanks again for setting this up," she said, a little unwillingly. She still wished Shaw had let her go alone. But he'd insisted.

"That's what I'm here for—among about a million other

things." He chuckled, then went serious. "I want to caution you again, by the way—"

"I think you've cautioned me enough, Harrison."

He quirked his eyebrows, but seemed to decide on silence as the best riposte. The car began to move. Though no sound or vibration reached the passengers, the scenery began to slide by. The embassy grounds dropped away, giving place to the new city of Riyadh.

She'd last seen the capital of what was arguably the richest nation on earth five years before. Then it had been a small but growing oasis, still with a sleepy air. Now it was transformed, as if it had fast-forwarded from the seventeenth century directly into the twenty-first. The palms, though, still lined the new highways, and for that she was grateful. She loved their delicate extensions toward the sky, the penislike curve of their trunks.

She smoothed her skirt over her lap. She'd let Shaw advise her on her clothing. This was the longest skirt she owned, mid-calf. She wore a high-collared ecru blouse under the camel-hair blazer, black flats, and for jewelry, simple onyx earrings—square ones. She'd even disciplined her hair into a french braid, a process that took an hour. In her purse was a paisley scarf, in case she needed to cover it.

As the car whispered onward, she ran over what she had to do in the upcoming interview. They'd be essentially the same facts and questions she'd already presented to ruling figures in the United Arab Emirates and Qatar. Only the Saudis were far more powerful, and pivotal, than any of the sheikhdoms. Their attitudes would be decisive in her final report to Talmadge. And in the final determination of what policy the United States should pursue in the Gulf.

It would be delicate, however. Ismail didn't have to see her. He didn't have to agree to a thing. He could toss her out if he felt like it. She had very little power here.

"Remember now," said Shaw, leaning again across the seat, "be gentle. Gentle! These people don't like to be approached directly, or presented with ultimatums. They don't bargain, either. Every concession has to be a gift, a gesture of friendship between equals. And if he asks you personal questions—"

"Harrison," she said, "please shut up."

Prince Ismail was nearly as tall as she, a glossy man in his late thirties. His quizzical, up-from-under half-smile had been all

over the papers at the Inter-Continental, where she was staying.

He was standing in the driveway as they swung through the
gates. She wondered for a moment how he'd known; then understood; of course, the chauffeur had a phone. He was wearing
a double-breasted Savile Row blazer, salt and pepper slacks,
and a white Arab headdress. He wasn't tall, but neither was he
afflicted yet by the paunchiness that transformed so many Arab
men after thirty from Omar Sharifs to Sidney Greenstreets.
Clean-shaven, except for an ambitious but rather sparse mustache. No candidate for *Playgirl*, but good-looking. His smile
said he knew it.

He and Shaw greeted each other with a handshake, held
longer than two Americans would have. Then he turned to her,
glittering dark eyes looking her up and down and frankly ap-
proving what they saw. "And this is Miss Titus?"

"Prince Ismail Bin Faisal Bin Turki Al Abdullah Al Saud, let
me introduce Ms. Blair Titus, senior staffer for Senator Talmadge." For a moment, she wondered whether she ought to
curtsey. No, that was only for the king.

The prince released her hand, leaving it smelling of lavender,
and led them inside.

She'd expected something like this, but still she blinked.
Every exposed inch of the floor and walls was marble, and the
rooms were gilded—no, not gilded, it was *gold*. Roses in cloi-
sonné stork vases tall as a man, Sung Dynasty temple lions, a
wall of carved jade and ivory figures in glass cases, gilded
temple carvings with scenes of warriors in battle. . . . Ismail,
or his decorator, had a taste for Chinese. The carpets had that
flat, drab shabbiness that meant incredible age and incredible
expense.

The prince led them slowly through room after room, glancing back as if enjoying her reaction. They went down a curved
cascade of stairs and she found herself again under the late-
afternoon sky, this time in a garden thronged with roses. Amid
them, between two fountains, a table had been set, European-
style, with lacquered Chinese chairs.

"I thought we'd dine outside this evening. Please don't tell
me you're allergic to roses."

"I love them." The funny part was, she did. She stared
around, only then noticing that despite the 120-degree heat,
dew glistened on nodding petals. Air-conditioned the old way,
by the fountains. A splash startled her; golden koi inlaid with
coral and opal gaped, gulped air, and sank again into glittering
transparence. "It's beautiful."

"Gardens are an Arab tradition. Small paradises, hidden away from the violent and ugly world outside. The rose is often identified in our poetry with Woman—wooed, captured, and then protected within enclosing walls."

He fingered a pale pink blossom, but he was gazing at her rather than it. "The Isfahan, for example. It has an intense, spicy scent, not unmixed with a faint bitterness . . . like love itself, perhaps?"

"It's beautiful," she said again, deliberately obtuse to his allusions. "You must spend all your time here."

"I only wish I could. Harry, you *did* tell her not to admire things too much, that as a good host I'm obliged to give them to her?"

"In that case, yes, I'll take the garden," she said firmly. Both men laughed.

"How is Washington?" Ismail went on, apparently abandoning the language of flowers.

"Hot and busy."

"I spent four years there in the seventies. At American U. It was a peaceful town then. After Vietnam, and before crack." He sighed. "I often wish I was a student again. No responsibilities, you see. And no wives."

"How many do you have, Your Highness?"

"How many? Four." He shrugged. "Just now I regret it, making the acquaintance of such a lovely woman. But that is our limit, you see."

"Will we meet them tonight?"

She caught Shaw's wince out of the corner of her eye. However, Ismail seemed to take it in stride. He said casually, "No, I'm afraid business bores them. And two are in Paris at the moment. No, there'll only be five of us. We three, Mr. Nawwab, the Defense Minister, and a poet. One of our more honored men, though I don't think he's well known in the West. Dr. Ibn Ubaiyidh."

The inclusion of a poet in what she'd understood to be a political dinner seemed odd to her, but she didn't remark on it. "I hope he'll be able to . . . recite something," she ventured.

"Perhaps. If we stroke him. You have any Arabic at all, Miss Titus?"

"Just *'is-salaam alaykum'* and *'min fadlak,'* I'm afraid."

"Certainly the two most useful phrases in any language."

Really, Blair thought, he was exquisitely polite. Except for that casual dismissal of his wives. He hadn't picked those manners up in the United States.

A butler and several servers appeared, threading their way

among the roses. One came directly to them, balancing a tray, and the prince said, "Champagne?"

"I didn't think—"

"No alcohol. It's our version—apple juice, soda, and orange juice."

"Thank you, that sounds delicious."

"Are you from Washington, Ms. Titus?"

"My family's from the Midwest, but I grew up in Maryland. Charles County."

"That's horse country, isn't it? Didn't Harry tell me you rode?"

"Well, less now than I used to."

"Hunting, yes? You shake your head a little—jumping, that was it! See, Harry, I have a memory after all, don't I? I have a mare you will have to ride. She's taken honors in England. Tell me you'll make an afternoon, fly to my farm in Ushayrah."

Blair smiled, almost sarcastically. For a moment she thought of asking who *he* planned to ride. But a glance at Shaw's warning eyebrows made it easier not to. Sure enough, Ismail's next question was "And are you married?"

"No."

"A woman like you, unmarried? What a waste."

"I'm not sure I look at it that way," she said, cutting another glance toward Shaw. Was this customary, this personal cross-examination? For a moment, she wished she'd listened more closely. But the ambassador's buffed smile held no guidance now.

She looked back at Ismail, to find the dark eyes focused on hers from a foot away. She stepped back instinctively. "American men, Your Highness, don't seem to understand that I have a career, too."

"Perhaps the problem is not wholly with them." He'd moved forward when she moved back; she could smell his breath now. "Certainly one area in which we Arabs differ from you—please don't take this personally—is the belief that man and woman were created for different tasks. Could it be that you'd be happier married, with children, making a home for someone?"

Children. Was that all that was on their minds? "I doubt it," she said, barely keeping herself from snapping at him.

Perhaps Ismail felt how angry she was getting. At any rate, he dropped it, explaining quietly he'd have to leave them for a moment. The other guests were arriving. Alone again with Shaw, she said, "He seems easy enough to get along with."

The ambassador pondered this. "Personally, yes. Diplomati-

cally . . . well, you'll find out," he said at last. "Really, Blair, I
don't know what you hope to do here. You're not going to get
anything out of Ismail that State hasn't, that I haven't."

"I only want to ask some questions."

"Wonderful, but *please* don't anger him. I've spent months
building a relationship. I wouldn't care to have all that work
lost."

"Relax, Harry. I'll try not to commit any incredible gaucher-
ies. But he can't live in a rose garden. There are realities out
there, and if he won't face them, we have to force him to."

Shaw, frowning, had almost computed his reply when a murmur of voices neared.

The minister and the doctor turned out to be short, chubby,
middle-aged men with King Fahd-style goatees. They both were
wearing blue suits and she could see immediately that sometime tonight she was going to call one of them by the other's
name. The poet was wearing a red tie, the defense minister,
blue. She hoped she could remember that.

"Come, let's eat," said Ismail, smiling.

The table was set for five but there was food for three times
that number. Stuffed pigeons, turkey, beef and lamb pies, salad,
broiled mutton, lamb with rice, dates, and innumerable dishes
of sweet pastries and cakes, the courses kept coming, borne in
relays by silent servers, supervised by the butler. She watched
the others for any little points of usage, but save for using the
fork in the continental manner, and the fact that all the utensils
were gold, there was no difference from any other diplomatic
dinner. However, there was almost no talking. The poet ne-
glected the silverware; he wolfed his food, getting his fingers
and tie greasy as he dipped into dish after dish. Now that she
was closer to him, she could see that he was older than she'd
thought, his little goat's beard streaked with gray.

When the prince leaned back and said *"Bismillah,"* it
seemed to be a signal. She placed her fork carefully on the last
dish, feeling stuffed. Then she jumped as Shaw, beside her,
belched loudly. *"Bismillah,"* he said.

"Bismillah," Blair said. She wasn't about to belch, though
she remembered now that was good form; but she managed a
small burp.

The defense minister excused himself for eating so little; it
was, he said sadly, his ulcer. The poet looked startled to find the
others were done. His eyes followed the dishes as they were
whisked away.

A servant, a veiled woman, brought towels, soap, and water.

Blair followed the lead of the Arabs and washed. After, not
before the meal, but after watching Ibn Ubaiyidh she understood why. As the woman poured cologne over her hands, Blair
tried to catch her eyes. But there seemed to be a veil over them,
too.

"It's growing dark," said the prince at last. "We faithful will
excuse ourselves now for a moment, if you don't mind. If you'll
go inside, we'll join you for coffee."

As they rose, she saw the servants spreading prayer rugs on
the flagstones.

The butler showed them to divans around a low table, so
deeply lacquered she could see her face not reflected but preserved deep within it, like a Sleeping Beauty entombed in
amber. The others came in perhaps ten minutes later. The chat
stayed light till the same woman brought in the coffee tray.
Blair wondered whether this was one of his wives, but decided
not to ask. "Coffee and oil, Arabia's two great gifts to the
world," rumbled Ibn Ubaiyidh, startling her; it was the first
sentence he'd spoken.

"I didn't know coffee was Arabic."

"Of course it is. *Quawha;* it reached your language through
the Italian. Very interesting history. We found that chewing
the bean helped us stay awake during long hours in the
mosque."

"The doctor is a learned man," said Ismail. Blair couldn't tell
what he meant by that—sarcasm, respect, or just his smooth
politeness. She tried to cover all the possibilities by saying, "His
Highness tells me you're Arabia's most famous poet. Unfortunately, I've read none of your work—"

"Oh, hardly the most famous." Ibn Ubaiyidh wobbled his
jowls, laughing silently. "But as you've been so kind as to ask,
I was playing with one during dinner. I've never worked in
English, so you must not laugh."

"I won't."

The old man looked directly at her, and chanted: "With ala-
baster throat and rising breasts, her hair shines more gold than
gold; like the rays of sun are her hair. Her hands are the cups
of river lotus. With narrow waist she, whose thighs dispute
each other's beauty, steals my heart when she walks into the
house of my Prince. All men turn their heads to watch this
unveiled houri, and I, old past the season of love, burn with
desire like a boy of twelve."

They were all looking at her. She felt her cheeks heat,
whether in a blush or annoyance, she wasn't really sure. For a

moment she trembled on the verge of rage. She took a deep breath, controlling her voice. "It's . . . very beautiful."

"Mashkuwr; but it would sound better in Arabic, I assure you. Did you know that God speaks Arabic, Ms. Titus?"

"Perhaps that's why I don't understand Him very well."

The Arabs all stared at her, Nawwab narrowing his gaze suspiciously. Shaw broke a tense moment by slurping his coffee. She followed suit. It was strong, bitter, and she decided the quarter cup she'd been served was quite enough. She shook it—that was the signal that you were done—and set it down.

"Now," she said, "About this matter of basing our ships—"

Shaw choked. The defense minister looked pained. The prince, though, simply said, "We've been through this matter at length with Mr. Shaw. Several times, in fact, with him and with his respected predecessor."

"I understand that. But matters have changed since then—"

The sad-eyed minister murmured to the veiled woman. She nodded and left, returning a moment later with something milky in a tall glass. *"Shukran,"* he said loudly, and began gulping it.

"We don't think they've changed," said Ismail, as if that ended the discussion. After a moment, he added, "Our policy, that of the Gulf Coordinating Council and the Saudi Government, is that our navies will cooperate with yours in pursuit of common objectives in the Gulf and Arabian Sea. Mr. Nawwab assures me this policy is being carried out. The surveillance data from the AWACs aircraft that you so kindly sold us, after two full years of pleading with Congress, is being shared with your ships. And we are happy to provide fueling facilities. It seems to me that we have reached a satisfactory balance of responsibilities."

"Senator Talmadge helped consummate that sale," murmured Shaw, almost too low to hear.

"We appreciated his assistance. But bases—that's out of the question. I hate to put things so bluntly, but I know Americans are impatient." He smiled at her. "You don't care for our coffee? I have tea coming, or we could serve you a lemon Pepsi."

"I'd like some more," said Shaw. His foot prodded her under the table.

She ignored it, and the offer of beverages. "It's not a satisfactory state of affairs."

"The Holy Qur'an says, 'Fight in the way of Allah against those who attack you; but begin not hostilities. Allah loveth not aggressors,' " rumbled the poet.

Ismail said, "What I believe the doctor means, Ms. Titus, is that we Saudis are a peace-loving people. Once the differences between our brothers are settled, we want to see the Gulf become a sea of peace. We have no intention of allowing it to become another arena of superpower rivalry. The British have left. We have no desire to see America, or any other external power, established in their place."

"What about Iran?"

"Pardon me, but Iran borders the Gulf. We don't see eye to eye with the current regime in that unhappy country, but they belong here in a way that America, however regrettably, does not."

Blair watched his hands flutter, then flatten themselves softly on the lacquered darkness. The effort of restraining herself was giving her a headache. She squeezed a last reserve of reasonableness into her voice. "We're not talking about a permanent base, Prince! Listen. Here is the situation. It is extremely expensive for us to maintain such a large naval force so far from home without facilities for repair, overhaul, and liberty. Every six months, we have to rotate ships nine thousand miles back to the United States. The senator is asking, Can we reduce this expenditure? Could we work out a way to base a squadron from, say, Jubail or Dhahran?"

Nawwab murmured something. Ismail said, with a hint of annoyance, "Say it to *her*. I'm not your translator."

"You have Bahrain," said the minister.

"We have part-time use of one pier. That's not enough. Frankly, if we can't reduce the cost of our deployments, or scale back the number of ships we send, we may have to end our escort and patrol program."

The prince shrugged. "I would personally regret that very much. We have evolved such a close partnership, such good relations. We've bought most of our ships from you; your Navy has trained ours. Nevertheless, if we were forced to look elsewhere, we would, of course, do so. Perhaps some other maritime power might be willing to undertake a guarantee."

He meant the Soviet Union. She'd expected it sooner or later. She also knew it was a bluff. There was no way the Saudi ruling house would invite the Soviets in. So she said, "Let's be reasonable, Your Highness. We are providing protection for trade. For Kuwaiti ships directly; for yours indirectly, but nonetheless effectively. We don't want to maintain our forces where they aren't welcome. But neither can we undertake to support allies who aren't willing to cooperate in their defense."

"Most of this trade is oil," said Nawwab. "Let us look at it in economic terms. If it is interrupted, the price goes up. We can ship overland to the Red Sea and Mediterranean with the new pipelines. The West, Japan, and the southern emirates may suffer, but we won't. Our total income might rise. Why don't you ask the Japanese to pay some of your expenses? That would be more rational."

Ismail said, "Let me also point out, Miss Titus, that your Congress, too, wants to have things both ways. They sold us AWACs, but they refused to sell us modern fighters."

"That's a side issue. And you know why the F-18 sale fell through. Because they might be used against Israel."

"Exactly . . . though I would say, against the illegal state in Palestine. But we have offered guarantees against that, and still you refuse. If we had modern weaponry, we could protect our own trade, could we not? So who is being unreasonable?"

"We have no wish to be drawn into Middle Eastern wars. We worry that our military people may . . . that we may be drawn into war with Iran."

"Nor do we want you to be. That would be a disaster for all concerned. Obviously, we trust that your people will behave with restraint.

"However, the temporary introduction of American seapower is a useful buffer, I admit that. Let's say this"—Ismail hesitated, looking, for some reason, at Ibn Ubaiyidh—"if the maintenance work truly cannot be done in Dhubai or Bahrain, I will undertake to persuade the government to offer you the use of the Saudi naval facility at Ar Ruways. However! There must be no liberty of American personnel beyond the gates of the yard."

"I'm not familiar with that base. What type of ship—"

The prince fluttered his fingers in irritation. "You will have to discuss the details with the Minister."

"I see," she said. "Well . . . I will. Then there's one other thing that Senator Talmadge asked me to raise with you."

"I am at your disposal," said the Saudi, but he no longer sounded quite so courteous as he had.

"That's the matter of Robert Patterson."

"Robert Patterson . . . I know no Pattersons. Do I?"

"He's a constituent of the senator's. Mr. Patterson was employed as a building inspector in the new hospital program. About a year ago, he noticed irregularities in the way anesthetic and oxygen lines were being installed. The valves were confusingly placed, so that the wrong gases might be administered."

The ambassador said, "Blair, there are people down the line we can take this up with. Really, the prince is not—"

"Excuse me, Harrison, I'm not done. He reported this. He was immediately arrested, held without charges for three months, and suffered broken knees and back injuries while in custody. He was released and repatriated and is now pressing a suit for damages."

Ismail said distantly, "I have told you already, I know no Robert Patterson. As Mr. Shaw has said, perhaps you should pursue your investigations regarding him elsewhere—say at the Ministry of Health."

He rose abruptly and clapped his hands. The woman, who must have been waiting just outside, came in with a smoking censer. The dark sweetness of incense permeated the room. The others had risen with the prince. One by one, they wafted the cloying smoke into their beards, hair, and clothes.

That, apparently, was the signal for the end of the audience. Ismail escorted them to the door and followed them out to the car.

Outside, it had become dark. She shivered in the sudden, unexpected chill of the Arab night. There was no more mention of riding afternoons. He kissed her hand briefly, bowed himself away, then turned and disappeared. "That's unlike him," said Shaw, frowning, as they got in. "He usually waits till I'm out of the driveway. You upset him. You were invited here as a guest. I'd hoped you wouldn't do that."

"You think I was too blunt."

"Damn it, Blair! *Nobody* talks to a member of the ruling family like that. Much less, a woman. You can't jump in here and in one day force them to make a commitment they obviously don't want to make. Most likely, given their domestic situation, they *can't* make."

"It was necessary. I had to find out how serious they were."

"You mean my reports aren't enough? Or is it just that Congress doesn't bother to read anything State generates?"

Blair said patiently, "Your reports are fine, Harry, and I read them all. But I have my orders from Bankey: independent investigation. All right? Anyway, we got something out of him. Ar Ruways."

"Yes, that's a real breakthrough, all right. That channel's only twelve feet deep. We can't get warships in there. It's a patrol-boat base."

"Oh," she said.

"I told you you wouldn't get anything out of Ismail. And— God damn it, why did you bring up that Patterson nonsense? We can't meddle in their internal affairs. Now I'll have to apologize for you."

She didn't want to say it, but he *had* laid himself out arranging the dinner. "I'm sorry, Harry."

"You're asking Ismail for something he just can't do, Blair." He glanced through the glass at the chauffeur. "You must know that. Congress has to know that. I know this isn't your doing, but they act as if the Saudis don't want to help us. It's not that; they can't."

"Of course they can."

"Never. They're too unstable. The GCC regimes are medieval autocracies trying to keep the lid on all the problems of the twentieth century. Expatriate labor, minorities, internal factions—as long as there's prosperity and relative peace, the emirs and kings can play them off against the others and stay in power. But a war, a defeat? There'd be a coup in days. Even a victory would be dangerous; it'd encourage the military to take over. Their only hope is American protection. Unfortunately, the Shi'a minority is so large that they can't even ask for that overtly." Shaw shook his head. "Ismail's a worried man. I'm glad I'm not in his shoes."

Blair thought about apologizing again, then thought, Forget it. Once was enough. "I find it hard to feel sorry for him," she said. "For a palace like that, I could accept a little mental strain."

"You may be right, may be right. Well . . . where do you go from here?"

"Back to Bahrain. I've arranged to look at some of our ships."

"Arranged with whom? Stan Hart?"

"Yes."

Shaw was silent then. He looked out at the passing night-lit highways, the wide lanes of new concrete, empty save for an occasional Caprice or Mercedes. Finally, he said, "This proposal, this initiative I guess, to invoke the War Powers Act . . . how serious is Talmadge about it?"

"He's serious. Not committed, but he's considering it."

"I think it would be a mistake. I'm not a fan of military intervention. But we've committed ourselves out here, Blair. It would look very bad to the Saudis if we backed out. They'd be okay till the war ended, probably, but then they'd have to reach some understanding with the winner. Be that Iraq or Iran, the result would be a tilt against the West, higher prices, undependable supplies. Not to mention our loss of face as a dependable ally. Just when we've recovered from our lousy performance with the Shah."

"Slight correction, Harry: the *administration* has committed us. Not Congress. We're not in business to keep the Saudis happy, whatever they, or State, may think. That fighter deal Ismail referred to—there are important interests in Congress opposed to letting them have long-range arms like that."

"They'll just buy them from France. Or Britain. There's a British Aerospace team here now trying to sell them Tornados. That could be twenty, thirty billion dollars over the next ten years. . . ."

He went on, but she had stopped listening. It was true that American influence was limited. But decisions had to be made. Piecemeal commitment was a favorite tactic of the Executive. If the policy was wrong, this was the time to step in, before annoyance raids and reprisals degenerated into war. Only when the tone of his voice changed did she tune back in. "Anyway, I'll get it patched up. What do you say to a late drink?"

She was suddenly tired. Of the prince, of the leering old poet, of Shaw's polished urbanity. She was tired of men. "Thanks, but I'd rather just turn in."

"As you wish," said the ambassador, his voice cold now. Nor did another word pass between them for the rest of the trip.

12

U.S.S. Audacity

TWO hundred miles south of the Azores, a thousand west of Gibraltar, surrounded by a heaving waste of gray sea beneath gray sky, John Gordon, his shorts and bare chest wet with sweat and spray, dug his fingers into wood and grunted his trembling legs into the air again. Then he scissored them open and closed to Maudit's bawl: *"One,* two, t'ree . . . *two,* two, t'ree . . . *t'ree,* two, t'ree. . . ."

A sea the color of a shark's back, yet with a blue-green heart, hurtled over the stern and exploded over the wallowing minesweeper. It rattled down on five men spaced across the deck between cable reels, tie-down points, and lashed-down paravanes. The paramedic spluttered and stopped counting. *"Ah, j'ai eu plein le cul de ce foutu temps, moi,"* he cried above the whistle of wind in the sweep gear.

"Ain't it about time to wrap this up, Senior?" grunted Burgee through a dripping mustache.

Gordon didn't answer. His legs ached, too, from flutter kicks, sit-ups, push-ups, and the raise-and-opens known hopefully as "hello darlings." He rested them for a moment against the splintery coldness of the deck and checked his watch.

"Two more sets."

"Christ!"

"Merde."

Gordon told them passionlessly to shut up. Finally, when it was time, he rolled over and hoisted himself to his feet.

"About fucking time," muttered Burgee. "Jesus, I'm starting to feel my age on those Goddamned flutter-kicks."

Maudit, Terger, and Burgee went immediately below, the squat contractor squeegeeing salt water out of his mustache with the flat of his hand. Everett got up slowly, pulling on a soaked sweat shirt he'd wedged under a padeye. Gordon squatted on a coil of line, waiting for his thighs to stop quivering. The banker looked around for a moment, then lurched toward him as the stern dropped. Gordon made room, and they sat silently together on the little ship's fantail, looking forward and holding on.

The sea boiled around them. Combers the color of old aluminum hissed as they came in. *Audacity* was the last ship in the tow. They couldn't see the cable from here, but Gordon knew from the wake that it was still up there, a three-inch-thick rope of braided steel that led five hundred yards in a great submerged catenary to the stern of *Resolute*. Ahead of that, off to starboard, when the sea lifted them the two men could see the horned shadow of U.S.S. *Sumter*, LST-1181, their motive power and mother for this long and painful voyage.

The minesweepers had been under way for three weeks now. Their progress was glacial. Hunnicutt announced the miles made every day at morning quarters, just to keep the crew's spirits up. Just to reassure them, Gordon suspected, that they were making progress, and not slipping back. It worked out to between 125 and 190 miles a day. Their best distance—250 miles between midnight and midnight—was the first week out, when all the sweeps had engines. Since then, many of the aged Waukeshas had broken down. And they'd wallowed along like a string of pack mules on rough terrain, rolling and pitching, yawing and bucking stubbornly at their bonds.

The crews were thoroughly sick of it. With the engines secured, fresh water had to be rationed; without exhaust heat, it had to be made electrically, with heaters on the evaps. The fresh food, milk and vegetables, had been used up and they lived now out of cans and dry stores.

Everett sat silent beside him. The combers swept toward them, hesitated above the little ship, as if saying grace, then toppled forward, shattering into leaping showers of white foam. Then Gordon heard him muttering. " 'Those images that yet, Fresh images beget, That dolphin-torn, that gong-tormented sea.' "

"Poetry?"

"Yup."

"Yours? That long thing you said you're working on?"

"I wish," said Everett. "Yeats. 'Byzantium.' "

"Nice . . . well, guess I'll go see Honey." Gordon watched the next crest, waited for it, wondering at the same time how this all looked to Lem. How differently he must see the world. A farmer, now, didn't have much use for imagination.

The sweep rose sickeningly, tilting her stern up, he thought, like a randy she-cat. With a bellow like an angry bull, the sea burst over them, raining green water over the sweep gear, laying a transparent gloss over the splintered teak of the deck, like the cobalt glaze Ola fired on her art pieces. As it ran out the freeing ports, he jumped up, crab-walked forward, and gained the hatch.

The interior was hot and dark. Like bugs shaken in a jar, sailors braced themselves foursquare in the tilting passage-way. The galley was unlit, shut down. There hadn't been hot meals for two days, since they hit this low-pressure area. Gordon stopped in forward berthing, close as a sealed tomb, the bunks swaying with silent bodies tied in with bungee cords and light line. He hung his wet gear on a pipe to drip, pulled on his greens, rank with old sweat—no laundry, either—and headed for the bridge.

He had to stop at the top of the narrow aluminum ladder. His fingers whitened on the coaming.

The bridge was only twenty feet wide, but it was packed with a full watch: the captain, two officers, boatswain's mate, quartermaster. The wheel and engine order telegraph were a deck below, in the pilothouse proper, and the conning officer was shouting his orders down through a voice tube. Heavy manila spanned it diagonally and horizontally, and the watch standers had entwined themselves like flies dressed by a spider. The fabric overhead rattled and boomed. A familiar stench came up from buckets lashed into the corners.

Audacity paused. Leaning drunkenly at the extremity of her roll, she gave a deep, tortured groan, unlike anything he'd heard from a metal ship. As she passed through the vertical again, the eerie multiple whine of the wind returned. He tried to let go of the frame, but the sensation of swooping through the air was too powerful. He had to take himself firmly in hand and just let go, stagger to the nearest line, and work his way up hand over hand till he reached the captain.

Hunnicutt, strapped into his chair, was staring straight ahead through the windows. He looked pale. He was gripping a plastic trash bag in his lap. Gordon followed his glance, and found *Illusive,* off to starboard, rolling so wildly he could see her bottom paint. The next moment, he was looking down her stack.

The captain jerked his face around. "Hello, Senior," he said through white lips. "Guess this's a change from Vermont."

"Kind of, sir."

"How's your gear doing?"

"All lashed solid."

"And your men?"

"They'll make it." Gordon tightened his grip as the deck began another buck. "How bad we in for, Captain?"

"It's hard to say. We had a route laid out to avoid storms, but we're so slow, we can't dodge when they change course." He hesitated. "I've been talking to the other sweep COs. If it gets any worse, we're going to ask *Sumter* to head into the seas. I don't know how much longer we can take this beam beating."

The cooks made cold sandwiches for dinner. Shortly after that, Lieutenant Kearn's voice, over the 1MC, told all hands to stay off the weather decks, and for those not on watch to lay to their bunks. Gordon had been riding a chair back and forth across the chief's quarters, grimly memorizing the render-safe procedure for a new Italian mine. But at that he gave up, locked the publication up, and went below.

He was dreaming about Jezebel's breech birthing when a hand came out of the darkness. The compartment was dark, filled with the screech of stressing timbers and the crash of waves.

"What. Lem? What is it?"

"Yeah. We got to get suited up. They want us to dive."

Dive. Gordon came fully awake at that and tried to swing his legs out. Unsuccessfully. Then he remembered, and unhooked the bunk strap.

The deck fell away and he shot out as if spring loaded. He crashed into Everett and they both went down, scrabbling across slick wet tile on hands and knees. At last, he hit the bulkhead and got his legs braced. "What the hell do you mean?" he panted into the other chief's ear.

"Don't know. Lieutenant Caliban rousted us out, told us to get suited up."

"Hold off till I find out what's going on."

Gordon pulled on trousers and boots and went up and forward. He rapped at Hunnicutt's door and went in.

There were three men already there: the captain himself, Kearn, and the engineer, a bulky, bald lieutenant named Parini. The divers got along with him; Burgee had found an intermittent short for him in one of the switchboards.

"You people ready to go?" asked the sweep officer, turning his furrowed face slightly. "No? Well, goddamnit, get them—"

"Wait a minute, Lieutenant. I understand you're ordering my

men into the water. It doesn't work that way. They take their
operational orders through me."

None of the officers said anything. So he added, "Now, what's
going on?"

"We need you to go down," said Hunnicutt.

The deck slanted and Gordon grabbed a pipe in the overhead.
No one asked him to sit, though there was a place on the bunk,
next to Kearn.

"We were running the engines about an hour ago," said the
captain. "Normal, we run 'em fifteen minutes a day, keep the
sleeves and pumps lubricated. Unfortunately, this time we got
a problem, a leak in the cooling system."

"A leak?"

"Zeke, draw him a picture."

The engineer's grease-blackened coveralls were wet from the
knees down. He didn't look at Gordon, just pushed a ship's plan
across the table. "Here, inboard of the main sea suction valve.
Probably a fatigue crack. Any other time, we'd just close the
valve, dry the area from inside, and braze it up. But that isn't
working. The flapper won't hold water. It's probably shredded;
it's rubber and pretty old."

"How bad is it?" said Gordon.

"We're taking two hundred gallons a minute. Pumps can
keep up with that running both generators, but thing is, it could
just rupture on us. That's a nine-inch intake, that'd flood out the
engine room in about fifteen minutes."

Kearn said, a sneer in his voice, "I been wondering what you
people were here for, Chief. Calisthenics and cribbage is all I
seen so far. Well, y'all are going to go down and put a cofferdam
into place. Once we got that over the intake, we can pull the
whole shebang, valve, pipe, replace the flapper and weld it up."

"We're in a storm," said Gordon.

"Course we are," said Parini mildly. "That's probably what
made it crack."

"Forget what made it crack, it's fuckin' cracked. Now break
out your fuckin' gear and—"

"I don't think we can do that."

They all looked at him. After a few seconds, Kearn bent
forward. "What the *fuck* does that mean, you 'don't think you
can do it?'"

"I mean I'm *not* doing it, Lieutenant. When the sea's this
high, you lose control of your divers. It's dangerous."

"More dangerous than mines?"

"We're trained for mines. We're equipped for mines. Jump-

ing over the side in a storm to do something we don't know how
to do—that's the way you hurt people."

"Well, what do you need?" said Hunnicutt. "For precautions?
Jesus, Chief, sometimes you have to accept a little risk in the
Navy."

Gordon turned to him. He didn't like the way the captain
looked, white, drawn, that intimidated look in his eyes. Sometimes you have to accept risks. Where had he heard that
before? This wasn't the time to try to remember. "I understand
that, sir. But the answer's still no."

"You know what I think, Dick?" interrupted Kearn. "We
thought we had EOD hotshots on board. What we really got's
a bunch of egotistical civilians who when the crunch comes
start shiverin' like a pup shittin' peach pits."

Gordon didn't say anything.

"Captain, if these asshole Reserves won't do it, I will. I used
to swim pretty good. You hazardous-pay part-timers are too
weak-kneed to take a chance for the ship, I'm not."

"Wait, wait, Sapper." Hunnicutt looked pleadingly at Gordon. "Senior, I understand your concern. But look at it from
. . . Look. If the engine room floods, this ship could go down.
We'd have to evacuate to *Sumter*. We could lose a combat unit
the Navy badly needs right now. That's why I'd like—"

"*Order* him to do it," muttered Kearn in his ear as a roll
swayed him forward on the bunk. "It's simple, Honey. Apply
some size-nine leadership. Then if he won't, relieve him and put
his second in charge."

Hunnicutt didn't answer for a moment. He passed a hand
across his scalp. Gordon saw the sweat glitter.

"Okay, you want to push me to it," he said. "What do you say
to that, Senior Chief?"

"What I said before, sir. We don't dive in rough seas in open
ocean. It's too dangerous."

The captain said then, and for the first time his voice sounded
calm: "So the bottom line is, you're refusing a direct order."

"I can't, sir. I can't risk my men in this."

"Maybe that's the problem. 'Your men.' " Hunnicutt was
looking at his hands. "You Reserves train together, work together, stay together a long time. Right? Know each other's
families? Sometimes that doesn't comport with getting the mission done, Senior. If you might have to pay for it in lives."

"I don't think that's the issue here, sir." But just for a moment, he wondered whether Hunnicutt could be right.

It must have shown on his face, because just then the sweep
officer sniggered. "Changed your mind?"

Gordon said slowly, "I'll do it. *Sir.* But when we get to the Gulf, I'm going to take this up with our bosses."

"You do that," said Kearn, lighting a cigar. He blew the smoke into the air and squinted through it at Gordon. "Why don't you just do that. But meanwhile, Farmer John, just lay your ass aft, and do as you're goddamn well told."

"Now EOD team, lay to the fantail."

Gordon shook his head angrily; they were all already there. He ducked under a burst of cold Atlantic and circled a finger in the close-it-up sign they used underwater.

"We got to cut out an intake," he began, and ignoring Terger's startled mutter, explained the situation. He finished, "I don't think it's right but I've been overruled."

"What about *Sumter*'s CO, John? Isn't he in charge of the group?"

"He'll back Hunnicutt. I don't think they understand what they're asking us to do."

"Yeah, but if we all refuse—"

"There're no strikes in the Navy. That's enough discussion," Gordon said sharply. "Okay, listen. I'll be diving alone. I'll use the nineties and standard regulator—"

"No, *you* won't," said Everett. "You are *not* going down alone. You're going down with me."

"Can't do it, Lem, I need a qualified dive supe topside."

"*Alors,* you are going with me, John."

"No, me!"

Gordon saw how it was. "Okay, shut *up!* It'll be Leroy and me. Lem'll supervise. Tony, you're tender. Clint, you're standby."

"Hold on!" shouted Maudit. They grabbed for handholds as a sea the color of distant mountains lifted to port. So high the wind stopped, its steady pressure left their bodies, cut off by the wave. It hung above the little ship so long Gordon could have memorized every ripple on its glass-slick, curving belly. Beyond it, almost on them, was the gray wall of a squall.

Then it broke, slamming down like a wet white avalanche. When they could breathe again, they stared at one another. "Nobody can dive in this," shouted Burgee. "This is crazy."

"You aren't going, Clint, so just listen up. The intake's on the port quarter, just above the turn of the bilge. Any questions? Let's go. I want to get this done before it gets dark. And stay alert up here, too. I don't want anybody washed overboard."

When he came up again, carrying his gear, the motion was less violent, the seas slightly less mountainous. He looked out and saw why. A hundred yards off, between them and the wind, rose the gray flank of the landing ship. Heaving, glistening dully with spray, *Sumter* was rolling almost as badly as the sweeps. To the west, her other ducklings, *Resolute* and *Illusive*, had lengthened their tows and were riding nose to the swells.

"Heads up!"

He hadn't heard the shot over the wind's howl, but now Kearn's gang swarmed out on deck. The shot line, bellied by the wind, drifted gracefully down out of the sky. They grabbed it and began hauling off. The chief boatswain leaned to his ear. "Gonna make up with a line forward, one aft, keep her steady while you're down, buds."

Gordon nodded wordlessly as the squall hit. Cold rain rattled on the deck. He shucked off his instantly soaked greens and stepped naked into the wet-suit bottoms. He zipped the top on and sat down on a chock. Maudit handed him in turn buoyancy compensator, knife, fins, depth gauge, and gloves.

He turned his head to see Terger's face disappear under a hood. He shook his head, preferring to leave his off. Everett finished making up the tank set and lifted it with a grunt. Gordon stood. He thrust his arms through the straps and pulled them taut. Bit the mouthpiece, and took a tentative breath.

He nodded. His mouth was dusty-dry, and not only from the canned air. Supported by his dressers, he shuffled through the dancing rain toward the side.

"Hold up, damn it," shouted the boatswain. "We're not fast to *Sumter* yet."

He returned to his perch, turning his mask this way and that. Terger waited too, the black rubber over his barrel chest bleeding with rain. He shouted, "Actually I'd rather be teaching electron balances."

Gordon grinned back, but his heart wasn't in it.

A capstan hummed. The after line rose dripping from a wave, then suddenly grew taut as nine hundred tons of minesweeper lunged against it. He glanced at the seething gray above the masthead, then at his watch. Dusk would be falling soon.

"What the hell are you waiting for?" Kearn's voice, high, pissed-off.

"You ready for me to go?"

"All intakes closed. Ship's tagged out and word's been passed we got divers over. Get moving, we can't hold this fucking lee all day."

The cofferdam, a heavy pine box about the size of a peach

crate, was already over, hanging on a hogging line. Gordon
waddled to the side—the boatswain had taken down a section
of the brass railings aft of the sweep gear—and without stopping or saying anything grabbed his regulator with one hand,
his tank boot with the other, and went in feet first.

He hit hard, and wrong. The roll was faster than he'd expected and he fell an extra five feet. The flat of a wave smashed
him in the face and dislodged his mask. He let himself sink
through the shock, and eight or ten feet down came to a stop.

And hung there, suddenly suspended in peace like a fly in
gray amber. The demented howl of the wind, the shouting, the
clatter of blocks, all were obliterated by the sea. All it held was
a deep thrum, the landing ship's screws, and the hammer thud
of his heart.

He got his mask adjusted and cleared just as he bobbed back
up. Terger was at the deck edge. A wave covered him; when it
passed, his partner was gone. In the lower half of his mask, a
vague plume of bubbles blossomed.

Gordon took a last look around, at the iron-gray sky, the
dripping line from *Sumter* leaping again into that terrible taut-
ness. Faces lined the rail of the reeling minesweeper: Maudit
dressed and ready; Everett gripping the lifeline, the other hand
holding a stopwatch, his eyes fixed on the sea.

Gordon's left hand moved then. Bubbles roaring in his ears,
he sank away from the light.

Visibility was okay, but there was even less illumination penetrating than he'd feared. This would have to be done quickly.

Terger came into view. A double trail of bubbles showed he
too was valving buoyancy. Gordon pulled out his buddy line.
One end snap-hooked to his belt, the other to the other diver's
line. That should give them enough room to work. He glanced
at his gauge and signaled. Terger nodded and they finned toward the vague shadow above.

The stern came into clear view, the twin screws and rudders
motionless, sharp-edged and black. They were heaving up and
down, dragging down clouds of salt foam. Again Gordon felt
the same dry dread he'd breathed on deck, waiting to go in.

*There are things, if a man's promised to do them, he ought
to no matter what.*

He swam forward along the port side until the cofferdam
came into view. A dirge boomed through the water as it battered against the planks, twisting and turning on the hogging
line. He waved Terger off and made for it.

As he passed the turn of the bilge, the surge caught him, sucking him violently up and down, five or six feet with every roll. He didn't try to fight or resist, just kept grimly swimming until he was up on the flailing box. He stopped a few feet off, sculling with his hands, searching along the hull.

A faint tapping forward . . . he moved up a few feet and saw it. The inlet was covered with a slimy bronze grating. He saw Terger's eyes fasten to it, too.

Well, no point in waiting. He finned forward and grabbed the box with both arms.

The surge spun him instantly and slammed him headfirst into the hull. He blinked broken light out of his eyes and tried to fend off with his elbows. He soared up till it was bright, then down till it was dark. Bubbles seethed around him. The box was too high. He yanked on the line, and it suddenly came loose and fell over his head. Holding his breath, he untangled it from his regulator, then vented the last bit of air from his vest.

Should be a rope inside the box . . . there it was, the end neatly whipped with small stuff. This had to go through the grate. Hugging the splintered pine to his chest, he fought his way back to the inlet. It went up and down at a dizzying rate. Again the surge sent him tumbling. Confused, disoriented by repeated blows, he began to suspect this wasn't going to work.

He felt Terger next to him. The other diver grabbed the cofferdam and shook the rope at him. Gordon nodded, released the box, and got the fingers of his left hand into the grate.

It was like grabbing a maddened whale. His arm was almost wrenched off as the hull dragged him through the water. He hugged it, reducing his resistance, and poked the whipped end through. He fed in four feet of it before letting go. As he did so, he pulled out his knife and rapped hard three times with the butt.

A pinging crack in his ears. One of the cherry bombs they signaled with. He'd come up in a minute. They were almost done.

Suction, and lots of it. They must have opened the flapper. He pushed off from the grate, signaling to Terger. The other diver, six feet away, had oriented the box with its open side toward the ship, and now lunged in with it.

It suck-slammed into place over the grate. They hammered with fists and knife until it slid sideways, centered. Simultaneously, they thrust themselves away and swam clear.

Or tried to. But the ship's motion had changed. They were being sucked backward. He saw with horror Terger slammed against the skeg, then dragged aft toward the screws. Sharp as they were . . . he twisted to brace himself and hauled with all his strength on the buddy line. The other man saw his danger, too, and kicked, fought, till his shadow separated from the hull.

They surfaced into a rage of water, wind, and rain. Lifted on a monstrous crest, Gordon saw for just a second the mine-sweeper drifted sideways out of the lee, the steadying line trailing from her stern. Then the squall wiped everything away.

He felt rather than saw Terger surface beside him, then fight his way over. When they were face-to-face, he raised his wrist. Gordon nodded. There was blood on the other diver's mask, but he'd gotten a compass bearing. He raised his hand and jabbed his thumb down violently.

At ten feet, they joined up and swam due east. The sea had gone mad, tossing them about so swiftly the needle on his depth gauge ticked like a windshield wiper. Then something dragged across his back. He flinched, then realized what it was. He turned over, grabbing for the wonderful rough thickness of the steadying line, snapped near the mother ship but streaming back from the minesweeper's stern.

They pulled themselves up hand over hand, and broke surface again thirty feet off *Audacity*'s stern. It loomed above Gordon huge and unclimbable as a bucking cliff, stained and splintered with decades of collisions and patches. At one moment, he could see the eroded tips of the screw blades; at the next, green sea gnawed at the deck and he looked down at the now brightly lit fantail. There was no hope of yelling above the scream of the wind, but he waved.

One of the boatswains saw him. Faces swung. A moment later, a heaving line uncoiled in the air, the yellow monkey's-fist wind-lofted far beyond them. He ignored it. There was no way they were going back aboard over the stern.

Or the side, either. In fact, he had no idea how they were getting back aboard.

The sea lifted them again and he glimpsed Lem Everett, momentarily at eye level, hanging on to the boatswain, shouting into his ear. The wave dropped away and Gordon sank dizzily. But the next time he came up he saw seamen at the starboard davit, struggling to swing it outboard.

They waited till the yellow horse collar was in the water, then submerged and swam up the starboard side. It was almost dark now. Finally, they collided with it. Gordon helped Terger in first. Four men hauled at the tackle. The first-class dangled slowly up, streaming water, and was swung inboard.

Then it was his turn. When the tackle slacked and his feet hit the deck, he lost his balance and fell, banging his tanks on wood with the toll of a muffled bell.

Everett helped him up. Other hands tripped his tanks, stripped his belt and vest off. "She snapped all of a sudden," the banker shouted over the wind. "Didn't you hear my signal?"

"We were just about done by then. I wanted to finish up."

Glancing beyond him, Gordon saw *Sumter*'s stern, the towline coming taut again; they were gathering away. He turned his attention to the deck, and to Terger. He was sitting down, and Maudit was working off his hood.

Under it the grizzled hair was clotted black. The paramedic probed it with his fingers, then shrugged suddenly. "Scalp. She bleeds like hell, Leroy, but we get her stitched up, feed you a brandy, you feel like new."

"Senior Chief."

Gordon turned, to confront the captain, hatless and bulky in foul-weather gear. "Glad you made it," Hunnicutt said.

"So am I. Sir."

The captain looked at Terger. "He okay?"

"Just cuts. He was sucked into the props."

"Good thing they weren't turning." He looked back at Gordon. "Uh, Senior . . . thanks."

"We follow orders, Captain. But I still intend to file that protest."

Hunnicutt's face went still. Then he turned away, suddenly, and went below.

"Okay, let's get this gear below!" shouted Everett. "All of it! Clean it and dry it out. Burgee, grab that tank before it goes over the side!"

Gordon sat on the deck, working his fingers. He'd hurt them in that wrestle with the grating. But they'd got it done. Got it done, all right, and thank God none of his men had died.

When he looked up again, Kearn's eyes were on him. But the sweep officer only scowled.

13

U.S.S. *Turner Van Zandt*

THREE hundred miles southeast of Hormuz, the Arabian Sea was clear as cobalt glass, marbled with streaks of foam that glowed in the sunlight. The crests, up to fifteen feet in the Gulf of Oman, had dropped to eight to ten, chivvied along by a northwesterly wind. The scattered clouds looked as if they'd just been dry-cleaned. The horizon was a serrated blade to the throat of a sky so clear and high it made Dan's eyes tear.

It was hard to look away. Even the busiest man will glance at a passing girl, and today Thalassa was more beautiful than any human woman. After the narrow Gulf, the Indian Ocean was like being released from a dirty prison cell. One you had to share with two homicidal maniacs.

Shaking his head at the analogy—it was just too apt—he blinked, tugged his cap down to shade his eyes, and concentrated on the chart.

Chief McQueen's 1100 fix showed them an hour east of Point Orange, the convoy rendezvous. Dan confirmed the satellite fix with loran and advised the OOD to adjust course left three degrees.

Navigation hadn't always been that easy. When he'd first gone to sea, the Navy had still depended on sextants and chronometers. Now the phrase *star fix* had a quaint sound, like *raising steam.* He smiled faintly as he entered their position in the log, then strolled out on the wing.

It was comfortable, warm, but the wind, not long out of Central Asia, remembered its mountain passage. He leaned against the coaming, gazing out.

Astern, a shrinking speck, was *San Jose.* They'd just finished an hour alongside her. Underway replenishments were never quite routine. When two hulls were a hundred feet apart, speed sucked them together, and several ships every year scarred

their sides and their captains' careers. But Shaker had taken
Van Zandt in with dash. He'd made the approach at twenty
knots and cut speed just as his bow passed the AFS's stern,
settling into the notch like a housewife parking at a Safeway.
In ten minutes, the black hoses were turgid, ramming JP-5 into
the frigate's voids.

Farther aft, the traffic went the other way. Clamped-down
pallets of combustible gear swayed across from the flight deck
and disappeared into the oiler's capacious holds. In return came
spare parts, ammunition, and food. In sixty minutes, the evolu-
tion was complete and Shaker commenced his turnaway. A
degree or two of rudder at first, then a whine of power as she
surged into a hard turn west.

Back for her third convoy. Back to the Gulf.

More deliberately—there was no hurry for her—the stores
ship had come about, too, headed east to rejoin the Indian Ocean
Battle Group: seven combatants, including *Forrestal* and the
new *Ticonderoga*-class cruiser *Mobile Bay*. They would trail
the convoy to the mouth of the Strait. From there, the escorts
would proceed alone.

That's the life, Dan thought now, looking after her. No worries. Just leisurely two-hundred-mile squares and every couple
of months volleyball and beer in Diego Garcia.

But it didn't take much soul-searching to know he'd rather be
where he was. Beans and bullets were necessities. Carriers,
Tridents, laser programs—they were great. For some other
kind of war. But this one had caught the Pentagon off base. The
deep-water task forces were almost irrelevant. It was the small
boys, frigates, minesweepers, destroyers, that would hold or
lose the Middle East.

Dan didn't think of himself as a man of war. He didn't love
violence, or talk as though he did. But if the country needed him
here, here was where he wanted to be.

He wondered again whether he really belonged in the service.
So far, the answer had always come up yes. Sometimes, though,
the margin had been narrower than the flip of a coin.

In the end, it wasn't pay or living conditions that mattered.
It was patriotism that kept men in and leadership that drove
them out. Too often, the peacetime Navy bred overcautious,
unimaginative careerists, officers and chiefs more concerned
with promotions and benefits than with their men or their pro-
fession.

But now he was seeing something new. A new kind of leader,
forceful, fearless, ready and even eager for battle. Something
the Navy had evolved, before, only in wartime.

But mightn't this unexpected war produce an unexpected kind of leader? It was something to think about. Wonder about. And hope for.

Because without it, he had the feeling they were going to lose.

Half an hour later, they were at lunch when the captain's phone buzzed. Shaker unhooked it as the conversation died. When he hung up, he wiped his lips, then slipped the napkin into its silver ring. His arms bulged under rolled-up sleeves as he hoisted himself to his feet. "Excuse me, gentlemen," he said. "The convoy's in sight."

Dan followed him topside. They stood together as white specks slowly pushed over the horizon into huge ships, sheer-walled, their empty hulls looming out of the water.

The merchant captains had been asked to form a line. As usual, they hadn't been able to agree how, or hadn't cared to try. They were all over the sea, steaming slowly on five different courses.

Shaker asked Steve Charaler, who had the deck, whether anyone else had shown up. The lieutenant said *Gallery* had reported by radio, but *Charles Adams* was still enroute.

"Who've we got here?" was his next question. Dan reached for the op order. It listed two American merchants, *Exxon Pacific*, New Orleans, and *Borinquen*, San Juan; and three reflagged Kuwaitis. There were three warships in the escort. *Gallery* and *Van Zandt* would be under tactical command of Commodore Bartholomew Nauman, embarked on *Charles Adams*. *Mobile Bay* would trail them in through Hormuz, tracking the air picture.

"Well, he ain't here yet," said Shaker, apparently meaning the commodore. He tilted his ball cap back and squinted out at the merchants. "Dan, you've done this before, what's the best way to get these jokers pointed in the same direction?"

"Basically just talk 'em in, Captain. They don't have secure comms, so we use bridge-to-bridge, channel twelve. Some of them can take flashing light, if you go slow."

Shaker seized the handset and scowled at the radar screen. "Yeah, but which one's which? What a clusterfuck. Uh, *Gas Prince*, this is U.S.S. *Van Zandt*, hull number nine-one, over."

It took over an hour to jockey, cajole, and threaten the tankers into a line. *Borinquen*, the Puerto Rican flag, didn't want to lead. Shaker gave her captain a choice: Take his assigned position or head for Kuwait alone. This silenced him, and gradually order emerged.

Meanwhile *Gallery* had poked up her mast top to southward.
Dan studied her through the Big Eyes, twenty-power binoculars hard-mounted on the coaming. It was unsettling, like an
out-of-body experience, watching a sister ship under way. Bow
on, the *Perry*s were good-looking ships. Only from astern did
they remind you of cracker boxes, or tractor-trailers painted
gray.

Charles Adams came on the net half an hour later. The old
DDG was forty miles away, closing at twenty-eight knots.
Shaker shifted to a scrambled circuit and discussed the first leg
with the commodore. Nauman wanted them on two-nine-zero.
They put the change out to *Borinquen*. The others followed her
casually around, sheering out several hundred yards to either
side.

"Good God," muttered Shaker. "How far have we got to walk
these dogs?"

"Nine hundred miles. All the way to Kuwait."

"Jesus Christ. . . . Okay, OTC wants us off the convoy's port
bow. Let's double-time over there, Steve. Say zero-five-zero on
the leader, five thousand."

Charaler gave the order for full speed and came left, estimat-
ing the course to station, then refining his solution on a maneuvering board. Dan liked the way he did it, smooth, smart,
correct. He and Wise were neck and neck for number one
among *Van Zandt*'s 0-3s, come fitness report time.

"What have we got set up down in Sonar, XO?" Shaker asked
him.

"Condition II Red, Captain. Full wartime watch."

"Let's make sure." Shaker pressed the intercom. "Sonar,
Bridge."

"Sonar aye."

"You guys on the bubble down there? What kind of search
are we running?"

"We're pinging active on the SQS-56, Captain. Boundary conditions give us a predicted range of ten thousand yards."

Dan wondered why he was bothering with the sonar. Shaker
gazed blankly at the lead tanker, then pressed transmit again.
"That's not too good."

"It'll get a lot worse in the Goo, Captain." That was sailor
slang for the Gulf of Oman. "And once we get past the Strait,
sonar picture turns to shit. Too shallow, and thermoclines up
the ying-yang. He could be counting the blades on our prop and
we'd never see him."

"Great . . . Lieutenant Pensker down there?"

"No, sir. He was here about an hour ago, then he left."

"Okay, do the best you can. If you see anything suspicious, I'll send the fly-boys out for a look."

"Aye, sir."

Shaker signed off. He looked around the bridge. "Dan, you know where Pensker is?"

"Not at the moment. Wait, maybe I do."

He leaned to the window and looked down. On the forecastle, a long white weapon, fins folded, rested on the launcher rail. Two gunner's mates in coveralls were working its nose cone over with scrubbing cleanser. A third figure, trailing the wires of a headset, was the black weapons officer.

"He's up forward, inspecting the missiles."

"I'm going down to talk to him. Let me know if anything comes over the net, or if these guys get too far out of formation."

"Aye, sir."

Lenson moved out on the port wing again. He leaned against the coaming, enjoying the clean bite of sun and wind on his face. Off their starboard beam, the tankers rolled along like elephants in a circus parade, spaced half a mile from stern to bow. Beyond them—square root of the sums of the legs, that'd be seven thousand yards—he could make out *Gallery*, a bone of foam in her teeth, sliding into station to the north.

Standing there, the wind brushing his wet hair, he thought for just a moment of what lay ahead.

The convoy, limited to the speed of the slowest ship and to deep-draft channels, would take four days to move up the gut of the Gulf. There would be danger the whole way, but it would peak at three points en route.

The first, of course, was Hormuz. Hiding in its incredible congestion, Iranian gunboats had operated on and off throughout the war from the base at Bandar 'Abbās. The United States had fought several small-scale actions with them. In each case, the Navy had come off the victor, destroying the smaller vessels or chasing them back under air and missile cover.

The second danger point was eighty miles on, where the shipping lanes passed Abu Musa. The barren little island was smack in the middle of the Gulf. Intelligence said the Pasdaran had fortified it. Occasionally, their small boats would ambush unescorted tankers or freighters with machine guns and rocket-propelled grenades. So far, none of their victims had sunk, but several had turned back, or limped into port with holes in their tanks or superstructures. And of course there were casualties and deaths.

A sudden clamor drew his eye back to the forecastle. Pensker

and the missile techs were backing away. The warning bell rang
steadily for ten seconds.

Suddenly the missile came to life. The launcher, quivering
like a tensed muscle, whipped it to point left and right, up and
down. Its speed and agility were frightening. Then it aimed
straight up. The missile poised on its tail, gleaming in the sun,
for perhaps two seconds before the blast-resistant hatch in the
deck popped open. In less time than it took to blink, the twenty-
foot weapon disappeared, whisked back within the hull like a
conjurer's trick. A blink later, hidden motors whined and another leapt up out of the magazine.

The bell died. The launcher quivered once more, suddenly lost
its uncanny imitation of life, and returned to being metal and
hydraulics. The techs picked up their buckets, scrub brushes,
and test kits, and moved in again, like wary ministrants to a
powerful and only partially tamed beast.

The wind brought him the smells of lubricants and electricity.
Dan rested his elbows on the coaming as his mind returned to
the transit.

The middle Gulf should be relatively safe. There were no
islands, no Pasdaran bases, and it was too wide for cruise-
missile targeting. The few destroyers and frigates left in the
Iranian Navy seldom ventured out of port. The threat there
would be mines, laid at night from coasters and commandeered
fishing boats.

As they neared the end, though, the last hundred miles into
Kuwait, they'd come into range of small boats and missiles
from Farsi Island, another IRG base, and cruise missiles and
aircraft from Bushehr. This last leg was the most dangerous of
the voyage. Tankers carrying Iraqi crude from the offshore
terminals at Khor el Amaya and Mina al Bakr were fair game
for the Iranians, and Iraqi Mirages made frequent strikes at
Cyrus terminal and Khārk Island.

Unfortunately, neither side could identify their targets very
well. Iraqi aircraft had attacked Iraqi tankers, Iranians Iranian,
and both sides had sunk and damaged neutral shipping. And
that, of course, was why Kuwait had asked to participate in the
American escorting program.

So far, *Van Zandt* had been lucky. Her previous convoys had
gone through unscathed. Though there had been scares: unidentified boats at night, aircraft approaching them, objects in
the water. He remembered a camel floating on its side, swollen
like a full wineskin in the sun.

Thinking of that, he realized they hadn't set the mine watch

yet. He considered it, then decided they were still too far out.
There'd be little enough rest for the men in the days ahead.
Tonight would be soon enough, when they hit Hormuz.

Dan rubbed his eyes—there hadn't been much sleep for him
either since Manama—and looked forward again. The check
was complete, apparently, and the foredeck was deserted. Then
he saw it wasn't. Up in the eyes of the ship, by the ground
tackle, two khakied figures stood close together: Shaker and
Pensker.

The JOOD's binoculars were wedged beside him. He picked
them up idly.

He was looking out at the lead tanker when he caught the two
men at the corner of the field. He shifted focus to them for a
moment. The black lieutenant was looking at his feet, his face
attentive. The captain was looking steadily at him. His right
hand gestured; turned over, palm up; then made a fist and
tapped the other palm lightly.

It looked like the captain was reassuring him, trying to build
up his confidence. Great, Dan thought, setting the glasses back
in their holders. He was glad he could stop worrying about
that. If Shaker had really been prejudiced . . . something like
that could tear a ship, a crew, apart. He'd seen it happen before.

His mind moved on to the reams of paper building on his
desk. Personnel matters, correspondence, required reports. He
ought to put in some hours this afternoon. It was time to rough
out their postdeployment operating schedule. He had to balance
the operating funds. Two men had reported their allotments
weren't coming through. The squadron staff wanted hearing-
conservation surveys, retention-program updates, and heat-
stress reports. Third-class evals were due. Their 3-M report
rejection rate was up to 20 percent and COMNAVSURFLANT
wanted a letter explaining why. . . .

He sighed. He checked their course one last time, then left
the sun and wind behind. Swinging down the ladder, he resigned himself once more to the gray steel honeycomb.

He jerked awake, a gong insistent in his ears. He'd been dreaming he was back at the Academy, late for noon formation. For
a moment, he wasn't sure which was real. Was he a lieutenant
commander, fourteen years of active duty behind him, dreaming himself a raw youth? Or seventeen, dreaming himself
thirty-five?

But this wasn't his room in Fifth Batt. He was in his stateroom, he'd zonked out over the laundry report, and *Van Zandt* was going to general quarters.

But Shaker had said there'd be no more drills after convoy joinup.

The tally of jumpers and khakis dry-cleaned last month hit the deck as he leapt for the passageway. The words *"General quarters, General quarters, no drill, air attack!"* accelerated him into a sprint.

Combat was fully manned, though OSs were still passing around life jackets and knocking their masks into consoles. He blinked in the near dark and tried to hoist himself into his usual chair.

Blue light gleamed off silver oak leaves. "Get off my lap, XO," Shaker snarled. "Lieutenant Wise! What's he squawking?"

"No squawk, Captain."

The gabble faded quickly as Dan shouted, "Keep it down, damn it! Make your reports and then maintain silence!" He swung around, stared at the air scope. They were just outside the Strait. The air picture showed confusion, scores of aircraft. Nothing showed over Iran, though.

Then he saw it.

A single pip had detached itself from the northward air route, heading for the center of the scope. Heading for *Van Zandt.* "No squawk" meant he was showing no electronic identification, neither civilian nor military, neither friend nor foe.

"What's going on, Al?" he muttered.

The ops officer spoke in an undertone, his eyes still soldered to the scope. "Incoming plane. It left the Dhubai–Bandar 'Abbās commercial air route five minutes ago. It'll be overhead in five. AWACs has no I.D. on it."

"Does *Gallery* have it?"

"Wait one, I'll ask him . . . what number track?"

"Thirteen forty," said Chief Custer.

"No, they just hold him incoming, unidentified."

"Range," said Shaker, his voice unhurried and even a little detached.

"Thirty-three miles, sir."

"Warn him."

Beside the captain, the radarman chief picked up the radio handset. He spoke slowly and distinctly. "Unidentified aircraft on course zero-two-zero, speed four hundred knots, altitude twelve thousand, you are approaching a U.S. Navy warship operating in international waters. Bearing zero-one-zero, range thirty miles from you. Request you identify yourself and state your intentions. Over."

They waited, the room silent except for the soft rush of blowers and the distant whale song of the sonar. The speaker gave them back only a whining clatter of interference, distant bleedover voices in Arabic and Farsi.

"No answer, Captain."

"Okay, cover TN thirteen forty," said Shaker.

"Weps control," shouted Wise. "Air target, bearing one-nine-zero. Load one Standard, range twenty-eight, fire on command, next round same. ECM, see if you can get a radar emission off him."

A confused clamor as three men shouted at once.

"Trying, sir, nothing yet."

"*Mobile Bay* calling us. They want to know if we hold the incoming."

"Yes! Ask them to identify it."

"They can't. They're alerting us to it."

"He's coming in silent," said Shaker. Dan looked at him; he was bent over the air picture, his hands out to either side of the screen. In the green flicker his face was strangely peaceful, almost content. "Al, have we got a lock-on with STIR yet?"

"Yessir, locked on with Mark 92."

The captain turned his head slightly, but his eyes stayed on the screen. "Dan, what do you think?"

Lenson took a deep breath. The pip was distinct now, emerging from the mountain clutter, still headed for them. The symbology showed it "Air Unknown."

"It might be a passenger plane, sir. With its electronics down. That way, it wouldn't radiate identification, wouldn't have its radar going, wouldn't respond to a radio call—"

"Or it could be a fighter pulling a fast one. He could tuck himself into the commercial stream over Bandar 'Abbās, cross the Gulf in the corridor, orbit over Dhubai, and come out of there headed for us. Completely silent so we and the Omani airspace authorities'd think just what you said. If he's one of their F-14s, he may have a Maverick. Or iron bombs."

Dan couldn't say anything to that except "Yes, sir, he could."

"He's only at twelve thousand. Isn't that low for an airliner?"

"He could be trying to find out where he is. If his radar's out, he won't know."

Beside them, Custer was speaking again into the radio. "Unidentified aircraft on course zero-two-zero, speed four hundred knots, altitude twelve thousand, you are approaching a U.S. Navy warship bearing zero-one-one, range twenty miles from you. Your intentions are unclear. You are standing into danger and may be subject to United States defensive measures. Request—"

"What is all this legalistic bullshit?" shouted Shaker suddenly. "God damn it, I don't *care* about the proper format. Tell him to alter course right now or I'll shoot him down!"

"Unidentified aircraft: alter your course now to zero-nine-zero or I will shoot you down."

Dan felt sweat break under his shirt. "If he's a hostile, how would he know we were here?"

"They've got coastal radar. They know what our convoys look like."

Dan picked up the spare handset and dialed the JL circuit. "Lookouts, Combat," he said rapidly, "we've got an incoming aircraft slightly forward of the port beam. We need a visual I.D., right now."

The lookouts saw nothing; one said it was too dark. Dan glanced at the bulkhead clock. It was almost eleven.

"Nineteen miles, still closing," said the radar operator. "Time on top two minutes, forty-five seconds. He's losing altitude! Down to ten thousand feet!"

"All ahead flank, come hard left," shouted Shaker. "ESM! God damn it, get me a signature!"

"There's no radar signature, sir!" The boy's voice went high and broke.

"Okay, calm down, son. Mr. Pensker: Phalanx to automatic."

"CIWS in AA auto, release hold-fire," confirmed the weapons officer. Dan stepped forward to check the setup, and for a split second saw the dark face, lit by the cold radiance of the WCC display, turn toward the weapons-control petty officer beside him. He looked intent now, cool, even eager. Whatever the captain had told him, Dan thought fleetingly, there was no longer any trace of strain or nerves. The button clicked as it depressed. The ON light glowed through Pensker's palm, tinted with the color of his blood.

"Twelve miles!"

The deck was slanting now, shaking as the turbines came up to flank. Shaker glanced at Dan; across the glowing circle of the scope, their eyes met. Lenson suddenly remembered another moment like this, in the Mediterranean. Unidentified aircraft closing, the formation socked in by fog and rain, and in charge then a man who couldn't make up his mind. He heard again Isaac Sundstrom's whine, begging for justification, support, sympathy, advice. . . .

Pensker said, "Sir, minimum range—"

"I know. Steady on course one-six-zero. Stand by to fire," said the captain.

Wise spoke rapidly into his headset. Pensker's hand moved up, flipped up the red cover over the FIRE button, rested over it. Dan saw Shaker take a deep breath. "All right—"

"Combat, Bridge: Lookouts report air contact, showing red and green lights and a white strobe, off port bow."

"Silence," shouted Shaker.

Everyone froze. Hands came up off switches and keyboards. They lifted their heads, eyes remote, mouths open a little. Waiting.

The green blip on the radar jumped ahead, and merged with the blot of light that was *Van Zandt.*

"Combat, Bridge: A plane just went over us. Headed northeast."

"What kind?"

"Can't tell, all we could see were the lights. A big one."

"Phalanx to hold fire," ordered Shaker. A switch snapped in the silence and the READY light blinked to orange. On the scope, the pip emerged from the blur at the center, still headed north. As they watched, it changed suddenly into a semicircle.

"AWACs identifies: commercial airliner," said Custer. His voice shook a little.

"Holy shit," said Wise. They looked at each other. Dan felt his knees begin to tremble.

They'd almost shot it down. If they hadn't still been at sea, where the lookouts could see more clearly than in the dust-shrouded Gulf, they would have. He could smell his own sweat. He looked at the captain. He, too, seemed frozen, looking into the green shimmer after the departing aircraft.

He never asked me, Dan thought through the aftershock of fear. Shaker had held off till there was not an extra second. He'd done everything possible to establish the bogey's identity. Then he'd made his decision. As a commanding officer had to.

So that was right. He was decisive. But had the decision he made been right?

What, Dan asked himself soberly, would I have done?

As soon as he asked it, he knew the answer. Given that choice—between taking a possible hit and shooting down a civilian airliner with who knew how many innocent souls aboard—he knew what his decision would have been.

He wouldn't have fired. Not with the volume of civilian traffic here. With chaff, electronics, and the Phalanx, they'd have a decent chance even if a fighter launched its weapons first. Only then, when he was sure, would he shoot to kill.

But Shaker hadn't seen it that way. He'd decided to fire first.

Which of them was right? Was it Shaker—with *Strong*'s agony still vivid in his memory, and probably his nightmares— or Dan himself, perhaps more detached, better able to deal with the situation rationally?

He remembered the old Navy saying: "I'd rather be judged by twelve than carried by six." The captain's first duty was to preserve his ship and the lives of his men. By that standard, Benjamin Shaker had acted properly. No senior commander, no board of inquiry could fault his response. A situation like this was beyond written rules. It had to be left to the commanding officer's judgment. No matter what that incoming contact had turned out to be, by Hart's rules of engagement Shaker would have been justified in firing on it.

He hadn't. But only by a fluke. When the lookouts had reported lights, he'd called "silence," the old powder-magazine command that meant don't move, don't breathe, don't do anything.

And the airliner had gone right over their heads.

So it had all turned out all right.

This time.

But what did his choice say about Benjamin Shaker? What would he do the next time he had to make an instantaneous decision on the basis of inadequate data? Would he always choose to fire when the situation was doubtful?

Had the loss of *Strong*, the resolve never to let himself be taken by surprise again, affected his judgment?

"Message from *Mobile Bay* to *Charles Adams*, sir, info to us."

"What's it say?"

"Relaying an SOS. A Greek tanker, north of us. Attacked by small boats, on fire. COMIDEASTFOR wants to know if one of us can render assistance."

"Range, location, damn it!"

Custer gave him the range and bearing and Wise marked it on the scope. Shaker lit a cigarette as he studied it. Dan saw that his hands were rock-steady. After a moment, he said, "I can get there in two hours. Al, ask the commodore if he wants me to try."

Wise spoke briefly into his headset. Then clicked off. "He says he'd rather send *Gallery*, she's north of us, but he wants us to scramble our chopper for a possible rescue. Apparently the fire's pretty bad."

"Okay, flight quarters," said Shaker loudly. "Let's get 'em in the air like now. No weapon load, we'll cover them. Minimum brief, vector 'em after launch. Go! Go! Go!"

Dan pushed his thoughts from his mind. It was his privilege to second-guess. But his actions, his speech, they were not his own.

He was Benjamin Shaker's executive officer. And he had his duty to do.

14

U.S.S. *Turner Van Zandt*

"**W**HAT you got under the towel, Buck? Tent pole?"

"Hell, you're supposed to make it littler in the showers, Hayes, not bigger."

Buck Hayes two-pointed his soap into the sink. His bare feet made wet question marks on the deck. "Okay, smart guys. What's eleven inches long and white?"

"What?" said Schweinberg suspiciously.

"Nothing." He whipped off the bath towel and polished his butt with it, then began rooting through his locker for shorts.

The pilots were sitting around the stateroom drinking Orange Crushes and Frescas from the mess decks. Woolton was beside Schweinberg on the latter's bunk. "Smiley" Bonner, Woollie's ATO and the junior flier aboard, was perched on Hayes's chair. Schweinberg had been telling a story, and now he started over, motioning with his hands.

"So like I was saying, these two Jews just got married. And they're already fighting over the toilet seat, right? He leaves it up, she wants it down. Well, one night she sits down without looking and bingo! She's stuck. She screams for him to get her out, but the harder he pulls, the more she wiggles and the tighter her ass gets wedged in.

"So finally, they call the plumber. They can't think of anything else to do. When he's at the door, the guy suddenly realizes his wife's naked. So he takes off his yarmulke and puts it in her lap. And then he takes the plumber in the bathroom.

"And he just stands there. Finally, the guy asks him, "So, what do you think?" And the plumber says, "Well, I think I can save the broad, but I'm afraid the rabbi's a goner.""

They laughed. Bonner said eagerly, "Hey, I got one. Knock, knock."

"Oh, hell, Bonner, what you wasting our time with that high-school stuff for?"

"Come on, boot camp, that's oldern' buffalo shit."

"You know why Smiley went helicopters?" Woolton said. "It's the only aircraft where you can masturbate without any hand motion."

Schweinberg said, "Did I ever tell you guys about my old OIC, Max Suck?"

"The Red Max? Sure, he was on the *Aubrey Fitch* when I was on the *Doyle.* I remember when we had our thousand-hour party, and he called our bridge and told 'em he was gonna render honors." Woolton grinned. "So the shoes all went out on the wing. Suck comes roaring past at a hundred feet, they salute, and there's the gunner's, the SENSO's, and the ATO's moons hanging out at them."

"That's him. Well, Max was our det CO on the *Fitch,* in the Med. And they were about to ship his crewman over to the JFK to see a shrink. Whenever they flew at night, he'd start screaming "ground fire, ground fire," and Suck would go evasive. Only there was never anything on the radar. The guy would come back shaking, swearing he'd seen tracers. Then one day Suck swapped with my ATO. Halfway through the flight, I noticed he was smoking."

"In the cockpit?"

"Yeah, holding it down by his leg. I don't know how he got it lit. Anyway, he'd put his butt down to the air vent there and tap the ashes off. Sure enough, all of a sudden our SENSO comes up on the ICS screaming "Tracers! Tracers! Break right, for Christ's sake!""

The pilots laughed. Schweinberg went on deadpan: "Our captain had this hard-on for the pilots. The Rocket Ranger, that was his code name. Well, when we first come aboard, every time we make an approach, the ship's right on the hairy lips of the envelope. He'd have the wind ninety degrees to port at fifteen knots, or someplace else where we're sweating baseballs the whole way in.

"So Max goes up to the bridge and says, 'Captain, we need to talk.' And the Ranger says, 'I know it's tough, I'm giving you a challenge.' Suck gets a little steamed at this and he tells the guy we get enough pulse-pounders, we want to see Mom and the kids again.

"So this dickhead takes a pencil and draws a little triangle way inside the limits on the relative-wind diagram, and marks it 'P.E.' Then he gives it to the OOD, and says, 'This is the Pussy Envelope for our no-balls helo pilots, Lieutenant.'

"Well, after that, every time the Ranger wants a photo hop, or a parts run, funny, the helo's always down. Then one day

COMSIXTHFLEET flies over to see what's new, and it's late, so he decides to stay. So the Ranger gives the admiral his cabin and moves down with the XO.

"Well, meanwhile one of the det guys, his wife sent him this rubber fuck-me doll. It's human-size and like everything works. Suck gets an idea. While the admiral and the Ranger are eating dinner, he sneaks into the CO's head. He leaves the doll in the shower stall along with a big jar of vaseline and some pieces of hose, electrical tools, carrots, that type of stuff. Then he closes the curtain and takes off. The next morning, soon as the admiral leaves, Suck's in there and sneaks it out again. The Ranger never understood why the admiral wouldn't shake hands with him anymore."

When they were done laughing, Schweinberg turned serious. "Woollie, talking about that, we got to do something about the way Lenson's screwing with our guys."

"What happened now?"

"He found our mechs flaked out in the hangar. Got torqued and chewed Mattocks out. Now, those guys worked all night getting the bird back up. They couldn't rack out in their berthing compartment because there were people tearing the deck apart."

"Right." Woolton nodded. "You're preaching to the choir, Chunky."

"Well, you preach to Lenson, then! Another thing, he made some crack a couple days ago about us usin' too much water. Well, we sweat in that cockpit. We *need* showers."

"They've got a water problem," said Woolton. "The CHENG, Guerra, he was telling me how the seawater's so hot here, the condensers aren't as efficient—"

"Woollie, you can't start takin' the shoes' side! You got to represent our side!"

Hayes got up. He flexed in front of the mirror, still naked except for shorts.

"Knock it off, Buck, you're givin' Boot Camp a hard-on. Woollie, when you figure we'll fly next?" asked Schweinberg.

"Pretty soon. It'll be double-pumps all the way up the Gulf, dhow-herding and mine-hunting."

"Waste of gas. The ragheads are running scared. This is a big sweatex, that's all, they won't pull anything with the *Forrestal* offshore."

"How about those F-14s that bounced us?" said Hayes. "My personal pucker factor's been way up since then."

There was a moment of silence, then Woolton got up. Schweinberg said, "Hey, one more before you go."

"What?"

"How do they know Adam and Eve weren't black?"

"How?"

"You ever try to take a rib away from a black guy?"

The white officers glanced at Hayes. He didn't laugh. There was another silence, awkward this time. Then, slowly, the little party broke up.

The dark thing almost had him. He'd tried to get away on his bike but it broke. Finally, he just ran, screaming "Dad! Dad!" Screaming for his father, the pilot, the strongest man in the world—

Suddenly he understood how to escape. Wake up. That was all. Knowing it was the first step. But it wasn't the whole way. Halfway across yet caught, like a calf in a fence, he fought toward consciousness with the mindless desperation of any being that must be born or die.

But its growls and his screams still rang in his ears. Then he heard its pad, pad behind him, the click of claws, and its rotten-flesh breath on his neck. He wasn't sure there was anything on the other side. He just had to jump.

When Hayes got his eyes open, the sheets were twisted around him tight as a coat of paint. It took a struggle just to get an arm out.

When the bunk light clicked on he saw it was 2235. The growling came from beneath him. But he couldn't close his eyes again. Not with that thing waiting in his head. What did Dustin call it—the Eater Monster—

He realized suddenly that in the dream he'd been his son, powerless, terrified, four years old. And at the same moment, he understood the terror. It was what he felt when his engineer's mind retraced some narrow escape and realized that one more bad break, one wrong command or move by his HAC, his crewman, or himself, would have killed them all.

That terror was too real. He preferred the nameless horror of his son's nightmares. But as he blinked at his watch it faded back into its dream jungle, casting back one lingering gleaming glance.

As if to say: I'll be here.

He'd just clicked the light off when the GQ alarm brought him upright again. Then came "This is not a drill. Aircraft incoming."

"Holy shit!" Schweinberg's feet hit the deck like two steaks. The overhead light flickered on, showing him pulling on his flight suit. Hayes grabbed a pipe and swung himself down.

Flight suit, socks, flight boots. They hit the door simultaneously, like a comedy team, but got through somehow and sprinted for the hangar.

When Schweinberg got there, the enlisted were already mustered. Four Two One was at ready position, nose within the ship, fuselage out on deck. He snapped to Mattocks: "Chief, got fire gear manned?"

"Thass right, sir. Skirla! Lynch! Get them tools put away."

Woolton came in, boot laces trailing. "What's goin' on, Woollie?" said Hayes.

"I don't know." At that moment, there was a roar overhead. Two ATs ran out to the flight deck. "Four-engined," one of them called back.

A few minutes later the bogen beeped. Woolton listened, then turned. "You got her tits up, Chief?" he called across the hangar.

"Yessir. We was just getting the cowling back on the tail rotor servo."

"What's wrong with it?"

"Nothin', sir, just had to vacuum; this fuckin' red dust gets into everything."

Woolton said, "Yessir," "Yessir," and then, "Aye aye, sir, right away." When he hung up, he looked around at the waiting men. "So, what was it?" said Schweinberg, popping his fist into his palm.

"I don't know what that flyby was, if that's what you mean. But the Pasdaran just rocketed a merchie. It's out there on fire."

"Combat search and rescue?"

"You got it."

"Move, move!" shouted Mattocks. "Mount the gun! Kane, get your SAR bag, first-aid gear, litters, line!"

The crew jumped into motion. At the same time, the 1MC keened. "Flight quarters, flight quarters! All hands man your flight quarters stations."

The det commander was reaching for his helmet when Schweinberg grabbed his arm. "What the fuck, Woollie? It's our turn."

"My mission, Chunks."

"Hell it is. We go by turns in this det! Get suited, Buck!" Before the OIC could protest, Schweinberg was buckling on the survival vest. Hayes lingered for a moment, waiting to see whether Woolton would assert himself, then grabbed for his gear, too.

Outside it was windy and dark. Only the red glow of the hangar lights eddied out onto the flight deck. Hayes stared around, feeling a breath of the dream-terror. Christ! Night search and rescue, with hostiles somewhere . . . Windy as hell tonight . . . They should have been dark-adapted long before now.

"Buck, you got everything?" A bulky shadow beside him. He patted down hastily. Dog tags on his boots, survival vest, PRC-90, knife, two flare packs, pistol, pocket checklist, knee board, emergency air bottle . . . "Yeah."

"Hokay, les' boogie."

A flashlight came on, red-lensed, and they began the pre-flight, not wasting any time, but careful not to skimp, either. If they had to abort, they wouldn't do anybody any good. At last they climbed in. "You want to take it?" asked Schweinberg, his voice subdued by darkness. "You need a nighttime bounce, don't you?"

"Uh . . . yeah! Thanks, Chunky."

Schweinberg grunted and glanced back into the cabin. For combat rescues, all four seats were manned. The machine gun poked its pronged snout out the cargo door. Christer, the gunner and hoist operator, was thrashing around back in the cabin, getting into a wet suit.

Outside, the flight deck was dim amber. Beyond the deck-edge lights, the sea was invisible. Schweinberg jotted down flight data as Buck started the engines, engaged rotors, and reported ready to lift.

The interior of the cockpit was a spilled jewel box. The engine and transmission strips were a bright jade green. The flight instruments were mother-of-pearl, and the tactical display a flickering emerald. The only luminescences outside were the deck-edge and the lineup lights. The strobe bounced scarlet off their rotors into the night. Kane sneezed into his mike and Hayes jumped.

The deck status light blinked from orange to green. Schweinberg made a last sweep of the panel.

As they lifted, the ship became something separate, then a distant set of faint lights. Finally it vanished. But not before Hayes had seen, behind it, a fan of cold green fire, roiled mysteriously from the dark sea by her passing.

Schweinberg: "Three rates of climb."

"Roger."

"After-takeoff checklist complete."

"Roger."

"Coming up on radar. ATACO, ATO, gimme a vector to this merchie."

CIC pointed them northwest. Beneath their hurtling passage, the darkness was crowded as an interstate on a summer weekend. Two long columns of lights stretched from the black Gulf out into the Goo; out to the ends of the earth. . . .

Schweinberg said, "Christer, rig for rescue. Clear the gun and get the hoist ready. Hoist power coming *on.*"

Hayes said tensely to the ship, "ATACO, pilot, we're bustering inbound at a hundred fifty or so. You got any comms with this guy that's been attacked?"

The ship said they didn't. He told Schweinberg to punch up international search and rescue and maritime distress frequencies.

"Hold you left of contact, Two One, come right" came the disembodied voice, pursuing them through the lengthening miles of darkness.

"What looks good?"

"Make it five degrees right, Two One."

"Five degrees, roger—Kane, got it yet?"

"I got a lot of stuff, sir. There's a whole slew of contacts out in front of us."

"Uh oh," said Schweinberg. Hayes glanced at him. "ATACO, pilot. How far are we gonna be from Iran, here?"

"About twenty miles, Two One."

"Holy creepin' crap . . . look, keep an eye on your scopes and shit back there, awright, guys? If we get visitors, I want to know in advance."

Twenty minutes went by. And then, growing steadily brighter on the horizon ahead, a yellow flicker, like an infernal aurora. Chunky took it at first for another flare-off tower. Then he realized the coordinates matched. Hayes rogered, came right, and headed for the loom.

"That's him, all right. Slowing to sixty."

"Start lowering your altitude, Buck. Better approach from upwind, stay out of the smoke."

"Good thinking," Hayes muttered. "Kane, what you got on the tube?"

"Stay clear of the starboard side, sir. I got four, five small contacts over there, maybe three miles."

"Roger. What's the wind?"

"Still showing three-five-oh at twenty, twenty-five."

High wind for a close hover. Hayes circled to port as he shed speed and altitude, steadying at five hundred feet. The smoke, sucked into the cockpit from outside, stank of petroleum. As he came out of it, he saw the ship clearly and whole for the first time.

It was a medium-sized freighter, the deck piled with fire. He could see the holes on the side where the rockets had hit.

He got down to a hundred and did a close sweep. The ship loomed suddenly huge. Bow to the wind; in the fire glow, he could see everything clearly. The whole superstructure was ablaze. The deck aft was burning, too. The crew was huddled near the bow. As he swept over them he caught a glimpse of waving arms, open mouths. "They look kind of anxious," he muttered.

"I would be, too, if my lifeboats were on fire."

"What are they throwing into the water?"

"Lumber, looks like. Deck cargo." Schweinberg flexed his fingers like a pianist warming up, then grasped the controls. *Click.* "ATACO, Killer Two One. We're on top. Twelve to fifteen people in a huddled mass, superstructure shot up, she's a bonfire. Permission to go in for rescue."

"Two One, ATACO: Captain says do it."

"Roger, going in at this time." Schweinberg clicked off the net and back onto ICS. "Okay, I got her, Buck."

"Hey! Just when it gets interesting—"

"This is where them extra hours count, buds. Christy, get the door open. We'll get a guy first pass, no dicking around. Be ready to shear that cable ASAP if you hear me scream."

The cabin door came open behind them and the noise level increased. Schweinberg slowed, watching the airspeed indicator. "Hoist checks good," said the crewman.

"Roger, pay out fifty feet or so."

Chunky squinted at the burning ship. She had no list, thank God. And it was funny how she kept pointing into the wind. Then he realized they'd dropped the anchor. He didn't like the looks of the flames aft. Not oil. Too white. It looked like naphtha, or gasoline. He adjusted the rearview and told Hayes to watch his ass.

"Will do." Buck uncinched his shoulder harness and turned in the seat. "You got a good two hundred yards to the bridge. Chunky, why don't you come in nose first?"

"No can do, wind's too high for that fancy shit. SENSO, pilot."

"Yessir."

"Help Christy with the hoist, but keep an eye on the radar. Lemme know if those little blips start moving in. And yell if it gets too hot back there. Buck, punch up the hover bars. Christy, call my position."

"Easy back, sir."

The hoist whined behind them. Fixed over the open cargo door, on the starboard side, it was run by the gunner. Hayes ran hoist procedures over in his mind. "Hundred yards to the bow. Easy back," he said.

"How's it now?"

"Easy back . . . fifty . . . forty, thirty, ten . . . easy. Easy!"

"Got it in the mirror. Christy! Watch the hook, don't let it snag. If they attach it to the ship, cut it right away."

"Rog."

"Crossing the deck edge."

"Ah, roger that . . . height!"

"Fifty."

"Gauges are in the green."

As they slid over it, the ship enfolded them with light and heat. Yellow flickered inside the cockpit. Hayes couldn't hear anything over the wing beat of their rotors. But he could imagine the roar of that immense mass of flame. Then he jerked his mind away. No imagining. He had to help fly this bitch.

"Fifteen knots, slowing."

"ATO, ATACO."

"Go, *Van Zandt*." Hayes kept his eyes on the instruments. "Looking good, Chunky."

"Where are you, Two One? Lost you on the scope."

"ATACO, Two One, we're playing marshmallow over the merchant. Hook's going down now."

"Roger. Two One, we have comms with a Royal Navy frigate. She's prepping a Lynx for launch. *Scylla*'s closer to the freighter than we are. After pickup, proceed two-seven-two twenty-eight miles to offload survivors."

"Copy vector two-seven-two, twenty-eight, HMS *Scylla*."

"You're drifting aft," Hayes said.

"Roger that." Schweinberg was sweating. He could see nothing in the rearviews but yellow flame. When he looked away, his night vision was shit; he got floating red patches instead of dial readings. He was flying by hover bars, but he didn't think it was going to work for long. The bird lurched to the right and he brought it back. Was the wind shifting? "Get that fucking sling down there, Christy!" he shouted.

"It's down. They're putting a wounded guy in it first, looks like."

"Well, make 'em hurry the fuck up!"

"Yessir!"

Hayes glanced back to see him pump his arm. Doubted if they'd understand that. "You're drifting aft!" he shouted. "Going into the bridge!"

"Shit, shit, *shit*. Get him *aboard*, gunner!"

The hoist whined. As soon as Schweinberg felt the weight, he increased lift and moved forward. When they were over the water, he relaxed his grip a bit, but still kept tight formation on the ship. Hayes, looking back, saw Christer, harness taut, lean out to pull a dark bundle into the cabin. "First guy's aboard" crackled over the ICS.

"How's he look?"

"Not so good."

"How many more?"

"Eleven, twelve?"

"We'll get two more and then go find that Brit."

"Roger that."

Schweinberg decided backing in sucked. He made the second approach from port, transitioning to a hover over the bow with wind abeam. This way he got immediate hand-eye feedback. He parked himself forty feet above the deck, holding with the cyclic and only adjusting the collective when the weight came on the hoist. One man came up and was swung in. The hoist went down again. "Yeah, this works better," he muttered.

"Number three in the horse collar, sir."

Up, up, and away. When the gunner reported the man aboard, he hauled around to the west and brought airspeed up to 150.

Hayes glanced back. The rescuees were huddling in the fuselage tunnel. One was sitting there smiling, looking around. He snapped his head back as Schweinberg asked him for altitude.

When they found her, the British destroyer was on the move, tossing up a sparkling bow wave visible from miles off. Her pad looked smaller than *Van Zandt*'s. Schweinberg came in athwartships. They took some nasty buffeting but thudded down safely. Christer and Kane slid the wounded out to goggled corpsmen. A moment later, Two One had lifted again.

When they came up on the freighter again, the other helicopter was over the bow. Schweinberg held a tight circle, staying in the firelight, but climbed as he came round the starboard side; he had no wish to be silhouetted. "See if you can get that guy on the radio," he said.

Hayes puzzled for a moment, then called *Van Zandt*. The ATACO answered and Buck asked him to get the frequency of the Lynx. He came back a few minutes later with 283.0. Buck keypadded this into the UHF and was rewarded with a light-hearted voice in midsentence: " . . . Right through the focking centerline."

"British Lynx, this is U.S. Navy SH-60, call sign Killer Two One, over."

"This is *Scylla* Prime, and how are you this evening, Yank Two One."

"Oh, smashing. How many did you get on that last pass?"

"We have five souls on board, five souls."

"Does he have radar on that thing?" he asked Schweinberg. The pilot shrugged. Hayes clicked to transmit again. "*Scylla* Prime, be advised we hold several small boats on radar bearing oh-five-oh. Suspect they're the bastards who hit the ship in the first place."

"Rojah, we hold them, too, and will avoid, thank you. Now lifting, clearing the area to the west."

Schweinberg said, "Let's finish these fuckers up; we're gonna need gas pretty soon."

"Maybe we can get a drink from the Limeys."

"Now you're thinkin'. . . . Okay, here we go."

The second load went perfectly. Four uninjured men came up on the sling one after the other; Kane secured the hatch; Schweinberg tiptoed forward till he was clear of ship's structure and could bank off toward the west. En route, Hayes called *Scylla* and set up the refuelling. The Lynx was gone when they got there and Schweinberg put 421 down again with her tail hanging over the side and held her there with the rotors while the rescuees debarked and she drank three thousand pounds of JP-5 equivalent. When they were in the air again, he said, "Okay, Bucky-boy. You wanta fly this last one?"

Hayes grinned through his nervousness. He was scared, but anybody who wasn't scared occasionally flying a helicopter didn't understand the situation. He tested the controls, then steadied up. This time, he took a moment to look, really look, at the burning ship as they closed. At the long tapered flames groping at the stars; at the dance and glitter of the firelight on the sea. He could see flame within the ship now through the rocket holes. He thought again of that naphthalene stink, then erased it from his mind.

He made his approach, as Schweinberg had, from the port side, and transitioned into a hover sixty feet up. It wasn't hard to get there, but holding position was a different story in the gusting and dropping *shamal*.

"How you doin'?" Schweinberg glanced across the cockpit. The dark face was sheened with sweat. Could his ATO handle it? The cross-cockpit hover was harder and maybe not too smart, but it gave him a break. He needed it.

"Great. Great!" Hayes was surprised first at the question, and then at the answer.

Suddenly he wasn't nervous anymore. He was psyched. He glanced to starboard, to see the windows of the bridge staring out at him like the lit eyes of a Jack-o'-lantern, the flames blown back like glowing hair by the rotor blast. Two One hung magically, dipping and swaying.

Flying. Flying! How could he live without this?

"Sling going down." Kane said, over the hoist whine. " . . . Guy's in it. Weight comin' on."

They dipped and Hayes added power. Too much; they started to rise; he dropped it, too much again. "You're overcorrecting," said Schweinberg. "Take it slow, take it easy. You got room."

"Comin' up," said Kane again. "Hal, get ready for his legs, there, haul him in—"

A red light came on suddenly above the center console. Simultaneously, Hayes felt a bump, like a pickup going over a jackrabbit. The left rudder pedal kicked his boot. The plane came up, yawed right, and staggered back toward the pyre. He tried to correct, but the cyclic was mushy.

"Control problem," he shouted, unable to look away from the looming superstructure long enough to fixate on the indicator. "Chunky, I'm losing it! Need some help!"

"Holy shit. Boost failure! Beef those controls!"

"What are you guys doing?" came Kane's voice. "We got a man on the wire here!"

Hayes had his legs locked against the rudder pedals. The torque of the rotors fought his rigid thigh muscles in the motionless agonizing balance of arm wrestlers. "Ah, get him aboard fast; we got a flight control problem up here."

"Shit! The fucking cable's jammed!"

"Get away from the ship," said Schweinberg. "Get away! Get clear, Hayes!"

"There's a guy on the wire!"

"Forget him, right? Get clear of this tub and then we'll figure out—"

"Okay, I get the idea. Transitioning to forward flight." He hauled up on collective, but it didn't move much, either.

A boost failure meant there were no hydraulics to amplify

their control inputs. They had to fly a ten-ton helicopter by main strength.

"Chunky, gimme a hand! Gimme left pedal, help me pull some power!"

They braced themselves in the seats and hauled together, cursing between clenched teeth. The torque climbed, and the ship crept away a little, then a little more.

Then, suddenly, the heading indicator rolled. Four Two One spiraled to the left, hammered as it flew through the updraft of smoke and hot air, and curved off into the darkness. "Gimme some right pedal, right pedal," Buck said very distinctly into the ICS. "Okay. Kane, what's your guy doing back there, you got him in yet?"

"He's too heavy. He ain't coming up."

"Look, we're kind of wrapped up flying this crowd-killer. Either pull him in by hand or cut him. I can't screw with him anymore."

"I can't move him, sir."

"Okay, he goes. Standby to cut, now, now, *now.*" A flat crack came from outside the fuselage.

He was looking down, out of the aircraft, into the blackness that lay north of the burning ship, when below him there was a flash. Then a ripple of them, white flashes, and a moment later a string of red Christmas lights floated past. "They're firing at us!" shouted Kane.

"No shit, Sherlock," muttered Schweinberg. "Forget 'em, Bucko. You see a tracer, it's already missed you. We lose control now and we're crab meat. Straight and level's the only way we're gettin' home."

Hayes suddenly remembered he'd left his body armor in his stateroom. The one time he'd decided he didn't need it . . . *"Where* do you think you're going?" shouted Schweinberg.

"Scylla."

"Like hell, hotshot, no way we're doing a boost-off landing on that Ping-Pong table. . . . ATACO, Two One: we got a major glitch here, feels like a pilot assist module leak. Request emergency flight quarters, break from the convoy and give us best wind over the bow. I got controls. Gimme RADALT hold, Buck."

"You have the controls," said Hayes. He didn't like Schweinberg's tone but this was no time to argue over it.

"Help me out, left rudder, straighten up."

"Coming left."

"Scylla Prime, this is Killer Two One: we got a flight-control problem. Request you pick up a guy we cut loose off the bow.

Two more left aboard." Schweinberg clicked off UHF without waiting for a response. "Kane! Gimme home plate range."

"Seventy miles, sir."

"Anything else flat around here? Any icebergs?"

"Got an island, sir."

"That's Abu Musa, that's where these gun-happy sheepfuckers came from. It's *Van Zandt* or swim, boys. Hang on tight."

Hayes got the checklist open and the light on it. This would not be easy. Putting a machine the size of the 60 on a frigate required delicacy. Just what they didn't have. Yaw control was tough with no boost. Especially over a rolling flight deck. Schweinberg would have to do this right the first time.

Shaker came up on the link. Hayes explained the situation, interrupted from time to time as Schweinberg shouted for help. He could feel sweat pooling under his buttocks.

"Two One, LSO." It was Woolton's voice. "Emergency flight quarters set, crash team manning up."

"Roger that, Woollie, what's deck motion?"

"Wind's ten to port at twenty-two, pitch one, roll two, altimeter twenty-nine point eighty-two, say your ETA."

"Roger that, on top in plus five."

Schweinberg said, "I'm gonna try a slow approach, see how the controls feel, then start descent."

"Roger, green deck. Good luck, guys."

"What's your feel for this, Buck?"

"Not exactly warm 'n' fuzzy, Chunky."

"Christer, Kane, you guys strapped in back there? Got your emergency air handy?"

"Ready for impact, sir."

Schweinberg cinched his straps. The ship came up suddenly bright ahead, as if every light had been turned on at once.

He blew out. It's simple, boy, he told himself. All you got to do is squat this bitch in one piece. On the deck is number one. Second best's in the water, clear of the ship. Some of us ought to make it out then before she sinks. Hitting the superstructure, you get no points for that. We all go crispy critter then. His arms were cramping. "Hummmbaby," he muttered, then, "Help me out, some right pedal."

"Two One, LSO: green deck for port recovery; say your position."

"Roger that, six miles on your stern."

"Roger."

"Death," Schweinberg muttered through his teeth. "But first—*cheech.*"

"Two One, LSO: roger your cheech. These lights good?"

"Look good from here."

The ship changed from a distant glitter to a place. Hayes noted the topaz glow of the glide-slope indicator, saw it fade to ruby as they sank too fast. Beside him, Schweinberg wheezed, and he grunted too as they hauled the plane up bodily. Out of nowhere, he remembered the summer he'd worked in the cemetery in Creston. His arms felt as if he'd been digging graves. Green luminescence unrolled beneath the stern, spinning like blurry green galaxies above the invisibly turning screw.

"LSO, Two One: on your one five-five at two miles, got an amber, starting my approach. Clear the deck."

"Roger, deck cleared, this final?"

"Affirmative. I'm committed. One mile."

"Two One, Paddles got you in sight. Say what seat."

"Right seat."

They were sliding inexorably downward. The glide-slope indicator went green again; too high. The two pilots thought like the two halves of one brain now, hardly speaking, moving the controls together. "Checks complete," said Hayes after several silent seconds.

"Roger. Half mile, looking good, coming through fifty-five knots. Help me on the pedals."

"More left pedal," warned Hayes.

"Quarter-mile, one hundred twenty-five feet, looking good, thirty-five knots. Here comes translation."

The fuselage shuddered. "Drifting left!"

"Crossing deck edge. Over the deck!"

The dark mass, light-outlined, of the hangar loomed in front of them. A graze with a rotor tip and it would all be over. "Right pedal," Schweinberg grunted. "Jesus. Help me out, Buck, for Christ's sake!"

"We're drifting."

"Roger—"

"*Easy* back."

"Looking good. Down, down, down—"

The wheels hit the deck with a *whomp* that brought Buck's helmet off. "Two One, all right, you're down, nice landing," said Woolton.

"Chocks and chains, please," said Schweinberg, breathing hard. To Hayes he said, "Cut her, disengage, shut down, get me a beer."

"Nice flying, Chunky."

"Thanks, Montana, you done a nice job too."

The ship was steel-solid under them. The engines wound

down, juddering the fuselage. The two pilots sat motionless, sweat dripping off their noses and running down their backs, for several seconds before they were able to trip their harnesses.

Schweinberg, stepping down from the right seat, found himself looking down into blackness. The right tire was six inches from the deck edge. He found he couldn't walk real well. So he straddled the landing gear and unwrapped a stick of Big Red.

Hayes found he had Gummi Bear legs, too. He made it to the hangar, then had to prop up a bulkhead. But that was all that was different. The hangar looked the same, the faces looked the same, the hollow metallic voice that said now "Secure from flight quarters; set the normal underway watch" was the same.

He felt a hand on his shoulder, and turned his head, expecting Schweinberg or Woolton or Bonner—one of the fliers. But it was Terry Pensker. The faded khakis of a surface officer looked out of place among the flight suits.

"I was following you in on the radar, up in CIC," he said. "And listening. I'm glad you made it, Virg."

"Thanks, Terry."

"We got to take care of ourselves, man."

"You got that right."

Pensker said nothing more. Just slapped him on the back, nodded to the other pilots, and left the hangar. Hayes looked after him, blinking off a sense of déjà vu. Then he remembered; the night in Manama, the encounter when he was lit and Pensker was CDO. Well, it must be lonely being the only black officer in a ship's wardroom.

He steadied his legs and strolled outside again. Four Two One squatted in the glow of the deck edges, looking fatigued somehow, her blade tips quivering. Already, panels were hinged down, mech were crawling over her. Everything was routine. Everything was familiar.

He lifted his eyes to the sky. Up there, down here: How different the two worlds were.

The strangest thing was that nothing had changed at all.

15

U.S.S. *Mobile Bay,* CG-53

SHE arrived at dusk, crammed into the back seat of a tiny and extremely fast helicopter. She'd looked forward, between the pilots, unsure whether what she was seeing—a tiny gray thing blending in the failing light with the sea—was really a ship.

But it was.

Blair thought, Surely we're not going to land on that.

However, it looked as if they were planning to try. She craned forward, trying to hear what was going on above the howl of engines. But the helmets ignored her, talking silently into throat mikes as the horizon stopped rolling and the gray structure, larger now, settled into the center of the windscreen.

She leaned back, wedged her briefcase and tote bag yet more firmly under the seat, and concentrated on not vomiting. She shut her eyes, then opened them. Open was bad, but closed was worse; at least she could see which way was up.

She'd thought she was used to helicopters. And she'd been aboard ships before. But she'd never been in anything this little and this fast, and she'd never made a landing at sea. She hadn't realized it would feel this dangerous.

The seat suddenly dropped away, slamming her dinner against the top of her stomach. The aircraft jolted, then steadied again, closer now to the deck, which every moment grew harder to distinguish from the sea.

The little helicopter had barely enough room for three. But now, all at once, she was glad it was small, seeing the postage stamp of a flight deck. Distant detail became guns and missile launchers. The ship swelled with steady menace, bigger, bigger, closer, *closer—*

She caught a scream, thinking for a moment they were going to fly into one of the square smokestacks. Then came a sudden heaviness, a bump and grate, and they were down.

The pilot turned, his mouth moving. She leaned forward. "What? I can't hear you."

"Said, go on and disembark."

"Oh, right." She tripped the seat belt, gathered up her belongings, and edged hunched over toward the door. Men in colored jerseys reached up. She balanced, glad she'd worn low-heeled boots, and jumped down into their arms.

Hands tugged at her head and the cloth helmet came off. Something caught in her hair; she winced as strands pulled out. Then she was being hustled forward. Behind her, much louder without her Mickey Mouse ears on, turbines screamed upward again. A loudspeaker echoed metallically. She didn't catch the words. She looked anxiously ahead, to where two officers waited.

"Can I help you with some of that, Ms. Titus?" shouted Jack Byrne, reaching for her bag.

"Yeah, thanks." She gave him the tote. The other man reached for the briefcase, but she said firmly, "I'll keep that, thank you."

The helicopter lifted suddenly in a blast of wind. Black-painted, lightless, it was gone as soon as it left the deck. The loudspeaker echoed again, garbled words she couldn't interpret. Apparently the crew could; they began straggling away, stripping off gloves and gear and lighting cigarettes.

"I didn't expect to see you here," she said to Byrne. "Really, how can I convince you people I don't need to be escorted everywhere."

The intelligence officer laughed. Blair noticed he was wearing aviator-type sunglasses despite what was now full night. "Relax. Relax! I'm not here for you. I'm here to set up for Hart. He'll be out tomorrow to cover the convoy transit. Blair, meet Lee Miller, skipper of *Mobile Bay*, the newest and hottest thing in cruisers."

Miller was over six feet, a gum-chewing Viking with an easy grin and sun freckles on his nose. Blair extended her hand. He almost broke it.

"This's a real good time for you to come and see us, Miz Titus. You'll get a real good introduction to the capabilities of this class ship."

"Thanks, I'm glad to be here—safely."

Both men chuckled. "C'mon," said Miller, turning. "Jack tells me you're cleared to see everything, and everything's what you want to see. That about right?"

"Essentially," she said to his back.

The passageways were brightly lit, wide, and immaculately

clean. She caught looks of surprise and admiration from the
crewmen as they hurried past, but their attention was obviously divided between her and the captain. Byrne brought up
the rear. "Where'd you get the MH-6?" said Miller, undogging
a door.

"The what?"

"Your transportation. That's an Army Special Ops helo."

"I really don't know. The State people arranged it." She
paused as a crowd blocked the passageway; then, at an anonymous shout of "Make a hole!" parted with mystic ease. "The
flight was . . . well, scary. We were about four feet off the water
the whole way from Bahrain."

"Those are useful people. Considering they're Army. Those
choppers are crammed with night-vision equipment. They've
helped us spot Iranian infiltration attempts, mining attempts,
nip 'em in the bud. Okay, CDC or my stateroom?"

"Why is that a choice?"

"Well, stateroom if you want coffee and a talk, or else we
could go right into the demonstration."

"I can't stay overnight. Or so they tell me. And it's getting
late. So let's go right to the operations room."

"That's the command direction center, Navy talk, ma'am."
Miller grinned and took off his cap. To her surprise, he was
almost bald.

The last time she'd been in the operations spaces of a ship—
aboard *Iowa*, one of the recommissioned battleships—they'd
been dim, cramped, and ghostly. *Mobile Bay*'s were huge, and
modern as a new operating theater, or the cockpit of a space
shuttle. Blair looked around, tossing back her hair.

Something about the room made her think of Sea World.
Computer monitors, radarscopes, display screens flickered in
eerie hues. Folding, light-absorbing partitions secreted off al-
coves and chambers. There was a subdued susurration of electronics, ventilation, and voices. The air was very cold. It moved
steadily over her skin, tasting charged, like the prodrome of a
thunderstorm.

The room was oriented toward three luminescent displays,
not as large as one might expect. Between the command level
and the displays, officers and technicians sat at plots and computer consoles. They all wore jackets and sweaters. She felt
their surreptitious glances, like the wary eyes of night animals.
When she caught them at it, their faces went blank and they
pretended to be looking at something beyond her.

"Ever seen anything like this before, Ms. Titus?"

She said dryly, "I've toured the Nuclear Operations Room at the Pentagon, Captain. And the National Command Center. It's more compact, but the layout's the same."

Miller took her comment in stride; or maybe he hadn't heard it, had just paused to let her express amazement. He went on, staring at the winking squares, carets, and half-circles.

"These screens allow us to look at any of the hot spots at the touch of a button. The computers are on the next deck down. At the moment, we have the lower Gulf up, from the Qatar Peninsula east. We network tactical data with all U.S. and British ships in the region, and of course with the Saudis, too.

"Our primary job is observation and coordination. If we see a threat developing, we're on an NTDS link with all forces. That's real time, with high resolution and high capacity. If we'd been here year before last, we could have warned *Strong* she had a missile inbound. But we can do more than warn people. We have long-range antiaircraft missiles, two types of cruise missiles, and guns for self-defense. There's not a more capable warship in the world."

"I know what NTDS is, Captain Miller. And I'm familiar with the Aegis program."

"Uh-huh . . . here, watch." He clicked rapidly on a keyboard by his chair and the leftmost screen flickered and changed. Yellow on luminescent blue, a finger of land poked up. At the top, more land curved around it, a gap of sea between. A chain of symbols, flickering and advancing, threaded the gap like a tapeworm in an intestine.

"That's surface traffic in the Strait. One of our convoys is transiting Hormuz now. See that highlighted symbol west of Ra's Sharitah? That's *Turner Van Zandt*, one of the escorts.

"Linking Aegis and AWACS like this, we can keep tabs on a million square miles of airspace. Not only do we have a complete picture of the entire Arabian Gulf, from this room, but this picture as we assemble it is available on every ship in the theater and even back in the Pentagon. *As it happens*. If we do our job right, there shouldn't be any surprises anymore."

"You're right, Captain. It's impressive."

She was thinking, but again did not say, that it wasn't that hard to startle people for a billion dollars. Which was what each *Ticonderoga* cost. The question was not whether it was a wonderful show. Nor even, did it work. The questions that came immediately to her mind were: Was it necessary? Was it cost-effective?

Who could answer questions like that? Not Miller. He was

proud of his ship, and rightly so—hardly an unprejudiced source. Not the shipbuilders, nor the electronics manufacturers, nor the admirals.

From all of them would come an unbroken chorus of praise. Yet, oddly, no matter how proud they were of their capabilities, it was never enough. There was always another incredibly advanced enemy threat. Always another generation of ever more expensive hardware for which to plan.

Yet none of these weapons, none of the training, none of the intent technicians below them came cheap. It was the taxpayer—worried about his or her job, many without medical coverage, tired of signing over half his income to various levels of government—who paid for ships like this. As well as for aircraft, missiles, turbine-powered tanks, and salaries, early retirements, and free medical care for the people who ran them.

Who could act as judge and watchdog? Could decide who deserved what share of defense resources that seemed to shrink with every year? Could calculate which program mix would deliver security at the lowest cost, supervise its execution, and change it if it failed to work as advertised?

Congress was responsible for appropriating the funds and overseeing their use. However, few of the attorneys and businessmen the American people elected to govern them knew the difference between an inertial guidance system and a phased-array radar, could calculate an optimal overhaul strategy, or had time for the Scholastic subtleties of nuclear deterrence theory.

So it came down to their staffs. Two or three hundred men and women who had to understand the military without being part of it, who had to reconcile the realities of budgets and politics with the dreams and nightmares of those entrusted with the country's defense.

Fortunately, she thought, I know what to look for.

Miller was talking now about patrol areas. She interrupted him: "Yes, I meant to ask about those. Who determines the distribution of our ships within the Gulf, how they're assigned and employed?"

"Those orders come from MIDEASTFOR."

"Admiral Hart?"

"His N-Three, I imagine. Commodore Ritchie. Jack?"

"That's right."

"And how does he determine where to put them?"

Silence; then Miller said, "I'm not sure I follow."

"They're different types and classes with different sensors and weapons. You have varying areas and levels of threat, which I imagine are constantly changing. How do you determine what areas are patrolled, and who patrols them?"

"We do that ourselves," said Byrne.

"But how, Mr. Byrne, *how?* How many times do I have to ask the same question?"

"Well, we just decide which ship ought to be where. Depending on where the threat's greatest. It's a complicated process, force allocation."

"Is it done by hand?"

"I don't see how else you could do it."

"I see." She bit her lip, then turned to the commanding officer, who looked puzzled by the whole exchange. "Captain, do you have a list of the ships available and their capabilities? And the Iranian and Iraqi threats?"

"Well . . . yes. We could get that pretty quick—"

"Please do so. And have them brought over to that computer."

She sat down at the PC and asked for a chart of the Gulf, for the threat overlay from the most recent operation order, and for a copy of *Jane's.* While Miller sent a master chief scurrying, she organized her thoughts.

A multi-attribute utility function, containing as a system of linear equations the weaponry and readiness of individual ships, could be set up in a three-dimensional matrix for the assigned force level. Then, after identifying the areas where patrols were required, they could be ranked in a separate matrix by threat sophistication and density. An allocation algorithm and queuing function would be the heart of the program.

She directoried the hard disk, found Lotus and GW BASIC installed, and set to work.

Eventually the printer began to rattle. It was a quick first iteration, but she was satisfied with it for demonstration. She tore off the printout and handed it to Byrne. "This is the optimal allocation of ships to patrol areas. High-capability units go to high-threat areas, low-capability to low-threat. Each ship spends a week on patrol and two days off for upkeep. They rotate between the Gulf and the carrier battle group. Every other month, there's a two-week out-of-area liberty."

Byrne and Miller studied it. They glanced at each other, then at the operations specialist who had hovered behind her.

"It looks reasonable, sir," said the master chief. "I couldn't follow some of it, never seen it done that way before, but it sure looks reasonable. This little girl knows her sh—knows her stuff."

"Where'd you learn to do that?" said Miller.

"Operations research degree. And a few years of practice."

"It's pretty much what we came out with," said Byrne. "See, *Mobile Bay* still comes out where we are now. We didn't need a computer, just did it by professional judgment."

"Of course, and I don't know as much about weapons systems and sensors as you do. But if you introduce some simple planning tools, you'll be able to come up with different options quickly in case a ship reports equipment failure, or you have a new threat emerge.

"The point is that informed judgment will give you *a* workable solution, but proper analysis combined with it will give you the most *efficient* workable solution. You see the difference, in terms of cost and force levels?"

"Very impressive," said Miller. "Can I have a copy of this?"

"It's on your hard disk now."

She looked at Byrne, but he was still examining the printout, an equivocal expression on his tan. She noticed he still hadn't taken the sunglasses off.

Someone cleared his throat behind them. It was an enlisted man with a clipboard. Miller handed it to her after initialing it. "Here's something you might be interested in. Minesweeping plan."

"Thank you. Areas to be cleared . . . this Farsi Channel, it's up north, isn't it?"

Miller reached for a keypad; one of the middle screens changed to show the upper Gulf. "Those green circles are the minesweepers," he said, highlighting an area. "They've just sortied from alongside *Coronado*. The Channel sweep will start tomorrow morning."

She asked a few questions about the antimine patrols, about intelligence collection. It had been obvious to everyone on the Hill that the Iranian mine laying had caught the Navy flat-footed. With the Reserve callup, though, it seemed as if they had a handle on the problem. She handed the message back without further comment.

"Well, now . . . how about that coffee?"

"I'm ready. Oh, and could you direct me to a rest room?"

"Let's just go up to my cabin. You can use the head there."

She took her time, repairing the ravages of the helicopter trip. When she came out, smoothing back her hair, a servant was laying out silver beneath a painting of Farragut. The officers stood; Miller introduced his exec. Byrne pulled her chair out for her. They can be so polite, she thought. As long as you know your place.

The steward served out coffee, cream, and pastries. "Now, Captain," she began, "I'd like to talk about your perceptions of how we're doing in the Gulf. What else do you need? What shortfalls do you see?"

Basically, Miller didn't see any. He talked about the ship's capability some more, then said, "This is the first high-tempo ops the Navy's seen since Vietnam. It's a tactically demanding mission: constrained rules of engagement, very narrow waters, and a dedicated enemy with a wide spectrum of weapons, some highly sophisticated.

"I don't think anybody will deny we've had setbacks. But when we did, we studied our errors, changed our tactics, and moved forward again. We've been flexible. When the enemy introduces new tactics, we have to change our warfighting approach to respond. I think Admiral Hart has done that."

"What about the speedboats? The Boghammers. They're small, fast, and have very little radar signature. Can you even pick them up?"

"We track them every day."

"In the Clarence Strait? And out of Abu Musa? But if you're tracking them, how come they're still hitting shipping in and out of Hormuz?"

Miller frowned. "As you said, they're fast. Since we're not officially at war, we can't attack them till they demonstrate hostile intent. So they wait till we're not around, duck out, hit a tanker or two, then duck back in. Occasionally we can scramble fighters or armed choppers to intercept them, but it's difficult. If we could go in and wipe them out, the attacks would stop."

"But their bases are in Iranian territory."

"Uh-huh," said Miller. He offered her a brownie. She shook her head. "We *have* responded to the small-boat threat. We've tuned our radars for small targets and outfitted Gulf-bound units with heavy machine guns and grenade launchers. I've read the 'experts' who say we ought to have our own speedboats out here. Pardon my French, but that's a crock. You don't fight small boats with small boats unless you have a lot of people to sacrifice. The U.S. Navy doesn't operate that way. Anyway, they know we're ready, and they don't attack our warships."

"They don't attack anyone's warships. They go after commercial traffic. Insurance rates have tripled this year for Gulf-bound tankers. Did you know that?"

"It doesn't surprise me."

"I can see it doesn't impress you, either. The Navy doesn't pay insurance, does it? But what it means, Captain, is that this multibillion-dollar fleet we're maintaining here is incapable of protecting shipping. It can deter sorties by what's left of the Iranian Navy and Air Force, it can escort a few ships at a time, but it can't stop what essentially is maritime terrorism."

"Now wait a minute," said Miller, suddenly flushing. "You're holding us responsible for not doing something that we're specifically restrained from doing. Those are safe havens for the Pasdaran, and it's Congress that's holding us back from hitting them."

Blair put her cup down. "Don't pull that stab-in-the-back bullshit on me. That's getting to be the standard response when you people fail, isn't it? Congress wouldn't let you win! If you were more efficiently organized—"

"Whoa, both of you," said Byrne soothingly. "Just let's back off now, and try to look at it calmly."

"I'm calm, Mr. Byrne, very calm. I just don't like to have utter *bullshit* served up to me as an excuse."

"If I get an order to go in, I'll go in," said Miller tightly.

"In this ship? No way! Captain, we paid too damn much for it to risk this floating Pentagon in anything less than defending a carrier against a full-scale Soviet air attack."

There was a rap on the door then, and the man with the clipboard let himself in. He paused, seeing perhaps the echo of angry words in their faces. But Miller waved him in. As he read, his face darkened.

"Bad news?"

"A few minutes ago, my tactical action officer alerted the convoy to an approaching air contact."

"What happened? Did they shoot it down?"

Miller cleared his throat. "Well, no. It was identified as a civilian airliner."

"Who identified it? Could you tell what it was from here?"

"Well, I'll be perfectly honest with you. Not always. In this case, the frigate made the final call. But the important thing is, she was ready." He paused. "Also, there's been another raid. On a Greek freighter. It's on fire. One of *Van Zandt*'s helicopters, and one from a British destroyer, are taking off survivors."

She wanted to say, And what about the attackers? Did you even see them on your expensive displays?

But there was a time to go easy, let the facts speak for themselves.

She, Byrne, and the two ship's officers sat in silence after the radioman left. Finally, she said, "So you see the problem. What can we do about it?"

"An air strike?" suggested the exec.

"Ineffective," said Byrne gloomily. "With the hand-held missiles the Pasdaran have now, the pilots can't go in low. And going in high, they'd never hit Boghammers."

"Well, all I can say is, you people had better think of something."

"We've also got to worry about that damned two-oh-nine," said Miller. "When and where it'll show up—"

Byrne started. Before he could speak, Blair said, "What's that?"

"It's a submarine. It's—"

"That's classified," said Byrne.

"You said she was cleared."

"Not for that."

"Not for what?" She turned on Byrne, who was hunched guiltily over a cherry tart. "The Admiral said *everything*, Mr. Byrne. Did he not? What's this about a submarine?"

"There may not be any. It's just a rumor."

"Let's have it." She was angry now. "Let's have it all. Is this what you were whispering about in Bahrain? Do you want me to call Talmadge, tell him you're holding out on me?"

"No. But I don't want you to overreact, either."

"You let me judge what I'll do. Now tell me what a 209 is, and why you're so worried about it."

The intel officer sighed. "It's a West German-made submarine. The Shah bought two. One was delivered, just before the revolution, but it was never operational.

"Now, though, we've"—he lowered his voice till it was almost inaudible over the hum of the ventilators—"This is highly classified, Blair, because it's derived from certain listening systems that we're not, uh, really supposed to have in the Indian Ocean. Our ships' COs know, but no one else."

"You mean you've been—no, don't tell me any more." She closed her eyes. "Okay, so you've detected a submarine. Where is it?"

"We don't know. Yet. We know it was under way for a brief period, possibly for training or system tests."

"Why is one submarine such a threat? Can't you deal with it?"

"We could in the open ocean. But the Gulf's so shallow, most of our gear won't work. Nobody's gear would. It's not a case of buying the wrong stuff, sonar's just not very effective there. We're talking about a very advanced, quiet boat, specifically designed for shallow-water operations. If the Iranians start torpedoing ships, that's a different matter than some fanatics firing rocket grenades. That would stop all the traffic. It would cut off oil to Japan and Europe."

"Entirely."

"That's right."

"Can our nuclear submarines track it?"

"Again, they'd deal with it easily in open ocean, but they're too big to go into the Gulf."

"So what does Admiral Hart plan to do, Mr. Byrne?"

"We're looking for it. Recon flights, satellite photos, and electronic intercept, as well as the listening stations. Sooner or later, if it's there, we'll spot it. Once we know where it is, then we can set up an antisubmarine screen outside its harbor."

"And then what? Sink it as it comes out?"

"Well, it'd have to show hostile intent first."

"Or we could sink it by mistake," said Miller thoughtfully.

She was about to ask exactly what he meant by that when a telephone buzzed. The CO reached under the table for it, listened, then said, "Thank you, she'll be back there in ten minutes—Ms. Titus, helo control reports your transportation is inbound. Let's see, think I saw your bag last in CDC. I'll send a man for it."

They got up. She hesitated, then said, "Captain, thank you for your time. I'm sorry, but you have to ask hard questions to get useful answers."

"I understand," said Miller, but his mouth was grim as he held the door for her. "I hope you find what you're looking for. Whatever the hell it is. And then go home, and let the professionals fight the war."

She stopped, there in the doorway, with enlisted men waiting outside. After a moment, she murmured, "Excuse me?"

"You heard me. I don't pussyfoot, Ms. Titus. I say what I think, and I think you don't belong here."

"Is that so."

"Here's your bag," said Byrne, emerging from a side door. "The helo should be waiting, let's—"

"Tell them to go back to the barge," she said, holding Miller's now-startled eyes. "We won't be needing it tonight. I'm staying aboard, Captain. Find me a bed, please."

"Blair—"

"You're not staying on this ship," said Miller flatly.

The enlisted men looked at each other and melted, unobtrusively but very suddenly, from sight.

"I'm not?"

"No. It's against the law. And I don't want you."

"Give me the briefcase, Mr. Byrne. Thank you. Captain Miller, do you see this letter? This authorizes me access to all military facilities in the Persian Gulf area for purposes of investigation on behalf of the Senate Armed Services Committee. This is a military facility, is it not?"

"It's not a Goddamned facility, it's a *warship*. There's no place to put a woman. Steward! Take her bag to the flight deck."

"That's mine. I'll need it tonight. Don't put your hands on it."

The man stopped, looking first scared and then glancing, in mute helplessness, at his commanding officer.

"Uh, Blair, overnight visits are not authorized—"

"Mr. Byrne, unless you are going to help me, please keep quiet. Captain, the only way I'm going on that helicopter will be kicking and screaming, and I don't think you'd enjoy what would happen once I got ashore. I need to see Admiral Hart tomorrow. So, I'm going to stay." She decided her sweetest smile was called for. "Now is the time for you to give in gracefully. Don't you think?"

Miller stared down at her for another five seconds, his face looking like a balloon about to pop, before he wheeled suddenly on Byrne. "You're Hart's Goddamned rep. Does he expect us to run a damn hotel for visiting . . . visiting . . ." He stalled, then spat out, *"civilians?"*

"Given the situation, Lee, I don't think we have a hell of a lot of choice."

Miller wheeled and began shouting. ". . . my inport cabin," he finished. "And hang some Goddamned sign on the door so people don't walk in. Jesus Christ!"

"That's not very graceful. But it'll do." She smiled at the enlisted man. "Now you can pick it up. Thank you. Follow us, please. Captain . . . lead on."

16

U.S.S. *Turner Van Zandt*

THE late-morning sunlight poured through the tempered glass like boiling water. Hayes's feet were cramping again. The helmet chafed against his neck, he was sweating under the body armor, and heat rash itched at his crotch.

Mattocks and the other mechanics had worked all night repairing Two One's hydraulics. The plane had passed its final check just before dawn. Since then, they'd been aloft, describing slow circles fifteen miles out in front of the convoy. He hadn't had the stick one minute of that time. He was uncomfortable, hungry, bored, and sleepy.

He glanced at Schweinberg. The dark curve of the visor hid his face from sight. Not that he was exactly longing to see the full red cheeks, the flat, stupid eyes.

Buck studied the stickers plastered on his HAC's helmet. The American flag, Day-Glo on Mylar backing; a Seminoles decal; SHIT HAPPENS; another, MUSTACHE RIDES 5¢; and the squadron insignia, a curvaceous angel in high-heeled boots plunging a sword into a submarine.

His own helmet was as bare as it was issued. He didn't think stickers for the NAACP, ACLU, and the Unitarian Church would go over real good.

Virgil Hayes thought he put on a good front. Weight lifting and an occasional street joke seemed to satisfy the men he worked with. But sometimes he felt surrounded.

Not that he disliked them, or disliked the Navy. His experience was that it was about as free of prejudice as you could expect of any organization run by human beings. But he felt out of place among men who were basically conservative, whose first response to any challenge was patriotism and violence.

On the other hand, it was true that his roommate didn't seem to care about money. Buck had to admire that in him.

The question was, should he stay in, or take ATI's offer? On paper, it looked good. At the moment, he was making $2,339 a month basic, $206 flight pay, and $110 for hazardous duty. Quarters, subsistence, and housing allowance for Joyce and the kids was another $741. Total, $3,400, or about $41,000 a year. The engineering job started at $47,000. But that wasn't the whole story. There'd be no more deployments, no dets, no duty days . . . just home being Daddy and husband.

The company would need a commitment soon; they couldn't hold the position open indefinitely. And Joyce wanted an answer, too. She'd have to set things up for Jesse's kindergarten and Dustin's school, find a house, get herself a job. He had to decide soon.

Beside him, Schweinberg stared down, hardly registering the uninterrupted surface of sea as it droned beneath him. His mind was in the past. In the night after the Old Miss game. He'd had three tackles and his first interception, and after the postgame party, two blonde juniors had decided to see whether they could exhaust the human football-and-fucking machine that was Claude Schweinberg at twenty.

And still was, goddammit. His fingers stealthily explored a hardness near the cyclic.

The plane thought for him. They were on RADALT hold, automatically maintaining altitude, and the rudder pedal depressed and rose slowly under his flight boots. From time to time, without engaging much of his brain, his eyes lifted from the sea and moved across the panel.

Gradually, the hum of rotors and transmission, the steady rush and whistle of wind gentled his mind, sanded smooth the edge of his lust. His head nodded in an involuntary dovening. The sunlight fell hot in his lap and the air hissed cool through the vent. Airspeed eighty, heading 210 and coming left again. They'd been in the air for three hours, refuelled in a hover, then gone back out without so much as touching the deck. They'd have six hours off that afternoon, then fly again that night.

It was a bear of a schedule. But convoy duty was like that—grind, grind, grind. With only one plane in the det, it was just that much worse.

He caught his head sagging and snapped it back. The ICS was silent. "Kane, Christy, you guys sharp back there?" he grunted.

Their voices were muzzy. The crewmen got even less sleep than the officers during a convoy. They flew, worked on the plane, then flew again. He'd have liked to let them sack out now, but he needed their eyeballs. He glanced at his copilot, and found him staring fixedly out the chin bubble. Cool and collected. His ATO was the wrong color, but he never seemed to get rattled. Schweinberg admired that.

Hayes caught the motion and blinked, recalling himself from his career decision. From a hundred feet up, the Gulf looked rough today. Not North Atlantic rough, but rough for a narrow, shallow sea. The waves uncoiled slowly, leaving patches of ivory foam. The sun accompanied them, sparkling and glittering to the southeast. It made his eyes water. He locked the visor up and rubbed them.

"See anything?" drawled Schweinberg.

"No."

"Well, I'm about passed out. You got it. Poke me in fifteen."

"Uh-huh."

The pilot eased his harness and slumped against the door. Buck took the stick. He ran his eyes over the panel. Main transmission pressure a tad low. Fuel consumption normal. Temperatures good. No odd sounds. He flexed his fingers on the cyclic, wishing he had some coffee or cola. Coming up on next circle . . . a slight bank, say five degrees, enough to let you look down at the translucent Gulf. . . .

The idea was to scan for anything out of the ordinary. Especially small boats and mines, but anything that might be evidence of Iranian chicanery. Hayes had never been able to decide how realistic this was. A properly laid mine couldn't be seen from the air. They were moored to the bottom and floated fifteen or twenty feet down, and even if the water was clear, nobody sweeping over at eighty knots was going to see one.

Drifting mines were different. The det from *Foster* had seen one last month and set it off with machine-gun fire. That would be a diversion. Schweinberg would love the noise.

He held the orbit, thinking how boring this all was. Tired, tired . . . when they got back and he put in his letter, maybe he and Joyce would leave the boys with her mom and head someplace to be alone. That would be a good idea. Get the arguments and tears that always followed a deployment over where they wouldn't upset the kids.

He realized then that for the first time he'd said *when*, and not *if*.

The lead ship of the convoy prickled into sight to the south, a flyspeck that boiled on the boiling horizon. Two One vibrated and droned, and Buck Hayes shook himself into the waking present again, realizing with something not far from horror that he'd nodded off, too.

"ATO, ATACO."

He clicked the transmit trigger on the stick. "ATO."

"Crossing contact to north, your zero-two-zero, fifteen, request you check it out." The petty officer sounded bored, too.

"Two One, wilco."

Schweinberg shifted in his seat. He muttered, "Don't say 'wilco' until I agree. Don't you know what that means?"

Hayes said between his teeth, "It means 'I will comply.'"

"Right, but I'm the helo commander. I'm the only one who can say 'wilco.'"

Hayes didn't bother to answer. He was sorry Chunky was awake again. It had been relaxing with him asleep. Except for the snore.

"What was that bearing?"

"Zero-two-zero, fifteen."

Schweinberg stretched and belched. "Okay, gimme the airplane. Coming right. How's my fuel?"

"MAD vector," said Kane suddenly, from the back.

"What?"

"Something registered on the magnetic detector, sir. Something big down there, something metal. Can we come around, take another sweep?"

"You're talking antisubmarine, right?" drawled Schweinberg. "Forget it. There ain't none out here."

"It was something, sir. Can't we check it out? We got no sonobuoys aboard, but maybe we could localize it with a couple passes. I think—"

"For*get* it," said Schweinberg, and his voice held exasperation and finality. "Told you, *ain't* no subs out here. It's just a wreck, some old ship or drilling rig on the bottom or something. Do what I tell you and quit thinking, Kane, quit your goddamn *thinking.*"

The SH-60 droned and vibrated through a huge arc. Hayes yawned luxuriously, still looking down. The Gulf rushed past blurry-swift directly under them, slower a mile away, and the horizon not moving at all. The black shadow of the bird rushed soundlessly over the sea, flying formation on them.

"There he is. Two o'clock," said Schweinberg.

The speck ahead grew, became a boat. Characteristic banana shape. White, green, blue stripes. They flashed over it at three hundred feet, then banked back in a great loop. Hayes said, "ATACO, ATO: We have contact in sight. Identify as dhow, course one-eight-zero."

Van Zandt acknowledged. As they came around, he saw the convoy on the horizon. They looked small and lost, caught in the

joining of the two vast bowls, placed lip to lip, of sky and water.
The ship came back. "ATO, Bridge: we hold his course inter-
secting ours."

"Concur," drawled Schweinberg.

"Try to change his mind. Commodore doesn't want him passing through the formation."

"Got it."

Bank again. The sun blazed suddenly through the windscreen, blinding them, heating the exposed skin under their
visors to the point of pain. Hayes wouldn't have been surprised
if the impact of those white-hot photons slowed their airspeed.

Schweinberg told Kane to open the cabin door. He eased back
on cyclic and the airframe gave an orgasmic shudder, transitioning to hover.

Killer Two One hung above the sea, moving with the dhow,
which was chugging stolidly along perhaps two hundred feet
away. "Wave him off," shouted Schweinberg.

Hayes caught Kane's lifted arm, and past him a glimpse of
the boat. The iron pipe of its exhaust rose perfectly vertical aft,
putt-putting along. Clothing decorated the rails. A few men
stood on deck. Around them, the topsides were littered with
wire cages, fish traps, line, orange plastic floats. He remembered the yard they'd visited on a tour, the patient artisans
carving ribs and stringers out of iron-hard teak. They'd said
each dhow was guaranteed for a hundred years. It was time-
less, biblical.

But now modern times had come, and a modern war with it.
Helicopters, fighters, missiles. And in the midst of it all, pung-
punging along in their eternal courses, moved the simple fishermen of the Gulf. What did they think of this strange
desultory war?

"Sonofabitch don't want to move, sir," said the gunner.

"He'll move," said Schweinberg.

"Let's not get too close to this guy, Chunky."

"No problem." Yet the nose stayed steady just ahead of the
nodding prow. "I'll go down the starboard side this time. Wave
him off, Buck."

The second pass had no more effect than the first. The ancient
boat plugged on, dragging its slow, straight burble of wake. A
thin stream of brown smoke jetted again and again out of the
rusty stack. The men on deck watched them. One of them, a
white-bearded ancient, was waving. "What is all that shit?"
said Schweinberg.

"Laundry day, looks like."

"Uh-huh. Well, what is it with this raghead? Is he dumb or just stubborn?"

"Probably headed for home."

"Not through my convoy he ain't." Two One banked left in a hairpin turn and this time dropped suddenly. Spray leapt up, a whirling mist that cut off everything around them. The forward airspeed indicator sank to zero, and they squatted, fifty feet up, directly in front of the dhow.

Schweinberg, staring through the spray into the oncoming painted eyes of the dhow, felt a surge of anger. *Fucking ignorant turbans. Greasy half-niggers. Want to play chicken, huh?* He moved the cyclic, and Two One tilted forward.

An artificial tornado of four thousand horsepower moved with them. Clothing fluttered and then tore away, sailing off toward Iran. The Arabs grabbed for handholds. They leaned forward into the rotorblast, shaking their fists up at the gray machine that menaced them.

When 421 came around from the close pass, Schweinberg saw with astonishment that the dhow was still plowing defiantly on. His mood changed instantly from contempt to alertness. They'd been warned against high-speed boats. The idea was they could dash in and drop off a bomb, or a mine, next to the hull of one of the escorts. But there was no reason not to suspect a dhow. They were slow, but you could pack a lot of explosive in that deep hull.

He slowed to a hover again beside it, not a hundred feet off, looking it over. The old man, the one who'd been waving, was staring out at them now.

Then suddenly, as Hayes watched, he bent. Tossed back a piece of canvas. And dragged up from under it something four feet long, metallically shiny, and shouldered it.

And the gunner, aft, wrestled his mount around frantically, and Schweinberg cursed, banking left, but too slow, far too slow to do any good. And the Arab swung his burden toward them, as the gunner still struggled helplessly with the belt feed, crew and pilots all caught in the impotence of nightmare, and held it up: the glittering tuna, long as he was, slim as the barrel of a missile launcher.

Hayes screamed, "Hold fire, Christer! It's a fish!"

"God damn it, sir, I was ready to shoot him!"

"Screw this pussyfooting," Schweinberg said. "Give him a burst, Christer. Right in front of those eyes."

"A burst, sir? We ain't supposed to—"

"Just do it, and keep your lip to yourself!"

They all watched the men on deck closely as they converged again. Watched for sudden motion, or for arms. The dingy wooden boat plowed on.

"Okay, shoot."

The machine gun blatted briefly. Six cones of white spray appeared spaced across the water, twenty or thirty yards ahead of the painted eyes.

The prow, curved like a Turkish slipper, wavered, then swung to port. All the crew, now, were waving their fists, their mouths black wells of defiance and hatred.

"Death, you bastards," Schweinberg muttered. "But first—cheech."

Hayes, beside him, was getting angry. He hadn't asked the ship for authority to fire. They had no right to fire on these people! They were probably friendlies, Saudis or Bahrainis. If they reported a helo had shot at them, there'd be hell to pay. Now, irritated, he said, "God damn it, what does that mean, Schweinberg?"

"What does what mean?"

"This 'cheech' shit."

"Oh, you never heard that?" Two One banked like a roller coaster and headed back toward the distant ships. Behind them, Hayes glimpsed the dhow, foreshortened and naked-looking, hove to under a vast ocher sky as tiny figures fished for their clothing with poles. "I thought I told you . . . Kane, Christy, listen up, this's a good one.

"There's these two missionaries that get captured by savages. They're tied up and took before the chief. The chief says, 'You invaded our territory and insulted our gods, and you have two choices: death, or cheech.' He asks the first missionary, 'Which do you pick?' And the missionary thinks, and then he says, 'Well, I don't know what it is, but it can't be worse than death. I choose—cheech.'

"The chief grunts, 'Huh. Cheech. Good!' And he makes a sign. The warriors grab the first missionary, fifty or sixty of them butt-fuck him, one after the other, and they throw him into the river.

"The chief turns to the second missionary, who's watched all this, and says, 'What is your choice? Death—or cheech?'

"And the second missionary, he's a real he-man, and he thinks, Well, no way these guys are going to do that to me. And he says, real proud, 'I choose—death.' And the chief nods and says, 'Huh. Death. Good! But first—cheech!' "

The enlisted men laughed. Hayes didn't. He looked out at the blurry horizon, the half-shapes of land melting into and out of their sight.

Near noon they set back down for refuel, crew swap, and some minor maintenance. The deck gang unreeled hoses and un- latched cowlings as the crew climbed out, stretched, and stared around the rolling tennis court of hot metal. Mattocks had Frescas packed in ice for them. Schweinberg grabbed his greed- ily, sucked it down. Hayes held out for water.

Woolton and Bonner were suiting up in the hangar. The OIC looked up as they came in. "You guys look beat," he said.

"We love it, Woolie. Sure you don't want us to take your six?"

"See anything interesting out there?"

"Not a thing."

"No mines?" said Bonner.

"Four or five, but we left 'em for you, Smiley."

Woolton asked, "How's the bird? Tits up?"

"Got a fire light in the engine compartment about an hour after launch. No smoke, no power loss, and after a minute, it went out. Figure it was a sun trigger; it comes through the seam there and hits the IR detector. The troops are reconnect- ing some fasteners on the tail-rotor gearbox. Four of 'em popped off. Otherwise, she's sweet, hot, and ready to go."

"Okay, I got her."

"What's for lunch?" said Hayes.

"Donkey dicks an' fries."

"Gut bombs and grease sticks, send 'em through the garden and hold the dirt," said Schweinberg.

They ditched their helmets and vests and strolled forward. Hayes felt light without the body armor. He stamped his feet. "Them cramps still bothering you?" asked Schweinberg.

"Uh-huh."

"You want to eat you some bananas; I heard that helps."

Hayes didn't answer. He was still angry over the warning burst. In part, it was anger at himself. Strictly speaking, he should report it. But he knew he wasn't going to.

When they got to the wardroom, the ship's officers were just sitting down. He caught Lenson's eye as he found a chair, and was suddenly conscious of his wringing-wet underwear, his not often enough washed flight suit, covered with red dust, his sweaty hair, unshaven face—they'd launched at 0600 and he just hadn't bothered.

But the XO was rising, folding his napkin. "Mr. Hayes, Mr. Schweinberg. Can I see you outside?"

Schweinberg muttered under his breath as he got up. They followed the exec out into the passageway. Once the door was closed, he said, "You men just landed, is that right?"

"Yessir."

"I see. Well, I'd appreciate it if you'd take a minute to clean up before you come into the wardroom."

Schweinberg muttered something. Lenson said, "What's that?"

"Nothing, sir."

"I have something to say," said Hayes. "We missed breakfast because we launched early. We've been flying for six hours. And it seems like whenever we need a shower, it's water hours. We just aren't on the same schedule as the rest of the ship. Now you're saying we can't even eat?"

"I understand that, and I'm not hammering you," said Lenson. "The stewards will save you a sandwich if you're going to be late."

"Well, we don't know if we're going to or not, that's the point, we go where you people tell us to."

"Lieutenant Hayes." Lenson took a deep breath. "I understand all that. But I assure you, everybody on this ship works as hard as you do. All the ship's officers stand watch. They don't get eight hours of sleep a day. They don't get special trips ashore for 'charts.' But they show up for meals in clean uniforms. The rules go for everybody, black shoes or brown."

"Come on, Buck, let's get some khakis on," said Schweinberg in an undertone.

Hayes turned away abruptly. But he couldn't resist saying, still in earshot, "Come on, Chunky, to hell with this happy horsesoap. Let's eat on the mess decks with our crewmen."

And it came through his angry mind that this, too, he would be leaving behind. In private industry, there'd be none of this about the right thing to wear and the right place to eat. The Navy hadn't been bad to him. He'd miss it. But all in all, he'd be happy, becoming a civilian again. There'd be flying in the ATI job, testing the displays. And he could pick up a private pilot's license, go in with somebody on a Cessna or Piper.

"Take it easy." Schweinberg glanced at him. "What's eating you, anyway, Montana? You've had your panties in a wad ever since this cruise started."

Hayes was on the brink of telling his roommate about it. But then his lips clamped shut.

It was hard enough living with Schweinberg as it was. Till he told them he was resigning, he'd be one of the gang. Afterward, he would be something subtly else.

Like that of the Arabs, the Navy view of the world was tribal and concentric. Squadron mates came before strange fliers, brown shoes before black, and the pure and dedicated military before the corrupt and money-hungry world outside the ranks. There were strange animals out in that night—reporters, lawyers, gays, peace activists. The moment a man announced he was leaving, he went from One of Us to One of Them, with the assumption unspoken but omnipresent that he *hadn't hacked it.*

Did bailing out make him unmanly? Did it mean he'd sold out? He didn't think so. He just thought he'd make a better engineer than a pilot, that was all. And a better husband and father than he could be at sea.

Crockery and silverware crashed from the scullery. They smelled the hot breath of the mess decks, the amalgam of fried foods, cabbage, spiced meat, and disinfectant, heard the babble of talk and clatter of forks against plastic trays.

Ahead of him in line, Claude Schweinberg had forgotten the scene outside the wardroom. He was reliving again the moment when the sea turned white under his bullets. He wished the men on the dhow had resisted. His hands crimped on the tray. He imagined it the neck of a swarthy man in a burnoose.

A foot behind him in the serving line, Virgil Hayes was nodding. He felt the rightness of his decision more with every passing second.

Then, unexpectedly, a chill fell across his mind, stalling him in front of the salad bowl. He stared into it. It was something about the flight just ended . . . something they'd known, but dismissed, or not understood.

It didn't come, and after a minute or two someone behind him, a little guy with glassy eyes, jostled him. He stopped thinking about it. Filling his tray, he followed Schweinberg's thick neck out into the mass of chattering, eating men.

17

U.S.S. Turner Van Zandt

PHELAN slid his tray along, smiling with vague delight at the good things. Meat and fish, vegetables, salads, Jell-O, red and shimmering like a sunset. He had to admit that about the Navy. They fed well. When you grew up hungry you appreciated that.

He thought, You done okay with your life, Bernard Newekwe. You done damn good.

Smiling benignly on the sweating schmuck on the serving line, he loaded salisbury steak, potatoes, salmon patty, shortcake, ice cream, till the battered plastic could hold no more. There were officers in front of him, pilots, but when he wanted to move on, he jostled the black one just like he would anybody else. Hell with 'em. They weren't supposed to eat here, anyway.

He floated out into the mess decks. Satisfaction burned in him like a mesquite fire on a foggy night. A good day, today. Busy, training the damage-control parties on first aid and CPR, but good.

A little yellow pill was the key to it all. It took care of him. Whispered encouragement whenever he felt inadequate or afraid. Took away all anxiety and fear. He wished everyone could feel this peace. Then there'd be no more wars. No more gray ships carrying death. They could be ships of life, bringing medicine to people who needed it.

It was a pleasant thought and he stayed with it, nodding and smiling to himself as the other sailors pushed by him. Not warships. Peace ships. He'd treat the kids. He liked kids.

Someone jostled him and he came back to the mess decks. His eyes drifted over the throng. For a hundred men packed together, it was almost quiet. He wondered why, then remembered the damage controlmen talking about some kind of channel, some place the ship had to get through. His lips twisted. It was like on the *Long Beach*, like in the Army, too. The brass was always pumping you up for something—inspections, parades, some kind of crap. You learned quick there was no point taking it serious.

As he sauntered forward, he mused on how the crew segregated themselves. Blacks had their own tables along the port side. The first-class took the booths, to starboard. The rest sat in an elbow-to-elbow mass. It looked mixed, but it, too, was sorted by work center and division and friendship, the men who drank and pulled libs together.

Phelan saw Fitch. The senior corpsman was alone at a four-man table. He thought, I got to work for him. Why eat with the prick, too? He veered away toward another seat. The dungarees around it were paint-stained and torn, but one of the faces . . . he clattered his tray down and sat, smiling around. They looked back blankly. Yeah, he knew one guy. "How's that thumb doing?" Phelan asked him.

"Huh?"

"Dontcha remember, I took that splinter out for you, couple days ago?"

"Oh. Oh, yeah! Thanks. It's all healed up."

"That's the job, man, you come to us, we fix you up." He was glad he was a corpsman. He was glad he was HN Bernard Phelan, USN. He started eating.

One of the men was telling a story. "So he rubs the bottle, there on the beach, and a genie comes out. The genie says, 'you got one wish.' So the guy makes it, but nothing happens. The genie says, 'Hey, I'm a slow genie. It'll probably take two, three days at the most. But you'll get your wish.'

"So the guy goes home. Next morning, he gets up and looks in the mirror and there's nothing. No change. Second day, he gets up and looks in the mirror. Nothing. So he goes to bed that night real up, thinking it's got to happen tomorrow, and when he gets up, he looks in the mirror.

"Nothing! Squat! So he's starting to get mad, when there's a knock at the door. And he opens it, and there's four guys with sheets over their heads carrying ropes. And the biggest one says, 'You the guy that wanted to be hung like a nigger?' "

The table laughed. The guy next to him, a big fat third-class with BB eyes, took a minute to get it. Then he guffawed and slapped the table, grinning around. Suddenly he looked startled. "Who the fuck are you?"

"Name's Phelan. I'm a corpsman."

"The new chancre mechanic? I'm Lester Orr. From Chicago."

Phelan nodded condescendingly as Orr told him the names of the others. The men in first division were peons. Still, a man needed friends.

Orr asked where he was from. He told them about the reservation, about New Mexico. They asked him the usual questions, whether Indians had to register for the draft, if they paid taxes. After that, it petered out again, each man withdrawing into a worried silence.

He wondered whether it was this channel thing. Then he wondered if he ought to be scared. Shit, let them worry. Why should he give a fuck?

When they were getting up, Orr said. "Say, Phelan, we generally play some poker in the evenings. Up in the bo's'n's locker."

"I'm broke-dick, man."

"Well, sit in, anyway."

He said okay. He had a couple of hours till his watch started in sick bay. When he shoved his tray through the scullery window, a dragon's breath of hot steam struck his face. Framed by it was the crowded hell of garbage and dirty trays and beyond that the cooks, stripped to soaked T-shirts and rushing about, shouting, scrubbing furiously at huge stainless pots.

He smiled sadly. Some people, that was all they were smart enough to do.

Orr hung back as they passed sick bay. "You know, I been trying to get some help from your first-class," he said.

"Fitch ain't much help to anybody."

"See, couple days ago I strained my back. I could feel it go. I was on the outhaul. It was just like a string snapped. Back here, around the shoulder blades, y'see? He give me some pills. Said it'd go away, but I can't hardly sleep."

"What'd he give you?"

"I don't know. White pills with squared-off edges. Whatever it is, it ain't for shit."

"Fitch don't care if a guy's hurting," said Phelan. The ship's store was open and he stopped for a minute for cigarettes. His last dollar disappeared across the counter. He lowered his voice. "It wasn't like that on *Long Beach.* Tell you what, come by tonight, I'll give you something that'll work."

The BM gaped at him. "Can you give them things out?"

"Sure. Tell the other guys, too. You deck apes work harder'n anybody. I'll take care of you. Just tell them, come by when I'm on duty."

Orr slapped his back, his squint brightening. "That's great.

That'd really help. Tell you what, just for that, I'll stake you tonight. Ten bucks?"

"Can you make it twenty?"

"Well, okay. Twenty. I really appreciate this."

"Shipmates got to help each other," Phelan said smiling.

"Letter for you," said Golden that night, as he let himself into sick bay. In the corner, the CPR dummy lay on its back, its mouth gaping at the overhead. Sometimes it looked foolish, sometimes ominous, sometimes flirtatious. Which it was depended on where his head was at, and also how horny he was. It was pretty in a way, and it had small breasts. Unfortunately, it ended at the waist.

Phelan caught a glimpse of himself in the mirror over the sink. His smile matched the plastic one. He'd won sixty bucks, a *New Jersey* Zippo, and a folding Buck knife with a leather case playing three-card burn. But he didn't like the way the dummy looked at him, wise, like it knew something about him the others didn't. He dropped his ball cap over its face.

"You hear me?"

"What?"

"Letter?" Golden held it up.

"Where'd that come from?"

"Didn't you say you were from Mexico?"

"New Mexico. I mean, how'd it get here?"

"I don't know. Don't you ever get mail?"

Phelan gave up. Golden answered everything with another question. He snatched it out of the seaman's hand and said, "Okay, I got it, get out of here, man." When Golden was gone, he sat down, looking at the return address. He shook out a butt, remembered where he was, and put it back.

The letter was from Denise. He looked at the postmark: a month ago. Not too bad considering it'd gone halfway around the world, then followed him from the Bitch to wherever the fuck they were now. He smiled, tore it open, and leaned back.

Dear Bernard,

I hope you are well and not drinking too much. You know I worried about your drinking. Anyway this is to let you know I'm marrying Paul Edaakie. He's been real good to us while you been gone. Like I said we have been having trouble. The welfare lady said we couldn't get anymore ADC because you were in the navy. We lost the trailer. I told the man about you were going to send the money but he said he couldn't wait. I couldn't work

anymore at the gas station because Little Coyote kept getting
sick.

Anyway Paul has been being real good to us. He has two kids
and they need a mother. I don't love him but I think this is best.
If you come back I don't think you ought to come by the house.
Paul is on the Council and they don't want you to come back. It
was alot of fun, I'll always remember, but that is Paul now and
I got to go.

Sincerely,
Denise

Phelan took the pack out again and slowly flamed the end of a
cigarette. He sucked smoke up his nose and breathed it out
again. For a minute, he thought somebody was playing a joke
on him. But it was on lined school paper like she always used.
It was her handwriting.

Oh, God damn it. He'd told her he'd take care of her and the
kid! Hell, that was why he'd joined up again! He *had* sent her
money. Last paycheck—no, he'd used the last one for the brick.
The one before that. He remembered getting the money order
at the post office. The base post office. In Coronado.

But then that would have been before they deployed. He'd
sent some after that, he'd—no, couldn't remember.

He covered his face with his hands, realizing suddenly it must
be three months since he'd sent her anything.

He sat there for a long time, anger and betrayal giving way
to shame and then despair. He deserved to lose her. He was
worthless, no good, just like her mom had said. He knew where
the money had gone: to get high and to get his friends high.

He found that he was crying. As the tears burned his cheeks,
he felt justified somehow. If only she could see him crying. Then
she'd realize what she'd done to him.

He remembered the place they used to go. Not a camp, just
a back road above Nutria Lake where you could park and then
scramble up a path through the dry dust, the juniper and scrub.
Till under the bluff you found a crumbling wall, and stone
circles on the ground, half filled in, like huge wells. Great Kivas,
they called it. There were sheltered places under the cliff paintings where you could spread a sleeping bag. He and Denise
would spend all weekend there, skinny-swimming, listening to
Rod Stewart and Robin Trower, and drinking take-out Bud-
weiser in quart bottles from Witch Wells under the ancient
spirals, lizards, man shapes, and crosses of the Anasazi. And

when your head was right, you suddenly understood they were telling you the secrets of life and death.

She'd told him one night when they were both high, he remembered it so clear. They'd built a roaring volcano of a fire out of piñon and old tires—so hot you couldn't get within twenty feet of it—and made love naked under the stars, half in and half out of the Zuni River. And she told him she'd always love him and that was one thing that would never change.

I don't understand, he whimpered in his mind. What's happening to me? Doesn't anybody care?

A few minutes later, there was a tapping from out in the passageway. He hesitated, wiped his nose with the back of his hand, then muttered "Shit," and got up. He wiped his eyes with a tissue, slammed it into the trash, and unlocked the door.

It was Orr, with another of the deck apes. "Think you can give me them pills now?" the big man muttered.

Phelan got the medication log out, and the prescription blanks. He spun the dial open and unlocked the safe. Then remembered and said, "You said you was having trouble sleeping, too, didn't you?"

"Hell, yeah, that compartment's real hard to sleep in."

He got out Tylenol with codeine and Valium. He wrote *50 CAPS* in the log and counted out thirty to Orr. The other guy hung back. Phelan asked him what his problem was. He had a bad cough, he said. Phelan looked at his eyes. He pulled out two half-pint bottles of Bayitussin with codeine and asked him to stay for a minute.

When Orr was gone, Bernard said, "You got anything to smoke?"

The guy looked at the cough syrup. Finally he said, not very willingly, "Couple ounces. But I ain't been smoking. Why?"

Phelan wished again he'd been able to buy more opium. The demand was here. Submerged, but here. Once he had something to deal with, he'd be in fat city. The tests were no problem. If one of his friends was on the list, well, he'd take care of it, that was all. Sure enough, the next sentence out of the guy's mouth was "Have *you* got anything?"

"Well, cough syrup for now, and the kind of stuff I gave Les." He remembered the safe. And the emergency kits in the life rafts. But he needed to take it slow, feel his way. "I might have some better stuff later, though. Some real righteous shit."

"Will this show up on the test?"

"Don't worry about it. You're on the sick list now, you rate taking it."

"Thanks," said the guy. He lowered his voice. "How much I owe you?"

"Forget it. This one's on the Navy. Say, what's your name?"

"Danny. Danny Quint."

"Glad to meet you, Danny."

At last, he had a friend. Phelan slid open a drawer and held up two little plastic dose cups. He set them on the bunk by the bottles and told Danny to pour.

The codeine-laced alcohol went down in a gulp, smooth, cherry-flavored, like a liqueur. His belly warmed and in minutes his earlobes went numb. He could feel it taking charge, taking care of his guilts and fears. It dissolved the bad news. It dissolved the feeling that Bernard Newekwe was worthless, not an Indian, not a white man, a liar, and . . . and whatever, he forgot now. In a few minutes, he'd feel fine. Smarter than the rest, wise, powerful, and generous. He popped one of the Valiums and after a moment offered one to Danny.

So she's gone, he thought. The pain, so keen at first, was already hard to feel through the beginning glow, the moment when it took hold and you knew you were going to feel good.

So? whispered the drug.

Really thought she loved me. Thought I was happy there.

I'll give you more. I'll give you all you want. San Diego, Subic, Honolulu, wherever you go. You got the stuff to deal, there'll be a sixteen-year-old nibbling your nuts every night.

If she'd really of loved me she'd of waited. I would of married her, like I said.

It was her missed out, Bernard. Edaakie, that fat old shit, he'll never make her happy like you did.

But it's better this way.

That's right. Get her off your hands.

My pay'll be my own again.

Life's good, Bernard. And it'll be better. Just stay with me.

Phelan poured another. He raised it to Danny, whose face was multiplying itself. Then he stopped, his hand trembling in midair.

The dummy was watching him. The cap had fallen off, revealing its face. Its smile was evil and knowing, the leer of a *kachina* doll with the eyes of a wolf.

Bernard Newekwe jerked his eyes away. He chuckled uneasily. Took a sip. Then laughed again, louder. When he looked back, it was a dummy again, lifeless and sprawling.

"Danny," he said, "Who else do you know who wants to get high?"

18

U.S.S. *Audacity*, Hawalli, Kuwait

Dear Ola,

I sent you a telegram and wrote from Spain, but I haven't gotten anything from you yet. Are you writing? I need to know how Mike is taking things. Is he helping out with the herd?

I mailed my first paycheck from Rota and you should have it by now. I'm holding out $75 a month. Everything else is going to you direct deposit. So you should be getting around three thousand a month. Hire a hand if you need help.

In case my letters aren't getting through, either, it took us a month to cross the Atlantic. We had a bad time with storms. It was smoother in the Med. We went through the Suez Canal and stopped at Jidda. They make a goat's milk cheese there that gives you the runs for a week. Then another long transit through the Arabian Sea and up into the Gulf.

We're anchored off Kuwait right now, finishing repairs and getting ready for our first sweep. It's hot, over 110 every day. We can hear artillery sometimes from where the Iraqis and Iranians are fighting. There are French, Italian, and Dutch minesweepers here, too. I had dinner on a French ship yesterday and it was much better than we get. If you make something that will keep in the heat, send it.

Hope you're getting a little time for your pottery by now.

Please keep writing. I'll probably get all your letters in a batch. There's no phone service from the nest, but I'll call as soon as I can, probably when we put into Bahrain.

Love,
John.

Gordon sucked his ballpoint. Then he scratched the back of his neck with it, staring out the porthole in the chief's mess. Finally he added:

PS: I miss you and Mike. Be sure and tell him that.

"Now all concerned personnel report on board *Coronado* for presweep briefing."

Gordon sighed, sealed the letter, and gave himself a once-over in the mirror. Khakis, decorations, insignia, shined combat boots. He smelled mildew and realized it was his shirt.

"Give 'em hell, Senior," said the chief boatswain. He nodded grimly, centered his pisscutter, and headed up the ladder.

Audacity was moored in a nest with U.S.S. *Coronado*, AGF-11, and her sister sweeps. A Dutch minesweeper was made up on the far side. The rafted ships rode to anchor two miles off the city in a sea that burned like a million Fourth of July sparklers. The air smelled of the oil that thousands of men were dying for a few miles north of them. Sweat prickled at his shoulder blades as he fell in behind Hunnicutt and Kearn. The captain nodded coldly; the sweep officer ignored him.

The Middle East Force flagship, painted white to lessen the air-conditioning load, loomed over them like a cliff of ice. They crossed *Resolute*'s fantail and clambered up a zigzag boarding ladder to an entry port. Up close, the white was chalky, streaked with running rust.

The command ship's passageways seemed enormous and very clean after two months on "Rowdy Owdy." Gordon made a detour to the post office, then rejoined the officers outside a briefing room. There was a scuttlebutt there with all the cold water you could drink. He joined the line of sweep sailors that immediately formed.

The door opened at 0850 and they found seats. A master chief called "attention on deck" sharp at 0900. Gordon rose with the rest. He wasn't surprised when an admiral entered. But he took another look at the unfamiliar uniforms that followed him in.

Coronado's CO, a four-striper with five rows of ribbons, tapped the mike at the podium and gave "seats." Gordon settled back to listen.

Operation "Pandora," the large-scale sweep to begin the next day, would be a thorough resanitization of the tanker lanes between Bahrain and Kuwait. COMIDEASTFOR had ordered it in response to reports of unidentified coasters lingering in the vicinity.

"First slide, please," said the captain.

The operating area had been divided into national areas of responsibility, from the French in the Kuwaiti approaches to the Dutch off Qatar. The Americans, Saudis, and British had drawn areas in between. A chief moved through the room, passing out copies of the operation order. The U.S. assignment was the Farsi Channel.

The slide changed. Helicopters from *Iwo Jima* were sledding the area today for influence mines. The minesweepers would follow, their on-board EOD teams dealing with any older-style mines.

Hunnicutt leaned across and whispered, "You getting all this, Gordon?"

"Yessir."

The captain asked for questions. Gordon raised his hand. "Senior Chief Gordon, EOD off *Audacity*. Does anybody have any idea what type of devices we'll be looking for?"

"The Iranians have a large and varied inventory. They've got U.S. types, contact and influence, moored and bottom-laid. We've also encountered Russian, Chinese, and North Korean mines."

"Yessir, but is there any indication—"

"No. I'm sorry, Chief, but we have no intelligence on the specific models we will be facing."

"Thank you, sir." He sat down, feeling Kearn's eyes sharp on him.

One of the Dutch officers asked about helicopter support; the captain repeated what he'd said about the H-53s. There seemed to be no more questions. The room stirred then as Admiral Hart was introduced. Gordon sat up. It was always nice to see the man you worked for, and hear from the horse's mouth just what he expected you to do.

"Thank you, Captain, gentlemen," he began. "I just wanted to add a few words, first of all welcoming our new team members, *Audacity*, *Illusive*, and *Resolute*, fresh from the States. I'm relieved to have you here. You effectively double my afloat assets.

"Now, a few words about 'Pandora.' There are those—I talked to one a few days ago, a congressional analyst—who probably understand the big picture, what the U.S. and our allies are attempting to achieve in the Gulf, better than I do. But we all know we have to keep those convoys coming.

"It's been said that mines are the weapons of the weaker power. I think that's true, if only because you don't want to foul up the sea if you expect to control it. The Iranians consider themselves at war with us. We don't, and that makes things difficult. We can't board their ships and search unless we actually catch them dropping large black things in the water.

"However. We still have to fulfill our commitment to protect the shipping of the neutral states, and the interests of our allies elsewhere who depend on oil from the region. Pandora will ensure this freedom of the seas."

Hart looked at the overhead for a moment. "There's a possibility we may not find any mines. In that case, we simply go back into port and keep an eye on the area. If we do find them, though, I don't intend to stop at just clearing them. That's a losing game. At some point, we'll miss one, or they'll sneak them in between sweeps. If you find mines, and we can trace them to Iran, I'll ask Washington for permission to take appropriate retaliatory action."

Hart paused. The four-striper murmured something. He nodded curtly, then went on. "This is an international operation, and we're indebted to the other navies and patrol forces involved. I want to thank Captains Fittipaldi, Grubb, Obenauf, and Beuningen, as well as our Kuwaiti and Bahraini liaisons, Lieutenants Jafurah and Quisaba. We aren't officially recognized as a multinational peacekeeping force. But I think we'll rate that honor when this war's over and they start writing books about it.

"So, thank you, and let's carry on as we've begun."

The master chief called "attention" once more. They stood in silence till Hart left, then were dismissed. Gordon saw another man he'd trained with at Fort Story and talked to him for a while. They decided to raid the ship's store, and stocked up on candy, fresh film, and underwear, all items in short supply on the sweeps. He went through his billfold on the way back. He had fifty dollars to last the rest of the month.

It didn't matter. It sounded like it was time to go to war.

The sweeps got under way at noon—it was a simple matter of taking in their nesting lines and putting the engines ahead— and proceeded in line ahead down the Gulf, following *Resolute*, the senior skipper. It was well over a hundred miles to their assigned area and they plugged along at low speed, zigzagging occasionally to avoid oil fields as the afternoon waned into dusk.

The next morning, Gordon lay on the fantail with the other EOD men, watching the sun come up as the sweeps maneuvered into a line of bearing across an unmarked scarlet-shimmering expanse. The rumble of diesels was reassuring under him. It was nice to be under way on their own power. The MSOs were spaced a mile apart, and he could see the other teams waiting, too.

As the morning wore on, they moved steadily ahead, like combines, he thought, each harvesting its own strip of a vast gently undulating field. Occasionally, one or the other would heave to, and a signal would flutter up its halyards and then hang limp, barely stirring; he wondered how the signalmen could read them. There was not a breath of wind. The air felt ominous and dense, like some intermediate medium between atmosphere and water. The divers lay silent in the inflated rafts; it was too hot to talk.

Finally he felt the need for a change. He got up, stretched, and wandered up to combat.

CIC was snug and dark, a grottolike retreat, and the coolest place on the ship. He stood for a while behind the petty officer on the SQQ-14. Though they still carried cutter cables and paravanes, sweepers didn't use them much anymore. With the "Squeaky Fourteen," a sensitive short-range sonar, they could see in front of them, see the ground below. "How's bottom, there, Hicks?" he asked at last.

The sonarman half-turned, then faced the screen again. "Hey, Senior. It's smooth at ninety feet. Looks like sand."

Beside the console was a lat-long gridded bottom chart, computer-generated, with every oil drum and discarded pipe and sunken dhow marked as a chatter of black dots. It was dated the year before. Anything new since then would be regarded with suspicion. The sonarman turned a dial and a shimmering wedge of amber searched out. There was another, fainter shimmer off to starboard, the sonar of the other sweeps.

"Don't be afraid to call me. If there's anything questionable. We'll be glad to check it out."

The sonarman nodded. Gordon stood there for a few more minutes, till he felt chilled. His trunks and T-shirt were soaked and the air conditioning turned them into liquid ice. He considered going up to the bridge, then decided against it. He went back to the stern instead, stopping on the mess decks on the way for a jug of bug juice and some Styrofoam cups.

The other divers were glad to see it. He shared out the pink fluid, then settled back beside Everett. The banker had been quiet all morning, jotting from time to time in a daybook.

He muttered, "Lem, how's Rosemary takin' this, your being gone?"

The banker pursed his lips, glanced away, just as he had when Gordon discussed his mortgage with him. "All right."

"You getting letters?"

"Yup."

"Regular?"

"Yup." He put the notebook away and looked at Gordon. "Ola hasn't been writing?"

"No."

"Uh-huh."

They sat silent together for a while longer, then Gordon tried again. "We haven't been married all that long."

"How long?"

"Three years."

"That's long enough."

"What do you mean?"

"I mean, that's long enough," said Everett. "I been married twenty-three, and that's too long. Three sounds about right. You ain't worried about her, are you, John?"

"Not exactly."

"Ola's a steady girl. She appreciates you. She put up with a lot from that bum she was married to before."

There was nothing much more to say after that. So Terger brought out cards, and they played cribbage until it was time for lunch.

At two-thirty, the beat of the diesels suddenly ceased. A signal licked up the mast as *Audacity* coasted forward, her stern skating around to the east. The phone talker, comatose since he came on watch, sat up from his slump against the bulkhead. He said, "Fantail, aye," and his eyes met Gordon's. "EOD team, man up!"

- Kearn came aft along the port side. His cheroot probed the air like an insect's antennae. "On deck, look alive!" he shouted. "Time to earn that hazardous-duty pay."

"Espèce d'enfoire ... Let's take that bastard down with us," muttered Maudit. "With halothane in his tanks—"

"Pipe down, Tony. Lem, hand our gear down once we're in the water. Lieutenant, hold this."

Kearn took the sea painter reflexively, then looked even more sour as he realized he'd just been pressed into duty as boat tender. Burgee, Terger, and Maudit seized the body of the raft. Gordon took the bow.

The thirteen-foot Z-bird scraped over the side and hit with a hollow splash. *Audacity* still had way on, and Kearn almost went in after it when its drag came on the line. He cursed them all and took a turn around the life rail. No one answered or even looked at him.

"In we go." They scrambled over in tennis shoes and swim trunks. Gordon held the walkie-talkie high. The boat rocked dangerously till he sat down. Everett began lowering gear from the deck. Evinrude and gas tank. Wet suits, three Mark 16 UBAs, fins, and masks. Net bags with tools, time fuzes, and smaller gear.

Last came the tricky stuff: two twenty-pound haversacks of C-4, already made up with det cord. Gordon stowed these carefully under the overhang at the front of the raft. It was supposed to be stable to shock and heat, but it wasn't good practice to take chances. Not till you had to.

Lem squatted on the sheer strake, then jumped down. Gordon nodded to the lieutenant to cast off as Burgee yanked the starter. The motor caught at the first pull and they curved off to port, bobbing as the wake caught up to them.

He turned on the walkie-talkie, holding the stub antenna vertical. "Hicks, this is Chief Gordon."

"Hello, Senior."

"What have we got?"

"A nice solid return. Survey shows nothing at that position. It's out along two-two-zero from us, about four hundred yards."

"Do you hold us on the fourteen?"

"Not yet. Have you got the marker over?"

Gordon looked aft. Terger was just lowering it. The metal reflector, diamond-shaped to show up clearly to sonar, went down on twenty feet of bright yellow polyethylene. "It's going in now."

Apparently an officer, Kearn or Hunnicutt, had come in; the scope operator's tone went suddenly formal. "*Audacity* One, this is *Audacity*, I hold you now. Proceed on two-two . . . correction, two-one-zero till I tell you to stop."

Gordon rogered and repeated the course to Burgee. The boat lifted her nose and began porpoising through the swell. Spray arched up and blew over them. He tasted for the first time the bitterness of the Gulf.

Back at the sonar, safely out of range of danger, Hicks would be watching the two pings—the possible mine, and the smaller return of the nonmagnetic marker on the raft—converging. The gray hull of the sweep shrank steadily.

"*Audacity* One: Slow down. I see you twenty yards right of track."

"Slowing, coming left to two-oh-five magnetic."

Burgee had already reduced speed; Gordon motioned to cut it even more. Slow and quiet, that was how you approached a possible mine. All their gear was designed for low magnetic signature, but it still had some, and a gradual approach reduced their impression on any sensors. The Evinrude was barely audible now, and with its above-water exhaust, they'd be putting even less noise into the sea. A few minutes later, the radio said, *"Audacity* One . . . stop."

The purr eased to an idle. They lost way at once and began to bob, jostling men and gear about on the floorboards. "Where do you hold us now?" Gordon asked the radio.

"Wait a minute . . . okay, got you. A little ahead." The sonarman jockeyed them about for a few more minutes, then abruptly told them to drop. Gordon nodded and Terger popped a buoy. He lowered the little mushroom anchor cautiously. A moment later, the red buoy, still inflating, bobbed up hissing on a wave.

"Let's get moving," Gordon said.

Not knowing what kind of mines they'd be facing, he'd decided to use the Mark 16s. This was a low-magnetic-signature rig compared to standard gear, and since it was semiclosed, recycling used air instead of releasing it to the sea, it was quieter, too. This might be important. There were mines that could listen, feel, sense metal near them, count, do everything but smell.

The others helped them into the UBAs. The oxygen tank, CO_2 scrubber, and breathing bag were housed in smooth plastic on the diver's back. Breathing was through twin hoses, like the old "Sea Hunt" scubas. Gordon finished adjusting his straps. He set the handwheel and turned the flow valve, tucking the mouthpiece between his teeth and lips. He took five slow breaths, sucking it in deep. Some said they couldn't tell any difference, but to him the helium-oxygen mixture felt cold and thick and tasted steely. He finished the last breath, pinched off the tube, tongued out the mouthpiece. "How do I sound?" he asked Burgee.

"Donald Duck himself."

He nodded. Helium gave your voice that quack. He stared over the side, his fingers moving over his gear. He clipped the electronic oxygen readout onto the side of his mask, sprayed the faceplate with defogger, and put it on.

The red buoy waited a few feet away, tossing nervously at the entrance to the deep.

"Tony, you ready to go?"

"Helium check."

"You sound like a real Frenchman, talking through his nose."

"Ça pue le fauve, les français."

He raised the walkie-talkie again, told the ship they were going in, and handed it to Everett. He looked around one last time. The sky was so bright.

He picked up the net bag and thrust his legs over the side. Without a ripple, he merged feetfirst with the sea.

The water was warm as urine and faintly tinged the same color. Still, visibility was good; he could see the buoy line thirty feet away. He twisted in a slow circle beneath the raft, checking for snakes. But there was nothing in the water with him but a slow mist of plankton. There was a distant eerie crackle, shrimp or some other bottom dweller. The sea was never silent. It always reminded him how transient their presence in it was.

Maudit appeared feetfirst, the usual conservative EOD water entry. He oriented and did a three-sixty search, too. Gordon grinned around his mouthpiece, then stopped. It wouldn't hurt to keep an eye over their shoulders. The list of nasties here was longer than in Lake Champlain. Sea snakes, scorpion fish, sharks, sea wasps so poisonous they could paralyze a man.

He'd seen a buddy die off Kwajalein from carelessness. They'd stopped to refuel on their way to Vietnam, and decided to go for a dip beside the runway. The man had reached for a pretty shell on the bottom. It had stung him. He'd lived for about half an hour, smoking a cigarette at first, then going slowly rigid till he could no longer breathe or blink or even beat his heart.

Above them, the prop began to sing, then faded slowly into the distance. Gordon located the buoy line, yellow against sepia, ducked his head, and began swimming down it.

There didn't seem to be a current. He cleared his ears twice as he dropped. The air hissed past his teeth and chilled his tongue. Something jangled in his tool bag and he shifted it around till it stopped.

He waved Maudit a hold-up signal at thirty feet. If it was a moored mine, it shouldn't be much deeper than this. He pulled out his buddy line, clipped a second one to that, and snapped the pair to the buoy line.

They swam in a twenty-foot circle without seeing anything. Maudit added his line and they made another, much wider circle. But still they found only the sea, darker, still seething with the fine soup of near-microscopic organisms. He wondered what they ate. Then he wondered what ate them. Probably the shrimp. Their clicking was louder now. He examined the darkness below, a drab, ominous green-brown.

He looked at the compass again. Their target, the metal thing that hadn't been here a year before, couldn't be far away. Maybe it was deeper. Maybe he was swimming just past it. Maybe it was off to the side.

At that moment, Gordon sensed something ahead of him.

He reached out to snag Maudit by the backpack. They hovered, and then, together, moved forward, very slowly indeed.

Through the seething murk something took shape, a presence darker than the surrounding sea. A shadow, looming up from the deep. A roundness, with points crowning its smooth curvature.

He knew what it was before there was time to think. He'd seen them the first time he'd gone through Mine Warfare School, twenty years before. He'd flash-carded this patient silhouette a thousand times.

A KMB-9. Old, but deadly still. It hung motionless in the gloom, a black sphere a meter across. Five hundred pounds of cast explosive, enough to snap the keel of anything up to a battleship.

He glanced at his depth gauge. Set at thirty-five feet, just right for a fully loaded tanker. A cable led down into the gloom, into the mad, shrill chorus of clicking and whistling, as if a million devils waited down there for him.

He signaled to his partner and approached the mine, sculling with his arms at a creeping pace. Foot by foot, it grew more distinct. Corrosion and slime coated the black body. He let himself rise a little and examined the horns. This was a contact mine. When they were pressed in, struck by a passing ship or tossed back into the hull as the bow wave passed, they shattered a glass capsule of acid, sending a current to the detonator.

It hung patiently in the gloom, silent, obsolete, simple, and deadly.

Okay, to deal with it. A contact mine could be rendered safe, but there was no point in disarming this one. They'd explode it in place. First, though, he had to make sure of one thing. He valved off a little air and sank, swam beneath it, past the cable, and came up the other side.

He circled it very slowly with his mask two feet away. He was looking not only for identification but for signs of tampering, new bolts or attachments.

Gordon couldn't help thinking just then of a pineapple mine, years before.

There was a scratch in the paint of the bottom hemisphere.

A few barnacles had already attached themselves to the shiny metal. He decided it was accidental, dinged when unknown hands had shoved it off the stern of a dhow or coaster.

He realized then he'd been holding his breath. He inhaled and exhaled several times, flushing his lungs, and checked the oxygen readout. It glowed a reassuring green.

Okay? Maudit, holding up the copacetic sign, with his eyebrows raised behind tempered glass.

Okay. He backed off, fumbled in his bag, came up with a yellow Nikonos.

When he was done taking pictures, he motioned the other man forward and took the haversack from him. He pulled a bungee cord from his belt. This would be the dangerous part. And thinking this, he signaled clumsily in alphabet code: *Tell them mine.* And he pointed up.

His partner nodded and began finning sunward. When he was out of sight, Gordon took several slow breaths, flushing his lungs again.

When he felt better, he slung the haversack over his shoulder and took the bungee in both hands. Moving very slowly, like a man trying to rope a squirrel, he edged up on the sphere from below. It was supposed to take a hefty impact to crush the ampuls, but the wires leading into them could corrode. Then a bump would set them off. After all, these things were fifty, sixty years old, some of them. He hoped they weren't too fragile. He was going to bump it around some. Right now.

His hands brushed it. The first time he'd actually touched it. The metal was cold and rough.

Gordon attached one of the bungee hooks to one of the grommets in the haversack, then held the charge in his left hand while he reached around the mine with his right. He pulled the elastic taut and made the other hook fast on the far side. Then, holding the haversack against it, he reached round the mine, keeping the bungee taut, and hooked it up over a padeye.

He let go and backed away. He began breathing again, then noticed that his oxygen light was blinking. Time to valve off. He retreated to twelve feet just for good practice, purged bubbles into the sea, and waited till the light glowed solid again. Then, hand extended for the dangling sling of the haversack, he went in again.

Maudit reappeared above, dropping toward him out of the light like a descending angel. The far-above sun sprayed topaz rays from his black silhouette. Gordon hesitated for a long moment with the strap, then dropped its loop over a horn. He

was careful not to touch the prong itself. It settled into place
and he backed off again.

It looked good. The bungee held the olive-drab pack against
the curved black belly, about where Australia would be on a
globe. Then he recalled he hadn't gotten the det cord. Stupid.
He unbuttoned the haversack and pulled out the coil of explosive cord. Maudit came around the mine—he'd been checking
the placement—and Gordon handed it to him.

There. He backpedaled another three feet and breathed
again, surveying his work one last time. The mine spun on its
cable, disturbed, but already damping out as the horns swayed
leisurely through the water. He glanced at Maudit; the other
diver's eye closed in a wink behind the mask.

Gordon gave him a thumbs-up.

The pale thread spun out behind them as they ascended.
When they broke surface, he thrust back his mask, blinking as
salt water splashed into his eyes. Then he kicked himself high,
craning around for the boat. He caught it four or five hundred
yards off. A faint shout came across the water. He raised his
arm and signaled them in.

"What was it?" Everett asked as he pulled them in.

"KMB-9. Russian. Got the popper set?"

"Almost ready." Burgee lifted the plastic float to show him,
then resumed work. Maudit handed him the bitter end of the det
cord. He carefully divided it and attached the blasting cap and
time fuze. He held it up and looked at Gordon, who nodded.

"Want to pull it?"

"Live dangerous, Clint."

The electrician grinned. There was a double crack, a puff of
white smoke, and the fuzes began hissing. He pitched the float
over the side. "Fire in the hole!"

The ship grew much more slowly, it seemed to him, than it
had receded. Burgee had the engine all out and they skipped
over the waves. Finally, they reached the minesweeper. They
tossed gear up to the deck, scrambled up, catching splinters on
the wooden hull, and hauled the raft up after them as the MSO
gathered way. The Z-bird seemed a hell of a lot lighter now.
Adrenaline, Gordon thought.

"Time yet, John?"

He checked his watch. "About a minute more."

There was a familiar, sour voice above him. He looked up to
see Kearn leaning on the rail on the next deck, looking down
at them. "Back already?" he sneered. "I heard there was a
mine. But I didn't hear no bang."

For answer, Gordon straightened. The sweep second on his watch pressed on, on, and came up on the mark he'd set when Burgee popped the primer.

"Right . . . about . . . now," he breathed.

A mile behind them a water plume suddenly appeared. The deck under them jumped, then shuddered as the energy of the explosion bounced from surface to bottom and back again. The thunder arrived a few seconds later, a rumble like a falling mountain. All this time, the white pyramid had been rising, incredibly slowly, till it towered now into the smoky sky.

They all stared at it, their mouths open. The thunder rolled past them, and the pyramid began slowly to unbuild itself, collapsing back into a welter of foam and tossing sea.

"Imagine what that would do to a ship," he heard Maudit say. And Lem Everett, almost under his breath: "It's beautiful. Like an iceberg, or a mountain, seen at a million years a second."

The last rumble of its collapse shuddered away past them, out over the calm sea, out to the four corners of the earth, out to where, as they ran their eyes tentatively around the once more flat and lusterless horizon, something enormous and dark stained the air, black as a thunderhead, in the first beginnings of a hot and hissing wind.

19

U.S.S. *Turner Van Zandt*

THE little night-light burned dim as an icon candle over the bogen. If he looked hard, he could make out the outline of a door beside it, limned in the deep red radiance from the corridor. Aside from that, it was dark around him—dark, but not silent.

Dan lay awake, listening to the ship.

Here in the upper Gulf, the seas were choppy, piled low and quick in the short fetch by the northwest *shamal*. It had started late yesterday, darkening the sky. He could hear the scratch of sand-laden wind on the outer hull, next to his ear. Like a beast with a million claws, scrabbling to get in.

But louder than that was the ship. The vast gray life-support system that enclosed, protected, informed, and nourished him and two hundred others. His ear drifted from the hiss of cooled air to the creak of flexing steel to the murmur of distant voices in CIC. Teletypes rattled faintly down the passageway in Radio, a sporadic punctuation to the steady throb of pumps, the tremolo of turbines, the endless double jingle of the fathometer.

When he'd finally snapped off his bunk lamp, at 0230, his body had craved nothing more than sleep. Not sex, not food, just nirvanic unconsciousness. For three days, since Point Orange, he and Shaker had alternated port and starboard on the bridge and CIC. Six hours on, six off, and the time off consumed in navigation, inspections, underway routine.

Like most Navymen, he'd learned to cope with at-sea schedules. He'd gone three, four, even five days without sleep. The body adapted. But with age it became more difficult. He was only thirty-five, but he had more sympathy now for the older men he'd served under. Now he knew what a toll it took, just staying awake.

At last, out on his feet, he'd told Guerra he'd go over the

maintenance package later. Minutes later he'd been fathoms past the level of dream. Then, some indeterminable time later, something had jerked him upward again.

Now his mind ran on and on and would not stop. He tried the little drill he used instead of counting sheep: tracing systems. Reviewing in his head the recirculating duct work on the 02 level, or tracing chill water lines through compartments and pumps and valves. Then he'd throw in various leaks or battle damage, and try to figure out the best places for cutouts and repairs.

This time, it didn't work. So finally, he just fixed his eyes on the night-light and let go. Released his mind, dropped its string and watched to see where it went.

It moved in zigzags at first. To the last time he saw Nan. She was thirteen now, willowy and snide. They'd played tennis at her stepfather's club. She'd whomped him. Tall like me, he thought. But the golden skin, the glossy dark hair, those were Susan's.

It surprised him sometimes that he so seldom thought about his ex-wife. They'd been together five years. Not long for a civilian marriage, but a good run for a Navy one. After the hostage situation in Syria, she'd decided she wanted out. He'd fought to keep her. Fought with all he had, because he loved her more than he'd ever loved anyone, even himself. But it came down to a single choice: either he left the Navy or she was through.

It hadn't been an easy decision, but he'd made it. If it was that kind of choice, after all, he'd lost her already. And now, looking back, he couldn't regret the way things had turned out.

All is for the best. Wasn't that what Alan Evlin had told him as *Reynolds Ryan* fought thirty-foot Arctic seas, the old destroyer foredoomed to a fiery death, and Evlin doomed with her? Dan had been fresh out of the Academy then, *Ryan* his first ship. Odd, how he still felt that somewhere, somehow, the gentle lieutenant who believed all men were worth loving still wished him well.

After the divorce, he'd gone, in a way, insane. It was a common craziness in those crazy years, with the heady prospect of sex with every woman you met. Instant intimacy, if thrusting yourself within another's body was intimacy. Driven by resentment and self-hatred, he'd raided and left woman after woman. And that was when he started to drink, nearly every night, glass after glass of neat scotch or gin till the bottle slipped from his hand.

Dan closed his eyes in the dark, remembering an artist he'd

met at a party. She was drunk as he was, her breasts falling out
of her dress. They did it an hour later in the garden, against a
trellis that shook, raining down the wilted petals of late roses.
He'd seen her ten or eleven times that fall. Around her futon
in her loft, her paintings, angular and stylized, conveyed aliena-
tion and fear, like those of a battered child. And then she'd said
she loved him. He'd left her that same night.

Once he'd been proud of his conquests. Now he was ashamed.
He'd always tried to do what was right, as he understood it,
except in his relationships with women. To them, he'd lied,
behaved badly, hurt them. Now he was sorry, but it was too
late. For the last couple of years, he'd lived alone. And, of
course, he spent a lot of time at sea.

Sea duty, the path to command . . . but beyond lieutenant
commander, promotion grew increasingly rigorous. About half
made it to commander, and only a third of those to captain. He
had no illusions about how his record would look to a board.
They'd react the way Shaker had. Regardless of what anyone
thought, he had no special pull, through Niles or anyone else.

Not that he cared. He'd given up ambition long ago. No, he
was here because he wanted to be, and because the Navy, once
in a long while, needed someone who cared more about being
right than being an admiral.

His mind moved on. He watched it coldly, wishing above all
that it would stop and let him sleep. But now it decided to think
about Terry Pensker.

The black officer's unease had come back. Dan didn't think it
was fear. Pensker did fine when the heat was on. When they'd
nearly fired on the airliner, for instance. It was when things
were calm he acted jittery. He'd known men like that before.
Their imaginations were their worst enemy.

Dan had discussed it with him the day before. He went back
to that conversation now, trying again to make sense of it.

It had been during XO's inspection. The ship had gotten
steadily dirtier since they'd picked up the convoy. Watch and
maintenance, that was all Shaker wanted their minds on. Dan
kept up his rounds, though. An exec had to know what was
going on in the corners. But he shifted his priorities, to damage
control and fire hazards.

Yesterday, he'd decided to start with the missile magazine.
One of the torpedomen was sitting by the scuttle in a folding
chair, reading a coverless Louis L'Amour paperback. He put it
away quickly when Lenson came in sight, stood up, fiddled with
his pistol belt.

"Hello, Thompson. Catching up on your professional reading?"

"Uh, sort of, sir."

"If you've got nothing to do on watch, study for your second-class exam. You need to."

"Yes, sir. Uh, you got to sign here, XO, before I can let you go below."

To his surprise, he'd found Pensker in the ready service room. This was a small compartment deep below the rotary magazine. It was usually unmanned, a bare space with rust stains like old blood on the deck and the air musty from the recirc unit that kept mold off the missiles. Pensker was sitting alone when he came down the ladder, pausing en route to check the linkages for the CO_2 flooding system. Dan saw he was studying one of the ordnance publications. A diagram of the launching system was folded out of it.

"Hi, Terry."

"Hello, XO." Pensker flipped the pub closed, stood up, and stretched.

"Getting some quals in?"

"No, we got an intermittent in the test today. I thought it might be in ship's systems, but it looks like a bad missile."

"Harpoon or Standard?"

"Standard."

"Did you find the problem?"

"I think so, sir." Pensker paused. "Maybe we can get a card ordered in, fix it aboard."

"Are we authorized to work on the missiles?"

"Not *authorized*. But if I can, we don't have to offload it, go through all the rigging for sending it back to *San Jose*. It'd save us a lot of man-hours. Hell, XO, the Navy couldn't operate if everybody did exactly what the regs say. Could it?"

Dan gave him a faint grin back. "It depends on the reg. And the reason we have to shave it."

Pensker fell silent. It was then Dan caught the shadow in his eyes. And noticed that the lieutenant's hand was dancing lightly against his leg.

That nervousness, that elusive wariness again. He'd thought it was over. Pensker had been doing fine on the bridge and in CIC. So now what?

Well, this was private enough to find out. And maybe it was time to. He said with forced heartiness, "I've been meaning to have a talk with you, Terry. Just been so much going on. . . . Have you got a minute? Go ahead, sit down."

As Pensker unfolded another chair for him, Dan hesitated. How to begin? He decided to plunge right in. "I noticed on and off, this cruise, you seem kind of on edge, kind of tense. Is anything wrong at home?"

"Oh, no, Lena's good."

"I remember her at Glynda Bell's party. She seemed like a nice girl. You staying in touch?"

"Yeah. She sends cards. Pictures."

"Uh-huh. Well, I see you talking to the captain. He grooming you for my replacement, or what?" They both chuckled. "Seriously, how are you getting along with him?"

"Good."

"What do you talk about?"

"Well, this and that, XO. Weapons-department business most of the time."

"Keep me cut in, Terry. The department heads have direct access to the CO at all times. But you need to keep me informed of what's going on, so I can track possible interference with the work of the other departments, coordinate the schedule . . . you know how it goes."

"Yes, sir. Will do."

They looked at each other for a long moment. Finally, Dan cleared his throat. "Well, don't make me pull teeth. What's eating you, then? Go ahead, confide in your understanding executive officer."

Pensker grinned unwillingly. "Hey, nothing. Well, there is one thing."

"What's that?"

"I was wondering, well . . . it sounds silly, sir."

"Not if it's bothering you, Terry. Believe me."

"Okay." The lieutenant's voice went suddenly soft. "Why the hell are we here, anyway? Steaming around, escorting these guys, waiting to get hit like *Strong* . . . what's the point, sir? I think I must have missed something."

Dan looked up. Through an open magazine access, he could see the nozzle of a missile booster. "I thought that *was* the point. Protecting trade. Protecting these merchants we're convoying."

"That's not—" The lieutenant hesitated. "Can I say this, sir? It doesn't sound real gung ho."

"Let's call it off the record, Terry."

"Okay, man to man, that doesn't sound like a hell of a lot to die for. Defending a lot of oil-company ships, so they can keep their dividends up. So people can pay a nickel a gallon less for gas to get to the beach."

"I can't disagree with that," said Dan. "I feel that way sometimes myself. It isn't like World War Two, when we were fighting for our lives."

"I maybe feel it more than the other guys, I know."

"Because you're black?"

Pensker said slowly, "I feel closer to other blacks, sure. Especially when they're in danger, or when they get . . . the shaft . . . from the white world. But I didn't mean just that.

"See, my dad died in 1969. He was on Swift boats, a gunner."

Dan waited him out as Pensker's eyes hunted into the corners. Finally, he said, all in a rush, "I've always felt like his life was wasted. I remember him; I was three when he left. He's just a name on a wall now. And what for? We lost. We sent people—black people, way more than should have gone, if you look at the proportions—away to fight a war. And they died. Like him. And we still lost.

"What we're doing here, it feels the same way to me."

"We're not losing here."

"We're not even *fighting* here!" Pensker slammed his open hand against the booster-suppression tank. "The Iranians sink our ships, they blow up people, take hostages . . . we don't do a thing! It's the same kind of limited-war bullshit they tried in Vietnam. Ho Chi Minh just outlasted us, till Congress wimped out and pulled the plug. The Ayatollah's playing the same game."

"When the Iranians push us too far, we push back."

"I don't see any pushing back. Why have we got ships and planes? Why've we got missiles? As long as we're out here, we ought to do something."

"You can't start a war by yourself, Terry."

"News flash, XO. We *are* at war. Drugs, oil, terrorists—everybody in the world thinks they can fuck us over and laugh. We ought to teach somebody they can't."

"Take it easy." Dan leaned his chair back, thinking how appealing it was. Especially to Americans: to see themselves as patsy and victim, and the panacea as violence. It had made sense to him once, too. Till he saw what the outcome was. "It's a hell of a lot more complicated than that. But one thing's for sure. The U.S. military doesn't make policy. We're here on this ship to do what we're told. Period, full stop. And that, even just that, isn't going to be easy."

The weapons officer's eyes had gone strange then. Dan had been looking right at him when it happened. His clenched hands relaxed and opened; his fingers worked. He looked away. "Maybe so, XO," he said. "Maybe you're right."

Now, lying in the dark, Dan stared sightlessly at the overhead. Cool air brushed his face like the fingers of a ghost. Why did he have the feeling that ever since that conversation Pensker had been on the far side of a wall from him? Why did he feel that something had been left unsaid?

Why did he feel that he'd failed?

At 0530 the bogen jerked him awake. After the clarity of his waking interlude, then sleep again, his brain felt as if it had been frozen and then microwaved once too often. At the fifth buzz, he got it to where he figured his mouth should be. "XO."

"Dan, Ben here. How about takin' over, I'll grab early breakfast."

"Yessir. Be right up." He lay back, fell asleep again for six seconds, then forced the animal he was chained to to roll out. He folded the bunk into a sofa, pulled on khakis, decided to shave later, and headed once again for the bridge.

Topside dawn was an eerie buff. Visibility was a mile in blowing sand. To starboard, one of the tankers was a horizontal shadow, fading in and out of sight as the storm thickened and waned. He looked at the radar, checked the track, and talked briefly to Firzhak. Shaker was slumped in his padded chair. He looked dead. When Dan was ready, he went over. "Good morning, Cap'n."

The Captain opened those malamute eyes; his mouth twitched. Dan saw that the furrows had deepened. "Morning, Dan. You awake?"

"Not sure, but I'm here."

"Coffee in the thermos. Get alert now, we'll be in the Narrows in the next few hours."

Shaker went over the formation disposition—opened to two thousand yards to minimize the risk of collision—and told him he intended to go to GQ around ten, as they closed Farsi Island. They'd be passing within twenty miles of it, and Nauman wanted them ready.

At last, he went below. Dan waited till Stanko announced his departure, then swung himself into the chair. A Camel smoldered in the butt kit. He stubbed it to death, then poured himself coffee. It was lukewarm, left from the midwatch, by the taste.

Farsi Island. The big Pasdaran base. They'd have to get a grip here, tired as they were.

He worried about that for a while. They'd been balls to the wall for three days now, since leaving Manama, everyone aboard working day and night with strip ship and drills.

But a crew could stay cutting-sharp for only so long. Overwork, heat, stress, lack of sleep—combined they made men not just less alert but less alert in a certain way. They blanked out for seconds at a time; could be staring at a screen but not see a new contact. Port and starboard watches, six on and six off, was a bad arrangement. A man got only five hours sleep at a time, and lost that to eating, maintenance, and musters. It also upset his sense of day and night.

Dan had often thought it was self-defeating to subject human beings to this and expect them to perform effectively. The U.S. Navy had always worked both its men and its ships harder than other navies, since at least the turn of the century. Even in port, twelve-hour days weren't uncommon, and at sea this was more like sixteen or eighteen. The idea seemed to be that this gave you better readiness, a more professional crew.

As a junior officer, he'd just accepted it. Now he thought it might have been realistic when equipment was simple and the consequences of error small. Neither condition held in the modern Navy. Submariners had studied fatigue and tried to prevent it. The aviation community insisted on regular rest. Yet the surface fleet seemed to take pride in subjecting its men to conditions guaranteed to reduce their effectiveness. It wasn't generally discussed—no one liked to appear weak or unenthusiastic—but fatigue-induced sickness, hallucinations, falling asleep standing up weren't uncommon at sea. Granted, an error in the air could cause an accident faster than a momentary lapse at twenty or thirty knots. But dopiness or poor judgment on the bridge, at a weapons-control console, or in main control could kill a lot more people.

Not that he had any alternative at the moment. The danger was real. They'd just have to stay alert. Shaker's remedy—no cleaning, no administration—was feasible short-term, in a battle zone. Someday, though, someone would have to look at all the requirements laid on men at sea, demanded piecemeal by different authorities, but aggregating to a crushing load.

He struggled with his eyelids through the morning. The sandstorm added to his anxiety and isolation. At 1000, he called Shaker and told him they'd be entering the Narrows in half an hour.

The captain ordered GQ. As Stanko passed the word, Dan pulled on his gear and settled the steel bucket on his head.

Shaker came up a few minutes later, yawning. "XO, you ready for a boat ride?"

"Anytime, sir, but what do you mean?"

"Just got a message from Nauman. He wants somebody on the lead merchie's bridge. In case anything happens. I thought I'd put you over there."

"Okay."

"I'd send you by helo but the sand's too thick to launch. Take one of our walkie-talkies. And today's code page. I don't think you'll need anything else."

"Got it," said Dan. "When do you want me to go?"

"Soon as he gives us the word."

"Do I have time for a head call, maybe a shave?"

"Go ahead. I'll pass the word for you when we get the signal."

Dan got a radio, checked the batteries, and stuffed the code pamphlet in his back pocket. On second thought, he buttoned it in. He went below.

He finished shaving, heard nothing over the 1MC, and decided coffee might help. He banged the wardroom door open, then stopped. On the TV screen, two women were engaged in noisy cunnilingus. The pilots were slouched on the sofa, stocking feet up, muzzle-deep in ice cream.

He was instantly angry. "Haven't you people got anything better to do?"

The fat one, Schweinberg, muttered something shamefacedly.

"Speak up," Lenson snapped.

"Uh, I said, we can't fly till this sand clears up, sir."

"Then maybe I can suggest some things. This ship is a shithouse. And your people aren't helping. For one, down in your hangar, they're leaving cans all over—"

"Hell with that," said the black pilot suddenly.

"What's that?"

"I said, the hell with that! They're working twenty-hour days in that hangar. There's no air conditioning. They drink Cokes to keep cool, to keep awake—so what! Lieutenant Schweinberg and I have been flying heavy hours this convoy, most of it at night. So there's a sandstorm, we can't fly, anyway—we take a break—so what! We're doing our job aboard *Van Zandt*, XO. Maybe you ought to go jump in somebody else's shit."

Dan bit back his first response. His sudden irrational anger frightened him. He delayed by drawing coffee. What had he been thinking on the bridge, about overwork. It was possible Hayes was right.

On the other hand, no one was going to address him in that tone of voice. *Ever.*

"Away the motor whaleboat," said the 1MC just then.

He said, trying not to snarl like an animal, "Mr. Hayes, I'm going over to *Borinquen.* I think, when I get back, you and I need to have a talk." He turned, saying nothing more, and carried the cup up two ladders and out into the sand-laden air.

Outside the heat was oppressive. The wind, coated with hot sand fine and sharp as powdered diamond, scorched and stung his face and hands. He shielded his eyes, letting the *shamal* take the paper cup. Two sailors were posting themselves on the 02 level, one donning headphones, the other shrugging himself into a Stinger harness. The latter swept the four-foot tube around, peering through the sight. A hollow clang came from forward; belts were going into the .50 machine guns.

Dan found himself looking at the sealed end of the Stinger. Behind it was an encapsulated antiaircraft missile. "Hey, Lorton," he said. "Watch where you're pointing that thing."

The seaman lowered the weapon. He looked barely old enough to trust with a bikeload of Sunday papers. "Oh, sorry, XO."

"You know how to fire that?"

"Just aim it, listen for the lock-on tone, then press this, that's all I got to do. The ragheads on the other end got it easy, too. All they got to do is bend over and kiss their ass goodbye."

Dan wondered how he'd see what to shoot at, in a sandstorm, but didn't say anything. Certainly their morale was good.

BM2 Stanko came back, relieved from the bridge, and began shouting orders. Yellow grease peeled from the cables as the whaleboat swayed out over the sea. Dan stepped into it, reaching for a monkey line.

"Lower away," shouted the boatswain. The davit jerked, almost knocking them off their feet, and then they were descending. The gray walls of the frigate's hull rose, stained with salt and rust—he'd have to get on Charaler about that, after this convoy—till the keel smacked into the water. Winokur, the boat engineer, tripped the hook and they were suddenly under way, plunging up and down in a confused chop, the gray sheer sides drawing away, melting like a ghost back into the abrasive fog.

"What's your heading?"

"East by southeast," shouted Stanko. "You got a radio, sir?"

"Yeah."

"Ask 'em to track us. I can't see diddley out here."

"*Van Zandt,* this is *Van Zandt* One. Heading"—Dan craned to see the compass—"one-four-oh magnetic."

"You're headed fair, sir," came McQueen's voice back. "Only about a mile to go."

The diesel hammered. A sea came over the bow and spattered

him. He licked his lips. Salt and sand, gritty and bitter and warm.

Ten minutes later, something huge and black darkened the airborne desert to starboard. Stanko altered course toward it. They passed under the stern and found a jacob's ladder rigged off her beam. Dan looked up at it. It seemed to go up forever.

"Ready, sir?"

"Yeah, take her in." He thrust the radio into his belt and screwed his cap tight. The whaleboat neared, slowed, pitched up and down, and slammed violently into rusty steel. Stanko fired a stream of curses at the tanker, the storm, and the whaleboat as Dan crouched by the gunwale. He waited for the crest of a sea, then jumped.

As the boat dropped away, he used his momentum to gain two more rungs. Behind him the motor roared. Good, Stanko was getting clear fast. It wouldn't be hard to get crushed between the boat and the hull.

The hull: Six inches from his eyes, it was black and rough, coated with paint so heavy it looked like tar. As the sea licked his boots and fell back, it bared the stinking foulness of barnacles, mineral encrustation, and seaweed that accumulated so quickly in warm seas. He lifted his left arm to climb, and hissed between his teeth at the sudden pain.

Above his head, a steel cliff loomed, fifty feet straight up. At the very top, a tiny head looked down at him.

He clamped his teeth on grit and began climbing. Christ, his arm . . . he couldn't get it above his shoulder. So he used it to grip, pulling with his right, pushing with his legs. His boondockers slipped, the leather soles losing the treads, and he dangled, kicking high above the waves. But he got himself back on the rungs, and finally gained the rail. A mustached man gave him a hand. "Hello, Navy," he said. "I'm Guterman, the master. Say, you all right?"

"Yeah." Dan rubbed his shoulder—the captain, in greasy coveralls? Then his hand stopped. Guterman was motioning him to a bicycle.

He wobbled into motion—it had been a while—and followed him along a broad way. The deck was endless, black steel covered with piping, valves, risers. It stank of oil, and NO SMOKING signs were painted in red every few feet.

"You've got a big one here."

"Four hundred thousand tons," said Guterman.

Another NO SMOKING sign, thirty feet high, frowned down from the superstructure. They reached it at last, parked the bikes in a rack, and took an elevator to the bridge.

Borinquen's pilothouse was like an empty barn after *Van Zandt*'s. Two men in slacks and short-sleeved shirts gave Dan half-salutes as he came in. Guterman introduced them as the second mate and the purser, then said to the younger one, "Bring her up to six."

The mate moved a control. Dan stared around. On a big surface scope, he could see the tracks and predicted movements of every ship from here to the coast of Saudi Arabia. Sure enough, there were only two men on the bridge. There didn't even seem to be a helmsman. He couldn't decide whether to be horrified or impressed.

When they entered the Narrows the sea looked no different, but the fathometer showed shoaling. He kept going back to look at the radar. There was a group of boats to the south, maybe ten miles off. Fishermen, most likely, but that was the hell of it and the anxiety. They were navigating a body of water that 95 percent of the time was at peace. Trading, fishing, passenger traffic, pilgrimages to Mecca, it all went on as it had for millennia. Only occasionally, when their opponents chose, did it erupt into war. He kept his eyes on the pips, waiting for one to turn toward them and accelerate.

They were halfway through the channel and he was standing on the centerline, admiring the computerized radar display and wondering when the Navy would get around to buying them, when the deck shuddered under him. He grabbed for the console. The shudder built to a whipping that went on and on, shaking books and pencils to the deck. The purser fell to his hands and knees; the second mate grabbed a rail.

"What the *hell* was that?"

"Don't know. Better go to all stop."

"I just did," said the mate.

The shuddering died away. Guterman appeared from nowhere, like a summoned demon. "What did we hit?" he said. "What's the depth?"

The mate glanced at a readout. "It's gone dead . . . but we had eleven meters under the keel, Captain. I don't think it was bottom."

Dan went outside. Suddenly he was angry. From the tanker's huge wing, he leaned out, sweeping the hull with his eyes. He could see the stern, but the bow faded out of visibility in the sand fog. He ran to the starboard side. There was nothing there, either—no smoke trails from missiles or rocket-propelled grenades, no small boats. Only the sullen sea, sliding by out of nothingness into vacancy.

"*Borinquen*, this is U.S.S. *Van Zandt*."

He raised the radio. "*Van Zandt, Borinquen;* Lenson here."

"This is the Captain. What's going on? We just heard a hell of an explosion over your way. Sonar says it blanked their display."

"I don't know, sir. Something happened; we felt it on the bridge."

Just then, with horror, Dan remembered they were at all stop. He instantly clicked the transceiver to channel twelve. "All ships in convoy, this is S.S. *Borinquen.* We have gone to all stop. Suspect mine detonation. I say again, we have shut down our engines. All ships acknowledge."

The merchants answered one by one. He made sure they understood, then went back to ten. "Sorry, Captain, I had to get the word to the guys behind us. We're heaving to till we figure out what it was. How do you hold our position?"

"I hold you in the middle of the channel, Dan. Check it out and get back to me."

As soon as Shaker signed off, the commodore broke in. Dan gave him the situation quickly and promised more in a moment.

In the pilothouse, the mate was studying a tank chart on the bulkhead. The master was on the phone. As Dan came up, he said, "We're taking water in two of the starboard tanks. Midships."

"Empty?"

"Yes."

"Any danger of fire?"

"Shouldn't be; they're blanketed. We've got plenty of reserve buoyancy . . . hold on . . . yeah. Yeah. Okay." The master hung up. "Engineer's headed down to check."

"Do you think it was a mine?"

"How could it be a mine? You guys swept here, didn't you?" The sarcasm was clear. "What's the story, Commander?"

"I'll let you know when I do. Can I use your bridge-to-bridge?"

He called Commodore Nauman back first. "Sir, this is Lieutenant Commander Lenson from *Van Zandt,* on *Borinquen.* We think we've hit a mine. Was this part of the channel swept?"

"Yes. But that doesn't mean there aren't more there now."

Nauman paused. Dan glanced at the master; Guterman was on the phone again. "I understand you've gone dead in the water. What's the situation?"

"We didn't go DIW, sir, we shut down the engines. I don't think we've sustained major damage. Two tanks flooding. No exterior damage visible from the bridge."

"Right. Okay, I'm going to reorient, put *Gallery* . . . no, I'll put *Charles Adams* in front and launch *Gallery*'s helo for a visual search on the bow."

"Uh, with all due respect, sir, I'm not sure that's a good idea."

"What's that, Mr. Nelson?"

"Lenson, sir." He thought quickly. "I'm not so sure it's a good idea putting a destroyer in the van, sir. If one of us hits a mine, we're screwed. We're a hundredth the displacement of these tankers and our machinery's a lot closer to the skin of the ship."

"So what are you suggesting?"

"Leave *Borinquen* in the lead, sir. These guys can absorb mines better than we can. I'll get up on the bow with a walkie-talkie. Have the escorts fall in astern."

Dan glanced toward Guterman; he didn't look happy, but he nodded. "Ship's master concurs with that, sir."

"What about the helo?"

"Visibility's terrible, sir. But that's up to you."

"Okay, do it," came the commodore's voice. "Let me know when you resume speed."

"I'm ready," said Guterman. "The tank's sealed off and we're pumping. I may counterflood later to stay on an even keel. Shall we start up six knots, see how she rides?"

"Sounds good," said Dan.

For the next two hours he stood at the bow, straining his eyes into the storm. The mate had given him a set of goggles. He was glad of that. The confectionery-fine sand filtered inside his uniform and turned to warm mud, gritted his teeth, drifted up in tiny dunes behind his boonies.

Still, it wasn't as bad as he'd seen it. Their worst sandstorm, on radar picket down south, had come in riding a sixty-knot wind. It had stripped *Van Zandt*'s port side down to bare metal, leaving Charaler undecided whether to celebrate or cry.

The worst of this was the reduction of visibility. He could see perhaps half a mile, not far with 400,000 tons of poorly maneuverable steel behind him. Not only that, but when he thought about it, it was unlikely he'd see a mine. If it had already survived a sweeping, it was probably bottom-laid, and pretty sophisticated.

But as it turned out, he saw only cardboard boxes, trash, and one drifting oil drum.

At last the dun curtain thinned, then lifted, its gracefully curved skirts sweeping off to the south. Shortly thereafter, the master called him on the walkie-talkie. One of the ship's officers was on his way forward to relieve him.

He heard the pulse of approaching rotor blades as he pedaled back. Slowly, because the tires kept slipping on the sand, and because now that he wasn't concentrating on the sea, he was very thirsty, hot, and tired.

It was a Navy helicopter, but not 421, as he'd half-expected. It circled them and landed forward of the superstructure. When he got there, a quarter-mile later, two men were standing beside it as the rotors ticked around, talking with Guterman. As he set the kickstand, he suddenly recognized Jack Byrne, then the short man in the flight suit. He hastily brushed off his uniform.

"Dan! Can we have a few words?"

As he saluted a grim-looking Hart, a blonde woman in slacks joined them from inside the fuselage. The admiral introduced her as Blair Titus. Dan saluted her, too, wondering who she was. Press? Some visiting celebrity? It seemed discourteous to ask. She was good-looking, with a confident air. Maybe he was supposed to recognize her.

Hart said, "She's congressional, Dan. We can talk in front of her. Now, how about telling me about the mine damage."

"Well, Captain Guterman can give you more detail than I can, sir. Actually, we don't know for sure if it was a mine."

"Here," said Guterman. Dan turned to him, and before he could say anything, he found an ice-cold bottle of Heineken in his hand.

While he was wondering what to do with it, what with Commander, Middle East Force looking at him, Hart snapped, "What do you mean?"

"The damage is amidships. It seems to me a mine would explode near the bow."

"Only if it was a moored type," said Byrne. His eyes were unreadable behind the sunglasses. "An influence type would go off nearer the screws."

"Yessir, but it wasn't really near the screw, either."

Hart began questioning Guterman. Dan was wiping red grit and sweat from his forehead when the woman said, "Can I ask you a few things?"

"Sure. What do you want to know?"

"Are you in charge of this ship?"

"No, no. This is a civilian vessel. That's the master, Captain Guterman. I'm Dan Lenson, XO of *Van Zandt*, one of the frigates escorting the convoy."

She turned to Guterman. "What do you think we ought to do about these latest incidents, Captain?"

"Make the Navy do their damn job, I think that would be good."

Incidents. Dan was wondering dully why she was using the plural when she swung on him again. "How about you, Mr. Lenson?"

"I'd just like to get some sleep."

The woman asked a few more questions, mainly about their convoy procedures and how effective he thought they were. He wasn't sure his answers made much sense. Finally, they drifted back toward the helicopter. He got rid of the beer over the side, not without regret; he was thirsty, and the master had meant well. "Dan," said Hart, turning back at the hatchway, "can we give you a lift back to *Van Zandt?*"

"Commodore Nauman's assigned me here, sir."

"He did so at my request. No reflection on you, but now that we've taken damage, I'm leaving Captain Byrne here as my representative."

That sounded like an order. He shook Byrne's hand, muttered to him to go easy on the Heineken, and climbed in.

From the air, he could see the entire convoy, eight ships strung out in a line ten miles long. It looked strange with the merchants in front. When they touched down on *Van Zandt,* the woman wanted to look around there, too, but Hart said they had to get back. She waved to Dan as it lifted, blowing sand off the flight deck, and disappeared to the west.

Dan stopped at the first scuttlebutt and drank greedily for some time.

He met Pensker in the midships passageway as he was going forward. The weapons officer didn't look nervous anymore. He looked mad, and his hands were fists. "You just back, sir?" he said.

"Yeah."

"You hear about our helo?"

"Yeah, I just got off it."

"No, I mean *our* helo. With our guys."

He remembered then his unfinished business with the two pilots. And suddenly was enraged again. "No. What did those two idiots do now?"

Pensker looked shocked. "They got shot down. We think. Anyway, they don't answer on the radio. You better get up to the bridge."

"Oh, no," said Dan. He began to run.

20

U.S.S. *Turner Van Zandt*

BUCKY Hayes came awake slowly that morning, drifting in and out of dream—a good one, for a change. Instead of a nightmare beast, his pursuer was a wanton Joyce. But gradually a recurrent grinding penetrated. It sounded like an empty cruise box being dragged over nonskid.

At last, he identified it as Schweinberg. He raised his arm and pressed the stud on his watch. When he blinked his eyes clear enough to see the little lighted window, he sat up suddenly. They'd overslept.

No, no one overslept aboard ship; if you weren't where you were supposed to be, you found out about it quick. But it was still 0654, and no one had called them, buzzed them, or shaken them awake with a flashlight in their eyes.

That meant they weren't launching at dawn. For a moment, he snuggled the skimpy GI pillow closer, then pushed it away and sat up. If they hadn't been called, that meant something was wrong. After all, they were transiting the Narrows this morning.

The most likely explanation was that Two One was down, grounded for repairs. He lay back, then realized he had only a few minutes left if he wanted breakfast. He clicked on his bunk light, clambered down, and found yesterday's khakis. He didn't bother to be quiet. There was no way Schweinberg could hear him over the snoring he was putting out.

The ship was strangely silent as he relieved himself, braced against the urinal, and went on toward the wardroom. The enlisted men in the passageways nodded to him with blank faces, the minimum of military courtesy. Gradually, he became aware of a whisper, a distant susurration, as if an audience waited on the far side of the steel walls. On impulse, he swung the dogs clear on a weather-deck door. He looked out into the breaker, and beyond it at the sea.

It wasn't there. Instead, the handle jerked out of his hands and something slashed his face. The abrading hiss came from all around him. The russet grit streamed over the painted surfaces of the ship, curled round the scuppers. It was only a little paler than dried blood. A thin scum of it tossed on the passing sea. Beyond that, he could see nothing, not only for the sand fog but because his lids kept jerking closed in protective reflex.

No wonder they weren't flying. Christ, the plane, the turbine blades! Then he relaxed. Mattocks would have her buttoned up in the hangar, with even the joints in the sliding door sealed with duct tape.

He yanked against the wind and finally got the door dogged again. So there was nothing else to do but eat. And then maybe sleep some more. He needed it. Since Hormuz, air ops had been nearly continuous, identifying contacts, herding dhows, electronic surveillance, shuttling back and forth across the route watching for mines and boats.

He wasn't happy about not flying. He knew having them aloft was important to the safety of *Van Zandt* and the merchants she was escorting.

But just between you and me, Virgil, he thought, I'm ready for a break.

In the wardroom, several of the ship's officers were eating in a sort of hasty apathy. The XO wasn't there. He didn't mind that at all. Terry Pensker gave him a quick smile. Hayes pulled out a chair beside him. They talked briefly about the storm. And then his plate came, carried by a sleepy, pimpled enlisted man, and he set to work.

Schweinberg slept heavily through dawn and through breakfast. He snorted and turned over when Hayes came back in and climbed over him to the upper, but he was still three-quarters asleep. And a moment later, the black depths closed again.

It was a Super Bowl. His side had gold helmets and a white and yellow uniform. He wondered what team it was. But it seemed dumb to ask in the middle of a game. In the huddle, he got a look at the QB. He was Phil Simms, but somehow, too, an older face, one you saw on television selling beer or motor oil.

But when the rush came the strangeness dropped away and he was hungry to take somebody down. He had the speed and lightness he'd had in high school, at 180, and at the same time the bulk and power of 230 and all muscle. Through a flashing gap in the line, he saw a man with a ball.

He knew suddenly this was the final quarter, final seconds,

and this down would decide the game. The roar from the stands was like the roar of engines. He wanted this sack. He wove through a falling knot and was in the open, and the opposing quarterback was just ahead, falling back, cocking his arm and craning for an opening.

Suddenly there was a wall in front of him. The left guard had to be over three hundred, seven feet tall. Schweinberg had just time to notice that both he and the quarterback were not just black but in black. All black, with little silver crosses on their helmets.

They slammed into each other face on. He took the impact with his mask. It knocked him out for a moment. When he shook his head, mumbling, coming back, the guard was still there, down in a three-point, his cleats dug deep, snarling down at him, ready to do it again.

Okay, fuckhead! Claude the Bod is gonna make you eat them little red eyes! And again he surged forward, yelling " 'Noles!" high and keen till the earthshaking slam and clatter of armored bodies made it an explosive grunt. But the guard didn't move. There was no give at all. He fell back, bruised and panting, and heard suddenly from behind him the coach's hoarse scream: "Get in there, Schweinberg! You pansy ass again and you're off my goddamn team, boy!"

Desperate, Chunky lunged in again. This time, he fed Death an elbow over the mouth guard. But it was his own teeth that came loose. He put his taped fingers to his jaw and took them out, one after the other, bit deep into the tough jelly plastic of the mouth guard.

"Buck. Hey, *Buck!*"

"What's doing?"

"Might as well get up. I'm about slept out."

Hayes rolled over and looked down. Schweinberg was standing moodily in front of the mirror in green boxers and a Marine Corps–issue T-shirt. He turned sideways to the mirror, then back; tensed his shoulders; sneered; picked his nose. Hayes watched, entranced and entertained. Now that he'd decided to leave the Navy behind, he felt almost nostalgic for his red-neck roommate.

"What are you doing, Chunky?"

"Nothing."

"Think they've got lunch up yet?"

"I doubt it. They're all still at GQ. They're so tight-assed about this convoy, it's pathetic."

They found a plate of corned-beef sandwiches undefended in the wardroom. Schweinberg went into the pantry. He came out with mustard, sweet rolls, carrot sticks, radishes, sweet gherkins, and a glass of iced milk. He sat down and said, surveying it, "There's Rocky Road in the freezer. Be good with walnuts and Hershey's."

"Chunky, you're gonna be flying alone in two or three years. SH-60's not going to have enough lift for you and crew, too."

"I'll have you know I weigh within ten pounds of what I carried in the Seminole line." He bit off half the sandwich. Through the beef and homemade bread came "Hey, wanna see a flick? What we got we ain't watched yet?"

"We've seen them all two or three times."

"Well, take a look. I'm in the mood."

Hayes rooted through the cabinet. Most of the tapes and books had been offloaded during strip ship, but the wardroom's private stock had crept out again. Schweinberg wanted to see *Librarians in Heat* and Hayes gave in.

They were sitting watching it, spooning up nuts and chocolate syrup, when Lenson came in. They looked up at him innocently. He was wearing a life jacket and carrying a radio; his uniform was rumpled and his eyes bleary. He was headed for the coffee, but when he saw them, his look went suddenly hostile. And Schweinberg muttered, "Uh oh. Here it comes."

"Mr. Hayes, I'm going over to *Borinquen.* I think, when I get back, you and I need to have a talk."

When the door closed behind a man whose face had gone white with suppressed fury, neither of the pilots said anything for a moment. Finally, Hayes said, "Jesus, he's in bad shape."

Schweinberg found his voice. "Christ, what's with you? Fucking with the exec—that'll get us all in hot water."

"What's he going to do to me, Chunky? Send me to sea?"

"He can submit a concurrent fitness report."

"I don't think he's that much of a prick. But if he wants to, fine."

"What's going on, Bucky? I don't get it. You was always a regulation type back at squadron. But out here, the last couple weeks, you're turning into a real give-a-shit."

"Can you keep a secret?"

"What?"

Hayes thought about it one last time. Then he took a breath, and told him.

* * *

They followed the porn film with a Rambo—just to celebrate his decision, as Schweinberg said. Midway through it, a distant vibration merged with the explosions on the screen, but neither got up to investigate.

When it was over, they drifted back to the hangar. It was dead silent and filled with snoozing crewmen. They were considering going back to sleep themselves when Hayes became conscious that something in the air had changed. He cracked a hatch and peered out. "Hey, storm's over," he said.

At the same moment, the 1MC came on. "Flight quarters, flight quarters, all hands man your flight quarters stations."

Fortunately they had spare suits in the hangar. As they pulled them on, the doors rumbled up behind them. Crewmen swarmed over Two One, removing intake plugs, spreading the blades and tail pylon.

The launch went fast and normal. Still, Schweinberg kept shouting irritably to hurry; he wanted to get aloft before the sand closed in again.

When they were strapped in, Hayes punched the ship's coordinates into the navigation computer. The engines whined, and the rotors began turning. Slowly at first, like the hands of a clock, then faster and faster till they seemed to disappear. Through them came the power that wrenched Two One suddenly off the deck and instantly, violently, into the sky.

The convoy and its escorts marched away below them till they disappeared into the heavy hazy air. The storms suspended dust as high as ten thousand feet. Today it was still murky at angels two. From there, though, they could see the departing storm, a tan mist as of disintegration, returning the sea and sky and the land that their radar said lay to the south to a vague chaos that might be anything or nothing.

Schweinberg gave his copilot the controls. He stretched and lifted a cheek, then followed the fart with a sigh. The heavy lunch sat uneasily in his gut.

He loosened his harness, then twisted to look back into the cabin. This was a one-crewman flight. He'd decided he didn't need Christer. If they had to detonate a mine, or fire a warning burst, as they had at the dhow, Kane could do it.

A moment later, he looked back at the ships. Narrowed his eyes. Then clicked onto the data link. "ATACO, Killer Two One."

"Go, Two One."

"Hey, what's with the convoy? Why've we got a merchie up front?"

The voice was silent for a moment; then it told them about the mine strike and the reorientation. "You mean you didn't know that? I thought everybody aboard knew that. Where were you, asleep?"

"Don't get smart," Schweinberg growled. "Nobody bothered to tell us, that's all. A mine, huh. Well, what do you know."

"Wouldn't have happened with us out here," said Kane, from aft.

"I hope not. But, jeez . . . let's lose some altitude here and get to work."

They skimmed ahead of the lead ship, keeping their eyes overboard. Shit, Chunky was thinking. He wished he'd been up here earlier, wished he'd seen the mine first. But then, what if somebody hit one in an area they'd checked out? As it was, the air arm was in the clear. He decided to be happy with things as they were and not try to improve them in his head.

They patrolled back and forth in front of the convoy for some time. Once, Hayes caught a dark object in the water; they dropped still lower as they approached it, Kane swinging out the M60. It was a sheep. Schweinberg wanted to give it a burst anyway, but the ship nixed that without comment. He lapsed into a sulk.

Hayes sat slumped, moving the stick slightly from time to time. He was getting bored again. Bored and hot. His mind drifted. They'd have to move. Joyce didn't like new houses and she didn't like suburbs. She liked older homes in settled neighborhoods. Four bedrooms should do it. Maybe they could find something for eighty, ninety thousand. . . .

"Want to play a tape, sir?"

"Yeah, go ahead, something country," muttered Schweinberg.

There was a pop and then a hiss on the ICS circuit. Then the jury-rigged Walkman cut in. "Oh, shit, not that goddamn disco tape again," he howled. "Kane, you little prick, I'm gonna tear your arms off when we get back."

A transmission from the ship overrode the enlisted man's comeback. "ATO, ATACO: vector zero-eight-five to investigate small contact."

"Oh, wilco . . . I mean, roger." Hayes clicked off and banked, not bothering to ask Schweinberg's permission. They came around and headed east, picking up speed till the needle nudged 150. The wind rose to a steady whistle. "Turn that thing down, Kane. ATACO, how far away is he?"

"Twelve miles, in and out of the big oil field."

"Roger." Hayes had the derricks now. Their tops pricked the

sky fine as needles. Schweinberg said nothing. Behind them, he could hear Kane whistling, breaking up as the voice-actuated mike cut on and off. The rigs marched over the curve of the sea like the flat video-game reality of a flight simulator. Two One droned and rumbled like an old pickup on a gravel road. The waves flashed by. From sheer habit, both men scanned the gauges, then lifted their eyes again.

"Got him yet?"

"Nope."

"He's probably oil-rig service, in and out of the structures."

"ATACO, ATO: gimme a re-vector, we got *nada* here."

"Hold him . . . wait . . . hold him zero-nine-five from you, between two platforms. Wait. There's more than one."

"More than one, aye. Coming right."

"Let's drop some, Buck; if they're small, we need to get down to two-three hundred."

"Got to watch these towers."

"Well, no shit. Let's just do what Uncle Claude says, shed some fucking altitude, okay? And do it now. These could be the guys laid that mine."

The water came up close, its corrugated surface flashing past. They were so low they could see sea snakes, plastic trash, a sheen of slick trailing from one rig. This low, the water was a grim tan-green, flat, as if the storm had sanded off the tops of the waves.

"Should be headed right for him."

"What size are these guys, ATACO?"

"We don't hold them anymore, Two One. Lost in the clutter. Don't you have visual yet?"

"Negat . . . negat. Hey, Chunky, is that something over there? See there, by the smoke? It's moving, got a wave system behind it—"

Two One, still descending, came right. The dot ahead, trailing rippled Vs on the sea, grew rapidly larger. Hayes bored in straight and level. He wanted to get it identified and get back to the convoy. Schweinberg focused the binoculars. He caught a vibration-blurred glimpse, and frowned. Not a boat. Smaller than a boat, but kicking up a plume. Something narrow and vertical. Not masts, but . . .

Then, just for an instant, the field steadied and he saw it. A vertical line, swelling at its tip to a black bulb. The sea flung apart in white cascades as it rolled. Behind that, a stouter, shorter pipe, with a faired black protrusion, trailing a brown haze of exhaust. A third vertical, thin and bent: an antenna.

And beneath, a shadow slipping through the tan-green Gulf.

"Holy *shit*," he whispered.

"What is it?"

"ATACO, Two One: We got a fucking sub out here! I mean, mark, datum! Headed zero-five-zero, looks like ten knots, scope and snorkel out of the water, black in color—"

"Two One, ATACO, say again your last—"

Bucky Hayes, jerking his head around as they rocketed over it, saw it, too. And lifting his eyes, he saw something else. Something beyond it, sliding out from between two oil rigs. A boat. Two big outboard motors; four men, seated well forward; a dark green tube . . .

"Look out, Chunky, they've got an escort!"

At the same moment he shouted, Hayes wrenched them into a violent turn. Two One responded instantly, the horizon and sky and rigs all swinging up, the black derricks reaching for them like spears. She shuddered as the rotors lost their grip on hot air. He grabbed for the collective at the same moment he saw, out of the corner of his vision, a white-hot brightness climbing toward them from the crazy tilt of the sea, building a pillar of billowing white. It curved inward rapidly, then disappeared behind them.

Kane's voice broke scared over the ICS. "Missile, rear sector! *Missile!*"

"Flares," screamed Schweinberg just as Hayes's finger hit the button. The dispenser fired twice.

There was a blow against the back of their seats and a sheet of flame shot forward between them. Hayes felt things tear through his seat back, flak jacket, lungs. Schweinberg felt his left eye shrivel and blacken. "Son of a bitch," he shouted, and the air he drew back in was suddenly burning hot. "We're hit—ATACO, Two One, we're hit—got a—did you get what I said about the submarine—looks like he's diving now—fuck it, we're going down! Buck, Kane, prepare to ditch."

Hayes didn't answer. Chunky couldn't see him real clearly, but his ATO seemed to have no chest, like in the scene in *Alien* where the thing comes out of the guy.

His mind scrambled over a cascade of sensations, terror, thought, while at the same time it tried to estimate damage. The rocket must have hit as they turned, exploding back by number-one engine exhaust. Two One was quivering like a wounded quail. Anyway, they were falling, and he couldn't seem to get the collective down to autorotate. And there was no way out of the aircraft, no nice rocket seats like the jet jocks had.

The gray machine fell like a shot bird, dying but still with lateral control. Okay, Chunky boy, his voice said calmly in his brain. You're the shit-hot pilot, let's see you fly your way out of this. He still had 120 knots forward airspeed. Lot of kinetic energy there. He could choose where he'd hit, within say a five-hundred-foot circle. And that was it. They were going to ride it in.

"Death," muttered Claude Schweinberg. "Good. But first— *cheech*, you terrorist raghead *motherfuckers!*"

"Roger that," muttered Hayes's suddenly airless lips. He stared straight forward. He couldn't move his arms or anything. He couldn't even breathe.

There wasn't really time, there at the end, for them to think. But during those two or two and a half seconds, Claude Schweinberg found time to grin tightly between clenched teeth. He hadn't flinched. And Buck Hayes found time to think: Joyce. Dustin. Jesse.

And blink forward through the bloody mist at upturned, suddenly frozen faces, a dark green motorboat emerging from a white smoke cloud. Directly in the path of ten tons of falling, burning Killer Angel, side number 421.

21

U.S.S. Mobile Bay

THE first thing Blair said that morning was "Damn."

She threw back the rough gray blanket, unrolled herself from the sheets, and began hunting around, crossing bare goosefleshed arms over her breasts. A memory of winter mornings in Minnesota crossed her mind, her mother bundling her up, the world-changing wonder of the snow.

She grinned sleepily. And what would her mother think of her now, in her sheer undies, surrounded by three hundred sailors?

She finally found the source of the electronic beeping that had brought her awake. Now she remembered answering it twice during the night. Male voices, asking for the captain. When she'd said he wasn't there, there was silence, then the rattle of a handset hastily hung up. She grinned again, picked it up, and said, tentatively, "Hello."

"Ms. Titus? Jack Byrne. Thought you might appreciate a breakfast call. It's oh-seven-hundred. They'll only be serving for fifteen more minutes."

"Thanks."

"Are you all right? You sound—"

"I'm just cold. I'll be right down."

She dressed quickly, choosing her heaviest panty hose, a cotton sweater, and a pair of parachute slacks she'd brought for shipboard. Actually, it had been astonishingly restful. Her bed swayed gently and each time she'd drifted up, the murmur of machinery had comforted her, a distant, soothing rhythm, a robot's lullaby.

For a moment she wished she belonged here. How simple to be told what to do. To know your place in an iron universe, free of decisions, personalities, politics. She stared at herself in the mirror over the sink as she brushed her hair, liking the man smell of leather and oil and the faint fragrance of shaving cream. For some reason, she was hungry as a horse. Wasn't sea air supposed to do that to you?

When she opened her door, there was a sailor outside, leaning against a pipe. As he came to attention, she said, startled as he was, "Who are *you?* How long have *you* been there?"

I'm one of the masters-at-arms, ma'am. We stood watch all night out here. Can I escort you somewheres?"

"I'm going to breakfast. Where's that?"

"I imagine the wardroom . . . follow me. Hold tight on this ladder, they're kind of tricky. Specially in shoes like that."

The officers sprang to their feet as she came in. She said coolly, "Please sit down, please." Across the room she caught a flat, angry look: Miller's. When she smiled at him, he dropped his eyes and shouted irritably for coffee.

She ordered from a mimeographed slip. Creamed chipped beef on toast, egg over easy, juice. The men around her seemed shy. Finally one asked her where she was from. She said Washington. The captain shot a glare at him like a laser. He didn't ask any more questions, just fidgeted with his fork for a moment, dropped it, then excused himself.

They'd all finished and she was sitting alone when Byrne came in. He hung up his cap, drew coffee, and sat down across from her. "Sleep all right?"

"Wonderful. Where did everyone go?"

"Quarters, then off to work. We start early at sea."

"When will Admiral Hart be here?"

"Flight plan says a little after eight."

"This is to oversee the convoy transit—is that correct?"

"That's right. *Coronado*'s his flagship, but he can get a better picture of the situation from an Aegis cruiser. He likes to be on the scene whenever there's a possibility the Pasdaran will come out."

"Commendable."

"He's a good man," said Byrne. He swirled his coffee, squinting as if looking through it into the past. "Speaking as one who's served with some who weren't."

"I know you find this hard to believe, Mr. Byrne—"

"Why not Jack?"

"I'll think about that. As I was saying, I'm not out here to cast for the Crucifixion. I see nothing to indicate he's not a good commander. I'm only trying to see that our overall policy is correct, and that within that context our resources are efficiently used."

"There are those who feel you're going about it in an unnecessarily abrasive manner."

"I'm sorry if it strikes them that way. It's how I have to operate sometimes. Otherwise, I'm ignored."

"I can understand that, I guess. By the way, these came in for you last night." He slid a SECRET-stamped manila across the table.

She set her cup down and unbent the clip on the envelope. They were press summaries, a short message from Shaw, in Riyadh, and a long one from Bankey. She laid the others aside and propped her head over the last.

Talmadge had talked to Tower, Nichols, and Kennedy. Together, they'd decided it was time to put War Powers to a vote. A committee resolution wouldn't bind the administration, but it would place the question before the committee of the whole. He was happy with her reports from Riyadh and Dhubai, but unhappy with the information on the armed-services side.

Specifically, he needed to know whether there was any expiration date on the administration's commitments. He knew this depended on the war, but still he needed some idea of whether U.S. forces were helping end it or acting to spread hostilities. He'd talked to Weinberger informally but hadn't got anything useful. (Talmadge didn't like Weinberger, but then he hadn't liked Brown, Rumsfeld, or Schlesinger, either; she suspected he wanted to be Secretary of Defense himself someday.) He needed to know quickly, in twenty-four hours. He wanted her to call him back so they could discuss it in detail.

"The following is a test of the ship's alarms. General. Chemical. Collision. Flight crash," announced a grille above her head, piercingly loud. A succession of wheeps, whoops, and beeps followed. "Regard all further alarms."

"Do we have a secure telephone here?" she asked Byrne.

"Eight or nine, different types. Why?"

"Could I talk to the States on one of them?"

"Satellite voice relay? No problem. We just need to get Miller's chop on it, and set up a frequency."

"Could you do that, please? Late this afternoon will be fine, after I'm done with Hart."

The intel officer nodded. "Now flight quarters, flight quarters, all hands man your flight quarters stations," said the grille. "That'll be him," Byrne said, getting up. "Want to get back there, grab him before Miller crawls in his ear?"

She glanced up, surprised. Byrne, she realized suddenly, was trying to help her. So there were people who didn't think she was an intruder, who didn't see her as a total imposition, or bad luck.

But it annoyed her, though, that her eyes went to his hand,

to the wedding ring. "Sure," she said, then smiled. "Sure
. . . Jack."

The admiral was businesslike and brisk. To Blair, he seemed
tense. Perhaps it had something to do with the convoy. He
greeted her courteously, though. She stayed beside him on the
walk forward from the helicopter pad. Miller wouldn't look at
her. It was plain he was still smoldering.

In CDC, Hart swung himself up into the leather chair, grunting thanks as the master chief brought over a cup of black
coffee so hot it smoked. There were two other seats on the
command level. "Why don't you all sit down," he said, rubbing
his short hair abstractedly. "Take a load off. We'll probably be
here all day. Jack, did you bring the Linebacker op order?"

"Yessir, stateroom safe, I'll be right back."

Miller ensconced himself next to Hart; Blair, on the far left.
Ensigns and lieutenants sat below them at consoles, talking in
low voices. The two men went silent, absorbed in the displays.
She studied them, too.

It was the upper Gulf. The coast of Saudi Arabia hugged the
left of the screen, slanting to the northwest. Several islands lay
offshore. A track among them was outlined by glowing yellow
lines. It was wide at the bottom of the screen but narrowed to
a passage perhaps a mile wide. Northeast of it, marked by a
steadily blinking symbol, was another island.

She knew this was Farsi, and that the narrows were the
Channel, the choke point for supertankers in transit to and
from Kuwait, Khārk, and Ābādān.

Hart leaned forward, peering around Miller. "Blair, let me
explain what's going on.

"We have our fourth reflagged convoy on that middle screen.
It's being escorted by three of our small-boy assets: *Adams,
Van Zandt,* and *Gallery.* They provide surface and air protection. The Narrows are also in range of the Kuwaiti Air Force
if the Iraqis or Iranians get to feeling lucky. The fighters are
on five-minute runway alert.

"The convoy's been escorted in from the Arabian Sea. So far,
no incidents. This morning, they're going to transit the Narrows. Since we just swept it, I don't expect mines. What I expect
is a sortie from Farsi Island. We have"—he glanced around,
apparently looking for Byrne, but he wasn't back yet—"we
have intel reports they may try something. If the bugs come out
from under the stove, I'm ready to stomp on them."

"You mean, if they initiate hostilities?" said Blair.

"Uh-huh . . . Captain Miller, could you give me a close-up of the channel . . . thank you. There, you can see the convoy approaching from the south. The tankers will stick to the deepest part. Our escorts are on the flanks, with *Gallery* and *Adams* to the east, between them and the threat bearing, and *Van Zandt* to port. Lee, how far away are they from us?"

"*Mobile Bay*'s two hundred miles from the convoy centroid, Admiral."

"Yet we can see every movement in the channel, and we can talk directly to the COs of each ship." He picked up a red phone, glanced at a tote board, and said crisply, "Bounty Hunter, this is Trail Boss, over."

The answer came instantly from a speaker. "Bounty Hunter, over."

"Admiral Hart, for the Commodore."

"This is Commodore Nauman, sir."

"How's it going, Snatch? What's the situation?"

"Visibility's lousy, Admiral. We've got half the Sahara out here with us. I've opened the interval to reduce risk of collision. We'll go through slow, at ten knots."

"Are all your units at general quarters?"

"Affirmative, sir."

"Do you have any liaison aboard the tankers?"

"No, sir, not at present."

"I'd like to have an officer aboard the lead merchie. For coordination, if we need it, and to reassure them."

"Aye, sir, I'll take care of that."

"We've got you up on the big screen. A perfect picture. As soon as we see anything cooking from Farsi, we'll give you a heads-up and pass targeting data."

"Thanks, we're not doing too well radar-wise in this stuff."

"Keep me informed, Barry. Good luck. Trail Boss out."

"Bounty Hunter, out."

Hart hung up. Blair said, "No code, or anything? What if they're listening to you?"

"It's a covered net. It's just a garble unless you've got the key list."

She hoped he was right, though after the Walker revelations it seemed as if one shouldn't assume things like that. But she didn't say anything. Hart stretched. "Now comes the hard part."

"What's that?"

"Waiting," said Miller. He shifted on his chair and finally said, "More coffee, sir? Ms. Titus?"

They declined. He fidgeted some more and then burst out, "Admiral, about civilians staying aboard—"

"What about it?"

"Well, I have no facilities for women. It's awkward. And you know it's against the law."

Hart said, *"She* stayed here last night, I take it."

"Yes, sir."

"Captain Miller gave me a fine stateroom. His own, in fact. He's been very accommodating."

Hart yawned. "Maybe I'll take a refill, at that. Black and bitter, please. My advice is, don't bust a gut over it. You're not staying aboard tonight, too, are you, Blair?"

"I hadn't planned to. But if I do, I expect shuffleboard and daiquiris." She smiled at the captain. He looked away, chewing gum like a pile driver.

"Mark, first tanker, entering the channel now," said a loudspeaker. They fell silent, their attention absorbed again by the glowing, omniscient displays.

When Nauman reported the damage to *Borinquen,* Hart sat up, punching his fist into the leather. They watched the column bunch up, stop, and begin to drift toward the lane boundaries. Miller ordered Farsi Island brought up on another screen, large scale. They all stared at it. There were dots offshore, but none of them were moving. The admiral said through clenched teeth, "We just *swept* that channel! Those Goddamned reservists . . . God *damn* it!"

"They must have snuck in and mined it last night," Miller said.

"I sure as hell don't see how. I had two Saudi PGs and the Special Forces out there watching. Those *bastards!"*

He reached for the radio. Nauman answered, his voice irate and apologetic. "Yes sir, she's taking water . . . the officer aboard tells me there's no danger of sinking, though. They've sealed off the damaged compartments. I'm reorienting the screen."

"What do you mean?"

"Uh, this was at the suggestion of *Borinquen's* master . . . he thinks if there are more mines, the tankers can take hits better than we can. He recommended we reorient to Form One, line ahead, with the escorts bringing up the rear."

Hart glanced sideways at Blair. His eyes were like little glinting steel balls. Into the phone he said, "And you concur?"

"I think it's the prudent thing to do, sir. We have no minesweeping assets with us." The distant voice paused.

"What about helo cover?"

"I'll put one in the air as soon as this sand lets up. Get them looking out in front of the convoy."

Hart, his lips rigid as iron, told him to do it. Blair relaxed. For a moment she'd feared he'd disapprove the suggestion, put the warships in front just to avoid embarrassing the Navy. She'd known senior officers, yes, and politicians, too, who thought just that way.

He signed off. He took out his pipe, started to pack it, then set it aside with an irritated gesture. "Has anybody got a cigarette?"

The master chief gave him half a pack of Merits. Hart lit one and sat puffing angrily as additional reports came in.

Early that afternoon a flash message came in direct from *Van Zandt*. It reported loss of contact with their helicopter. It also relayed that the pilot's last message, though garbled, had said something about sighting a submarine.

She saw them forget about her, saw them lean forward. "Call them back," Hart snapped. "Right now, Jack. Did the pilot send back any specifics before he went down? Description? Course and speed?"

Byrne busied himself on the red phone while Miller waved the master chief over. After a short discussion, they retrieved the last recorded radar position of side number 421. It had been shot down north of the convoy, not far from the Hasbah oil field.

Now the chief recalled the tactical data picture from the computer's memory. The screen showed them the semicircular symbol of a friendly aircraft frozen near a surface contact. A scatter of small returns surrounded them: the derricks and buoys of an oil field.

Then, to the clicking of a keyboard, time began. Blair leaned forward, tensing as the helicopter suddenly altered course. There was nothing on the screen to show why—or at least nothing large enough, or high enough above sea return, for the long-range radars to pick up. Four Two One then turned, passing directly over the surface contact. The two symbols merged for a moment, winking as they coalesced.

Then, abruptly, both disappeared.

There was utter silence in CDC. Finally, Byrne murmured, "Something small, intermittent, where he made that sudden turn . . . that could have been a sub. At periscope depth. Then he submerged, after his escort boat fired."

"Hasbah—that's Iranian?" Hart snapped.

"Yessir, Hasbah's Iranian."

Abruptly he jumped down and said, not looking at them, "Captain Byrne. Charts, please. Northern Gulf."

"Yessir."

"What are you doing?" she said.

"We're going to hit back."

"Hit the submarine? Is that what you're talking about?"

"It's long gone. We'll never pick it up in those rigs and pipelines." Beneath the explanation, the admiral's voice smoked with rage.

"Then what are you talking about?"

"A reprisal."

Byrne handed up the charts. Hart looked around for a work area, and at last smoothed them out on a radarscope. Then he went on. "I don't know how they got to *Borinquen*. But they did. And we won't have the full story on what happened to *Van Zandt*'s helo for a while, either. If it's a sub, a successful attack on a U.S.-escorted convoy, we're in trouble, Miss Titus. Deep trouble. We've got to find it and kill it. But that's not going to be easy. We never saw it approach, and we only saw it leaving by accident.

"But I'm not going to stand still for this. We're here to show force when necessary. I think it's necessary now."

He turned. "Captain Byrne! I want a plan for a strike on their oil rigs, today, after the convoy detaches. Announce that it's in retaliation for a submarine attack. Get on the horn and work it out with ASU. I want it transmitted here, copies to *Adams*, *Van Zandt*, and *Gallery*. Notify the usual allies and diplomats. I want it here in two hours."

Byrne stood for a moment, tapping his glasses against his lips. Then he said, "Aye aye, sir. But do you want to revisit that one point . . . about announcing a possible submarine contact?"

"Should I?"

"If we can for a moment, sir. We still don't have any hard evidence that the 209 is operational. Do we really want to announce that it is? As I see it, even if that pilot was right, announcing it to the world is counterproductive. They'll go to ground and be twice as hard to detect next time. Why not exercise a little cover and deception?"

"C & D? How?"

"Like this: Just announce that *Borinquen* was hit by a mine. Let them think they've put one over on us. Meanwhile, alert our commanding officers, rearm and reorient to the extent we can for shallow-water ASW, and, above all, get our intelligence people on the stick. If the Iranians think they're invisible, sooner or later they'll get careless. And we'll see them again. When they do, we'll jump on them with everything we've got."

Hart stuck his lower lip out. He pulled out another cigarette and lit it. At last, he nodded, short, sharp, bending to the chart. "It's a thought, Jack. It has its appeal, doesn't it?"

Blair had been sucking a pencil, running over things in her mind. Now she cleared her throat. "Admiral, I don't think that's wise."

Hart straightened slowly. "I don't recall asking for your input, Miss Titus."

"I'm not quarreling with the fact of a reprisal. You're the on-scene commander. That's your prerogative. But I don't think it should be an oil rig. Nor do I think you should conceal the fact there's a submarine loose in the Gulf."

Beyond Hart, the screens flickered, updating second by second; the smooth, steady hum of voices and radio circuits went on. So much data, so much research and engineering and expense, she thought. But it all came down to this—to the decision of the man in charge.

He said sharply, "I'm listening."

"The submarine first. If there's really one out there, or if you suspect there is, it's only fair to release the news. Allow the shipping companies to reroute, or delay. Secrets don't do anyone any good, Admiral. Most of them are just a form of military masturbation."

Hart looked away, blinking once at the last word. "And the reprisal?"

"I say no. For two reasons. One, it's too easy for them to counterstrike, burn another—Saudi, Kuwaiti, or another of our allies'. Second, I don't perceive Iran as a unitary rational actor."

Behind her Miller snorted. "What does *that* mean?"

"It means that the Pasdaran, Navy, and oil ministry are not coordinated at the national level. They formulate policy independently and act independently. Ergo, attacking an oil rig won't be perceived by the Pasdaran, or the Navy, or whoever set up this attack as a punishment, nor will it deter further aggressive moves."

"They're all Iranians," Miller said. "Their other assets are too hard to hit without a major action, major planning."

"Then do a major action. Against the Pasdaran."

The admiral said angrily, "And take how long? Jack's idea about playing dumb as far as the 209's concerned—that's good. The alternative is shutting down the whole Gulf. We'll do that. For now.

"And Lee's right about the reprisal. Those are valid targets.

Those oil fields earn foreign exchange. For sure, hitting one's going to hurt."

"Yes, but—"

"Will you please, Miss Titus, *leave it to me!*"

The last words were shouted and the hum in the windowless space quieted, the enlisted men and junior officers looking up. Hart lowered his voice but steel still braced it as he said, "*As* you pointed out, I'm the commander on the scene. Now, you can hang me after the fact, if what I do doesn't work, but by God you are not in my chain of command and you will *not* tell me what to do! Is that clear?"

"Perfectly clear, Admiral."

He swung away from her, shouting again for Byrne. Together, the three men bent over the charts.

She found her own way to the mess decks, and had a late lunch among the enlisted men. Or rather, by herself. She seemed surrounded by a protective magic; sailors came out of the serving line, saw her, and quickly found themselves seats elsewhere. Blair smiled grimly. She could imagine how fast the story of her confronting Miller, and then Hart himself, had gone through the ship.

The Bitch from Washington picked at overcooked roast turkey, baked beans, and a yellow scum meant to be macaroni and cheese. They don't eat any better here than in the House of Representatives, she thought.

When she was done, she went back up, the master-at-arms still tagging along behind her. Hart was sitting with his feet propped on an intercom, staring at the screen. The convoy was past the Narrows, headed north. A fresh pack of cigarettes lay on the console. When he saw her, he swung his feet down. "Well," he said. "Where've you been?"

"Eating. Are your plans complete?"

"Concept of operations, target selection, yes . . . the rest the staff's working out. It won't be too complicated. We've done oil-field strikes before."

She wanted to ask, And did they accomplish what you wanted them to, Admiral? But she didn't. Part of her wanted to reassure this cornered, lonely man, with a weight on his shoulders that, after all, she'd never had. She had the ear of the powerful. But she had no accountability. And for that, suddenly, looking at his strain-engraved face, she was grateful.

"I'm going out there," Hart said. "To Linebacker Four. Byrne's taking my gear down to the flight deck. Miller will get Bahrain to send somebody out here for you."

"Admiral—"

"Yes, Miss Titus."

"May I come? You promised me a look at a convoy."

Hart looked surprised. Then he laughed, a short ugly bark. "I did, didn't I? Sure, let's show you what it's really like out here. Lee, say goodbye to your guest. Call away flight quarters, please."

Mobile Bay had been steaming northwest all morning. So the flight out, in Hart's command helicopter, took a little over an hour.

"*Adams*, sir?" shouted the pilot when the lumbering forms of the merchants, the gray sheep dogs of the destroyers, came into view ahead.

"No. Put us down on the lead tanker. I want to see the damage for myself."

She was surprised at the ship's sheer size. It was huge; so long that the far end was misty in the dust. It didn't look as if the explosion had hurt it badly. It just steamed ahead with a very slight slant to the right. But she supposed most of the damage was underwater. She walked around on the sand-gritty deck, talked briefly to the master and the engineer, and then to a commander from the destroyer, Lenson. He was attractive, tall, but he looked tired. Hart lifted again shortly after that, and after brief touchdowns on *Van Zandt* and then *Adams*, they headed back toward Bahrain. She and Hart sat silently in the passenger compartment.

She was thinking, again, about the report she had to write, and the call she had to make. Tomorrow . . . no, in the excitement she'd forgotten, it was due today. She ought to call from the embassy when she got in. Or no, they'd be landing at the Admin Support Unit. Perhaps she could use a secure phone there.

Only what would she say?

She decided then to advise Talmadge to postpone the vote. Tell him there were operations in progress now that might enable her to make a firm recommendation.

And basically that was the truth. She just wasn't sure yet. She thought, for one thing, that the number of ships committed could be reduced . . . to, say, twenty. And they could do without the *Forrestal*. The Navy needed more minesweepers and light units here, perhaps the squadron of hydrofoils based at Key West. These could replace the more expensive ships without loss of effectiveness. Hart, of course, would argue that it was just that, the overwhelming force available, that limited the scope of Iranian aggression. However, she didn't think so, looking at the broad picture. Iran was being bled white by war. The regime's energies were concentrated on the all-important Iraqi front.

Though as to the larger question, what role American power had to play here . . . to that she could not yet formulate an answer she could back up in quantitative terms.

It was obvious that the Navy was a major player in the area. It was the keystone holding the GCC together. As the Royal Navy had been once. The Gulf states were too weak, rich, and internally unstable to last long without outside support.

But could the United States midwife a lasting peace? Would a "barrier" policy, a Kennan-type containment, turn Iran toward better relations after the war wound down? Or would it exacerbate the regime's demands? The Pasdaran was the sticking point. Was the U.S. presence keeping them small, limiting them to hit-and-run tactics? Was it goading them into more? Or was it totally ineffective as far as the half-terrorist, half-military revolutionary guard was concerned?

And what about this new element in the balance? The submarine?

It was possible that the retaliation Hart had just ordered would clarify the question. But she thought it more likely it would just muddy it further.

Maybe the only real test was a full-scale attack, *on the Pasdaran.*

She recalled now Miller's response to this the day before. "If I get an order to go in, I'll go in." "Those are safe havens . . . and it's Congress that's holding us back from hitting them."

But what if Congress lifted the restraints?

What if, when she talked to Talmadge, she explained the situation—and asked him to lobby the other Senate leaders for a one-time exception?

It would be a gamble. In fact, it would risk all-out war, closure of the Gulf, and pushing Iran into the waiting bear hug of the Soviets.

By all the tenets of her training and experience, she believed in avoiding risk. To have to gamble meant poor planning. Yet still, with the force levels they'd built up, wasn't this the best time for a showdown?

It might be a disaster. If it was, it would have her name on it. But if it failed, their course would at last be clear. Talmadge, with a majority on the committee, could call for a vote on War Powers and win. The administration would have to pull out, and the region would settle into a new, more stable pattern of power. Sometimes you had to be realistic. Sometimes prestige and even national interest just weren't worth what you had to pay for them.

And maybe it was time to put her name on something, even if to history it would be Bankey Talmadge's. To take responsibility—as Hart did, as Miller did, as even Prince Ismail did in his way.

The helicopter droned on, and inch by inch her head, still buzzing with the complexities of economics, trade balance, diplomacy, and possible war, sank until her golden hair fell forward, hiding her eyes.

22

U.S.S. *Turner Van Zandt*

THE rest of the convoy was uneventful. The doubled lookouts reported fishing floats, drift nets, garbage, but no mines. The only incident worth note was off Ras al Khafji, when three ships came into view at 20,000 yards. One had the lines of a warship.

Gallery's helicopter identified them as two merchants escorted by a *Krivak*-class destroyer. Dan had already recognized the silhouette. Recognized it with a feeling of doom, remembering a hot day in the Caribbean, the silence of the hove-to *Barrett*.... He monitored the exchange as the commodore called them on channel twelve. The *Krivak* didn't answer, but at last one of the others came up. "This is Soviet Union merchant ship," was all he said.

"Soviet merchant, this is the American convoy on your bow. I want to report to you that we have encountered a mined area in the Farsi Narrows."

"*Americanyets* warship, *Americanyets* warship, please say if that confirmed."

"That is confirmed. Advise you stay clear of that area until swept."

"Thank you, *Americanyets* warship," said the Russian. "Thank you for the warning."

"Crazy damned war," Shaker had muttered. "Us telling *them* to look out for mines."

They dropped the convoy off Hawalli, leaving them in custody of two gunboats. U.S. warships were not welcome in Kuwaiti waters. The sleek craft ran circles around the listing *Borinquen*, tossing up rooster tails higher than their masts, acting as if they were out there just for fun. The three escorts lay hove to until they were out of sight.

And now they were steaming south, toward Manama and stand-down.

When the intercom came on, Dan was thinking about the times he'd chewed out Schweinberg and Hayes. It was Radio. He leaned on the answer switch. "Bridge aye."

"Is the captain there, sir? Flash coming in." Behind the voice, he could hear the teletype chattering, the bell signaling a special message.

"I'm here," said Shaker, speaking past him from his chair. "Get it up soon as you can."

Flash was the highest priority the Navy had, reserved for Pearl Harbor–type warnings and orders requiring instant action. The radioman arrived two minutes later, puffing from his run. The captain leaned back, squinting at the message board. Dan looked away, wanting to snatch it out of his hands; why couldn't they bring up two copies? At last Shaker, frowning, tilted it toward him. He glanced down it, skipping the headers.

FLASH SECRET

1. (S) Upon detachment of *LINEBACKER IV ADAMS, GALLERY, VAN ZANDT* proceed at best speed to radar picket station KILO off Kuwait. UK frigate *CARDIFF* will join en route. Commodore B. S. Nauman will assume tactical coordination of combined surface battle group. SBG will loiter vicinity point KILO until EXECUTE order is received. At that time proceed by shortest route at flank speed across Exclusionary Zone to vicinity Ardeshir oil field.

2. (S) At Ardeshir OTC will select one gas/oil separation platform and destroy it with gunfire. Remain in area no longer than one hour. Avoid civilian casualties. Minimize collateral damage and adverse environmental effects. If approached or threatened by Iranian air or sea units respond in accordance with COMIDEASTFOR Rules of Engagement, ref (A). Do not proceed east of selected target. Do not engage other platforms, surface craft, or aircraft unless necessary to preempt attack. Do not approach Iranian mainland closer than 50 (fifty) nautical miles.

3. (S) Return at highest possible speed. Upon crossing zonal boundary detach HMS *CARDIFF*. *ADAMS, GALLERY, VAN ZANDT* return to Bahrain as previously directed ref (B).

4. (S) Commanding officers will ensure that all units and personnel are at highest degree of readiness during execution of this order. Maintain Condition II Red against surprise attack until south of 28 degrees latitude.

BT
DO NOT DECLASSIFY WITHOUT PERMISSION OF
ORIGINATOR
SECRET

"Reprisal," said Dan.

"And about goddamn time," said Shaker. He took the pen the radioman held out and scribbled his initials. "Officer of the deck! Get Lieutenant Pensker up here. We're going to need to shuffle our ammo around."

"Aye, sir."

"All units Sagebrush, this is Bounty Hunter. Message follows. Immediate execute. Break." Lenson, Firzhak, and Shaker grabbed for pencils as McQueen turned up the Tactical Coordination speaker. "Bravo Tango Two tack zero-four-five. Sierra two niner. Yankee Hotel two. Alfa Charlie niner one. I say again"—the calm voice from *Charles Adams* reread it—"nine one. Standby, execute. Over."

"Roger that," shouted Shaker. "OOD, come right to zero-four-five. All ahead flank, kick her up to twenty-seven knots."

Meanwhile, Dan had grabbed the code book. The intercom beat him as *Van Zandt* heeled to full rudder. "Bridge, Combat: Break last signal as follows: Form line of bearing in order of hull numbers. Prepare for surface and/or air action. Intended target, fixed installation."

"Concur with Combat's break." Dan snapped the pub shut and made for the chart table. Sure enough, the next question out of Shaker's mouth was "Navigator, how far to Point Kilo?"

"Twenty-two miles, sir."

"From there to the Ardeshir field?"

"Wait one . . . forty-eight miles."

"Mister Firzhak! What's your course to station?"

"I'm steering by eye, sir, to come in astern of *Gallery.*"

"Okay. Boatswain! Call the mess decks, have them set up for early chow, sandwiches or whatever they got can be fixed quick."

Shaker busied himself with the intercom. He told Guerra, in main control, to put all pumps on line and bring up another generator. He reviewed weapons and electronic readiness with Al Wise, the TAO. Then he joined Lenson and McQueen over the chart.

Dan, glancing at him, could hardly believe this was the same man he'd found slumped in his chair that morning. Shaker was grinning, eyes lit like strobes. "I'll hold off GQ till the guys eat. Christ, I hope nobody up the line wimps out on that execute. What do you think, XO? Will the buggers come out and fight?"

"I don't know, sir."

"They've got the ships. *Sahand* and *Sabalan* are inport Bushehr. They could intercept us. And there's a fighter squadron there, too . . . those stupid bastards!" He battered his fist down on the tan coast of Asia. "That's where we should hit! Not some fucking oil platform; that doesn't do a thing but stir them up! Where the hell is Pensker?"

"Here, sir, behind you."

Shaker and the black officer went out on the wing. Dan could hear them discussing the proper ammo with which to destroy an oil rig. Then their voices fell, borne away by the fresh wind as *Van Zandt*, rolling as the sea kicked up, sliced her way eastward, toward Iran.

Cardiff joined ten miles west of the hold point. Dan watched her slide into line ahead, a trim modern frigate in the lighter British battle gray. The White Ensign fluttered at her masthead, matching the cream her stem peeled off of a sea that grew greener with each mile. She fell in astern of *Gallery*, just ahead of *Van Zandt*.

The execute order reached them shortly thereafter. At the picket station, Nauman ordered a turn-in-sequence to the east. They corpened around, each warship turning in the swirl left by the previous one's rudder. Under a burning sky, they increased speed gradually as *Adams* brought her boilers on line, and finally steadied at thirty.

The sea was empty. Not a dhow, not a craft of any kind showed on it or on their screens as they crossed the invisible line that marked Iranian-controlled sea. It looked the same on the far side, a sullen green with here and there a drifting slick, its edges refracting the dull sunlight into a thousand muted hues.

Shaker muttered, staring ahead through his binoculars, "Dan, you take CIC for this action. I'll stay here."

"Aye, sir."

Combat was as ever, cold and blue-lit, but someone had taped a placard over the plotting table. It read: SO WHAT IF IRANIANS ARE SHORT, DARK, AND SMELLY. SCREW 'EM ALL.

He circled the room, checking each scope and position, and at last settled into the chair. Al Wise grinned at him. The operations officer looked excited and at the same time scared. Pale and thin, a detail man, he was devoted to his cats; he had three, named after Soviet radars, which he boarded with his fiancée during deployments. "Good times, hey, XO?" he said now.

"Good times?" said Dan. "Sorry, I'm a little slow today."

"Never mind. You going to play TAO, or you want to second-guess me?"

"I'll do it. You back me up."

"Got it." The ops boss screwed his head back into earphones. He was on Air Defense Net Alfa; if speedboats or planes showed up, that was how the OTC would coordinate the SAG's defense.

Dan sat motionless, feeling the tension coil in his stomach, as if his guts had turned to springs. There was nothing to do now but wait.

An hour later, he could make out the field on radar. It looked like a glowing spiderweb. From each platform, glittering lines spun outward, pipelines to satellite wells. And each spider was itself woven, he knew, into the submerged pumping network back to Khārk. Pips moved within the web, service boats, probably guard boats, too; the new Boghammers that the Swedes—always happy to coin kroners from neutrality—had sold Khomeini in the face of an international embargo. Not that the Reagan administration could throw stones. . . . The range closed steadily. Down here he wouldn't see much of the action. If Iran took up their challenge, though, this was where the battle would be fought from.

Nauman slowed the group when they were ten miles away, and sprinted ahead in *Adams*. A loose routine had evolved for platform attacks. The men on them, civilian workers and a few guards with rifles, got ten minutes warning in Farsi, French, and English before the destroyers went in. It seemed to take hours. The men in CIC didn't fidget, didn't move. They were glued to the screens.

At last Nauman's signal came over PRITAC. Follow him in, and commence fire in turn.

Van Zandt accelerated instantly, heeling to hard rudder. Dan switched to the gunnery circuit as Wise said, "*Adams* has commenced firing."

"Very well."

Time crawled by. He stared at the screen. Occasionally, he could see speckles near the spider. Plumes of spray from ricochets and near misses. Wise, from the coordination net, announced who was firing.

At last, the captain's voice came on the line. "Mount thirty-one, load fifty rounds point det to last station screw feeder."

Terry Pensker, his voice hard and eager: "Fifty rounds PD loaded."

Shaker: "Stand by . . . commence fire."

Too bad they were last, he thought. *Adams* carried two five-inch mounts and was known in the fleet as a shooting ship. *Gallery* and *Cardiff* had taken their turns, too. No way Shaker would give up a chance, though. And the platforms, spiderweb frameworks of steel, were notoriously difficult to damage with shellfire.

The 76 slammed suddenly above them, making the plotting boards shudder. Three slow rounds followed, spotting rounds. He could hear the empty shell cases clang on the deck, and the whoosh of high-pressure air that cleared the bore. Then Pensker ordered rapid continuous and the firing began in earnest, as fast and steady as a good carpenter nails a wall, slam, slam, slam, till the ready magazine was empty.

A moment later the 1MC came on. "On the *Van Zandt:* This is the Captain speaking. For those of you below, we've just completed a firing run on an Iranian oil platform. It's on fire. I count ten hits. . . . Now the lead ship in our group is hauling around. Looks like we're going to make another pass. Petty officers, break off as many men as possible for a look-see. The fire is orange-red, hundreds of feet high. Loads of smoke, dense and black—"

Shaker went on talking, describing the flashes as the British ship's shells hit, for all the world like a sports announcer. Dan sat motionless in the padded chair, pulling at his earlobe. He thought of going outside, watching the shells tear apart what American or Dutch engineers had built. But it didn't tempt him. Not even Shaker thought this was the answer to the problems that had brought *Van Zandt* to the Gulf, or even a step toward them.

At least it was going smoothly. There'd been two boats near the platform, but they'd retreated eastward after picking up the crew. But if he were the Iranians—

"Tracks two-one-oh-one, two-one-oh-two, two-one-oh-three turning west."

"Say again," Dan said instantly to the man who was watching the air picture. "Al, better get on this."

"Got them. Three aircraft over the coast. Turning our way."

"Range?"

"Seventy miles, closing."

He leaned over the petty officer's chair. There they were,
three hostile-designated contacts, detaching themselves from
the Bushehr peninsula. They weren't showing on radar yet.
This data was digital, transmitted from the AWACs.

"Type?"

"F-4s, I think, sir," called the EW operator.

Lenson watched them for a long moment. Phantoms. U.S.-
made, supplied when Iran was the bulwark of the Nixon doctrine. Integral machine guns and cannon, and they could carry
rockets, iron bombs, or TV-guided Mavericks.

They were making for Ardeshir, all right. They'd be overhead
in ten minutes. It was almost like the encounter at Hormuz.
Only this time there was no doubt as to what they were.

"Lieutenant Pensker. Your target: three bogeys at one-two-
seven. Designate to STIR. Load Standard to the rail. Next
round same." He pressed the intercom. "Captain, CIC. Three
fighters heading our way from the mainland."

"Take good care of them, Dan. Does Nauman know about
'em?"

"He should, they're coming over NTDS."

"Call him, make sure. Keep me posted."

"Aye, sir." He snapped off and looked at Wise. The ops boss
nodded, already relaying the alert to the flagship.

Now, as the TAO brought designation and tracking up, Dan
backed off from the situation, forced himself to relax and think.
Nauman would most likely designate the incoming aircraft to
one of the frigates. Their missile systems and radars were
newer than the 1960-era *Adams*. But *Gallery* was off to starboard. Sure enough, the speaker said then, "Comanche, this is
Bounty Hunter. Your target, aircraft, track two-one-oh-one,
oh-two, oh-three, bearing one-one-zero, range fifty miles."

"Comanche" was *Van Zandt*. "Illuminate," said Dan.
Pensker, at the weapons console, acknowledged and called
back: "Illuminating. . . . lock-on! Solid track, good solution on
leading bogey."

"Designate to Standard. This will be a three-round engagement with setup for immediate refire."

"Designated."

"Missile on."

"First round, standing by to fire."

"Bridge, Combat: To the captain: Group of three tight bogeys
have been designated our target. We're locked on, awaiting
release authority for three-round engagement."

Shaker, tersely: "You have my permission to fire when OTC
orders."

"Roger that . . . Sound fire-warning bell," he told Pensker. No one was supposed to be near the launcher during GQ, but they might as well take the precaution.

Now he returned his attention to the screen. Turn back, he thought, trying to will the oncoming pilots to break off, to heed the warning the Mark 92 lock-on would be droning in their headphones. He remembered another man, far away and years ago, a man he'd had to kill with his bare hands. He didn't like to kill. But he didn't want his men to die, either. *Turn back. Don't make me fire.*

The pips jumped another mile forward. "Altitude?" he asked crisply.

"Ten thousand."

"Confirm IFF hostile." Unlikely they'd be anything else, out of Bushehr in a V formation, but it was another check.

"Squawking mode two. They're ragheads, all right, and military," said Pensker.

"Standard commands and responses, Lieutenant." He voiced the rebuke automatically. His mind was running independently now, like one of the computers around him. The range and altitude were within the missile envelope. They ought to fire soon, to allow for a second salvo in case the first missed.

He remembered another day when he'd waited for aircraft to come in, just like this. A stormy day in the Mediterranean. That time all he'd had were three-inch popguns, too slow to follow jets around, much less hit them. Now he had missiles, 76mm, Phalanx, multilayered defense. He had to admit, it felt a hell of a lot better.

"Thirty miles."

"Hard paint," said Pensker tightly. "We ought to fire now. Sir! We ought to—"

"Take it easy, Terry."

"Comanche, Bounty Hunter: weapons free," said the speaker. Dan paused for just a second. The moment he'd hoped would never come again was here.

He said, his voice devoid of all emotion, "Shoot."

The deck plates vibrated to the bellow of a rocket engine. It receded, and he visualized the second round, thrust up too fast for eye to follow out of its magazine onto the rail, twin probes locking in for the data feed, then the launcher swinging it down at the same time it trained, fast as a striking viper. Another howl dwindled off. One thousand. Two thousand. Three thousand. Four thousand. A third. "Missiles away," shouted Pensker, his voice charged, happy.

Dan stared at the screen. Their targets could still escape.

Turn tail and outrace the oncoming weapons . . . chaff wouldn't decoy a Standard, even if they carried it . . . the symbols jumped forward again.

Twenty miles. "Standby," said Pensker. "Intercept!"

The update came. There were only two symbols on the screen. At the next sweep, there was one.

"Bogey three's outbound."

"Combat, Bridge: We see smoke on the horizon. What's the scoop?"

"Two bogeys off the scope, sir, presume splashed. The third one"—Pensker hung fire for a moment, straining his eyes into the fluorescent glow—"third one's turned tail. Headed back for shore."

Shaker's voice again, boisterous as a boy's at recess: "Nice work! Damn nice work! Teach them to fuck with the U.S. Navy!"

Dan stood by the plotting table while the room went noisy around him, men slapping each other on the back, laughing and yelling. Something brushed his face and he glanced up.

IRANIANS ARE SHORT, DARK, AND

His hand came up without thought, and the paper tore, half staying with the tape, the rest coming free in his fist. Crumpled, it bounced on the deck, rolled under a repeater.

"Hey, XO!"

"What'd you do that for, sir?"

He almost couldn't speak through the sick feeling. "They were brave men. They died for their country."

"They were *ragheads*, XO!"

"You can bet *they* were cheering, Commander, when they shot down Buck and Chunky," put in another voice: Pensker's.

Someone gripped his arm. It was Al Wise. "Sit down, Dan," he murmured, steering him for the CO's chair. "Maybe you're right. But they don't want to hear that now. Right now, they think they've won."

Half an hour later, from the fantail, he looked back as *Van Zandt*, still last in line, hammered westward at flank speed.

Behind them the Gulf was burning. Flames guttered orange-red, licking upward along twisted steel. They writhed inside a cocoon of sooty smoke like snakes fighting to be born. And from them, welling and then slowly toppling to lie along the whole eastern horizon, was an implacable blackness, like an early and unnatural night.

He clung to the rail, and the weight of the helmet bent down his head.

Destruction! The sole and last communication possible between those who had defined each other as evil incarnate. Only the flight of weapons could cross the walls Iran and America had built between them. And like flames in oil, each act of revenge inflamed the other side to greater hate and greater vengeance.

If you are struck, you strike back twice as hard; this was the law every child learns on the playground, and the relationship among states. This time, America was lucky. This was a war fought at sea and in the air, where her technology, resources, and military skill gave her triumph after triumph. But her very success drove her enemy to the tactics of the weak: suicide craft, terrorism, hostage taking, the whole spectrum of "uncivilized" warfare.

But how could it ever end? How could the scales ever balance?

And now what horror would the other side commit?

"Now secure from general quarters. Set the condition two underway watch. On deck, watch section port, officers section port."

He sat listlessly in the padded chair in Combat. They'd passed the twenty-eight-degree line, then. He hadn't been up to the bridge to see. Now Wise groaned, got up, stretched. "What do you say, sir, grab some dinner?"

"I guess so."

He shuffled below unenthusiastically. Sat with the other officers in the TV nook, none of them speaking, avoiding even each others' eyes. Firzhak fiddled with the television. They could get a grainy black and white image of a man in a burnoose reading something, but no communication penetrated the sand hiss of static. At last, he snapped it off and picked up the February *Naval Engineers Journal*. On the end table, stripped of its walnut veneer to bare metal, lay a sweat-stained fore-and-aft cap with scratched lieutenant's bars. No one touched it, though they looked at it from time to time. It had been Schweinberg's.

Have to write a letter, Dan thought through the numbness. Parents. Next of kin. The last he'd heard, a patrol boat was searching for the wreckage. He doubted they'd find anything. No, the rowdy young pilots were gone. Just . . . like . . . that.

"Bastards," muttered Guerra. The engineer's pitted face was poisonous. No one asked who he meant.

"Sir, we're ready to serve," said the steward, leaning over Dan.

He started and glanced around. "Anyone seen the captain?"

"Still on the bridge, I think, XO."

He got up wearily and punched the bogen. Shaker answered. His voice dragged, too. They were all feeling it, Dan thought. He hung up. "He'll be down in a second."

The JOs took their positions around the table, standing behind their chairs. Shaker came in a few minutes later. "Sit down, guys."

Dan ordered the salad. When it came, he was suddenly hungry. For a while there was no sound but the clink of silver, a muttered request for salt.

"Well," said Shaker at last, clearing his throat. "Frank, Terry, your gear worked pretty good today."

"Yessir."

"I don't know how we looked overall out there, though. The four of us must have fired a thousand rounds at that thing. Saw a hell of a lot of misses. Right through the trusswork, or under the platform."

"I saw that," said Bob Ekdahl. "But if it was a ship, sir, one of their gunboats, those would all have been hits."

"Good point," said Shaker, his face lightening. "But those are bum gun targets. Tell you what, tell the gunners to brush up on their demolition. Next time, we'll just scare the Persians off it, send the whaleboat over, and blow it up."

Dan didn't say anything. He felt detached from this conversation, though he wasn't sure why. Shaker turned to him next. "Nice work down in CIC, Dan, Al. And I mean nice. Blew them out of the air clean as a whistle. Two out of three."

"I was thinking about that," said Proginelli eagerly. "Sorry, sir—"

"No, go ahead, let's hear what our CIC officer thinks."

"I think we fired too fast, sir. Three rounds, just like that. Could be two of them hit the same bogey." His eyes slid to Dan and he added hastily, "I don't want to ping on the guys in the hot seat, but maybe next time we fire on multiple targets we should space our rounds out."

They discussed that for a while, some arguing that on a gaggle of bogeys the thing to do was get ordnance there fast and lots of it, which was the way TAO school taught it, the others taking Proginelli's side. Dan said to the steward, "Yeah, coffee, black. Thanks."

"Now," said Shaker, "I understand we had one person who didn't think we did so well."

Dan registered the words after a moment. He glanced up. "Are you talking about me, Captain?"

"Uh-huh." The faces along the table turned his way; he saw their expressions—puzzlement mixed with polite interest. The captain pushed back his plate and shook out a Camel. He searched his pockets for a light; Guerra pushed him matches. Shaker poised the flame off the tip, looking past it at Dan. "I understand you don't think we did the right thing, sending those assholes to Paradise."

"That's not exactly how I feel, Captain."

"How exactly do you feel, XO?"

"I felt that cheering, like the men were doing, was inappropriate."

"Let's see, that's Naval Academy, isn't it? Mr. Ekdahl, supply the quotation."

The ensign flushed; junior man in the wardroom, just out of Annapolis, he was unused to being singled out, except for ragging. "Uh, yes it is, sir . . . let's see . . . 'Don't cheer, boys, the poor devils are dying.' Captain John W. Philip, USS *Texas*, at the Battle of Santiago, 1898."

"That kind of what you mean, Dan?"

"Kind of, Captain."

"Uh-huh. Well, that's not my attitude. I remember a little of that stuff myself. Georgie Patton, what'd he say . . . 'Nobody ever won a war by dying for his country. The object is to make the other poor son of a bitch die for his.' Or something like that."

The JOs chuckled. "Dessert, Captain?" said the steward, picking up his plate.

"What we got?"

"Peach cobbler and ice cream."

"I'll have that." Shaker winked at him. "As long as it's no-cal."

Dan refused with a shake of his head.

"In my view," the captain went on, "the operation was a success in spite of the stinking orders we were given. Dash in, shoot up a dime-a-dozen oil rig, then run for it with our tails tucked. Get real! We were just lucky they came out after us. We ought to go in there like we own the place. Blockade 'em. Dare 'em to come out and fight. This whole 'proportionate response' idea is a no-brainer. We ought to jam it in and break it off. When they get the picture we're mad dogs, the mining, hostage taking, all that'll stop."

"The Saudis wouldn't like that," said Dan.

"What have they got to do with it?"

"The Iranians can make real trouble for the little states. It's hard enough just getting them to let us refuel."

Shaker blew smoke at the overhead. "Jesus Christ! That's exactly my point, XO! Why won't they support us? Because they can't depend on us when things get tough. They think we'll cut and run! But if we took a hard line, the way the Soviets do . . . You see the Iranians taking any Soviet hostages? Like hell! They'd have bombers over Teheran the next day!"

Dan felt it wasn't that simple. First of all, there *were* Soviet hostages. He had a point to make, but he wasn't sure what it was. Maybe just that it was smart to think twice before taking on 60 million fanatical Iranians.

But the whole discussion seemed out of place to him. They'd killed some of the enemy, but lost three good men. The feeling of disgust, of futility, he couldn't seem to shake it off. Looking at the others, though, he could see this just wasn't the time.

"Well?"

"It's just not in our orders, sir. So I don't think it's a good thing to discuss."

Shaker stared at him. The JOs were deathly silent. Then, suddenly, he hoisted himself from his seat. "Okay, Mr. Lenson," he said. "Maybe we better have a little private confab."

"What's that, sir?"

"My cabin. Right now."

He followed the CO's short-legged roll through the passageways. The captain groped in his pockets for a moment, then unlocked the door. "Sit down," he said, jabbing at the chair. "We got to get some things understood here. Such as, whether you remember our first little talk when I took over."

Dan occupied the seat he pointed to, steeling himself for a reaming. He found himself facing the mutilated photograph. Shaker was angry, all right. His face, already picking up a Gulf sunburn, was drawn tight. "Yes sir, I remember that."

The captain wheeled suddenly and slammed his fist down on the table. "Then what the *hell* do you think you're doing, contradicting me in my wardroom? Telling the men there's something shameful about shooting down people who are attacking you? What the *hell* do you think we're doing here?"

"We're carrying out policy."

"The U.S. Navy wasn't built to 'carry out policy,' Lenson! It wasn't built to show the fucking flag and impress people! We're here to kick the living shit out of whoever gets in Uncle Sam's face! That's the kind of spirit I'm trying to build."

"I understand that, Captain. I think—"

"I'm not done. When I took this ship over, it was nothing but a showboat. And I don't think it was Charlie Bell's fault. I think you took charge when he got sick and, just coincidentally, the fighting spirit went to hell!"

"That's absolutely wrong."

"Shut your mouth when I'm talking to you! I'm telling you, Lenson, you piss me off. Your attitude pisses me off. I gave you your marching orders when I came aboard. You seemed to understand them then. What is it with you? Is it a moral problem, shooting down those assholes?"

"I gave the firing order, Captain. I just think we approach the issue differently. We're two different people."

"We're not two different people, God damn it! You're my *exec!* You're *me,* Lenson! Everything I want, you want! Everything I think, you think! And everything I say, you say! *Have you got that?"*

He shouted the last words. Dan knew the bridge watch, directly above, could hear them. He thought for a moment Shaker was going to come at him over the table. He'd never seen a commanding officer so angry. And he'd never had one curse him to his face. For a moment, he wondered whether Shaker was sane.

Then he stopped thinking. His fists crimped together under the table. Rage rose in him, blurring his sight. "What are you asking me to do, Captain? Swear unquestioning obedience to you? Then I'm telling you right now: you don't rate that. Nobody does. Even whatever made us, even he left us free will."

"I'm asking you to do your fucking job, that's all!"

"And I'm telling you I am!"

Shaker hung there, half over the table, and each man stared into the other's eyes. Then, slowly, the captain swayed back. He crossed the room, coughed violently, then dropped onto the settee and lit a cigarette. When he spoke again, his voice was soft. Without looking at Dan, he said, "Yeah. I *am* asking a lot. But think about it this way.

"I lost forty-two men on the *Strong.* And three more today. In the face of that, I conclude we're at war. In wartime, morale and leadership are all-important. Weapons are necessary, but it's fighting spirit and leadership that determine victory or defeat.

"And I intend to win! So I will *not* have you undermining me. Or debating me. You'll carry out my orders with unquestioning enthusiasm. If you disagree, you'll keep it to yourself! Is that clear enough?"

"Yes, sir."

"On this ship, you carry out my policies, Lenson. Your per-

sonal feelings are immaterial. It was that way for me when I
was number two. You'll want that from yours when you get
command."

"Yes, sir," said Dan again.

"Now get out of here," said Shaker. "Get ready for Manama.
We'll be there at dawn."

Outside, in the coffin-sized corridor between the captain's cabin
and CIC, he stood alone for several minutes, pressing his fists
to his head. They shook; his mouth was dry; rage still hammered in his blood. It wasn't only Shaker's anger that had
surprised him. His own had, too. And frightened him. He'd
almost hit Shaker in that moment they'd shouted at each other,
face-to-face.

Everyone in the Navy got his butt chewed to ribbons from
time to time. It was part of the experience. But Shaker hadn't
been putting this on for show. He was serious.

Dan found himself wondering whether he ought to have a
talk with someone on the staff about this. Maybe Byrne. He and
Jack went back a long way, back to Ike Sundstrom and the
Guam. . . . No. He'd been privately reprimanded for not supporting the commanding officer in front of the wardroom. For
that, Shaker was well within his rights.

Still, he wondered. He knew the captain had talked to all the
junior officers, individually, in private, since he came aboard.
Dan had set the appointments up. Had he talked to them like
this? And what had been their response?

He rubbed his mouth, thinking again about Shaker's face,
and then about Hayes . . . and Schweinberg . . . Kane, he'd
barely known the enlisted flier.

What was he supposed to think? He was too tired to know
what was right and what wasn't. He needed to be alert, rested,
to see what was really going on. Fortunately, now, they'd be in
port for a few days. A little liberty, a little time to unwind.

He needed it. They all did.

Still rubbing his lips, Dan turned and went below. Behind
him, a petty officer turned a switch marked DARKEN SHIP. And
in the corridors, the lights changed suddenly from white to deep
and bloody red.

III

THE STAND-DOWN

23

Mombasa, Kenya

THE C-5 flared out for the last few seconds, hanging above the rushing runway as if it feared the return to earth. Gordon peered past Terger through the window. The greenness was astonishing, unnatural, after the sun-blasted Middle East. As he stretched—he'd napped through most of the flight—he could just make out, beyond the plain, the blue fog of distant mountains.

"Now this, she looks like Africa," said Maudit from behind them.

Getting a hop to Kenya was unexpected luck. They'd pulled in after "Pandora" for a few days' maintenance, and the end-of-operation message had suggested that EOD personnel be included in the first liberty section. He'd thought Kearn's face would fall off with jealousy as he'd given him the word: a long weekend, to begin in six hours. It was *Audacity*'s chief boatswain who'd suggested they try to snag a space-available. "Get out of the fuckin' Gulf, *out*," he'd said. "Go someplace you can have some fun. Karachi, Sri Lanka—anyplace but Diego Garcia. The ugliest nurse there's dated solid till menopause."

At the terminal, they'd walked in, found the military desk, and asked the Spec-4 on duty what was available. Half an hour later they boarded, penciled in on the manifest of personnel and replacement parts heading for Mombasa and *Forrestal*, due in in four days.

The transport quivered as the wheels met pavement. Inertia dragged them forward as the turbofans went into reverse. Burgee, behind him, handed up a Special Services brochure he'd snagged from the flight crew. "Good news and bad news," he said.

"What's the good news, Clint?"

"Beer's cheap."

"The bad news?"

"Three-quarters of the prostitutes have AIDS."

"Says the Navy," Maudit muttered.

"No, that's Kenyan government figures."

"Jesus."

"Well, you're big boys," said Gordon. "I'm not going to tell you not to dip your wicks. But that'd make me think twice."

He ran his eyes down the brochure as they waited to disembark. Already there was a different smell in the cabin air, humid and earthy rich. Suddenly he was excited. Being a civilian had nothing to compare to this sudden depressurization, this absolute and unexpected freedom. Anything at all could happen on liberty—and usually did. He remembered three little girls in Bangkok. . . .

They took one of the yellow-stripe taxis in from the airport. Dusty herds of thin red cows driven by thin black children parted before them. It was now that a basic disagreement surfaced. Maudit and Burgee wanted to skip downtown Mombasa for a hotel with a beach. The older men wanted to see Kenya. Gordon was also strapped for money. This meant the Castle, the more or less official hotel, where the Shore Patrol was based. According to the brochure, it had a special U.S. Navy discount.

They agreed to disagree, but he made it plain where and when they'd join up again. After a short one to take the edge off, they split up. Terger was going west, to the national parks. The younger guys were going north, and he and Lem Everett had decided to entertain themselves in town.

"Just a minute," said the chemist, just as they were parting. "In case you get lucky." He opened a tote bag, and passed out four small bottles of his homemade perfume.

The road north was newly paved, a two-laner along the coast. The two divers relaxed in the rear seat, watching the countryside slide by. The air was steamy, hot, and wet. "Smells like a Laundromat," muttered Burgee, stroking his mustache.

Maudit didn't reply. He was counting the money he'd exchanged. You got an awful lot of Kenyan shillings for a dollar. He took a deep breath. *Balaise!* There was nothing like a spell of active duty to make you realize how good you had it as a civilian.

A few miles later, the taxi slowed, turned off through a whispering lane of palms, and rolled to a stop at a huge white building that looked as if it had been airlifted direct from Las Vegas. "Nyali Beach," the driver said, turning to face them. "Twenty shillings, gentlemen."

"How much is that?"

"Three dollars, I think."

"Jesus, Tony. I'm not sure I can afford these sky-high prices." They split it and added a tip, then piled out. Two porters were already hauling their bags out of the trunk.

The lobby was white marble and they stared around, a little intimidated. "Let's check things out before we get a room," said Burgee. "Make sure this is, uh, the right kind of place."

"Meaning the bar?"

"That and the beach."

They caught a glimpse of it across a patio; sand white as powdered sugar, blue water, the lazy parabola of a volleyball. They couldn't see the players. They went into the bar, blinked at the sudden dimness, and then stopped, together, ten feet inside. Their eyes traveled slowly around the interior. There'd been talking as they entered, but now the place was silent.

"Ha putain," muttered Maudit.

It was filled with women in bathing suits, and every one had her eyes fixed on the two sunburned, well-built divers. Burgee swallowed and fingered his mustache, fighting a sudden urge to turn and run. Instead, he swaggered to the bar.

They ordered Tuskers, and before they had them half-finished, there were five women lined up beside them. "Where are you girls from?" Burgee asked a pale-skinned, stunningly built honey blonde in a white two-piece and espadrilles.

"Most of us are from Germany and Norway. We came on a package tour. I'm Elena."

"Clint. This here's Etienne, we call him Tony. Uh . . . aren't there any men here?"

"There were supposed to be. This is supposed to be an adventure tour."

"No, a sex tour," said another woman, beside Maudit. He turned, intending to face her, but found his eyes channeled like pinballs down the front of her beach wrap. "I'm Brigid," she said, sliding her arm through his. "Und vhere are you boys from?"

"The U.S."

"Navy? We thought the carrier wasn't due till next week."

"You got good intelligence," said Burgee. "But we just flew in from the Gulf. Been clearing mines up there."

"Is it true all American sailors are tested?" said Brigid, fingering his sleeve as if she were branding him in some way, leaving a scent marker that would warn off other women.

"Tested," he said. "Tested?"

"For AIDS."

"Oh. Oh, yes, that is perfectly correct," said Maudit. "Tested and passed before we came on active duty. All the two of us."

There were women all around them now. "Let us buy you a drink," said a voice behind them. "There's a special beach not far from here. Would you like to go with us?"

"Well, we got to get our shorts—"

"You won't need clothes."

"We should see if we can get a room," said Maudit.

"Don't worry about that," said three voices, together, in varying accents of alarm, laughter, intoxication, and lust.

"*Ha putain,*" muttered Maudit again, then jumped suddenly off the stool as a hand insinuated itself down the back of his jeans. He and Burgee looked at each other. "Could be tough," he said.

"Could be deep water."

"Could be dangerous."

"Only one way to find out."

"Beach Time!" Burgee screamed, and they stampeded out of the bar, waving their Tuskers and scattering foam.

Lem Everett spent the next day buying things. There were plenty of things to buy. Shops lined the quay; there were shops outside the hotel.

The Old Kilindini Road was one huge shop. Its warren of alleyways harbored goldsmiths, batik dyers, brass foundries, and, for whenever you got weary, little dusty-floored bars selling strong, delicious Kenyan coffee, soft drinks, and the ubiquitous Tusker. He bought a Swahili flyswatter, a brass coffeepot, a malachite egg, three elephants carved in ebony, an Arab-style dagger in a hammered scabbard, a Swahili sari, and a Zanzibar chest bound with sand-cast brass. He smiled his thin banker's smile as he stalked from one stall to the next, haggling down old men with the eyelids of tortoises to prices that made them cry aloud to Allah to save them from this infidel whose ruthlessness would bring them bankruptcy and abandonment in their old age.

In the evening, he dined on an excellent curry, then sat for a long time over a White Horse and soda. From beneath an awning, he stared out over the darkening bay. It had been raining while he ate but at last eased off into a mist, the rain clouds moving past and inland, to die, he knew, this side of the mountains of the Masai.

From time to time, he opened a little book. Noted, in minuscule handwriting, a line or metaphor or sometimes even just a word that might work in a poem he was considering on the Gulf. Or better yet, into the big poem. He'd been working on it on and off for five years now, keeping the manuscript, crabbed and dirty with erasures, in a drawer in his desk at work. Two minutes between phone calls, twenty at lunchtime over an apple and soda. Its tentative title was "The Atonement."

Behind the mountains, the clouds trembled a tawny red. Somehow at that instant, it all fused, the idea of Africa, of Masai, the violent dying glare behind the overcast.

He opened the notebook and wrote carefully: "The sky was the color of a lion's open mouth."

It needed work, but there was something there. That was the way with words. Alone they were flat, non-numinous. But if you rubbed them together long enough, you would find a pair that threw mysterious sparks. Like pieces of fissionable metal machined to fit. "A matter that renders Self oblivion." Ginsberg— he loved the "Plutonian Ode."

He sat there for a long time. When he left, a tiny bottle lay beneath his chair, forgotten where it had slipped out of his jacket.

The rain had stopped, but the ancient stone of the waterfront was still wet and slick. Gordon strolled, hands sunk in the pockets of his slacks. The air was cool, fresh from the Indian Ocean, and ahead the old Portuguese bastion of Fort Jesus was a crenelated cutout against the fading day.

He was standing on the quay, looking out at the moored fishing boats—they had a vaguely Arab look to them, though they were older and more beat-up than the ones you saw in the Gulf—when he heard a heavy splash, then a keening so filled with terror and loss he broke into a run, thinking of a child in the water.

Three ragged black men, bony as beggars, were lifting their voices in sorrow and expostulation. When he reached them, they were standing beside a wooden litter, looking down from the quay wall to the stern of a fishing boat. Several limp-looking fish lay forgotten at their feet. An old man squatted on the boat's counter, staring into the water as if contemplating suicide. Tears streaked his cheeks and scurried into a gray beard.

Gordon followed his eyes. A few bubbles circled, an oily film reflected the last glimmer of scarlet over Africa.

"What's the trouble?" he said.

The nearest native looked startled. He looked Gordon up and down, then said, "My father, we have lost his motor."

"What? You dropped it?"

"It was very new. We don't leave it on the boat at night. They steal. And now it's gone." He looked down at the weeping ancient. "We will never be able to buy another one. We had to borrow. Now we lose our boat."

Gordon looked down, too. The water moved in sluggish swirls, black and evil-looking, denser somehow than water should be.

He said, "How deep is it here?"

"How deep? It is deep. Nine, ten meters, I think."

Twenty-seven, thirty feet. Not shallow, but not that hard for a man in good shape. He looked at the fishermen again. Their faces were blank with shock and fear.

He began peeling off his sports shirt. "Sir!" he shouted down to the old man. "You got a rope down there?"

The Kenyans looked startled. One said something angry; the others hissed at him, a sign, perhaps, to be quiet. There was some scattered coughing. The young one—the one who'd spoken English before—furrowed his brow at Gordon's bare chest, his black-taped dog tags. "You can get it for us?" he said.

"Might be able to. I'm a diver."

There was a rapid exchange of questions and opinions between the men on the pier and the old man. Finally, the young one hesitated, then bowed. He said, "If you can, we can be very happy. Very happy. Yes."

"Let's give it a try." The old father scrambled forward as Gordon squatted on the stone, then jumped down. The smack reeled violently; it was less stable than he'd expected. He grabbed a stay before he pitched overboard headfirst.

The old man spoke no English, but with his son translating, he produced a ballast stone and a rope. The others—brothers?—looked on in somber silence. Gordon lowered the stone at the position fixed by six pointing fingers. The old man tied the line off on a hand-carved cleat.

He took off his slacks and had his fingers under his shorts when the men gasped. He hesitated, then left them on. He asked for a second line, got a bowline around his waist, and tossed the end up. "You—"

"Tom."

"Tom, you tend me, all right? If I give you three pulls, I'm in trouble, you haul me up right away."

"I understand."

He slipped over the side. The water was warm and smelled like an open sewer. It was too late to back out now, though, not with those anxious faces looking down at him, hope in their eyes. And he'd had all those shots. . . .

He took a few deep breaths, flushing his lungs, and surface-dived.

The water was so murky he kept his eyes sealed as he pulled himself down the line. The pressure leaned on his ears and he cleared them. Hand over hand, deeper. Something soft brushed by. He had no idea what it was.

He cleared twice more and fought off an attack by an old fishing net. He was beginning to doubt the wisdom of this whole idea. Just then, his outstretched fingers found the stone. It had buried itself in muck. He held the line with one hand and frog-kicked around it.

Almost at once, his fingers touched something hard. He slipped the bowline off, fitted it around the shaft and throttle, and made for the surface. Now he wanted air. He blew out in a thin stream, imagining a straw in his mouth. Probably a minute and a half, maybe two so far . . . where was the surface?

His head popped up into an excited chatter. He grabbed an extended hand. His heart dilated in relief and he sucked in the cool sea air, blinking in the dusk. Finally he gasped out, "Tom, tell 'em they can haul her in. Careful, don't let it swing into the quay wall."

There was a wild ululation of victory and joy when the Suzuki emerged, spewing water from every orifice. The sons, grunting and coughing, pulled it up the quay and laid it carefully in the litter. He started to tell them to get the plugs out, then thought, They know motors as well as you do, Gordon.

The youngest son helped him up on the quay. "That was wonderful. Wonderful, sir. We saved for two years for that motor. We could not buy another one."

"It's okay." He was embarrassed at their gratitude. They were carrying on as if he'd saved their lives.

"You swim like a fish, sir. How can you do that?"

"Told you, I'm a diver."

"What is your name, sir?"

"John."

"Where are you from, John?"

"Vermont."

"Where?"

"The United States. America."

The old geezer had made shore now. He primed Gordon's hand twenty or thirty times, speaking rapidly the while. His son had fallen back, but now he said, grinning like a searchlight, "My father is very happy. He insists you come and have food with us."

"Oh, I don't know."

"You must come. We have nothing else to give you. We are Giryama, we make our lives fishing. You must let us give you food, be our guest. It is the custom."

Gordon shrugged, buttoning his shirt. They shouted again when he nodded. The sound was chilling, unless you were looking at their faces. It sounded like a war cry. Four of them picked up the litter, the others quickly shouldered the fish, and they went off down the quay. Then, after a couple of blocks, they struck back off down a side alley, still whooping and shouting to passersby, who grinned at them and then, their faces closing a little, at Gordon.

The quay had been unlighted save by the windows of the bars and in the night the alleys were absolutely black. The pavement stopped, and though he couldn't see, he could smell what he was walking in. The brochure had warned against going into slum areas alone. He was making his mind up to turn back when the party turned in to a bare yard, lit by a hissing Coleman, and set down the motor with relieved grunts.

Three minutes later he was sitting on plastic tatami mats, drinking a beer and dipping up a savory dish of yams and chick-peas with his fingers. "The fish is being cooked, come out later," said Tom. "You like our food?"

"It's very good," he said, and meant it.

When he finished the first dish, the old man offered him what looked like a handmade cigar. Gordon refused with a smile. They tried to converse, but it was impossible. So he motioned toward the engine, the old man nodded, and he began stripping it down.

He'd just gotten the plugs out when Tom came back from somewhere in the house. "Forget that, we do that," he said, and pointed to a door. "You go back in there. There is something for you."

"What?"

"Just go in, you will see."

They were all watching him, giggling. He had another moment of doubt, then thought, They've treated me all right so far. Moslems were supposed to be hospitable.

He stood in the darkness of the hut for a long time, smelling unfamiliar smells, before he saw her eyes shining in the half-light. She was standing right in front of him.

"My name is Leah. Tommie says you need company."

He couldn't see them in the darkness, but when she put his hands on her breasts, he could feel them, loose and slick with sweat.

"That's very nice, but I don't think—"

He tried to take his hands off her, but she held his wrists tight, holding his palms to her. "Listen. You don't have to pay. I live here. They feed me when the ships aren't in. Then I pay them back. Tommie wants you to have me."

He couldn't see her well, but she was tall. Firelight came through seams in the tin. It gleamed off bracelets and necklaces. Her breath smelled of beer and chick-peas.

"You are afraid," she said. "Are you afraid? I have a green card. You can see it if you like. That is Kenya government health card."

"I believe you. But I'm married."

She didn't speak, silent as darkness, and he was afraid he'd said something wrong, that she would scream and the brothers would swarm in. But when she spoke again, her voice had changed.

"You love her, you mean. That is good, you love somebody. . . . You are right to fear me. Shall I tell the truth? The green card means nothing. They cannot afford to test us; they only look at us and stamp it and laugh."

"It can't be—" He'd been about to say, It can't be that bad; but the words sank back halfway.

"It was not like that before. I worked at a guest ranch when I was small. We were happy. We made money from the German tourists. Now all the girls are dying. They say it came from here, from Africa. That is a lie. You brought it. The American sailors."

"Who told you that?"

"Well, that is what they say in the bazaar. Myself, I think it is a punishment from Jesus. I know I sinned. I deserve to die. So for me, it doesn't matter. Only now it is so many, men and women and little babies. Have we all sinned so bad? Are we so evil we have to die, and God send a new people to start again?"

He tried again to take his hands off her chest. This time she let him. He was too filled with horror to think. Sounds filled his empty brain. Laughter and coughing outside, the clink of bottles and spoons on tin plates, the sigh as she turned away in the darkness. On impulse, he fumbled in his pocket. "Wait! Leah.

I think you're beautiful. I'll always remember you. Will you tell Tommie and the others I did it with you?"

"I told you, no money."

"It's not money. It's perfume."

He heard the cap come off and then a jingle as she lifted it. "But this is very nice," she said. "I love perfume. What kind is it? Is it expensive?"

"It's rare. Only one place in the world makes it."

"Thank you. You are a good man, to help Tommie's family. Without the boat, they would all starve. I'll tell them you made love with me. That will make them happy. I don't think they know why they are all so sick. Jesus bless you, John."

"You're Christian?"

"Yes. I went to the mission school. I was going to be a teacher. Now I'm going to die. We're all going to, no one can help us, and it is not our fault."

Through the horror and disgust, the recoil too instantaneous and deep to be anything but instinctive, he stood motionless. Then, when he'd been able to think about it, he reached out. Her shoulders were smooth and slick. He wanted to say something consoling but there was nothing in all the world he could think of. All he could do was hold her, sharing for a moment her anger and her fear.

Outside, in the yard, a brushwood fire blazed and crackled, lighting a ring of jolly faces. The motor, cover off and plugs lying beside it, was propped up facing the flames. Tom moved over to let him sit down, and an old woman brought steaming fillets and another beer. He looked at the faces across from him. Now he understood their thinness, their drawn, wasted look.

He drank the beer and ate the hot fish. When he decided to go, they all walked back with him, holding his hands to guide him in the darkness of the slum, under the cloud-sealed sky.

He passed the last morning in the bazaar, but bought only a native pot he thought might interest Ola. That finished his cash. At noon, he was checked out and sitting at the Castle bar, where he'd told them to meet for the trip back.

Everett and Terger were already there. The banker had a heap of bags and taped-up boxes three feet high around his stool. The chemistry teacher swung around, saw him, and patted the seat beside him. Gordon asked him what he'd done with his liberty.

"Went out to Amboseli."

"See any elephants?"

"Bet your ass. Rhinos, lions, about six different kinds of cats—hell, I had to look them up just to know what I was looking at." Terger tapped his camera. "Lucky I wasn't carrying a rifle, I'd of run out of ammo the first day. The lodge I was in, you looked right out at Kilimanjaro when you woke up."

Burgee and Maudit came in. They were sunburned and peeling, with circles under their eyes and bruises on their necks. Their hands shook as they set down their overnight bags. "You look like you been TAD in hell," said Terger, looking them over.

"Yeah. We were. But thanks for that perfume, man. Wish I'd had a gallon; it didn't last long in the field."

"Want a beer before we hit the road?" asked Gordon.

Maudit flinched. *"Merde, pas de bibine, j'ai une super casquette plombee."*

"No alcohol," said Burgee, closing his eyes. "Please. No more beach. No more women. And no more liberty. You can have one if you want. Just don't let me see it."

Terger bolted a last one, then they whistled down a yellow stripe. They were well out of town, and the airport tower was lifting above the plain, when Gordon bent forward and tapped the driver's shoulder.

"Sir?"

"Pull over." He pointed to the side of the road.

The taxi's brakes locked and it skidded the last three yards to a halt, raising a cloud of red dust so thick it choked him when he swung the door open.

The boy was intent on his work, his wire-thin, scarred legs thrust up on either side of his hands as he squatted. A black cloud circled him, buzzing ferociously, and the flies crawled over his close-cropped head and over the red bristly hide and the calm slow liquid eyes that blinked slowly at him as Gordon hesitated, then stepped over the ditch and up the other side and stood beside the child and the cow.

"Excuse me."

The boy glanced up, his eyes white as the moon on a dark night. Gordon made the motions with his hands and held out a shilling. The cow boy grinned and held out a pale palm. Then he got up and began patting the beast's neck, gentling it in Swahili.

It was awkward to kneel, but everything else was the same. Gordon turned his head till his cheek rested against the warm flank. The good smell filled his head, foreign and at the same time homely, and his fingers found the teats.

"Senior Chief! Damn it, come on, we got to make this plane!"

He closed his eyes and ignored them. She was a little hard, but as his fingers remembered, she let down. Milk hissed into the jug. The tail stung his face. The flies droned in the solid, manure-smelling, dusty heat. He did not shake them away, only squeezed his eyes tighter, till the tears stopped trying to come.

24

Al Hadd, Bahrain

THE sun was a thousand times hotter than he remembered it ever getting in New Mexico. And there was nothing back home like the sand fleas. He felt as if he was melting, dissolving into the gritty black sand that smelled like the floor of a gas station.

Exotic Bahrain, my ass, Phelan thought bitterly. He'd been smoking a butt on *Van Zandt*'s fantail when the officers went ashore. That was their liberty: hotels, parties, diplomatic shit. But for the enlisted, the guys who'd just torn the guts out of the Iranians? A stinking patch of waste waterfront and a couple cases of year-old beer. That was good enough for them.

He lay stiff as a stick on the sand, hating them, hating everyone, till he couldn't stand himself anymore. He was trying to cut down and he hadn't brought anything but grass out with him this afternoon.

He realized now, too late, that this was a mistake.

Two o'clock, and the sand had soaked up enough energy to cook meat. The towels, issued one each by the supply department, were just long enough so you could choose to sear either your neck or your legs. He'd like to cook them out here, fry them in their own grease. . . .

Enough, God damn it, Bernard, *enough*. About to scream, he hoisted himself to his feet and began hiking up the narrow strip of beach that lay in back of the airport.

But he couldn't stop what was happening inside his skull. The invisible biting bugs had gotten inside it. The single joint he'd allotted himself and the three beers he'd chugged didn't seem to help. He scratched at his back. It felt as if sand was sticking to it. He scratched and scratched, till he saw bits of bleeding skin on his fingernails, but it wouldn't come off.

He glared around, wincing as a passenger jet roared over,

low enough that he could see the people laughing down at him.

Danny Quint, Golden, Orr, and the other guys were standing around the trash can they'd ferried over in the whaleboat. The ice had gone slushy before they even got here, and the water he plunged his hand into was tepid.

He came up with a Miller's and popped the tab like the pin of a grenade. His eyes searched the sky as he sluiced his throat. It was a fierce and cloudless blue-white, knife-scarred with contrails. Christ, if it was cooler, they could have some fun. But no one had touched the footballs and Frisbees. He slapped his neck suddenly, but missed. Only the flies were really partying down.

The warm beer left his mouth tasting like cardboard. Not really thinking, he fished out a cigarette. Only when it was lit did he realize it was one of the specials. But then it was too late to put it back.

Quint, staggering past, winking at him. Phelan's irritated gaze followed his erratic course down the beach. The Salems Danny was smoking weren't exactly regulation, either.

A patch of shadow detached itself from under a palm tree. He quickly dragged the butt to a lip-scorching end, dropped it, and scraped oily sand over it. It was the black lieutenant, the missile officer. He was in charge of the beach party.

Phelan didn't want to talk to him. He didn't like officers, didn't like blacks, and this black officer had something more than the sand fleas eating him. For a second, he wondered whether Pensker needed a supplier. He'd never known an officer who used. Though there had to be some. But, shit, why should they? They had it all. Special food, plush staterooms, lifers like Fitch sucking up to them all day. Shit, if he had all that, he wouldn't need to get high, either.

The sand was too hot to stand on, the air too hot to breathe, his skin too hot to wear. He wanted to shuck it off and leave it lying behind him. I should of gone into town, he thought. The scuttlebutt was the Arabs cut guys' hands off for dealing. But there had to be something, with all these ships and planes zipping in and out.

The ship. That was what was eating him. The ship and on it the safe. The safe with the neat blocks of pure morphine, stacked and numbered. Wrapped snugly virgin in their foil seals. Tamperproof, they were supposed to be, but he'd spent hours thinking about them. He almost wished now Fitch hadn't given him the combination. Because even worse than the blocks were the syrettes. Little tubes with needles attached, designed for self-administration by wounded men. Quick. Easy. Disposable. Sitting there watching him every time he swung the steel door open.

He lit another cigarette, scowling up the beach to where Pensker had stopped to talk to a chief. He wanted out of here. He wanted to go back to the ship. The pills were there. The morphine was there, too. But he didn't want to go back. For the same reason.

You are getting to be one fucked-up coyote, Newekwe. No, I'm doing all right. I haven't touched the syrettes. Or the blocks. The waiting neat little blocks. And I won't. All I need is to get out of the sun.

There was no way out, though. Not till the brass decided the party was over.

He sucked the can empty and hefted it, waiting till Golden turned his head. There was a hollow clunk as it hit. By then, he was already running for the water.

The Gulf boiled around his ankles, heated by the black bottom, flecked with mustardy scum like old vomit. They were only about four miles from the anchorage. If he cared to look, he could see *Van Zandt*, riding to anchor like a gray wolf among the tankers and freighters. Straight out was nothing but sea, shimmering like madness, and two hundred yards out the motor whaleboat, rolling casually as two gunner's mates smoked under a tarp, their rifles propped against a thwart.

A bigger wave than the rest rippled in. Phelan heard splashing behind him. He hesitated, then dove in as it reached him.

It was like diving into boiling soup. The water was so hot and salty, he had to close his eyes. He coasted along beneath it, suddenly yearning for the icy freshness of Nutria No. 2. He wanted the cold slickness of a woman's flesh against his, slippery and urgent as mating eels, and the stars, watching as they'd watched his ancestors making love on these same rocks for as long as there'd been Indians. He'd gone in the water to piss, but now he couldn't. His cock had gone suddenly steel-hard under his trunks.

A few feet out he came up. But whoever it was was still behind him, splashing and calling his name. He turned, letting his feet down gingerly, feeling for bottom.

It was Golden, the geek he'd beaned. But the other corpsman didn't seem bent on revenge. He called out again, something jolly Phelan didn't catch.

They swam along the shore together for a few yards. Then he yelped as a paintbrush of acid wiped his side. He tried to claw it away, but its invisible burning clung like a spiderweb. He paddled for shore, cursing through clenched teeth.

"Bernie," said Golden in a low voice as they waded through the last few inches of Gulf.

"I told you before, dickhead, don't call me that."

"Sorry. Bernard."

"Ah, *shit*, that hurts!" He touched his belly delicately. The welts were already puffing up. "Something fucking bit me. What the fuck you want, Golden?"

"Is that grass you and Quint're smoking?"

"Grass? *Grass?*" He laughed, then coughed. The harsh smoke made his throat itch. "You're fucking clueless, man, you know that?"

"Can I bum one, then?"

"No. I'm fresh out, I hadda borrow that jay myself."

Golden's sallow face peered up and down the beach as another jet roared over. A hundred yards away, a wall of great jumbled rocks ended the world. "Grab us a couple beers. Let's go over there," he said.

"What for?"

"Cause I wanna talk to you! That all right?"

He considered this as he fished around in the tub. Nothing left but warm Pabst and Fresca. . . . Somebody must of made a million selling fucking Fresca to the Navy. . . . Pensker was zonked under his private palm tree. . . . The other guys knelt glassy-eyed and swaying around a blanket, betting shells and coins on five-card stud. Beyond them shimmered the shark guard, the gunners leaning back motionless, caps tipped over their eyes.

He decided Golden wanted to get high. He hadn't expected that. But another buddy in *Van Zandt*'s medical department could only make things easier. As long as it was clear who was in charge. Soon, the next port they hit, he'd find better merchandise than grass, cough syrup, and poppers. There wouldn't be any more problems then. Shit made money, money made shit, till you were shitting money. He toweled off slowly and pulled his dungaree shirt on. The chambray felt like steel wool on his shoulders.

"Got the beer?" said Golden, coming up behind him. "Where's mine?"

"Go climb yourself, Golden. You want beer, get it yourself."

Heat came up in slow waves as they struggled toward the jetty. As they neared, Phelan saw it wasn't really stone. It was concrete, great blocks of it tumbled into a labyrinth of caves and crevices. In the merciless glare, the flat cast faces were crumbling and stained with lichen. As they approached, a faint scratching began, like leaves stirred by the wind, and for a moment he thought he'd done too much Mexican, or maybe should have eased off on the beer. Then he realized the tiny spider shapes were real: crabs, retreating into their aeries. Birds fluttered up from within the maze, swallows and sea gulls, and the fleet shadows swirled over them.

Golden jumped up on the first block. "Hey, where we goin'?" said Phelan, hanging back.

"Inside."

"Inside where? What for? We can talk here."

He took the pack out of his shirt, shook one free for himself, then held it out. Golden said, looking at it, "That looks like a regular cigarette. But you've got something else in it. Marijuana, or something. Am I right?"

Phelan frowned. What was the game? He couldn't figure it. So he didn't answer. Sweat crawled down his back. He flicked his Zippo and turned to shield the flame, staring over it at the placid, glittering Gulf. It was pretty today. But far too hot. Even going in the water hadn't done much good. Just got him stung. He drew in a lungful of hot smoke and held it. What was this, his third? He'd stretch this one.

He stared in tranced wonder at a sea that was dissolving into the soundless golden roar of atoms and void.

"Come on," Golden's voice floated down. The seaman was scaling a tilted slab like one of the crabs. As Phelan watched, blinking in the steadily increasing brightness, he disappeared.

He took another drag and held it. His heart pattered, struggling in his chest like a caged bird. Then, Bogarting the roach, he scrambled slowly up after Golden.

Just then, after teasing him all afternoon, the grass hit. All at once, the way it did sometimes. One moment he was straight; the next, deep, deep. The world disassembled into a bewildering complexity of infinite detail. He stopped, hanging by one arm, his eyes epoxied to the surface. A moment before it had been old concrete. A part of his mind remembered that. But now the close graining held pictures and stories and worlds.

It took him long ages filled with history to cross it. The beach vanished, cut off by the blocky jumble. The sun dipped from sight and only a jigsawed space of blue showed directly above. Furtive skitterings and cheepings came from beneath the tumbled chunks. He was in a ruined city, a bombed city, a thousand years after the war.

Golden sat in the shadow of an immense overhang of flaking concrete. He patted the sand beside him.

Phelan squatted very slowly, coming to rest Indian-fashion. The rocks had gone translucent. This was why he used. This penetration to the magic behind everything you saw.

Above him, swallows clicked across the sky. He could see each beat of their wings. Then, suddenly, he was flying high and cool and there down below him in a nest of rocks was a tiny face, squinting up in wonder.

There was no difference. It was all one. Hadn't his ancestors known that? Wasn't it part of the Shalako festivals? He remembered seeing them from his mother's lap. The twelve-foot figures, huge and horrible, their monstrous dancing attendants, the drums and chanting that lasted all the chill November night till dawn. The ceremony that renewed the world not just for the Zunis or even for the Indians but for everyone who lived in it, white, red, black, brown, or yellow, man animal fish bird or snake . . .

Golden's mouth was moving. Phelan stared at him. Through the peace, he smiled with infinite compassion. They were one, part of the same huge Oneness that was the world and whatever god or devil you wanted to make of it. And poor lost Golden was trying to communicate with words.

"I said, you all right, Bernard?"

He extended the pack once more. Again Golden looked at it. He reached out and took one.

Phelan shook out another and lit it. The part of his mind that never stopped watching decided that it was all right. He had plenty more back on the ship. The Mexican was more potent than he'd expected. But he hadn't been doing much grass. His tolerance was probably down. That didn't mean he could smoke it all up at once, like he had with the brick. But he rated a party once in a while. Slowly, carefully, he blew smoke to the four corners of the earth, then the sky, and then downward, toward the sand.

"What's that all about?" Golden wanted to know.

"It's like an Indian prayer, Goldie. Like, saluting the spirits, saying you're tight with them."

When he looked back at the seaman, he was dangling the unlit bone between his legs. Phelan searched his mind for a word and finally found one.

"Light?" he said. It oozed out. He could see it crossing the space between them, see the other man blink as he took it in, watch his brain interpret it. It was a hoot. Just like talking to a robot.

Golden took the lighter but didn't use it. Instead, he said, "Man, did you see that oil rig burn? I went up topside to see it when we was steaming away. Wasn't that something?"

Phelan grunted. He didn't give a shit about oil rigs. Or any of the other mind games they were playing out here. So he didn't answer.

"Where'd you get this stuff, Bernard?"

"What?"

"The grass."

"Mondo bizarro," said Phelan. "It's primo grass. Try some, Rich."

"Where . . . did . . . you . . . *get* . . . it, Bernard?"

"Oh, where, who cares?" He laughed. "Go on. It's a little old, Danny said—I mean, it's a little old. But it'll still kick your ass."

"Did you get it here?"

"What, here? Change channels, Rich. When I been ashore? Besides, you heard what these people do to people who enjoy themselves." He took a drag and whispered hoarsely around it. "Everything's everywhere. You just got to look for it. I had some shit in Pakistan . . . well, that shit just blow you away."

"I know what you been doing," said the seaman. His yellowish face was sweating, too. The heat, trapped among the rocks, was hellish, and there was no merest breath of wind. "You know that?"

"What have I been doing, Golden?"

"Selling drugs. On the ship."

Phelan grinned. There was something fascinating in the way Golden's face moved. Could there be a mind behind it? Sometimes when you were high you could see people thinking, like it was that Max Headroom on TV. Golden didn't worry him. He felt like he always did on grass. Everything was the way it was because. Nothing he could do was wrong and nothing bad could happen to him. He was immune. Safe. Not like the slaves and peons around him. He was part of something bigger.

He said casually, "You're way out of line, dude. I use once in a while. Who doesn't? But I don't sell nothing."

"Don't shit me, Bernard. I seen the pharmaceuticals log. And I counted what we got left in the counter stores. You're giving stuff out like M & M's. Enough to space out half the ship."

"Everything's covered, Goldie. Those guys are sick and I prescribe for 'em. Just the way it's supposed to be." He laughed. "It's all *kosher.*"

Golden, he noticed then, still hadn't lit the joint. In fact, he was putting it away, in his shirt pocket. His long hairy legs shifted a bit closer to Phelan's.

"So, hey, what's going down?"

"I'm thinking about turning you in, that's what's going
down," said Golden.

Phelan was tracing a finger through the sand. Back here it
wasn't oily, it was white, and he could feel each grain as it slid
past his skin.

"Well, Rich, you got to do what you got to do, I guess," he
said at last. To his faint surprise, the sand said *denise*. He tore
his eyes off it and tried to find the seaman in the storm of color
around him. It was so bright he had to squint or it would blind
him. "If you got to turn some poor scum-suckin' shipmate in
because he gets high once in a while, I feel sorry for you,
though."

He grinned again and took a deep hit. He could hear the wind
sighing past the wings of the gulls. He could hear the faint
clicking of the crabs, secreted among the rocks, hoping for their
departure, or possibly their deaths. He looked at Golden's
sweating face through the smoke. Would crabs eat a body?
Somewhere outside, apart from them, the sea hissed like a
waiting snake.

"Pensker's right out on the beach, man," he said. He could
feel the smile still on his face. Eating it, like a crab. "You'll
probably get third-class out of it. Shit or get off the pot, Rich."

"You really don't care?"

"Doesn't make a rat's ass to me."

It'd taken him a while, but he understood now what was
going down. But he could see his cool puzzled Golden. So he
decided to play the hand out. If the other corpsman went
through with his threat, he could always deny it. Ditch the pack
in the water. What did one joint prove? All he had to do was say
he bummed it from Quint.

If Golden had one joint. If he was alive at all sixty seconds
from now. Phelan watched him from beneath half-closed lids.
He was too skinny to be strong. You could slip running over
these rocks. Get banged up bad. Maybe even get your neck
broke. It wouldn't be like murder. It would just be changing
Golden into something else.

In the crevices the crabs clicked Morse like a thousand secret
signalmen.

Golden made a little circle in the sand with his bare toe.
"Well. I don't really want to do that. Not to you."

Phelan waited. The beer and the cannabis and the heat had
turned his eyelids to lead. It was some time before he realized
Golden was rubbing his back under the shirt. It felt good and

he bent his neck. "I sort of thought we should be friends," the seaman was saying from far away.

"Yeah, they're good to have."

"But you haven't been acting friendly, Bernard. You've been real irritable. Throwing that can at me, for example." His voice was a silky whisper.

"So what."

"I mean, we could be close. If we were close, we could do things together. I'm not into drugs. But that's not all there is to do."

Phelan considered, detached, lazy, but his skin thrilled as Golden's fingers slipped down his shirt. It came down real simple. It was either let him do what he wanted or kill him.

A whisper, almost lost in the hiss of the hidden sea. "We can be special to each other. I can do things you'd like. Better than you've ever had from women."

Phelan lay back, his eyes closed. The fingers moved over him like soft crabs. They rippled over him like the sea. He thought of Denise and the camp fire by the lake. He felt the tide rising, the waves rippling over his legs, his thighs, and reaching at last his rigid and suddenly voracious cock. He opened his eyes for just a moment, to see Golden's yellow face close to his, shining with love.

He decided it might be nice to be friends.

25

U.S.S. *Turner Van Zandt*

AT exactly 1000, the anchor let go with a jarring rumble, the running chain exploding a cloud of powdered rust, paint, and sand out of the hawse pipe to drift down onto the calm water of Sitra Bay.

Dan stood on the wing, feeling unneeded. With Bell ill, he'd gotten used to maneuvering, mooring, and anchoring. Judging the wind, tide, current, all the forces that could affect four thousand tons of ship. Then giving the orders that put *Van Zandt* where he wanted her to be.

A whistle echoed over the water. "Moored. Shift colors," said the 1MC. The jack fluttered upward, unfolding to a faint, hot breath.

But now she was another man's. He'd had nothing to do that morning but navigate, and the bridge team had been in and out of Sitra so often they could have reeled off the bearings in their sleep. Some of them had looked as if they were.

"Fifty fathoms on deck, chain tending two o'clock," said a phone talker. At the same moment, McQueen, at the chart table, held up two fingers, pointing up.

"Navigator holds us twenty yards north of assigned anchorage," called Dan.

"Close enough," said Shaker. "Pass the stoppers, secure engines, secure sea and anchor detail."

"Get some more white lead on that sumbich, slather her down good," Chief Kellam cried. Dan glanced down. Seamen in dungarees were evening up the stoppers. The rest of the forecastle detail stood staring landward, ball caps shoved back, fatigue and relief plain in their slouched bodies.

Shaker had pushed his back, too, the scrambled eggs on the bill gleaming in the sun. One black lock, wet from 100 percent humidity, curled over his forehead. In khakis, Dan thought, any

director would have typecast him as a hell-for-leather destroyer
captain. Big, a little paunchy, but impressive. Three rows of
ribbons beneath the Surface Warfare insignia civilians often
took for submariner's dolphins. Above that, the dull gold Command at Sea pin. The crow's-feet emphasized the eyes, penetrating and cold' beneath shadowing brows. He was talking to
Turani, whose launch had been standing off as they passed
Sitra Beacon. Now, seeing Dan watching, the captain waved
him over. "Hey, XO, Mr. Turani's got an invitation for us."

The husbanding agent was wearing the kind of shirt waiters
wear in Mexican restaurants. Four ball pens were stuck in his
pockets, one in each. "Hello, Achmed," Dan said heartily, extending a hand.

"Good morning, Commander Lenson. Nice to see you back.
I'm sorry about your pilots."

"I am, too, Achmed."

"You are all very brave, lions of the sea, and we Bahrainis
appreciate your assistance in this troubled time. Let us say this
is in their honor. I would like the two of you, and your officers,
to join me tonight to celebrate your return."

"Thanks. I'm sure some of our guys will be there, but I'm
afraid I've got a lot of work to—"

Shaker said, "Oh, horseshit, XO. Come on, enjoy yourself for
once."

When Dan looked at him, a little taken aback, the captain's
face was open and boyish. The angry man of the night before
had disappeared.

What I want, you want. He said to Turani, "Okay, thanks.
We'll be there. Just tell us where and when."

"The Regency. Around nine. I would entertain you at my
home, but my wife keeps a strict household. You might find
yourselves, ah, inhibited."

"Good point," said Shaker. "It's been a long, dry cruise. See
you there."

They stood together on the wing. The glittering bay, beyond
it Mina' Salman, and beyond it Manama, looked just the same,
smelled just the same.

Dan was looking toward one of the moored ships—a new
ro-ro flying Italian colors—when he saw a launch clear the pier.
He moved around Shaker, who was leaning on the coaming, and
swung the Big Eyes around. Even three miles away he could
identify the man who stood in the stern sheets, supporting
himself with one hand as the boat lifted into a plane.

"Admiral Hart's coming out to see us."

"What? When?"

"In about ten minutes. I'm looking right at him."

"Oh yeah? Hey, do me a favor. Call Crockett, tell him to lay out some iced tea in my cabin." Tilting his cap forward, Shaker made for the quarterdeck.

The admiral didn't stay long. Shaker left with him in his gig, leaving the whaleboat for the beach party that afternoon. Dan called Wise—he had the duty—and told him several things that needed to be done.

Then he went up to his stateroom. He peeled off his khakis and hung them up. He sat on his settee in his underwear and contemplated the uniform. It hung quietly, stirring a little now and then as the ship moved. The oak leaves glowed a dull gold.

They told you at Annapolis that was what you saluted, what you obeyed. Not the man, the uniform he wore.

He no longer believed everything he'd memorized in the halls of Mother Bancroft. Some of it was oversimplified. Some of it was obsolete. Gradually, you modified it, with experience.

But it wasn't a bad start.

Before he knew it he was asleep.

When the phone buzzed, he was lying not in but across his couch. The lights were all on. "Yeah," he grunted. "XO here."

"Dan, this is Al. Sorry, did I wake you up?"

"S'alright. What you got, Wise-off?"

"Got a boat alongside from the Bahraini Navy. They say they've got remains on board."

He propped himself on one elbow. "They've got what?"

"Remains. The lieutenant in charge says they tried to call on the way in but couldn't raise us on harbor net."

"I'll be right down."

He was instantly soaked with sweat as he came out under the open sky. The steel deck and every piece of metal was radiating heat after baking all day in the sun. Two Arab officers in British-style white shorts were waiting on the quarterdeck. He returned their salute, looking past them. Their boat rode docilely at *Van Zandt*'s boom, an orange sack in the bow.

The lieutenant said that this was all they'd been able to find of the crew. They'd also found floating fragments of gray fiberglass and one uninflated life jacket. The life jacket was stenciled HSL-52. Dan pondered this and then said to Wise, "We better get Doc up here."

"I already called him. He'll be up in a minute."

"Here, sir," said the corpsman a few seconds later. Fitch was a small, bald, middle-aged man with a submissive expression. Dan told him what they had. He nodded thoughtfully, looked at his hands, then edged his way out along the boom. A moment later he was back aboard, slinging the sack over his shoulder like a department-store Santa. He said in a low voice, "You want I should check it over, sir?"

"Please."

"And refrigerate it, sir?"

"We'll see. Call me when you figure out what you got. I'll be in the wardroom."

The Bahrainis left after Dan noted their ship and commanding officer in his wheel book. A message would be called for. Though from the looks of the sack, it might have been better to leave whatever it was out where they'd found it.

Fitch knocked at the door of the wardroom a few minutes later. He edged in and took off his hat. Dan looked up from the message blank. "Yeah," he said. "What was it?"

"Body parts, sir."

"Whose?"

"I can't really say, XO."

"Right. Well. Are they . . . are they black or white?"

"I can't really tell, sir," said Fitch again, respectfully. "Maybe an M.D. could, some kind of pathologist. But not me. Do you want to see them, sir?"

"No. Where'd you put them? One of the freezers?"

"Well, no, sir, I didn't think that was what you wanted me to do. I got some ice cubes from the galley and they're iced down in sick bay."

"I guess that's better than the meat locker. Okay, thanks, Doc, I'll let you know what we decide."

"We ought to do something pretty quick, sir."

"I know. I just want to ask the captain about it, get his input, that all right with you?"

"Yes, sir. That's fine, sir." He nodded, seemed about to say something else, then put on his cap and started to leave.

Dan sighed. "Fitch."

"Yes sir?" He paused.

"What were you going to say?"

"Well, it was just a thought, sir. That is, what to do with the remains."

"Shoot."

"We can't ship them back, sir. That wouldn't be right for the family. I mean, there's not enough there even for a closed casket. Couldn't we hold on to them till we get under way again, and do a burial at sea? I know it's too shallow to do a real one, with a chaplain and all, but—"

"That may be the best thing. Thanks, Doc."

Fitch left. Dan sat there for a while, playing with a salt shaker, then got up. He got an iced tea and sat down again. After a moment, he pulled the pad toward him again.

When the message was in Radio, the ship suddenly became too small to bear. He showered again and put on slacks and an open-necked shirt. Then he went out to the quarterdeck, slinging a sport coat over his shoulder. Lewis, Loamer, and Brocket were there waiting for the water taxi, which was doing one round-trip an hour from the anchorage to the fleet landing.

Most of the officers had had enough Arab food, so they agreed on a French restaurant not far from the Mubarraq causeway. At nine, slightly noisy, they piled into a taxi and headed for the Regency.

The streets of Manama were full of men and boys and a sprinkling of foreigners. The only women were very old and in black *chadors*. The Mercedes, smelling strongly of the driver's imitation Chanel, sped them through streets of clothing stores, perfume shops, jewelry shops, the windows shimmering with gold bangles and bracelets, heavy and gaudy to Western eyes, but not without an exotic charm. Dan leaned his head back on the seat. He was counting minarets. The slender needles were crowded in among new apartment complexes, malls, office buildings, cranes, power lines. As the late dusk fell the call to submission floated on the cooling air. Their driver, who had been pointing out where his friends had been killed trying to make left turns, pulled off the six-lane highway, got out, and unrolled his rug to pray.

The hotel was lit like a cruise ship when they arrived. The lobby was solid with Filipinos, Koreans, technical representatives, oil men. The bar was easy to find. So were *Van Zandt*'s officers, even in mufti. He followed the shouts and laughter. The sliding doors were open—with night, the air grew cooler, not a lot, but enough to permit human life—and beyond them palms nodded against the stars. Two European women played in the pool, their bodies outlined by light. The junior officers kept glancing their way.

Shaker had a glass of bourbon in front of him. By his looks, it wasn't his first. Turani was with him, smoking his Camels, and an older man, a Westerner; Dan didn't know him. Guerra, Bonner, Firzhak, and Charaler shoved their chairs together as the second wave hove into sight. Dan grabbed a spare from a nearby table and sat on it backward, across from the captain. A pretty Filipina took his order for orange juice.

The younger pilot was saying, "Another one he used to tell was this story about Adam and Eve. They're in the bushes; they've done it for the first time. Adam comes out and God's standing there. He says, 'What were the two of you doing in there?' And Adam says, 'Making love.' God says, 'Oh yeah? How was it?' And Adam gives him this big grin and says, 'It was great.' So God says, 'Where's Eve?' And Adam says, 'She's down by the river, washing up.' 'Oh, no,' says God. 'Now all the fish are going to smell like that forever.' "

Turani laughed harder than the rest of them. Dan saw he was nursing a milky-looking drink. Maybe it *was* milk.

Shaker turned to them. "You guys just get ashore? You got some catching up to do. We're telling Schweinberg stories."

A moment later, however, he seemed to recall something. He got up, unobtrusively motioning Dan along. Outside, by the pool, he said, "Is everything under control out there?"

"Yes sir. I checked the ground tackle before I came ashore. We're riding well, no vibration, no drift. Al's got the duty section turned to and a watch on the air picture."

One of the women was floating on her back. Shaker stared at her absently as he said, "Good. Now listen. That porky guy beside me's Commodore Ritchie, Hart's operations deputy. He told me some very interesting things this afternoon after the admiral had to leave.

"For one, that—this is real close-hold, Dan. Remember that last transmission from Two One? Al must have told you about it, what Chunky was screaming as he went down? Well, it looks like *Borinquen* didn't hit a mine. She was hit by a torpedo."

"A *torpedo?*"

"Keep it down. I gave them the same double take you just gave me. But they had a diver down this morning. The edges of the plates, where the hull was pierced, they're bent outward. Not in. That's what a torp does to a thin-hulled ship. It's just luck it went into an empty tank."

He could hardly grasp it. "It's too shallow, Ben. What did we have there—thirty meters? Less? A submarine'd be skating along on the bottom half the time."

"Maybe so. But this could be a 209. Forget I told you this, but we've been looking for the one the Shah bought. They may have gotten it running. And hey, if you're willing to die, what's a little shallow-water work?"

Dan chewed it over, feeling apprehensive. They hadn't picked up a thing on sonar. The AN/SQS-56 was powerful, but built for deep-ocean work. If there *was* a sub loose, it could wreck "Earnest Will," wreck the whole concept of escorting in the Gulf. No merchant would dare enter the Strait. And there wouldn't be a thing the U.S. Navy could do about it.

It would be the stranglehold the Iranians had always wanted on the West.

"Second thing." Shaker looked around the pool; the women were at the far end now, pulling themselves gracefully up, reaching for towels. Wet flesh jiggled gently. "The Iranians have started some kind of coordinated offensive."

Dan felt his stomach tense. It was too close to what he'd just been thinking. "What did they do?"

"Three attacks today. The first two, Boghammers out of Abu Musa. The usual type stuff, hit and run. Two ships hit with rocket grenades. Minor damage, couple of crewmen killed.

"But then something funny happened down south. A Japanese LNG tanker. Liquid natural gas. It was loaded to the gills, going out. There was a French destroyer two miles away. They said there was nothing on radar, no surface contacts, no sign of missiles or aircraft. Just suddenly this tremendous fireball. Ritchie says they could hear the explosion in Dhubai. The Frenchman took heavy topside damage. No survivors from the tanker."

"My God. No survivors . . ."

"So now you have the overall picture. Right? Hart's worried. He's sweating to get more antisubmarine assets deployed. He's got P-3s on their way from Sicily and Diego Garcia. He had *Klakring* out on picket duty. Now she's reported generator problems. She's losing power. If they don't get it back up by tomorrow, he's going to have to send somebody out in her place."

He forestalled Dan's protest with a lifted hand. "I know, I know, we just come off convoy, it's not our turn, all that shit. But it comes down to us or *Gallery*. And they're as tired as we are. So I volunteered us."

"Okay, sir. I understand."

He remembered then what he wanted to tell Shaker about. When he got to the details, the captain looked disturbed. He interrupted, "So, what do you want to do?"

"Doc suggested that we bury it at sea next time we got under way."

"Okay, that might work. Yeah. Let's plan on that, a ceremony. You preside."

"Me?"

"You. Maybe it'll give you a new attitude toward what we're doing out here."

"What's that mean, Captain?"

"It means this." Shaker leaned closer, exuding the sweet, strong smell of bourbon. "Means this. I don't intend to let them bastards push me around anymore. From now on, it's *Van Zandt* that's going to be doing the pushing."

Shaker waited for a moment or two; then, not getting any response, said, "Well, excuse me, I'm still feelin' sober. What are you drinking, there, XO? Are you into those godawful fruit things?"

"It's orange juice, Captain."

"OJ and what?"

"Just orange juice."

"Oh." He examined Dan with a puzzled expression, then slapped him on the back. "You know what your problem is? You need to bust loose once in a while. Come on, join the human race." He pulled out a cigarette and strolled away, rolling slightly, not from drink but just from being on solid land again.

When Dan went back, the party was in full swing. Shaker, Ritchie, and the junior officers were playing ship, captain, and crew. The dice skittered across the wet table and came up sixes. Charaler moaned and hauled out his wallet. A dance band began playing in the next room. The waitresses threaded the room, unloading drinks and joining in the song. Turani clapped his hands over his head and began to dance. Firzhak mimicked him.

Dan stood a few steps away, watching. Their faces were red, collars loose; Charaler was guffawing so hard, he couldn't catch his breath. Out of uniform, they could be a group of bankers, salesman, a convention . . . no. Their haircuts and youth, their trim builds, a certain aggressive boisterousness marked them instantly as military. As did the obvious deference they gave the big man near the window.

No, not deference. And even more than respect. He was the center of the group. Not by any virtue of rank. By something innate.

They deserved to relax. This fourth convoy had been by far the tensest and most dangerous. But he didn't feel like joining them. Shaker was already pressing him to drink, and other things could happen as inhibitions loosened.

He went by them, and found himself in the bar. It was packed with sound and bodies, Italian sailors, civilians, Pakistani and

Korean hired workers spending their pay in one of the few
places in the country they could get a drink.

   He was standing there, thinking about finding a taxi back,
when Blair Titus took his arm.

26

Regency Hotel, Bahrain

"YOU'RE Lenson, aren't you? The one I met on the *Borinquen?*"

He looked not down but into a level green gaze. For a moment his mind stalled, confronted with an aquamarine silk blouse, loose, cool-looking linen slacks, and casual braided-leather pumps. It had been on other subjects: body parts, torpedoes, an unexpected patrol against an enemy primed for revenge.

Then he had it. The lingering furnace smell of a sandstorm. And from a lifting helicopter, the wave of a hand.

"Ms. Titus. I didn't expect to see you here."

Blair still had his arm. Now she dropped it. "I was hoping I'd run into somebody I recognized. I was sitting in my room; I heard the band and thought I'd come down. Get my head out of politics."

"I'm glad you did." To be honest, he hadn't thought of her since Terry Pensker had told him 421 had been shot down. But she looked awfully good to a man after months at sea: Shoulder-length blonde hair, tall and slim and clean-looking, with that easy upper-class carriage he'd always admired and wished he had himself. And just now, she was smiling in what looked like amusement—at him.

"You look so surprised. We're not just going to stand here, are we? Where's the party?"

"Oh, there's no party. Just a bunch of us from the ship."

"Is that where you're headed, so pensive-looking?"

"Actually, I was leaving."

"That bad?"

"No, no—" He floundered for a moment. "I was just . . . leaving."

"I see. Well, want to stay a little longer and join me for a drink?"

"Uh, sure."

The bar was too noisy with the band and sixty men, and there weren't any seats. He suggested the pool. There were tables under the palms. A Korean waiter took their orders: a strawberry daiquiri and an orange juice and tonic.

Blair let herself down gingerly on the poolside lounger. She sighed, pushed her huaraches off, and wiggled her bare toes. It was warm and breezy, and the stars were an arm's length away. The pool was lit with varicolored lights, an underwater show.

She'd spoken to the Navy officer on impulse, recognizing him as he stood outside the lounge with that lost expression on his face. Now that she had, in essence, picked him up, part of her still wanted to be alone. But then again, part of her didn't. Two hours in her room with Anne Tyler had been about as much reconstructive solitude as she could take. She wanted to talk, dance, have a daiquiri or maybe even two. She wanted to relax and forget the defense of the West. If nothing clicked, there was always Saudi television, reruns of "I Love Lucy" and "Hawaii Five-O."

The drinks came. She tasted hers and made a face. "Whew!"

"Strong?"

"They meant business when they made this. Don't let me drink more than two or I'll fall over backward."

Dan decided to let that volley go by. She was damned attractive. He was thirty-five, celibate by circumstance but not by oath. His body wanted her already. But he wasn't sure even now, sitting knee to knee with her in the half-dark, that it would be a good idea. His life was complicated enough with Shaker, Pensker, the Pasdaran, and a shipful of sailors to take care of. Maybe just this—some fresh-squeezed fruit juice, an hour by a pool with someone not Navy, not part of it all—maybe just this was enough. And anyway, he was too bone-grinding tired to stay up much longer.

She didn't insist on an answer. Instead she said, "You don't drink?"

He shook his head.

"Just as well. Too many men where I work—bourbon and power, that's all they're interested in."

She looked up at the palm trees, remembering one of those men. They could still hear the band—"Take My Breath Away"—but it was muted, distant. The air smelled like spices.

"Did the admiral say you were from Washington?" Lenson said, startling her.

"Uh-huh. That's where I live now, in Alexandria."

"I was in Arlington for a couple of years. Pentagon, and school."

"Where'd you go?"

"George Washington. Poli Sci. Part time."

"You know Dr. Lewis? Dick Kugler? John Logsdon?"

"Yes, I had them."

"GW has a good rep. I went to Georgetown myself."

"Blair . . . I didn't quite get what you did, when Admiral Hart introduced you. You work for Congress, he said?"

"That's right, Senator Talmadge's office. I'm his defense aide."

"Senator *Talmadge?* His *defense* aide?"

"Don't get nervous. I'm off duty now . . . on liberty, is that how you put it?"

"You've got that Navy talk down, Blair."

They talked about Georgetown, about the bars and party joints and foreign films, and about Halloween, the throng of masquerading students, gays, and hoodlums so dense and crazy that the D.C. cops had backed off policing it. The waiter came round again and she hesitated, then ordered a second.

"That band sounds good," she said after a while. "You game?"

"Dancing?"

"Nothing less."

He didn't want to, wasn't really sure he wouldn't fall down from sheer fatigue. But he got up and followed her in through the patio doors, back into the noise and smoke.

The floor was totally empty. The only other women in the bar were the Filipina waitresses, and of course the singer. The men at the bar turned to watch as Blair stepped out, and there was a noticeable drop in the sound level. He caught familiar faces turned his way—Charaler and Brocket; great, now he'd have to listen to their ribbing tomorrow. He wondered again whether he ought to check out early. Just say good night, thanks, and head for the ship and an early bunk. But then he caught her smiling at him. The lights glittered in her hair.

He found that he was starting to enjoy himself.

After two fast numbers, the next turned slow. He was taking her hand when he became conscious of someone behind her. They both turned. It was the front-desk messenger. "Miss Titus?"

"That's me."

"There's an overseas call for you. Where would you like to take it?"

She dropped Lenson's hand, conscious suddenly of the whole

roomful of men watching her every move. "Can I take it at the
front desk?"

"Yes, ma'am."

Walking quickly after him, she thought then, No, it might be
Talmadge. In that case, she'd want privacy. "No, wait," she
said to the retreating uniform. "Have them put it through to my
room. I'll go up right now."

"Well," said Dan, "I guess I'd better be—"

"Where do you think you're going?"

"You seem to have business. And I've got to get back; we're
getting under way in the morning."

"It's a long time till then, Commander. I have some questions
for you. Grab your drink. This won't take long."

He stood for a moment alone on the polished marble, caught
by the sweep of lights, watching her walk away. The men at the
bar laughed. She glanced back, made a little impatient motion:
Come *on*.

He grinned, took a deep breath, and followed.

It was Talmadge, as she'd expected. His wheezy voice—he'd
taken a mortar fragment in the throat in Korea—ebbed and
boomed through seven thousand miles of microwave and satellite links. "Hey, Blair? Where are you, honey?"

"I'm here, Bankey. In Manama." She hesitated, then added,
"This is a commercial line. It isn't secure."

"Uh-huh. Well, look, about what we were talking about this
morning. You know?"

"I know."

"Well, look, I just got together with the boys. Ted, Al, Clai-
borne, and Sam. Know what we come up with?"

He sounded well liquored, but that was no impediment to
business on the Hill. She juggled time zones in her head; it was
his lunchtime double she was hearing. "No, Bankey, what?"

"They liked it." The far-off home-boy voice wheezed. "It don't
hurt none, the fuss that's blowing up here about them shooting
those boys down. In the helicopter. That got some time on the
evening news and people are askin' just what is going on.

"Course, there was some things we had to get straight. Like,
that this wasn't a blanket authorization. Didn't want no Tonkin
Gulf resolutions, we don't want to give those boys no blank
checks like last time, do we? But we kind of got an agreement
banged out, an' I think I can make it stick. Goin' to see Bill
tomorrow, get them on board, then maybe we'll see some action." He chuckled. "Pell, he started callin' it the Talmadge
Resolution. Kind of catchy, I thought."

"It's your idea, Bankey, why not take credit for it?"

"Well, it'll bear thinking about . . . how you doin' out there otherwise? Getting any answers?"

"I think I may be able to come back with some, yes."

While she talked, Dan stood on the balcony, trying not to overhear the few words that made it through the glass. He leaned forward, looking out.

The Regency was at the northern end of Manama, and ahead and below him was the black Gulf. Far off, fifteen or twenty miles—it had been invisible from the patio, hidden by the curve of the sea's dark breast—he could make out the electric sparkle of Ras Tanura, the big new Saudi tanker terminal. To his right, the causeway bridged blackness with yellow glare; beyond it were the gay lights of pleasure boats, yachts, and motor yachts sleeping in the lee of Al Mubarraq. The only sounds were the distant barking of dogs, the occasional whir of a late taxi, and the bass thud of the band, carried as much by the concrete against which he leaned as by the air. The sky was the color of new rose leaves, the eternal, far-off refinery flicker like a futile attempt to ignite the dawn.

On this side, light . . . and on the other, the eternal, hungry darkness of the empty Gulf.

For just a moment, he remembered another sea. Another balcony, and another woman—years before, and a thousand miles away.

Taormina. And Susan. He'd loved her, and in a way he always would. But she'd stopped loving him.

He'd never understood it and he couldn't now. How could you *stop loving* someone? He'd accepted, at last, that she didn't want to live with him anymore. But understand it—no.

He heard the rattle of a receiver. A few minutes later, a toilet flushed. He lingered still, though, drinking the warm, sweet air.

Blair stood just inside the plate glass, watching him. Against the flickering night, his silhouette was slim and erect. She was sure he'd heard her call his name. Yet still he leaned there, looking out.

Lieutenant Commander Daniel Lenson. He seemed so pensive, so . . . reluctant. Could he be married? But he'd said he wasn't, and there was no wedding band, nor the paleness above the joint that meant one slipped off for the occasion. Only the heavy gold Annapolis ring. And she'd felt, dancing, the evidence that she interested him.

Maybe it was her imagination. And she, too, was strangely reluctant—as if this might not be something quick and clean, but something that would grow. Was she ready for that?

She thought, It is the losers in love who must comfort one another. She tugged at the glass—surprisingly heavy—and it yielded, and she said, "Dan? Are you coming in?"

She stood by the bed, saying nothing. He stopped just before her and they stood, each waiting for the other to reach out, a few inches apart. The wind breathed softly through the open window, stirring the curtains.

Suddenly, he found it hard to breathe. "So," he said, clearing his throat. "You said, some questions—"

"I had some," she murmured. "But I can't remember now what they were."

Dan saw unhappiness in her eyes, and suddenly nothing seemed more important than to make it go away. Yet still he stood apart, his legs trembling with want and fear.

Finally he said, "I want to hold you."

"I want to be held," she said, and stepped forward into his arms.

She lay beside him in the warm night, stroking over and over the long muscles of his naked back. He hadn't wanted to be inside her. And she hadn't insisted. But still they were together. And she was happy.

They'd held each other for a long time, standing by the window, and she'd felt him trembling. His hands had explored her face, her closed eyes. Then her neck, brushing back her hair to find the fine silky nape beneath the collar.

She let her eyes slip closed as he unbuttoned the blouse. His cheeks scratched her breasts. Her fingers crept inside his shirt, feeling the hard muscle, and she burrowed her face into the good smells of sweat and cotton. "It feels so good just to hold someone," she murmured into the sparse wiring of his hair.

Dan laid his cheek against the warmth of her skin. Her breasts were small, almost boyish, a model's breasts. Under the slipped-down and kicked-off slacks, he found her belly flat and hips flowing with the easy streamline of fine design into the long bones of thigh and shin. Her skin was white against his sea-tanned arms. His hands smoothed her like a cat, hesitated, and moved inward.

There were petals of liquid silk under his fingers, then hot honey, and last, a yielding, hungry gulf. She sucked in her breath as his fingers spread her, entered her, found the focus of her want.

On the bed, he made no move to slide over her the way most men did, eager to enter and then eager to depart. Slowly, very slowly, his hand moved and moved until her stomach tensed and she shuddered and then cried out, over and over, small sobs lost in the immense silence of the night.

"Did you ever hear about women who have multiple orgasms?"
   "I've heard of them."
   "You just met one. I could do this all night," she whispered. "I don't like to do it very often. But when I do, I want it till I'm exhausted, till I'm no good for anything the next day, till I never want to have sex again. Let's do that, let's do it all night."
   "All right."
   "You're not tired? You don't want to sleep?"
   "No."
   "Do you want to come inside me now?"
   "No."
   "What do you want? Tell me what you want."
   "Just to lie here with you. To make you cry out. To make you scream, that's what I'd like."
   "You want to make me scream?"
   "Uh-huh."
She grabbed his ears and forced his head down. To her opened thighs. And caught her breath as his tongue found her.

She lay near fainting. After minutes of blinding wonder, she had begun to shake, feeling it build to something tormenting and painful. Then all at once, the center ceased to hold, and she broke apart into pleasure past agony. And he kept on! Till at last, barely conscious, she closed her legs and pushed him away. Then pulled him back, pillowing his face on her belly. She pinned him there, gasping helplessly, till the waves eased and she could wet her lips and murmur, "Oh, God, Dan."
   He kissed her navel and the waves gathered again. "Oh, Jesus, stop! You're going to make me—I don't know what you're going to make me do. I can't take any more of that."
   He kissed her. His lips smelled of her and she thought, This is what I taste like. She wrapped her arms and legs around him, a starfish on an oyster, and held him helpless against her. She couldn't let go.
   She ran her tongue around his ear. "I seem to be having all the fun here," she whispered. "What can I do for you?"
   "A handjob would be nice."
   "You really don't want to—?"
   "No. Not now."
   She didn't understand, not really. Really he was strange. So

she slid down him as he lay on his back, slid down him like a cat down a tree. She kissed him over and over as she descended.

"I don't really do those very well," she whispered. "I'm sorry."

He closed his eyes as her breath stirred his hair. Then he felt her tongue, and last, the warm fluid ring of her lips. She moved with maddening slowness, stopping whenever he tensed to bite his belly and flanks, then dropping her head again. He shivered at the brink and she held him there for long minutes as he sobbed, till at last flares and star shells burst in a shuddering fusillade.

They lay together, exhausted in each other's arms.

"What did you think when you saw me? Did you think I'd be like this?"

"No."

"What did you think? I want to know."

"On the tanker? I thought you looked cold. Businesslike. Tall, sensible shoes, blonde—Ice Maiden. Untouchable."

"Good." Her laugh was mischievous. "I want men to think that. I don't want them to know what I'm like."

"Why not?"

"It would be too dangerous."

"For you?"

"No, stupid, for them. But if you thought that about me— then why did you come up here?"

"I was lonely. I didn't think you'd be interested. But it was worth a try."

"Are you glad you came?"

"You know I am."

"Why didn't you want to have intercourse?" she asked him. "Do you think this was bad? What we just did, and what we're going to do again in a few minutes?"

He didn't answer for a while. She stroked his hair. Short and bristly, why couldn't the military understand how sexy hair was. . . . At last he said, "Well, there were worse things we could have done."

"Don't rationalize it," she said. She ran her hands over his shoulders. Not bulky—she hated musclemen—but his body was hard and well defined. "Don't. There are people who've been married their whole lives and who've never done what we just did."

Dan thought, But there are degrees. The fruit of the Tree of Knowledge is doubly bitter. No human being truly knows right from wrong. We only know the distinction exists, and must be made with every act. He didn't want to make her pregnant. She had the right to end it, as all human beings have the right to sin, but he didn't want that on his soul. Or hers.

He felt her fingers on his wrist. "Let's get this off you," she said, and he felt the wristband come off. Something light hit the carpet. "Do you care what time it is? Do you have to be anywhere?"

"Tomorrow. Dawn, I guess. I ought to be back tonight. We're getting under way." He realized then that any possibility of catching up on sleep was gone now, probably for days.

"What for?"

"Operations."

"What kind of—" She laughed. "You won't tell me. Will you?"

"No." He had to smile, too. "My Mata Hari."

"Your anything. For tonight." She snuggled close, throwing her leg over his belly, and suddenly he hated every other man who'd ever seen that graceful motion. Their damp bodies pressed tight as leaves in an old book. "Tomorrow we'll be other people, for other people. Tonight we'll be us, for ourselves. Can you reach . . . hand me that, please."

He lifted the glass over him and held it to her lips. "Oh, I forgot . . . you probably don't like the smell."

"I don't mind if you drink. I just don't myself."

"Why not? Is it your religion?"

"No. I found out I couldn't handle it."

"You're a good man, Dan Lenson. I wish I'd found you a long time ago. Before I got mixed up with people who didn't care." She heard, herself, the note of bitterness.

Suddenly, without premeditation, she was telling him about another man, how he'd wanted a family and she didn't, and how he'd left. And then she was crying, and didn't know how to stop.

He held her, smoothing her hair over and over, knowing there was nothing he could say to ease her pain. It would live inside her for a time and then die, and new love would paint it over, and it would sink into her heart like old varnish into wood. And she would be stronger, wiser, and deeper, simply and only because she had suffered.

But there was no way to put this into words. It was something each human being had to learn. And so he held her and stroked her until she stopped crying and lay first rigid and then soft against him, warm and perfumed.

For a moment or two, while he caressed her, another image

came unbidden to his mind: of a woman's face, slashed out of a family photo. There was pain there, too. Pain and loneliness.

Bennjamin Shaker had never offered to discuss his marriage and what had happened to it. Dan had wondered whether he ought to ask. Somehow, though, the time had never seemed right.

She whispered, "I don't know. Part of me wants children. Part of me says not yet, maybe never. Do you have any?"

"A girl. She's thirteen now."

"And you . . . you're not married."

"She left me. Years ago."

"Why?"

"I guess she didn't want to be married to me anymore."

"And you still love her? Your ex-wife?"

"Funny. That's what I was remembering, on the balcony. I do. I guess I always will. But you can live with that. You can go on, and love other people, too."

"So you loved her, and she had your child. And then she left you. Are you sorry you had your daughter? Dan—oh—I'm not sure I know what to do, or what to think."

He knew she needed something and he wasn't sure he had it. But he had to try. "Blair, whether or not you have a family is up to you. Don't be afraid of it. You've got the strength. But don't let anyone else tell you what to do. Don't have kids because someone else wants them. And don't cross them off because of your career.

"What's a career? It's over in a day if you make the wrong decision. Or the right one, if somebody above you doesn't like it. Hold lightly, Blair. It's over in a heartbeat. But a family's real. I've never regretted loving Susan and having Nan. You just have to decide. Then drive on and don't ever look back."

He was filled suddenly with both joy and sadness. Would he ever see this woman again? Was this it for them, one snatched night? He knew already that at the very least he'd always remember her. That in years to come he would see her likeness in others who passed him on the street, in malls, on beaches. She would be part of what made him himself; he would take the smell of her hair with him into the darkness.

But he needed someone to love, not for a night, but for nights without end.

And even if she was that someone, would they ever be able to, given their careers, his changes of duty, her commitment to the Hill?

"When do you have to leave?" she whispered, and he

breathed the warm scents of rum and lime and the sea-smell of woman.

"Soon."

"When?"

"Now."

"No, not now. You can't leave now. Hold me some more. I'll let you go. But not now."

"All right," he said. So he held her, not thinking anymore about the day ahead or the days ahead or forever. And for a while, just holding her was enough.

27

U.S.S. *Turner Van Zandt*

T HE next afternoon, sixty miles out, Lenson blinked away
gritty fatigue. Putting on his cap, he took a last slow look
round the flight deck.

The crew was ready. The honor guard was in place, three
ranks of ten along the port quarter. No more could be spared
from a ship at full readiness for attack. To his left, the rifle
squad waited at parade rest, M-14s grounded on a deck too hot
to touch. Behind him, in the shadow of the hangar, stood the
pallbearers.

The hull techs had welded a box out of stock aluminum and
spray-painted it black. It rested now on a tablecloth-covered
breadboard from the galley. Over it were draped three new
American flags. Six sailors in whites held it, swaying to the
sway of the ship, their bell-bottoms flapping in the hot, thick
wind.

He glanced at his watch once more, then raised his eyes. For
the last hour, a pod of dolphins had been following them, rolling
through the sea like black wheels. Yes. They were still there.

"Now all hands bury the dead."

As he stepped to the lectern, the ensign dropped, fluttering
down to half-mast. The whine of the turbines sighed away and
Van Zandt slowed, slowed, till she rolled uneasily in the center
of a vast blurry emptiness, a hazy circle giving no suggestion
that such a thing as land existed anywhere.

It looked different somehow now that he knew it held an
Iranian submarine.

He clicked on the mike. "Ship's company. Atten-*hut.*

"Parade . . . *rest.*

"We are here today to bury the mortal remains of shipmates
who fell in battle. Virgil Hayes, Claude Schweinberg, and Peter
Kane will long be remembered by all who knew them. They

gave their lives defending their country. May they rest in peace, and may their sacrifice carry them to eternal glory.

"Please bow your heads for the Scripture reading."

He bowed his, too, focusing on paper that burned and dazzled in the eternal glare of the Mideast. There was a flash of white to the side. It was Shaker, taking his position beside the rail.

" 'God is our refuge and strength, a very present help in trouble. Therefore will we not fear, though the earth do change, and though the mountains be shaken into the heart of the seas. For God is our God forever and ever. He will be our guide even unto death.'

" 'If God is for us, who is against us? He who did not spare his own Son but gave him up for all of us, will he not also give us all things with him? It is God who justifies; who is to condemn? It is Christ Jesus, who died, yes, who was raised from the dead, who is at the right hand of God, who indeed intercedes for us. Who shall separate us from the love of Christ? Shall tribulation, or distress, or persecution, or famine, or nakedness, or peril, or sword? No, in all these things we are more than conquerors through him who loved us. For I am sure that neither death, nor life, nor angels, nor principalities, nor things present, nor things to come, nor powers, nor height, nor depth, nor anything else in all creation, will be able to separate us from the love of God in Christ Jesus our Lord.' "

He paused to wipe sweat from his eyes. In the hot silence, the steady sigh of sea wind, the slap of waves seemed louder than they ought to be. Invisible seabirds pleaded from the blazing heavens. He let the pause linger—the service was brief enough as it was—then went on to the prayer. When it, too, was over, he paused again, then lifted his head.

"Ship's company: Atten—*hut*. Hand . . . *salute.*"

The men straightened. Their hands came up. The body bearers stiffened, exchanging glances.

"Unto Almighty God we commend the souls of our brothers departed, and we commit their bodies to the deep."

Dan waited, his eyes on the book, but nothing happened. He glanced toward the lifelines. The bearers were looking at him expectantly. He nodded. A moment later, there was a muffled splash.

" '. . . in the sure and certain hope of the Resurrection unto eternal life, through our Lord Jesus Christ.' "

"Amen."

The bearers stood rigid, holding the flags as they flapped over the now-empty board. Dan gave the order and the crew relaxed back to parade rest.

" 'The Lord bless you, and keep you. The Lord make his face to shine upon you, and be gracious unto you. The Lord lift up the light of his countenance upon you, and give you peace. Amen.' "

The gunner's mates came to present arms. Ensign Lewis muttered, "Aim . . . fire." The report cracked out over the green sea. Breeches rattled; empty brass tinkled on steel. "Aim . . . fire. Aim . . . fire."

The bugler played taps. When he was done, there was a long, hot pause while the bearers solemnly folded the flags. Dan found himself yawning and snapped his mouth closed. They handed the triangles to Shaker, who received them without word or expression. His face looked cast out of some marble substitute that would last for centuries without decay or change.

Dan looked at his notes again. There seemed to be nothing more. But the men were waiting. At last, he leaned forward again to the mike. "These proceedings are closed."

The crew broke ranks and straggled forward. The ensign climbed back into a hazy sky as exhaust burst from the stack again. As the ship gathered way, the gunnery officer handed Dan the spent cartridges. Along with the flags, charts, and a letter signed by the commanding officer, they would be mailed to the next of kin. He gathered up his notes. He turned the microphone off and was about to leave the flight deck when he saw that it wasn't empty.

Shaker was still standing by the rail, the flags under his arm. He was staring out at the murky blur that was their horizon.

Dan watched him for a time. Sweat trickled down his neck and he scratched it absently.

Only now did it occur to him that it was on this picket station—probably not far from this exact position—that *Strong* had been hit two years before.

After a while, he went over. He propped a shoe on a chock, keeping his whites clear of the sooty grit on the lines. Shaker glanced at him, but it was obvious his mind was far away. Dan wasn't even sure the pale eyes recognized him.

"Captain," he said at last.

"What?"

"I know how you feel."

Shaker turned his head at that. The furrows around his eyes were deep as graves. "You do, huh?"

"I do, Ben." He looked down at the Gulf as it slipped by, hollowed by *Van Zandt*'s bow wave. The sea he remembered was a slaty gray and miles deep. He debated with himself for a while whether to say it.

"I know about the nightmares," he murmured.

The big head jerked around, quick as the Phalanx locking on to a threat. "What nightmares?"

"The ones you have. About watching men die. And not being able to move. Not being able to help."

"How do you know?"

"Because I have them, too."

Shaker had returned his gaze to the distance. He said nothing more. But Dan saw the tension in his back, and the way his hands tightened on the lifeline.

Oh yes. He knew what the captain was seeing. He should have guessed it long before.

"*Ryan* was a good ship, too, Ben. With a good crew. Her captain made a mistake. It wasn't a big mistake. With any luck at all, he could have corrected it. Unfortunately, other men made mistakes, too. Because of that, a ship died.

"For a long time, I blamed myself. I was on the bridge when it happened. Junior officer of the deck. Because I didn't speak up when I realized the maneuver was dangerous."

He lifted his eyes to the horizon, half-afraid he would find there what had haunted him for years after: the bow of a carrier, wedged and deadly as a lifted ax. But there was only the tan sky, the equivocal, ever-shifting transition where it met the passing sea. The pain was still there, but it had changed. Been transmuted by time, into . . . wisdom? Acceptance? He pulled his mind back. It had value now, at this moment, only as it could help the man beside him.

"I guess all I've got to say is that it passes. We have to carry on for those who died. Carry on, and just—trust—that it all will turn out for the best."

Shaker stared out to sea. Dan stared at his motionless profile. What was he thinking? Could he be reached? Or would he have to find his own way through?

He waited in the hot wind for a long time. Then he lowered his head and went forward, leaving the captain standing by the rail alone.

He was very tired. Nevertheless, he worked late that night, drafting the loss report, the after-action report, and letters to the next of kin. Occasionally he got up and rinsed his face.

Staring into the mirror at his puffy, reddened eyelids, he would think for a moment about a woman, or about men who'd died years before outlined by flame.

Then he went back to work.

At midnight, he decided he couldn't work anymore. He called CIC for a late update. Everything was quiet over the Iranian coast, and inland as far as the Battle Group's E-2C and the AWACs could see. Then he undressed and turned off the lights. He was thinking again about Blair, wondering whether he should try to call her back in the States, when the edges of his mind blurred and he sank away.

Some indeterminable time later, he came awake again. His hand went by reflex to the bogen.

In the earpiece, he found only the distant drone of an empty line.

He hung it up again. It was long past midnight. Yet sleep was gone. He could feel that.

He got up and pulled on his trousers. A glass of milk might help. He slipped his feet into his boonies and decided that at this hour even the exec didn't have to be in full uniform. Halfway to the wardroom, he stopped, listening to the ship. To the steady eternal whine of blowers, the gentle creak as her hull worked.

Nothing was different. But he knew suddenly that something was wrong.

He knelt and laced his shoes, and debated for a moment going back to his room for his shirt. Then he decided not to. Not for a short look around. He climbed the ladder to the O1 deck and slipped into Combat.

Darkness, silent men, the green glow of scopes and the steady whalelike song of the sonar. The sonarmen had shortened the 56's ping length, hoping for a better shallow-water picture. Huxley had said it wouldn't help much, but it was all they could do.

Pensker was sitting at the weapons console. Dan stood behind him for a while. Lines of control code glowed green on the screen. At last, he said, "Hey, Terry."

Pensker swiveled. "Oh, hi, XO. What you doing up?"

"Couldn't sleep. Where's the captain?"

"I don't know, sir. Probably in his cabin. Can I help you with something?"

Dan shook his head. He paced around for a few minutes. The night watch was quiet and intent. OSs and EWs and STs sat at their displays, detached from their bodies, their attention projected into the sea and sky around them. He put his hand on Shaker's chair, ready to pull himself up.

But he didn't. Instead, he crossed the room and pressed the CO's buzzer.

Shaker didn't answer.

Dan stood holding the phone, biting his lips. There was nothing on the scope. Earlier in the day, they'd seen fighters airborne inland, to the south, out of Bandar 'Abbās. They seemed content to stay there, however. As far as he could tell, nothing was threatening them.

Then why did he feel as if there was?

And where was Shaker?

He pushed his way through the curtain into Sonar. Perhaps what he was feeling . . . but neither the SQS-56 nor the towed array, a passive listening system, had showed anything suspicious for hours. They had two hundred meters under their keel, about as deep as it got in the Gulf, and the sonar supervisor said their active range was 7,500 yards.

At last, he reached for the intercom. "Bridge, Combat. Is the captain up there?"

"He's not up there, sir."

"Where is he, Petty Officer Stanko? Any idea?"

"Don't know, XO, sorry."

He looked again at the scope; again, saw nothing out of the ordinary; but this time caught a glance from Pensker, across the consoles and displays. The weapons officer was slumped back in his chair. He dropped his eyes as Dan looked back.

He suddenly decided this was enough. "Pass the word for him, please, Bo's'n. Have him call CIC."

"For the captain, sir? After taps?"

"That's right, Stanko! Right now!"

A second or two later, over all circuits on the sleeping ship: "Commanding officer, call CIC."

The bogen went off immediately. "Shaker here. What's wrong?"

Dan felt relieved just hearing his voice. "Nothing specific, sir, but we lost track of you for a while. Where are you?"

"I'm in the goat locker."

Dan wondered what he was doing in chiefs' quarters in the middle of the night, but that wasn't the kind of question you asked a CO. It was his ship; he could go where he liked. "Will you be there for a while, sir?"

"Till I decide not to, I guess. That meet with your approval?"

"Yessir."

"Good." Shaker hung up.

Dan stood irresolute. For the moment Shaker had been on the line, he'd felt better. But even if you were captain only for a day, your nerves seemed to extend themselves. Your senses extended themselves, became part of the metal fabric around you. He'd picked some of that up when he'd understudied for Bell. And this sense was telling him, more distinctly by the minute, that something was wrong.

He considered calling general quarters away. But it wasn't a good idea crying wolf unless you had at least a pawprint. He thought, I'll see how the captain feels.

In the passageways, scarlet light glimmered in pools on the decks.

The only one awake in the CPO mess was the supply chief, Dorgan. He set aside a snatch magazine as Dan came in. Skipper wasn't there, he said. No, he hadn't seen him, and he'd been there since taps.

Dan rubbed his mouth, momentarily at a loss. Where the hell was he? And why had he told him he was where he wasn't?

He decided he'd better find him fast. He remembered how Shaker had stood by the rail after the burial at sea. He remembered the captain of the *Dickerson*, some years before, who'd disappeared one night under way. He, too, had been going through a divorce.

Then Dan remembered the bogen. That meant he wasn't topside.

He decided to start at the bow and search aft till he found him.

Forward, through a passageway and a berthing compartment. Muffled snores came from the dark. Past that, the passageways ran on again, a familiar labyrinth, yet unfamiliar now, haunted, ruby-lit, empty. Steel echoed under his steps.

He was standing at the dead end of the forepeak, the deserted warren of paint lockers, chain lockers, stowage, when he realized suddenly not that he'd seen something unexpected but that he hadn't seen what he ought.

There'd been no security guard at the missile magazine. No sailor named Thompson or Menendez sitting half-asleep by the scuttle leading down.

He whirled and ran back. The logbook was there, lying on the folding chair. But there was no sign of the guard. The scuttle was dogged but unlocked. He hauled it open, and looked down two decks into the ready service room.

He squinted in the sudden glare. Below him, the white lights were on.

"Hey!"

"Hey, what," came Shaker's voice, sounding surprised, and then, in the same breath, guarded.

"It's Dan. What's going on?"

"Nothing. Is something wrong?"

"No. Just wondered where you were." He hauled the heavy scuttle up the rest of the way and latched it. He had his boots on the ladder when Shaker's voice floated hollowly up from below.

"Stay up there, XO."

"Captain—" He let himself another step down, cursing under his breath at a stab in his shoulder.

Shaker's voice reverberated oddly in the compartment below, distorted by the maze of piping and duct work that cooled and dehumidified the missiles. "Dan. I said, don't come down."

He was debating whether to obey when he heard the clang of a pistol slide going forward. It froze him where he was, hanging by his right arm, crouched against the ladder. His heart began to hammer with sudden apprehension.

"Captain, what the hell is going on? Where's the guard? What are you doing down there?"

"Well . . . " The captain's voice was muffled, as if he was inside a closet. Though he couldn't see him, Dan figured he had his head up inside the rotary magazine. The ready service room had a scuttle leading up into it. He couldn't think why. All you could reach from there were the booster sections. It was a twenty-foot wriggle straight up after that, between the smooth white tubes of the Standards and Harpoons, to get to the blast door and the main deck. Dan had managed it once, barely, but he doubted Shaker could.

He wondered for a horrible moment whether the captain was contemplating doing something irregular, destroying them, or trying to launch one. But that didn't make any sense. He could launch missiles whenever he liked, just by giving an order. The only weapon they carried that had any restriction, any special procedure on it, was—

He suddenly felt cold.

"Ben," he said again, and this time his voice came out strange, high and tense.

"Shove off, Dan," came Shaker's voice again. He sounded angry, but at the same time preoccupied.

Dan moved down a step—very quietly—then another.

"Lenson!"

He looked down, to see Shaker, foreshortened, glaring up into the vertical tunnel of the magazine trunk. The painted steel

deck he stood on was the inner hull. He was hatless, and there
was a balding spot on the crown of his head. Strange, he hadn't
noticed it before. The guard's .45 was in his right hand.

"Where's Thompson?" Dan asked him.

"He wasn't feeling too good. I took over for him. Let him go
to the head. Thought I'd look around down here while I was at
it. This space is scuzzy, Dan. Lot of rust down here. I'm surprised at you letting it get by you."

He said nothing. After a moment, the captain went on.
"Okay? Satisfied? Go get some sleep. You need it, you're getting antsy."

"Not till you tell me what's going on."

"Just did. If you can't sleep, go back up to the bridge. We
could be attacked anytime. One of us ought to be up there."

"You ought to be there, sir. Instead of here." He paused. His
arm was getting fatigued; it was a cramped position, clinging
to the ladder. "What are you doing to the missiles, Captain?"

Shaker looked over his shoulder, as if he'd left a piece of work
half-finished. "Won't butt out, huh? Then I imagine you've
figured it out."

"I think so. But, Ben, you can't do it. You can't touch one of
those Mark IAs without permission."

"I might have permission. Ever think of that?"

"I didn't see a message."

"You think Stan Hart would put something like that in writing? Now get out of here and let me finish up."

He disappeared from the square of light.

Dan almost believed it. Then he didn't. Not that it mattered
whether COMIDEASTFOR had approved it or not. Special
weapons required National Command Authority release. Or if
there was no President anymore—if Washington was a smoking hole—then it could be ordered by one of the CINCs. In their
case, CINCCENT, a four-star, General Cannon.

For anything aboveboard, there would have been a message.
Because there was no way you could launch a nuke without one.

"Captain," he said again, in a low voice.

"Jesus *Christ! What?*"

"You said, you 'might' have permission. That's true. But *do*
you have permission?"

"Why don't you let me worry about that?" Up to now, Shaker
had sounded reasonable. Now he reappeared at the foot of the
ladder, staring up. His face was shiny with sweat. "God damn
it, I told you for the last time. You've got your own career to
worry about. Get your tit out of this wringer while you still
can!"

"I don't think I can do that."

"You'll do it, God damn it! You said you'd support me. Well, support me!"

"I'm not supporting you in this, Ben."

Quick as that, the captain half-lifted the automatic. He didn't actually aim it. But he'd started to. And Dan, just as quickly, had tripped the latch, dropping the scuttle—two inches of hardened steel—between him and the man below.

Now Shaker was trapped. Sealed below. But he couldn't keep him there forever.

Dan crouched there, trying to think. He was scared now. Christ, he thought. Christ!

The Mark IA, a 1960s-era weapon, had what was called a "Permissive Action Link" in the fire control system. Dan saw the PAL keys themselves only during the monthly inventory, when three people—CO, XO, and Weapons—had to sight and sign for them. The captain kept them in his stateroom safe. Inside the sealed pouches were perforated disks, perhaps two inches in diameter, made of a plastic that would shatter if it was drilled or punched.

Even with the PAL, though, Shaker still couldn't fire. The circuit board in Combat into which the disk had to be plugged also had a keypad lock. The combination was not aboard *Van Zandt*. It had to be received from the CINC and decoded.

Only after both elements were present—the PAL disk and the correct combination—would the Mark 92 Fire Control System initialize a Mark IA for launch.

Now, if Shaker had orders to fire, say as the result of a plot between him and someone higher in the chain of command, then he'd have the combination. And he already had the disk.

But if that was so, then he'd have no reason to be in the magazine with the missiles.

Was there any other way he could fire a nuclear weapon?

Even as he thought it, Dan realized the answer might be yes. It stemmed from the way the older warhead had been adapted to ride a new missile out of an even newer class of frigate. And that was, by applying an electrical impulse directly to the missile booster itself.

The problem there would be the booster suppression system. This was a pressurized water tank piped to a nozzle located directly beneath each missile. If one of the boosters fired by mistake, either from circuitry error or a conflagration in the magazine, a fusible plug in the nozzle melted at four hundred degrees. The water spray blew the engine apart and cooled the nearby missiles until the fire burned out.

However, if Shaker, down below, disabled the suppression system . . . cut off the water, or pinned out the trigger valve . . . then he might be able to fire the booster, and then the sustainer, without going through the internal logic in the Mark 92 computer—of which the PAL was a part.

So far what resulted was a complicated way of committing suicide. One booster burning in the magazine would cook off the others. They'd lose the whole forward half of the ship.

How could the missile be launched without the launcher? It sounded impossible. But as soon as Dan visualized it, he could see a way. If Shaker—or somebody in CIC, at the weapons-control console—rotated the magazine to the proper position, the missile, boosting "illegally" yet unsuppressed, would shear its umbilical and fly vertically up out of the missile-loading hatch. It would bypass the launcher rail, and it was the launcher, he realized suddenly, that fed it targeting data.

Without data, the missile—a modern Standard airframe, but an old-fashioned Terrier warhead, with semiactive backup homing in case its primary guidance circuitry failed—would beam-ride *Van Zandt*'s radar wherever it pointed. And detonate on command, the moment it was switched off.

It would be complicated. It would require careful timing, to acquire the missile before it left the cone of the guidance radar and self-destructed. He didn't think Shaker knew the system well enough to do it. But theoretically, at least, there was a way he could fire a nuke on his own.

Dan looked around quickly. The only thing of use he saw was the sound-powered phone by the guard's chair. He turned the dial to the weapons liaison circuit and spun the crank.

After three cranks, Shaker came up on the line. "Yeah, that you, Terry?"

Terry. Dan suddenly couldn't breathe.

The man whose father had died in a war that wasn't fought to the limit.

The man with a master's degree in electrical engineering.

The black man whose friend the Iranians had just shot down and killed.

Van Zandt's weapons officer said in his ear then, "Combat, Lieutenant Pensker."

"Terry, that you? Did you call me?"

"No. The growler just went off up here. Wasn't me, Captain."

"It wasn't me, either. Listen. The XO ran across me in the magazine. He's got me bottled down here. Can we fire yet?"

"Pretty soon now, sir. I'm through rewriting the program. Just have to enter initial fly-out bearing."

"Okay. Set it up."

"Captain," said Dan. "Listen. Don't cut me off. I'm going to tell you something very important."

A pause on the line. Then: "I told you to get lost, XO. You can't stop this. So just stand clear. I'll say you were asleep, you didn't know what was going on."

"Who's that?" said the black officer.

Dan ignored him, speaking directly to Shaker. "Where are you targeting this missile, Captain? They'll hang you for this."

"It'll be worth it. You know where we're sending this little love note, Dan? To Bushehr. The biggest base in Iran. They've got frigates there, Dan. Gunboats. Fighters." Shaker paused; his breathing was labored. "There . . . got it. Suppression valve's closed. By the way, that's where the missile that hit *Strong* came from. Bushehr."

"Ben, this isn't right. You know it isn't. Knock this off and come out. I'll let you out and we'll talk about it. I give you my word, I won't report it if you come out now."

"Forget it."

"You about ready down there, Captain?" The weapons officer's voice came through.

"I think that's it. You can rotate the magazine now."

A whir of electric motors came through the deck below Dan, through the steel of the locked scuttle.

He looked around again. He couldn't go into the magazine. He doubted whether Shaker would shoot to kill, but he wouldn't do much with bullets in his legs.

He couldn't go back to CIC, either, and stop Pensker there. It would take him two, three minutes getting there through all the dogged-down doors. By then, the missile would be on its way.

His eyes stopped. He stared at a red cylinder beside him. At a red, T-shaped toggle.

"Aligned," said the lieutenant's voice.

"Launcher vertical."

"Launcher vertical. Bringing up CWI."

Dan reached out and pulled the toggle. A bell began to ring below him, inside the magazine.

"What's that bell?" Shaker demanded.

Dan said into the phone, "That's the CO_2 flood alarm, Captain. You've got sixty seconds to get out of there. Then the space will be flooded with carbon dioxide."

There was a pause on the line. The bell rang steadily on. It had to be hellishly loud in the enclosed space. At last, Shaker said, "Lenson! God damn it! You mind securing that racket before I go deaf?"

He said evenly, "Ben, have you got a breathing device down there with you?"

"What? No, God damn it. Turn that thing off!"

"I'm not going to turn it off."

"Pensker! The fire-fighting system. Can you secure it from up there?"

"No, sir. You can trip it from DC central, but the only place you can turn it off is the guard station. Where he is."

"Christ!" For the first time he heard fear in Shaker's voice. Then it hardened. "Dan. Listen. You're making the wrong decision here. Maybe I'm out of line. But you got to admit, it's the kind of thing somebody should have done long ago."

Dan sat hunched on the folding chair. Thinking.

About loyalty, and about honor, and about the duty to obey.

"Why, Ben? Explain it to me."

"Because it'll save American lives. Just like the bombs at Hiroshima and Nagasaki did. You know that's the only way we're going to end this war."

He waited.

"Dan, listen. The Navy used to operate under the control of its commanders. They left it up to us, to decide what action was necessary. Now we're micromanaged from halfway around the world.

"And those people are wrong! They've got domestic politics on their minds. Whether they'll be reelected. A peacetime mind-set. They can't see, even if it's obvious to us, that there are times and places you've got to stand up to the enemy and show him what you're made of. Or there's no point in being there."

"Ben—"

"No, listen. Nobody under fifty remembers what it's like to see America win. They need to. That's why I'm right, XO. And you know it.

"Now, close the valve to the CO_2 flood."

For just a moment he felt like doing it. Because part of him agreed with Shaker. He'd seen the mess politicians made when they tried to direct military forces in contact with the enemy. Vietnam. Beirut. And once, personally, in Syria. And what he said about America—maybe that was true, too.

But this wasn't the way to protest. Shaker was asking him to abandon civilian leadership. Abandon the law. As well as murder who knew how many civilians. A beam-riding missile

. . . it would be a miracle if it hit anywhere near where it was aimed.

At last, he said, "I can't go along with it, Captain."

"Okay, Terry, you heard the man." Shaker suddenly sounded tired. "Launch it anyway."

"Aye, sir. Stand by for ignition."

Dan said quickly, "Hold it, Terry! You'll kill him if you do that!"

"I know that. And I accept it. Lieutenant Pensker!"

"Listen, Ben. You've got one chance to get out of there alive. Terry, are you still there?"

"Yeah, XO, but—"

"Just listen!" Dan looked at the dial on the red bottle. He had to talk fast now. "Captain. The scuttle to the rotary magazine. Climb through it. There's not much room up there, but you can squeeze in. Get up there, right now, and dog it behind you."

"No way."

"Ben, listen." He tried to sound friendly and reasonable. Actually, he was scared shitless. "Where you are, in ten more seconds, it'll be pure carbon dioxide. If you get up in the magazine, there'll be air there."

"Sure! And then the booster will cook me alive!"

"Only if Terry fires it," said Dan. "But he isn't going to. Are you, Terry?"

He could hear the lieutenant breathing. That was all.

"Pensker! Listen. Fire the fucking missile!"

"You're still in ready service, sir."

"That's right! And I ordered you to fire. Fire!"

"I can't," said Pensker, his voice suddenly hopeless. "I can't do that to you. Do what he says, sir. Get in the magazine and close the scuttle. I'll get a blower and clear the ready room. We'll talk to the XO and do it later."

At that moment, the bell stopped ringing. The muffled thump-hiss of releasing gas was clearly audible. Dan shouted, "Captain! Get out of there!"

"Close the scuttle, sir!" screamed Pensker.

"Fire the missile!"

Dan didn't say anything. He closed his eyes. It was all up to Terry Pensker now. How much he believed in this himself, and how much Shaker had convinced or intimidated him into it. *"Fire!"* the captain said again, his voice cracking.

"I'm not going to, sir. You might as well save yourself."

After a long moment came Shaker's voice, coughing: "Okay. God damn you both. Okay."

Dan dropped the handset and sprinted for the passageway.
He pounded through the berthing compartment and up a ladder. He went through two more watertight doors and up another deck. He bypassed Combat and stabbed at a combination
lock. The door to Radio Central buzzed and swung open.

The radiomen stared at him. He picked up the bogen and
dialed the bridge. Wise answered. A moment later, the general
quarters alarm began to bong.

Dan hung up. He wished he could think. He wasn't at all sure
this was right.

But there was no time to think. No time to ponder what he
was doing to Shaker, to himself, or to both their careers. He had
to go by the letter of the law.

The leading radioman came out of the transmitter room. Dan
said, "Chief, get a circuit up to COMIDEASTFOR, Manama. I
have an outgoing OPREP CERBERUS. Nuclear-access incident. I want it out in thirty seconds."

The radioman flicked a switch and sat down at the teletype.
"No problem. Flash precedence, XO?"

Dan said, grimly, "You bet your ass."

The answer came back in twelve minutes flat. By then,
Shaker was there, his face shining with sweat but inhumanly
controlled. The chief tore it off and handed it to him.

USS *VAN ZANDT* BREAK OFF PATROL. USS *GALLERY* WILL SORTIE TO
RELIEVE. RETURN BAHRAIN IMMEDIATELY FLANK SPEED. PREPARE
TO RECEIVE NAVAL INVESTIGATIVE SERVICE TEAM BY HELICOPTER.
HART.

28

U.S.S. *Turner Van Zandt*

THE NIS team arrived while they were still thirty miles out. Two men in civilian clothes and three armed Marine sergeants. The Marines double-timed directly from the flight deck to CIC and the missile magazine. They relieved the guard and snapped huge antiterrorist padlocks on the scuttle and the blast door. One of the men in civvies went to CIC, showed Proginelli his identification, and removed four printed circuit boards from the fire-control system.

Van Zandt was defenseless, her teeth drawn.

The second civilian convened an ad hoc investigation. He saw Shaker first, brushing aside his request to delay till they reached port. They were closeted in his cabin for almost an hour.

Finally, Dan was called. He waited outside the door. When Shaker came out, the flat blue eyes contemplated him for an endless moment. Then he shook his head, turned away, and pulled himself up the ladder toward the bridge.

Dan took a deep breath, tapped, and let himself in.

"Morning, Commander. I'm Bart Sturgis."

"Dan Lenson."

Sturgis was standing, and they shook hands. He was a little overweight, moon-faced, with slicked-back hair; he was wearing an off-the-rack polyester suit, dark blue, and a blue tie. It was held to his shirt by a Navy tie tack, the kind anyone could buy. He looked like a small-town realtor. Sturgis, he saw, was looking him over, too.

"Sit down." He extended a pack of Navy Exchange generics. "Smoke?"

"No, thanks."

The agent put the pack away without taking one for himself. Dan grinned inside his head. Till he noticed the recorder.

Sturgis removed a cassette from it and slipped it into his jacket. He put in a fresh one and closed it. Then he shoved a form across the table.

"This signifies consent to recording, Commander, as well as a legally binding agreement not to discuss this matter with anyone else until the investigation is complete. Please read it."

Dan took out his issue Skilcraft and signed. He licked his lips; his mouth was going dry.

"All right," said Sturgis. He turned the recorder on and looked at a steno pad beside it. "Now, you're the one who sent us the message, so you know why I'm here."

"That's right, sir."

"Don't call me sir. I don't have a rank as far as you're concerned. Just call me Mr. Sturgis." He paused, looking up. "This is a serious accusation. As I'm sure you realize."

"Of course it is, it's serious as hell. That's why I called for help."

"Right." Sturgis rubbed his face. He had a heavy shadow on his chin and neck. That and his weight gave him an air of simplicity and harmlessness. "Now, I talked to the captain first, but I want you to know that great old saying, The first liar gets believed, does not apply with me. I listen to everybody the same. My job is not to decide who's right and who's wrong, who's telling the truth and who's not. The Board of Inquiry does that. My job is to decide if there's something here ought to be investigated and, if so, what action has to be taken right now to prevent further damage."

"I understand."

"Okay, let's hear your story."

Dan began with Shaker's loss of *Strong*, and digressed to talk about Pensker, too. He tried to make it factual and dispassionate. He didn't want to vilify either of them. Just get it out in the open. He told the silent agent about the closeness between the two. He discussed briefly, a sentence each, their possible motivations for disgruntlement or revenge. Sturgis listened closely, making a note now and then.

Then, getting more detailed, he told of the confrontation in the magazine. He recounted the conversation, and went step by step through his reasoning, why he had concluded that Shaker meant to launch, and how he could do it.

He hesitated there. Then said, "Mr. Sturgis, who sent you here?"

The agent flicked up his gaze. "Admiral Hart. Why?"

"Because Captain Shaker implied at one point he had COMIDEASTFOR's permission to launch."

"No." Sturgis shook his head. "He called me himself. He told me to find out what was going on, no pussyfooting, get hard data so he could act. I know Hart. He's straight."

He paused, and for just a moment Dan saw a different, much more dangerous man under the jolly, bland exterior. "And if he isn't, Commander, the Naval Investigative Service reports directly to the Secretary of the Navy. If he's tampering with nuclear weapons, I don't give a fiddler's fart how many stars he's got. His relief will be on the next plane out of Dulles."

Somewhat reassured, Dan resumed with his decision to trip the CO_2 flood. Sturgis interrupted here with a question about what that would do, and he explained.

He finished with Pensker's decision not to fire, and with his own action in sounding general quarters and sending out a flash OPREP.

"Why did you call away GQ?" the agent asked, fiddling with his pencil.

"It got the whole Condition One team on station. Pensker had to turn over the weapons console. There were people on deck to see what was going on. I figure that was why Shaker was doing this at night. Only the people he'd co-opted would be on station. I don't think anyone else in the crew knew about it."

Sturgis put the eraser end into his ear. "Who all do you think was involved?"

"Shaker, Pensker, and the guard. I think it was Thompson. And maybe not him; the captain could have just told him to get lost and he'd do it. He's not the brightest guy aboard."

"Okay, that narrows it down," said Sturgis. He took the pencil out and looked at it. "Now, why did you send the CERBERUS?"

"Well . . . isn't that obvious? That's the message you send when the security of the special weapons is in danger. If someone's trying to launch a nuke by himself, that's a dangerous condition, isn't it? As bad as a group of terrorists trying to get hold of it."

"But the weapons officer had already refused to fire. You couldn't wait till you were back in port?"

"No! I had to get the word out then. Otherwise, they could wait me out—or put me out of circulation somehow. Then launch at their leisure."

"What do you think Captain Shaker would have done to you, Mr. Lenson?"

Sturgis's eyes were suddenly evaluating. Dan thought, What did Shaker tell him about me? That I'm paranoid? Fatigued? Subject to delusions? This was a dangerous question. So he said, trying to sound calm, "I don't know. He's never shown any inclination to personal violence, if that's what you mean."

"You don't think he'd have killed you? Or had Pensker do it?"

"That never occurred to me."

"Why not?"

Dan said slowly, "Because he's an honorable man. He has nothing against me or anyone else in the U.S. Navy, Mr. Sturgis. Only against the Iranians."

"Why do you think that is?"

"Well, again, that seems obvious. Because of the *Strong*."

"Do you think the Navy would have selected him for another Gulf command without a psychological evaluation?"

"I don't know. I know he was sent out here in a hurry, because of Captain Bell's illness. But that's beside the point. All I'm telling you is what I observed and what I concluded."

Sturgis sighed. He tossed the pencil on the table. "Mr. Lenson, Captain Shaker's record shows absolutely no indication of instability or poor judgment. Nor does he seem unbalanced to me. Do you think it's possible you may have been mistaken about his intentions?"

"No."

"Why not?"

"Because of the conversation. He told me specifically that he was launching a nuclear weapon on Bushehr."

"On the sound-powered phone."

"Yes."

"But we have no record of that, do we?"

Dan shifted in his chair. "No," he said.

"Or any witnesses?"

"Only Terry Pensker."

"Mr. Lenson, do you sleep properly?"

"As well as anyone sleeps under way in a war zone. Not very well, I guess. Why?"

"Because I think you hallucinated this," said Sturgis, his voice suddenly harsh. "Or made it up, to smear a captain you hated, a man whose only crime was to get the command you thought you deserved. I think you're despicable, Lenson, a disgrace to the service."

Dan glanced at the recorder. His hands tightened on the chair arms. Through his anger he said, "I understand what you're doing, Mr. Sturgis. But I didn't hallucinate it and I'm not out to get the captain. I heard every word I told you I heard. I saw everything I told you I saw. Ben Shaker's a good man. I'd be happy to serve with him again. But not in this part of the world."

"Tell me why I should believe you, and not him."

"Because I'm telling the truth!"

"Give me another reason."

"There should be evidence. Circumstantial, I guess it would be."

"What evidence? Tell me what to look for."

He thought rapidly, conscious that every word he said was being weighed—as well as preserved on tape. "Down in the ready room. His fingerprints will be all over."

"He has a perfect right to be there, Mr. Lenson. In fact, he's supposed to carry out periodic inspections. Isn't he?"

"Yes, but of the booster suppression system? Is he supposed to lock it out? And if Pensker did any fiddling with the launching circuitry, or with the missile, an expert—the other guy you brought along—he ought to be able to tell."

"Maybe that's true." Sturgis spun his pencil, frowning. "And maybe it isn't. Item one, I strongly doubt if the fact that his fingerprints are on the system—and even if they are, they may not be readable, if the part's been oiled recently—are sufficient to prove intent to tamper. And second, if I understand the Mark 92 FCS, most of the modifications, if any, would be in software. This weapons officer, Pensker, would probably find it pretty simple to erase them and substitute the original programming."

Dan stared at Sturgis. He hadn't thought of that. He'd assumed any tampering would be evident. Rerouted wiring, shorted boards, jumper cables. But the agent was right. His mind had been back in the hardware age. "In that case," he said slowly, "there's no proof anything happened at all."

The pudgy man cocked his head. He put the pencil to his lips and sucked it.

"Do you think I acted properly?"

"Oh, I couldn't say at this point, Commander. If you heard what you say you heard, yes. If you made it all up, no, and you're facing either an insanity discharge or a good many years in prison."

Sturgis made a slow check mark on the pad, letting that sink in. "I know I already confronted you, but I'd like you to think about that for a minute or two. It's not too late to modify your testimony. If you're at all uncertain about it, say so now. You'll be off the ship tomorrow, on your way back to the States, and I'll even promise you this: I'll do all I can to let you resign quietly."

"I'm sticking by what I said."

"Okay . . . but that makes this kind of . . ." The pencil point broke with a tiny snap. "See, Mr. Lenson, Captain Shaker's explanation of these events is rather different."

"What does he say?"

"He simply says he was on a tour of the ship, as his duty calls for, and that you began acting erratically in his absence. Roaming around half-dressed, passing the word for him, and so forth. Then you tracked him down, came on him in the magazine, got the wrong idea, locked the hatch on him, and tried to kill him."

Dan closed his eyes. Through this whole interview, he'd hoped that Shaker had, if not confessed, at least refused to lie. That would have been consistent with the man he knew, or had thought he knew; a man of integrity. "He said I tried to kill him?" he muttered.

"Well, I'm paraphrasing . . . I guess what he actually said was just that you pulled the flood on him and advised him to vacate toot sweet or else." Sturgis paused. "Not quite what you expected?"

Now his apprehension was growing moment by moment. He still didn't see what else he could have done. But it looked like it wasn't enough. Oh, he'd done what he set out to do. There was no way now Shaker could wipe out a city. Whatever happened to him personally, he was glad he'd accomplished that. If only he had some evidence!

But he didn't.

When he opened his eyes, Sturgis was operating on the pencil with a folding knife. He muttered, "Okay, I guess we've got what all there is for now. Commander, I'm inclined to believe that you heard, or saw, something that made you suspicious. Thing is, unless this Pensker lets something slip, or decides to come clean, we have no reason to disbelieve the captain. First off, there's kind of a presumption of sagacity on his part, just 'cause he's the CO. He's also pointed out that you have a history of acting, uh, independently of the command framework.

"We'll check out the firing logic and the PAL, and we'll certainly go through the ready room and magazine very carefully. But if there's nothing out of whack down there, it'll be hard to leave you aboard here with Shaker. Since there seems to be some personal conflict involved, that would be leaving the blasting cap with the dynamite, so to speak.

"On the other hand, we can't just dismiss what you say. The idea of a loose cannon in command of a nuclear-armed ship is pretty horrifying. Yeah"—Sturgis frowned at the recorder—"this has all the earmarks of a real dilemma for the pore ole investigator."

"Good luck," said Dan.

The agent grinned unwillingly. He made another check mark, harder and blacker this time.

"One more thing. I know you signed the paper. But I want to make sure you understand there could be serious consequences if rumors start before we can establish the truth. We'll have the ship isolated and guarded when we get alongside. You won't go ashore. And you won't talk to anyone not involved in the investigation."

"I understand."

Sturgis sighed and stood up. Dan didn't see quite how he did it, but he looked simple, fat, and harmless again. "Thank you for your cooperation. Please send Lieutenant Pensker in."

Outside the door, he found Pensker leaning against the bulkhead. Dan studied him. Finally he said softly, "Terry?"

"Yeah, XO?"

"You made the right decision this morning. Now finish it up. Tell the truth."

There was agony in the dark eyes. But he didn't nod, or say anything. Only slid past him, not quite touching, knocked, and went in.

Dan stood by the chart table as land grew into view ahead. The mercury shimmer gradually solidified into low reefs, fish traps, Bahrain. Had it only been two days ago they'd partied together here?

The bridge was dead quiet. There was no talk, not even the usual furtive grab-assing between the lookouts and the signalmen. Between the terse formalisms of maneuvering, the fathometer clicked in a strained silence. He caught Charaler's wary glance, Ekdahl's averted eyes. McQueen had nothing to say beyond ranges, bearings, set, and drift. Beyond it all, Shaker brooded in his padded chair, smoking and staring out to starboard as the pilot boat approached.

At the "all stop" order, he stepped back from the charts, rubbing his eyes—and bumped into Chief Nolan, who was standing behind him. The master-at-arms looked disturbed. "Sir, we got a problem. Caught one of the corpsmen giving himself a shot."

"A shot. Who?"

"The new man."

He'd have to see him. The world might end, but discipline had to be maintained. "Hold on to him for now; I'll talk to him later."

"When, sir?"

"After we dock. I'll see him in my cabin."

Nolan left. Dan looked out to starboard; the pilot was clambering aboard. He went back to the chart table and looked down at it.

He wondered again, as he had not stopped wondering since the night before, whether he'd acted properly. His heart said he had, but his mind wasn't sure. If he hadn't interfered, might Shaker have thought better of it? Had second thoughts? Decided his private revenge could be deferred?

But it was beyond them both now. As if his pulling the toggle had set a train of events in motion that could end only with his ruin or Shaker's. Neither he nor the captain could back down now. Now the decision as to whom to believe, and what to do about it, was out of their hands.

It occurred to Dan then that Hart, and Sturgis, and Cannon, and those above them might fully believe neither of them, but be unable to exonerate them, either. In a way, that would be worst of all. He and Shaker would both lose *Van Zandt*. Hart would have to relieve them both, just to be safe.

Oh, it would happen quietly, their professional deaths. It would hardly help the national interest, relations with allies, to advertise that what Shaker had almost done might be possible. They'd be sent back to the States with a vaguely worded reprimand in their jackets. Shaker could retire, he had enough time in. But he would have to linger on, certain now of never gaining a command, just crossing off the days in some shore-duty backwater. This could be the last time he stood on the deck of a Navy ship.

Charaler ordered ahead two-thirds. Dan stood rigidly at the chart table, recommending courses and speeds. The dawn showed them the pier, stark and shadowed in the flat rose-colored light. On it, as they approached, they could see the party of officers and technicians waiting.

He could see already that one of them was Stansfield Hart.

29

The U.S. Embassy, Manama, Bahrain

BLAIR stood at the conference table, watching as the men filed in. Twelve sharp, and it looked like everyone was here. Everyone—no, the two ambassadors were still absent.

There was a stir in the corridor, a murmur.

Shaw stalked in, impeccable, his distant smile sweeping the room like a radar. Beside him, an older man, green sport coat, glasses, slicked-back hair. Two Foreign Service types trotted behind them with briefcases and walkie-talkies.

And that, she thought, rounds it off. She moved forward and caught the older man's eye. "Hello, Jerry."

"Well, hello, Blair, nice to see you again." They shook hands, Weber grinning as if he was here for a flossing appointment.

Jerry Weber was a political appointee, a California banker whose years of support of the President had been rewarded in the usual way. Unfortunately, the exotic, harmless post he'd been assigned to—Bahrain—had turned unexpectedly turbulent for most of his tenure.

She glanced around at the mix of suits and uniforms. The attachés, of course, and Hart's staffers, Byrne, Trudell, Ritchie. One was in Army green, Colonel Saunders, General Cannon's rep from CENTCOM. No one made jokes about his name. She nodded to Shaw and got an air-conditioned smile in reply. Had he managed to smooth things over with Prince Ismail? It didn't seem like a good time to ask.

Weber, to an aide: "Time yet? Uh-huh? Okay—gentlemen, ladies, please follow me."

The Bubble opened off the regular conference room. It was a little larger than a walk-in closet, bare-walled except for framed photos of President Reagan and Sheikh al-Khalifa. The table looked like it had needed stripping and refinishing for longer than she'd been alive. A technician was just leaving; he waved a meter, murmuring "It's clean, sir" to Weber. There were only six chairs. He sent the attachés back for more.

At length, everyone had coffee who wanted it, the door was closed, and the ambassador, watching his aide fiddle with a cassette recorder, said to Hart, "We don't have very good ventilation in here, Admiral. If you don't mind—"

Hart grunted and looked around for an ashtray. There weren't any. He stubbed out his cigarette in a trash can and resumed his seat.

Weber kicked off. "Uh, gentlemen, Miss Titus, this is an ad hoc working group to coordinate a military initiative against irregular forces in the Gulf. The basis for it is a presidential order we received at four o'clock this morning. B.B., that thing on now?"

"Yessir, Mr. Ambassador."

"We have present the honorable Harrison Shaw, Ambassador to Saudi Arabia; attachés of the three services from this embassy; Mr. Dennis Hsiao, CIA; Ms. Blair Titus, Senate Armed Services Committee staff; and Rear Admiral Stansfield Hart, COMIDEASTFOR, who will be responsible for military planning and coordination, with his staff. Also present are myself, Gerald Weber, Ambassador to Bahrain, and my assistant, B. B. Mease. Uh, Admiral, would you like to chair?"

"I think you had better, sir. I'm not sure how these interagency things go."

"All right. Has everyone read the message?"

Everyone had. Weber's assistant read it aloud, anyway. From the Joint Chiefs of Staff, via CENTCOM, it directed COMIDEASTFOR to plan and execute a time-urgent reprisal against a Pasdaran base. He was directed to conduct preliminary liaison with local diplomatic and intelligence authorities to ensure that the action chosen would be suitable, feasible, and acceptable; that is, damaging to the Pasdaran, reasonably sure of success, and in accord with wider policy. The strike was to take place within seventy-two hours, to link it with recent Iranian attacks.

"Any questions on the order?" said Weber.

"What are we going to hit?" asked Hsiao.

"Uh, I think we'll need both your input and the Admiral's on that. Admiral?"

"I am rather constrained on what to recommend." Hart drummed his fingers on the table, examined a file Byrne handed him, and added, "By the fact that we have no hard intelligence yet on the location of our major threat."

"You're talking about your . . . submarine, I suppose," said Weber.

"That's right, sir. I've been running patrols, requested satellite reconaissance sweeps, and we've been listening around the clock for electronic emissions. Not a peep. Whoever's running that boat, he's good."

"But *is* there a submarine?" rumbled Saunders. "I hear there is from the Navy, but so far as I know, there's been no evidence—"

"There's been a sighting and one, possibly two torpedoings."

"A possible sighting, a possible torpedoing—"

"Let's stick to the issue, gentlemen. We need to settle on a target."

Hart gave Saunders a final glare and turned back to Weber. "Yessir. Therefore, I suggest either Farsi Island or, better yet, Bushehr. They're the biggest thorns in our side up here as far as fixed bases are concerned. There are six Boghammers forward-based at Farsi, supported from the mainland."

"Farsi Island or Bushehr. Any objections to those choices?"

With the doors closed, the little room was becoming stuffy. Blair was beginning to sweat. She shook her blouse loose under her arms and said, "Bushehr is on the mainland. It's an Iranian Navy base and air facility. Wouldn't you be taking on the regular armed forces as well as the Pasdaran, if you attacked there?"

"That's not a drawback, that's an advantage," said Hart. "If the wraps are off, I want to hurt them as much as I can. Go for their fleet. Sink some frigates, not just motorboats."

Shaw said, "I'd like to register an objection."

"Go ahead, Ambassador."

Again, as she'd noticed in Riyadh, he paused before he spoke. She could see him, like a chess player, computing several moves ahead. "I don't presume to speak for the Saudis, but perhaps that's my role here. I feel sure they would object to any attack on the mainland of Iran. They prefer deescalation, not escalation, in their end of the Gulf." He stopped, then added, "For the same reason, I would object to Farsi."

"Why?" said Blair.

"It's too close to their offshore fields. If Farsi alone is attacked, the losses can be quickly replaced, as Admiral Hart has pointed out. We'll see lots of rigs on fire then. Saudi rigs."

"I support that," said Weber.

"Excuse me?" said Hart.

"I mean, I support Mr. Shaw's objection to Farsi Island."

Hart said angrily, "Well, gentlemen, where does that leave me? You've just ruled out the two best targets in the northern Gulf. It seems to me—"

"In the *northern* Gulf, Admiral," said Blair. "Aren't there other Pasdaran bases? Not so close to the oil-producing areas?"

"Abu Musa," said Hsiao.

"Yes, Abu Musa, that was also on my short list."

"That would be more acceptable," said Shaw. "There isn't the high density of oil fields down there. It's also far enough away from the Saudis and Bahrainis to decouple a strike from them. They can denounce it, if they like."

"But what about the UAE and Oman?" said Saunders.

"I don't see anybody here representing them," said Weber. He smiled.

"How does Abu Musa look to you operationally?" Blair asked Hart.

"It's a tough nut. But not as challenging as Bushehr."

"Fewer air defenses," said Hsiao. "According to our sources."

"Fewer defenses, and it's close enough to get planes in for a suppressive strike. I'll have to get a message out to *Forrestal*, turn her around; she's on her way to Kenya right now."

"Wait a minute. Are we talking—what kind of strike are we talking about, I'm confused," said Weber. "Is it an air attack? Purely air, like Libya?"

"Can't do that, I'm afraid," said Hart. "I've thought a lot about that, about how to hit these Boghammers." He went over the high-attack versus low-level bombing problem. "Even an isolated base like Abu Musa is going to be equipped with antiair defenses. Mr. Hsaio, perhaps you could supply details—"

"Mostly Chinese. Peking's been selling them a lot of shoulder-fired weapons."

"Can we use B-52s?" said Weber then, smirking a little. They all looked at him.

"What B-52s?" said Saunders.

"The ones that are flying in. The wing that's going to base here."

This occasioned some discussion. Most of those present had heard the rumor. "It's got to be gonzo secret, if I've never heard of it," said the CENTCOM rep at last. "But anyway, they aren't here now, so let's plan with what we've got."

"What about Iranian air, out of Bandar 'Abbās?" asked one of the attachés.

"I think three or four F-18s will keep them in the icebox," said

Hart. "They've been pretty tame lately. Parts shortage, probably. Intel, you concur?"

Hsiao and Byrne both nodded, caught each other doing it, and traded scowls.

"One point I want to make," Blair said. Their heads turned. "This action must be decisive, whatever the target. This is a one-time dispensation, if you will, in response to media pressure about the shoot-down of Four Two One. Congress is taking a risk by conceding it to the administration. If it fails, or if the IRG continues to operate out of the base afterward, the Hill will share the blame. They'll look for a way to ensure it doesn't happen again. And it is quite possible that the result will be a sizable reduction, if not a complete withdrawal, of U.S. forces in the Gulf."

They were silent for a while, each pondering this in his own way. It was very hot in the room now. At last, Ambassador Weber cleared his throat. "Uh, I take it the consensus of the principals, then—have we agreed on Abu Musa?"

They seemed to have agreed. "Now," he went on, "I know this is your ball park, Admiral, how the strike will be carried out, but do you have any ideas? Can you give us, uh, a rough sketch?"

"It'll be pretty rough," said Hart. He stared at one of the portraits. "There's a mine field to contend with. That will have to be swept, or at least accessed with a cleared channel, to the anchorage, where the boats moor. The shore facilities include fuel dumps, workshops, barracks, and the like. Looks like light construction; they weren't there two years ago.

"My initial idea is to do a high-level strike with A-6s from *Forrestal*, concentrating on the shore installation. Then send in two or three low-value surface units and shell the dickens out of the Boghammers and any remaining facilities at close range."

"What's that, a 'low-value unit'?" said Weber. "I'm not familiar with the usage."

"A destroyer-type ship." Hart paused. "I have several currently unassigned to patrol duties. I have two specifically in mind for this tasking."

And Blair felt suddenly uneasy. Destroyer-type ships . . . didn't that mean frigates? And currently unassigned to patrol duties . . . no, his ship was supposed to be getting under way. . . . Before she thought through what she was asking she said, "Which two ships, Admiral?"

"Charles Adams. And *Turner Van Zandt."*

She summoned everything she had to look cool and distant. This was not what she was here for. It was a breach of professionalism even to ask.

But she did anyway. "Why those two?"

"Well, *Adams* is what we call a gunship. Older, faster, better-armed for shore bombardment. *Van Zandt*—she's well trained and the captain is aggressive. Maybe too aggressive. But I think he's a good choice for this kind of action." His eyes left the wall, suddenly sharpening on her. "Unless you know something I don't?"

She heard the weakness in her voice as she said, "Don't you have several frigates available?"

They were all looking at her now. "Blair?" said Weber. "What are you trying to say?"

"Nothing. The choice is up to you, of course."

"Admiral," said Shaw then, "these aircraft, these A-6s. How will they be armed?"

"I hadn't gotten down to that level yet, sir. That will be a decision for the air arm. They'll analyze the recon photos and calculate the optimal bomb load and type."

"It would be better if they didn't use cluster bomb units. That's my advice."

"No CBUs?"

"No."

Hart was reddening now. "And what in God's name, sir, is the rationale for that request?"

"The Saudis are sensitive to CBU use because the Israelis have used them in Lebanon, and we refused to sell them to the Arabs. Now, if we employ them against—granted, Iranians, but still Moslems—I don't think it would read well in the Arab states."

"Mr. Shaw, I am going to leave that to the carrier. I'm not going to make tactical decisions based on political PR."

Shaw said, gently, "You're to take the recommendations of this working group into consideration, Admiral. That's clearly indicated in your orders."

"Crap," said Hart. Several of the diplomats winced.

Shaw said, his voice just a shade grayer, "We're talking about an operation in support of U.S. policy, Admiral, and that would be a decided positive—"

"Crap," said Hart again, interrupting him in mid-sentence. "We're not talking about policy, we're talking about men's lives now. You've already moved me to Abu Musa. Now you're telling me what ordnance to use.

"Well, I'm not buying that. That's not advice, that's meddling in military operations. If CBUs are the safest way for my pilots to destroy this base, that's what I'll use. End of discussion." He swiveled away from Shaw, caught Blair in his sights, and let off a salvo at her, too. "Yes, meddling. Like *you*'ve been doing since you got here. What about it, Miss Titus? Any more 'recommendations,' 'advice,' or 'consultations'? *Are you done screwing around with us?*"

She was instantly angry. "That's unfair, Admiral. You complained to me about not having a free hand. I got it for you! Where do you think this order came from? From a negotiated agreement of both houses with the Executive. Stop whining and carry it out!"

Shaw tried to interrupt, but she went on. "You wanted a chance to hit them. Hit them, goddamn it, and face the consequences!"

Weber said, "Uh, I don't think we need to drag personalities into this discussion—"

"He's the one—" she said, but then stopped herself. No one else spoke.

"Abu Musa, then," said Weber. He shoved his chair back and turned off the recorder, looking relieved. "Abu Musa, seventy-some hours from now. And that's close-hold, everybody, no talking about it outside of this room or another secure space.

"Thank you all for attending. This conference is adjourned."

They got up. The door opened, and the attachés filed out. Blair lingered, however. Hart was gathering up his charts and files, his cheeks still flushed. As soon as the recorder went off, he'd lit another cigarette, and it hung now from his lips, shedding gray chips of ash on the table.

He ignored her, talking rapidly to Byrne. Finally, she said, "Admiral."

"What?"

"One last thing—the ships you're going to send in."

"We discussed that already."

She stood by the table, her arms crossed. She wasn't sure how she felt. Still angry—yes, at his accusations. But also—scared. And not only for Dan.

"I know, but I was wondering"—she heard the tremor in her voice with sudden terror, but pressed on—"wouldn't the *Mobile Bay* be a better ship to send in than the, the frigate? It's so much more capable. And it's on station there now, closer—"

"Wait a minute," said Hart. They were alone now. He brought his eyes up slowly, then narrowed them, tilting back his head as if, she thought, he was peering at her through bifocals. "Wait a minute! I know why you're asking me this. My chief of staff said he saw you with one of *Van Zandt*'s officers. Is that what this is all about? Something *personal?*"

He said it the way a doctor would say *malpractice lawyer*. Suddenly, just like that, she hated him.

She said in a tight, frozen voice, "All right. That's correct. I'm asking for a favor."

"A *favor.*"

"That's right."

"That I not send the ship your . . . friend is on; that I send another in her place."

"That's right," she said again, and her voice trailed off to nothingness in the insulated room.

"Forget it," said Hart. "*Van Zandt*'s the best I've got for the mission. For the mission *you* want done. And her assigned crew, *all* her regularly assigned crew, is going in on her."

The smoke made a circle in the air. Then he hesitated, half-turning back to her. She stopped breathing, torn between fear and hope. When she saw his eyes, though, she knew there was no ground for hope. Not from this man.

But now his voice wasn't angry. It was tired. And there was no hint of reproach anymore. "You know something, Miss Titus? I know Lenson, too. And Shaker. And a lot of other men on that ship and *Adams*. But I've got to send them, anyway.

"So you got us this deal, is that it? Thanks. For doing your job. But welcome to the real world. It's not all equations and budgets, is it? Now somebody's got to point at a man and tell him, Go out there, and be ready to die.

"I'm disappointed, Blair. It's kind of sad. I was starting to respect you."

She stood alone in the empty room, wanting to cry or scream but unable to do either. She felt as if part of her had died. Hart's last words echoed like a knell. *Starting to respect you.*

Till now, she'd thought of herself as a professional. Focused on the quantifiable, on the facts. Emotion prejudiced analysis. Therefore, it had no place in her business, which was *truth* and *efficiency;* no place in her career—the most important thing in her life.

Hold lightly, Blair. It's over in a heartbeat. . . .

And now she'd given way to it. In the worst, most degrading way.

Then something inside her heart said, horrified, Isn't it natural to protect those you love?

She shuddered. What was she doing? Where was she going from here?

She didn't know. But she couldn't think about it now. Someone was calling her from outside. Saunders. He sounded angry.

She squared her shoulders, lifted her chin, and went out.

30

U.S.S. *Turner Van Zandt*

SHAKING and with pounding heart, not with fear but with the insulted rage of innocence accused, Phelan stood at attention outside the executive officer's stateroom. Across from him, Chief Nolan leaned against a bulkhead. The humming air was cold. Colder, he thought with furious hatred, than it ever got where the enlisted lived.

He sniffled, and Nolan's eyes flicked. "Straighten up, you worthless piece of shit," he rasped.

He raised his shoulders a quarter-inch, then let them slump back. Fuck him. The chief master-at-arms. Big deal.

But no matter what he told himself, no matter how he sneered inside at the fat chief and all he represented, he couldn't stop trembling.

It had occurred to him more than once in the hour he'd been standing here that this time he was in real trouble.

He hadn't expected Nolan that early. Sick call wasn't till after quarters, and sick bay was off limits till then. After all, it was a medical space. People weren't supposed to just barge in. So when the door eased open and the fat face stuck itself in, he'd frozen, too deep in the rush to move or speak. The chief, glancing around absently, had asked him something—something about Fitch—and then, suddenly, seen what he was doing. Seen his arm palm up on the blotter, the paper and foil scattered, the little specimen cup.

And the needle.

Not that it was a big deal. It wasn't as if he was mainlining, like an addict. He'd just been skin-popping. It was just to be able to do his job; he wasn't worth a shit in the morning these days. But he'd realized then, in that moment of simultaneous euphoria and horror, that he'd forgotten to lock the door.

"Come to attention, Phelan," rasped Nolan again. Bernard

gave him a go-to-hell sneer. If he wanted him at attention, he could fuck a duck.

Boots rattled on the ladder. It was khaki, the XO. He looked tense already. Phelan came to a boot-camp attention, shoulders back, thumbs along the seams of his dungaree trou.

Dan blinked at the waiting CMAA, the mustached, swarthy man beside him. Remembered, and suppressed a sigh. "This him, Chief?"

"Yessir. Seaman Phelan."

"Hospitalman Phelan, *sir,"* the little man barked.

"Sorry to keep you waiting. There's a lot"—Dan paused—"a lot going on today."

"That's all right, sir. Waiting won't hurt this guy none. Give him time to get it out of his system."

Dan wondered what Nolan meant. Then thought, That's what we're here to find out. He slid past them, leaving the door open. The chief flicked his eyes for Phelan to follow.

Inside, Bernard glanced around enviously. Private desk, sofa, books. A porthole, pictures on the bulkheads. A lot nicer than a two-by-six bunk, with people playing cards all night, slamming doors, farting in your face as you lay in your rack. The only trouble was that the overhead lights were too bright. He thought of asking the XO to turn them off. No, that wouldn't be smart.

Lenson stood in front of the porthole for a moment, blinking into the morning. He was remembering how Sturgis had looked when it became evident there was no way of telling which version of events to believe, his or Shaker's. The agent was still pursuing the investigation, broadening it now to the rest of the officers and crew.

Phelan, watching him with the attention a rabbit gives a hawk, saw the XO hadn't shaved yet. He thought angrily: We got to, though. Take your fucking time, us peons got nothing better to do than wait on you.

Dan turned. "Where's the Doc?"

"I guess down below, sir."

"This man works for him. I want him here before we start."

"Aye, sir. Use your phone?"

Lenson nodded. Nolan spoke briefly on the bogen, then hung up. "He's on his way, sir."

"Lieutenant Wise; captain's cabin," announced the 1MC. Dan turned the speaker down, then sat and took a message out of a basket. He looked at it, massaging above his eyes with thumb and forefinger. He wondered what Pensker had told them.

Would he back Shaker up? Or would he figure it was time to come clean?

Phelan watched him, seething. Go ahead, ignore us, he thought. We're just dirt to you. Army, Navy, the officers were all the same.

He stayed braced, though. It seemed like the smart thing to do.

Fitch came in a few minutes later. "Shut the door, Doc," said Lenson, sliding the message out of sight and leaning forward.

"Uncover," barked Nolan. *"Two."*

Dan began, the words routine: "Hospitalman Phelan, this is XO's investigation. It's carried out to see if there's evidence to warrant writing up a formal charge. No punishment will be awarded here. However, the same rules for your protection apply as at captain's mast. You have the right to remain silent and to make no statement. You have the right to call witnesses to your defense. Do you understand everything I've said?"

"Yessir," Phelan snapped.

"Chief, what do we have here?"

Nolan cleared his throat. "Well, sir, like I said on the bridge, at approximately oh-six-forty-five I was coming back from the fantail. I stopped at sick bay to see if Doc was in. Wanted to ask him if he could retest my body-fat percentage. I've lost ten pounds since my last physical."

He paused, then resumed his official voice. "Petty Officer Fitch was not in sick bay. Hospitalman Phelan was. I observed that the safe was open, that there was drugs out in front of him, along with other paraphernalia, and that he had a needle in his arm. He looked spaced out and didn't answer at first when I spoke to him. I asked him what he thought he was doing.

"He said he was giving himself a vitamin shot. That didn't sound right, so I took charge of the syringe and the drugs and the candy, everything that was on the desk, and called the Doc. When he got there, I turned subject man over to his custody and went to notify you."

Dan nodded. He didn't think about what he'd just heard. He remembered it, but he hadn't thought yet. It was only one side of the story. "Okay. Doc?"

Fitch nodded solemnly. He looked grave and important, regretful and vindicated all at the same time. The prick, Phelan thought, this is just another chance for him to suck off an officer. . . . "Yessir. When the Chief got me down there, I first made the observation that the controlled-substances safe had been opened. I then—"

"Let's have the short version," Lenson interrupted. "What was he doing?"

"Injecting himself with morphine. Near as I can tell. I think what he did was open one of the blocks, dissolve it in water, heat it, then do a subcutaneous injection."

"Morphine? Medical morphine, from the emergency stock?"

"Yes, sir, that's right."

Dan felt sick. He took his cap off and set it to one side. Then, for the first time, he looked up. Phelan kept his eyes straight ahead.

"Okay, what have you got to say?"

"Nothing, sir."

"What do you mean, nothing? This is serious, Phelan."

"Yes, sir, I know it is." He'd been thinking all this time about what he was going to say. The bit about the vitamins had almost gone down with Nolan; he'd seen the doubt in his eyes. With Fitch here, though, that might not work. At last he said, "Sir, I don't know how this goes. I never was up to one of these before. Don't I get a lawyer or something?"

Dan stared up at him, trying to catch the eyes, but they slid around his like oiled marbles. "This is the first time you've ever been at mast?"

"Yessir."

"Never went to mast on the—what was it, the cruiser you missed movement on—"

"*Long Beach*, sir. No, sir."

"We still don't have your records, do we?"

"I don't think so, sir."

"Well, about a lawyer: This isn't an official mast yet. As I said. Now, if you want to talk lawyers, we can find out if there's one attached to the staff here. Only it won't be a mast then, it'll be a court-martial. Got that?"

"Yessir."

"Now tell me what you were doing in sick bay with a needle in your arm."

The stall had only bought him a minute, and he decided now to stick with what he already half-believed was the truth. "It was a vitamin shot. Like I told the chief. He's got it in for me; he's been hassling me since I got aboard. But that's what it was, that's the truth."

"Doc?"

"We don't give vitamins that way, sir. If they need 'em that bad, they're already in a shoreside hospital."

"The morphine was out of the safe. Is there any reason it should have been out?"

"No sir, I do the inventories. There was no reason one of those blocks should be open unless you're using it."

Dan said, "Right. Now, did I hear somebody mention candy? Does that have anything to do with this?"

"I think it might, sir," said Fitch. "That caramel they sell in the ship's store kind of looks like morphine. I figure he was going to mold some to the same shape, then wrap it up again somehow and replace it."

Dan closed his eyes. The emergency supplies . . . meant for burned men, major casualties . . . "Is there any way we can tell how long he's been doing this?"

"I'll have to check our whole stock, sir. Unwrap it and test it."

"What about the rest of the drugs?"

"I checked the pharmaceutical log against the stock log." Fitch looked at Phelan. "And I looked back at the prescription records. I haven't got numbers yet, but we're down in stimulants, analgesics, tranquilizers, too. It's covered as far as the log goes, but there's been more opiates and sedatives given out this week than I issue in a year."

"I thought you needed the CO's signature to dispense those."

"We do, sir. There's a signature on the forms that sort of looks like Captain Bell's."

"Captain *Bell's?*"

"Yessir. Those were the last prescriptions we did before Phelan came aboard. I figure he just traced them without realizing or thinking that we changed COs."

"Prescribing to whom? To himself?"

"No sir," said Fitch.

Dan fiddled with a pencil. At last, softly, he said, "Vitamins, Phelan?"

Phelan met the gray eyes straight on. "Yes, sir," he said sincerely. "I've had the flu or something since Karachi. I thought vitamin C might help. We didn't have any liquid, so I crushed some tablets up. The other stuff Petty Officer Fitch is talking about, those people were hurting, and I gave them what you're supposed to give them. I don't know nothing about any signature. That's all." He shrugged.

"Why was the morphine out?"

"I don't know, sir. It was laying there on the desk like that when I got to sick bay."

Lenson sighed. "And the caramel?"

"I like caramel, sir."

"Phelan, why are you doing this to yourself?"

"I'm not doing nothing, sir. You want the truth, I think maybe somebody was trying to trap me. Leaving it out like that."

"Sir?" said Fitch.

"Yeah, Doc."

"Chief tell you, I searched his locker?"

Phelan turned, forgetting his brace, suddenly outraged. "You little—hey! You got no right to do that. That's my fucking locker, man, I got rights—"

"Pipe down, sailor! You're at attention!" shouted Nolan.

"Shut up," said Lenson coldly to both of them. "What about the locker?"

Bernard stared down, trembling with anger, as Fitch laid out the tobacco pouch, followed by two pill bottles and half a pack of Marlboros. Lenson looked at them. He opened the pouch and sniffed it.

Nolan and Fitch leaned over the desktop, and Phelan, looking at the backs of their heads, thought for a moment of laying them out with the paper punch, closing the door softly behind him, crossing the quarterdeck, walking up the pier, and disappearing into the desert.

But he didn't.

"It's pot, all right," said Nolan. The leading corpsman nodded, too.

Dan pushed a bottle toward Fitch with the tips of his fingers. "You recognize these?"

"Navy stock, sir. Demerol and Catapres."

"What are those?"

"Demerol's a morphine derivative. Catapres, that's clonidine. It's a blood-pressure medication."

"Blood pressure?"

"Yessir."

"Is it something you get high with?"

"Not that I know of, sir. It's used in drug-treatment programs, though. To help them through withdrawal."

Lenson looked at the drugs. Finally, he said, still looking down, "Okay, Mr. Phelan, anything else?"

Bernard felt his lip trembling, so he sneered. "You got it all wrapped up, don't you? You don't give a shit about me. Why should I say anything?"

"Because I'd like to hear it." Dan paused. "The blood-pressure drug. You must have been trying to quit. Am I right?"

Phelan looked at the deck.

Dan sighed. He pushed the pills around on the desk. "You

tried to stop. But you're taking more and more. You tried to stay out of the morphine, didn't you? You're a corpsman, you know who that's for. But you couldn't help yourself. Because it's in charge now, not you."

Phelan said, scowling at the deck, "I got nothing to say."

"I'd like to help you, Bernard. But is there any way to get to you? Or do you have to ride this one down all the way?"

Now the XO was trying to trap him. "I told you, I got nothing to say."

Dan waited. But that was all. He straightened then. "Okay, you're tough. So we get tough, too. Who else have you been giving this to?"

"It's in the log. Why ask me?"

"Because of the grass," said Dan softly. "This is a *Van Zandt* tobacco pouch. So you didn't bring it aboard with you, did you? You got it here. Who else is using? Who've you been sharing with—or selling to?"

"I don't got nothing to say to you," said Phelan contemptuously. "You want to be some kind of detective, go ahead. I'm not playing your fucking games."

He suddenly realized then, just from Lenson's eyes, that he'd pushed the wrong button. The exec's face went hard and sharp as flaked quartz, and his hands went white on the desk. He opened his mouth to try to retrieve the words, but it was too late.

"So you don't play games," Dan said softly. "Well, you're not standing in front of me for our mutual amusement, Hospitalman Phelan. Are you? You're looking down the barrel of an Article One twelve court-martial. Wrongful use and possession aboard ship, intent to distribute, that's twenty years hard labor, my friend. Or death, if the court decides the war-zone provision applies."

"Sir, I didn't—"

"And I'd be happy to see it happen, Phelan. I don't care for people who use and sell on board. You see, I lost a lot of ship-mates once because of a bastard who was doing just that. You remind me of him, as a matter of fact."

"I didn't mean that, sir. I—"

"That's enough." The voice was flat. "I don't want to hear it, Phelan."

Bernard stood rigid again, sweating now despite the chill. He didn't believe what the exec was saying about death. That was just to scare him. But hard labor. Prison. Twenty years . . .

Lenson stared up at him for a moment more. He kept his

hands glued to the desk. Then, slowly, he raised one, and massaged his left shoulder for a few seconds. There were just too many parallels to the doomed *Ryan*. Too many things he didn't want to remember.

From outside came the roar of a truck engine, on the pier. At last he spun his chair around and pulled out a black-backed pub. He riffled through it, stopped to study a page, then snapped it closed and spun back. He still looked grim as he said, "How long were you on *Long Beach?*"

"Six months, sir."

"How'd you get along there?"

"All right, sir."

Nolan muttered something; Fitch snickered under his breath. Phelan ignored them. It was Lenson who was dangerous. "Why? Sir."

"Because, much as I'd like to, I don't know if it's practical to court-martial you aboard *Van Zandt.*" Dan looked toward the door, wondering what Sturgis was hearing at that moment; wondering at the irony of a man under suspicion sitting in judgment on another. "First off, we don't have time, we're . . . well, we don't have time. For sure not today, and it looks like not for a few days."

"What's going on, sir? I saw the troops on the pier—"

"Later, Chief. It would also not be strictly fair to try you here, Phelan. We don't know you; you don't have anybody who can go to bat for you. If you deserve it, that is." Dan paused again, looking toward the porthole. "What I had in mind was transferring you to CMEF headquarters. The legal beagles can decide whether to try you here or send you back to the States. Then again, they may remand you to *Long Beach.*

"Does that sound like fair treatment?"

Bernard didn't have to think too long about that. Looking at what Lenson was saying, maybe he better get that lawyer. He might be able to work something out ashore. For sure, this guy scared him. He didn't want to be around him anymore.

So he said, "Yessir, that might be better all around."

"Good. I believe I can persuade the captain to do that, Phelan, if you tell the three of us who else is using aboard this ship."

"Okay." He grinned. "Can do. But you got to do something else for me, too." He felt better now. Get them bargaining and you were halfway home.

Lenson didn't say anything, just waited, his face slightly turned away.

"You got to drop the dealing charge. Just say I was using what was in sick bay."

"No."

"Well . . . how about dropping the grass, then? I can tell them—how about just dropping the grass, sir? I never even smoked any; I was just holding it for somebody else."

"Who?" said Nolan. Phelan gave him a quick, angry look. Fuck it. They had him boxed.

"Okay, okay, you got it. The guys you want are Quint and two other guys, I think they're snipes. I forget their names, but one of 'em's got a tattoo on his left arm, a Confederate flag; and the other guy they call Ham. You check their lockers. You'll have 'em cold."

"Chief?"

"I know them," said Nolan grimly.

"Who else?" said Lenson.

"That's it. Just them. Oh, and Golden's a queer. Just thought you'd like to know." He grinned.

"Get this shit off my desk, Doc," said Dan. He stood up. "And this scum off my ship. He's got twenty minutes. Chief, watch him while he packs, then escort him off. The yeoman will have transfer papers on the quarterdeck. We'll send the charge sheet and the evidence over by guard mail this afternoon."

"Aye, sir. Armed escort to the compound, sir?"

"I don't think that's necessary. He hasn't been violent, and there's no place else he can go."

"Aye, sir. Seaman Phelan! Cover—*two*. About—*face*. Forward—*march*."

The last he saw of the exec, he was standing by his desk, looking down at the grass.

Nolan stood over him while he threw his shit into the seabag. The chief took the bottles of cough syrup and his knife and wouldn't give them back. He wanted a shower, his dungarees were sweated through, but he knew it was no good even asking. He got his whites on—he'd have to go through town to get to the compound—and lugged the duffel up two ladders to the main deck.

Topside it was hot, as usual. The yeoman was waiting with a manila envelope. There were a lot of other people standing around on the quarterdeck, too, officers and civilians, and some trucks on the pier. He didn't really see them. He was too mad. He realized too late how the fucking XO had outmaneuvered him. Got what he wanted, and given him nothing in return.

He walked past men with guns without seeing them. He broke out sweating again as he realized Lenson had shafted him royal. He'd just be a number at headquarters. What if they had a computer, they might dig up the desertion charge. Even *Long Beach* wouldn't be much better. Captain Golubovs hated druggies like poison.

He edged around a truck, shifted the bag on his shoulders, muttering to himself, and trudged on.

The pier was about a mile long and he was sweating through his jumper before he got a hundred yards. He was hot and his guts hurt. He hadn't had anything all day. Not even the skin-pop, Nolan had barged in before he'd finished. His hand moved absently about before he realized he was out of cigarettes, too.

When he was sure he was out of sight from the quarterdeck, he stopped and unslung the duffel, looking carefully around. A hungry-looking, dirty cat was watching him from a sliver of shadow by a bollard; that was all.

He tried to pat it, but it retreated. "You, too," he muttered. "Ain't it a bitch." Nobody cared. Not Denise, not the Navy, nobody. Self-pity flooded him.

Well, if that's the way they wanted it, Bernard Newekwe had ways to cope.

He stretched the ache out of his back, looking around again, and at last took the Zippo out of his crackerjacks. He pulled the lighting element out and extracted the cotton reservoir.

The tablet was damp with kerosene, but whole, and he rubbed his hand over his mouth and swallowed.

He'd needed it bad and it hit fast, putting a spring in his step and lightening the load in his mind. He was almost to the head of the pier and thinking about a taxi when he saw a whaleboat at the landing. Four guys in dungarees were loading cans. He stopped to watch them for a minute. The side of the boat read DDG-2.

"Hey," he called.

"Hey what," said one of the guys. They were working hard, piling the cans in lickety-split.

"Where you guys from?"

They were from something called the *Charles Adams*. She was out in the anchorage, standing by for them to come back.

He looked around. There was a dumpster a few steps away. It didn't take him long to swagger over behind it, squat down, and dig out the papers they'd given him on the quarterdeck. And the lighter still worked.

He ground the ashes into the concrete, shouldered the bag,

and went back to where the boat was tied up. "Hey," he said, making his voice plaintive, "I got a problem."

"Don't we all," said one of the guys. Phelan, looking at his arms, figured him for a boatswain third.

"No, listen. I'm a corpsman, supposed to go to *Long Beach*, but she ain't here. I don't have no place to go. Tried that frigate, but they're assholes, won't even let me on the mess decks. I ain't eaten all day."

They were squinting up at him now. "No shit? That's tough titty. Missing your ship out here, you're shit out of luck."

"You said it. Can you guys maybe take me out to your ship? Let me talk to your personnelman, see what they can do? I'd do the same for you."

"I don't know," said the boatswain. Phelan waited. At last, he said, "Oh, hell, can't just leave you here. Come on, get in. We can probably use a corpsman."

Phelan stepped over the thwart and settled in, smiling benevolently at the sweating men. He was glad he wasn't one of them. He bummed a cigarette and lit up as they shoved off. He was back in business. The world was rosy again.

He figured something would turn up.

31

U.S.S. Audacity

WHEN Gordon dropped his AWOL bag on the quarterdeck, they were waiting for him. Kearn, his face looking as if it had been twisted around a stick. Hunnicutt, the captain's bland eyes shaded with the dislike that had become ever more evident since their confrontation during the storm.

And three men he didn't know. They were in civvies, two in light sport coats, the third in a lightweight suit, standing quietly in the shade of an awning. At each one's leg, like a heeled dog, was a battered briefcase.

He caught himself start to salute, stopped, and nodded to the petty officer instead. He crossed to Hunnicutt. "What's going on, Cap'n?" he said slowly.

As usual, it was Kearn who answered for him. "God damn it, where've you people been? We've been trying to get hold of you all day."

"We were on liberty. You know that, Lieutenant. We checked out with you."

"Yeah, but God damn it, you're supposed to let us know *where*. I don't believe it, fucking reservists . . ." His voice trailed off. "Anyway, get the hell over there; those people want to talk to you."

"Want us to stay, John?" asked Everett, behind him.

"No, get the guys aboard. And see . . . hey, see if any mail came in while we were away." He looked around, suddenly realizing that *Audacity* was the only minesweeper still in the nest. He pushed sweat off his forehead—the Gulf felt even hotter after Mombasa—and followed the sweep officer to the far side of the fantail.

The civilians turned out to be from the States. The oldest, a fiftyish, paunchy man with a graying beard, introduced himself as Dr. Rothman, from Indian Head. Gordon turned this over in his mind as he shook hands. Indian Head, Maryland, was the Explosive Ordnance Disposal Technology Center. The laboratory, engineering, and intelligence brains of the entire EOD branch.

"Well, let's get down to business," said Rothman, picking up his briefcase. "There someplace we can talk?"

Hunnicutt offered his stateroom. Rothman hesitated for a moment, looking at the others. When they nodded, so did he.

When they were all introduced and the coffee had been poured, Rothman lit a cigarette. He clicked the lighter open, shut, open, shut. He examined the door, then the overhead. Then said to Hunnicutt, "Ah, Commander, is this a secure space?"

"Well—"

"Maybe it would be best to have a guard? Outside the door?"

"I can arrange that."

"And, if you don't mind." He made a little shooing motion with his hand at both Hunnicutt and Kearn. They took a moment to understand. Then the captain reddened, and the lieutenant went white. Rothman waited imperturbably. At last Hunnicutt muttered something, put his head down, and stalked toward the door.

That left Gordon and the three civilians. Rothman took a couple of puffs and clicked the lighter as he examined him. "How's things been for you boys out here?" he said at last.

"All right."

"I read your message. On the KMB-9s."

Gordon nodded.

"Unfortunately, they aren't all that easy."

Gordon waited.

"Ever work with Mark 36s?"

"In Haiphong."

"Oh, you were on the demining?"

"Yup."

"That's good. Haiphong, eh? That's very good." Rothman turned the lighter in his fingers for a moment, then seemed to make some decision. He reached down for his briefcase, unlocked it, and laid a technical manual, a blue-covered report, and a green box the size of a Michener paperback on the captain's table. He hitched his chair forward.

"This is a top-secret briefing, Senior Chief, on an operation that we—the U.S.—are going to undertake two days from now. We're going to go in and wipe out Abu Musa."

Gordon's hands twitched before he could stop them. He stuffed them into his pockets—he was still in civvies—and nodded, to show he was listening.

"Here's a copy of the operation order. Times, insertion, signaling, and so forth. You'll be inserted by helicopter. A night drop with full gear and rafts. Your men are jump-qualified—right?"

"Right."

"You'll have to clear a channel through a mine field. You won't have much time to do it. The mines are Thirty-sixes."

"How do you know that?" Gordon asked him.

"Mr. Hsiao?" Rothman said.

"We got a defector," said the second civilian. He looked Chinese, or part Chinese.

"Do we know what mod?"

"Eleven."

Gordon sucked in a little air. "That's no dumb piece of ordnance."

"Thanks," said the third. Gordon looked at him. Thin, colorless fellow in black-framed glasses.

"Richard designed the trigger logic. So you know the mod eleven, Senior Chief?"

"It's a destructor-type mine. Usually air-dropped. With acoustic, pressure, and magnetic sensors, tied in with logic and a counting circuit. Smart as hell."

Rothman said, "Do you remember the render-safe procedure?"

"Isn't one," said Gordon. "They're too dangerous to tinker with. Got to destroy them in place."

"Right again. Unfortunately," the senior scientist said, stubbing out his butt, "in this operation, they tell us, you can't do that. That would alert the enemy and lose the advantage of surprise. Fortunately, Rick had a project going that might do the trick. We haven't completed testing yet. But he put together a black box for you."

Gordon picked it up. It was welded aluminum, obviously waterproof, with a rubber-covered switch on the top and a peel-off sheet on the bottom. It was unmarked, and lighter than he'd expected. He put it back on the desk. "Not much explosive in there."

"Isn't any." The design engineer was talking now. "It's all electronic. The mod eleven was our first all-digital mine. The logic circuitry, what tells it to explode, is actually a sixteen-bit computer. What this gadget does is inject a signal. The Arm

Enable circuitry runs off a 74LS76 positive NAND gate, with a count-trigger pulse as part of the input. When you—"

Rothman said gently, "Why don't you boot up to system level for the Senior Chief, Rick."

"Sorry. What I mean is, this gives the mine an artificial Arm Inhibit signal. So it shouldn't go off. The batteries in the gadget will run it about three hours in seventy-degree water."

Gordon examined it again. He turned it over and picked at the peel-off paper with a fingernail. "This stuff underneath, is it sticky underwater?"

"Yes. Magnets would be better, but—"

"Right. Where does it go on the mine?"

"Over the smallest rear access plate. Align the long axis with fin number three."

"It's in the technical documentation," said Rothman. "The folder with the blue cover."

"What happens when the batteries go dead?"

"The arming circuit reverts to normal functioning."

Gordon looked at it, and then at them again. He wondered, just for a moment, how far he could trust them. Not their loyalty, but their skill. Then he realized the question meant nothing. He wasn't going to have any choice. "Okay," he said. "I guess that's clear. When do we go?"

Rothman nodded at the third man, the one in the gray suit. Up to now, except for the remark about a defector, he'd sat quietly in the background. "Mr. Hsiao here will take you to the airport this afternoon."

"What? I thought you said—"

"Tomorrow night, but that's the drop. We have to get you and your men down south, to *Iwo Jima*—that's where you'll launch from. Get your gear together, we've got a plane at four." Rothman clicked the lighter shut for the last time and dropped it into his briefcase. "Rick?"

The second briefcase came open. Four more green boxes came out and lay, their spray-painted surfaces gleaming dully, beside the first one.

"Any questions?" said Rothman, getting up.

Gordon had several. Whether they'd tested these things on live mines. How you could tell if they weren't working. Little things like that. But he knew the answer without asking: It's in the documentation. He shook his head and got up.

"Good luck," said Rothman. His hand was warm and large and soft. "We'll look forward to reading your message, after the action. Okay?"

"Sure," said Gordon, wondering already whether he would really get to write it.

He was carrying his duffel up the ladder when Kearn loomed at the top. The sweep officer pointed wordlessly off to the side of the quarterdeck.

He followed the lieutenant's back to the sweep gear. Then waited as Kearn, eyes narrowed, looked him up and down.

"What's going on, Senior? I see people walkin' off my ship. But I don't hear where they're going."

"We're going to clear some mines, Lieutenant."

"Yeah? Where?"

"I can't tell you that."

"Well," said Kearn. He chewed his cigar for a moment, squinting out at the sunlit sea. "Think you'll be coming back?"

"I don't know. They didn't say. Just grab gear and go."

"Okay," said Kearn again. Then he didn't say anything, just looked around, then suddenly stuck out his hand. Gordon looked down at it, too surprised to react.

"You don't got to take it, Senior. After the way I been riding you. It's my style. Too old to change it. But I just wanted to say—you fuckin' Reserves done all right. Come back any time. That's from Sapper Kearn."

"Okay, Sapper," said Gordon. They shook hands, hard and straight, and when they turned, the rest of the men on deck were grinning back at them. "Awright, you bastards!" Kearn howled. "Grab their gear there, goddamn it, bear a hand and help your shipmates out!"

Hsiao stayed with them all the way to the airport, and sat with them in the terminal. Gordon didn't wonder who he worked for. It was self-explanatory. He sat fidgeting for a time, then asked if he could make a phone call. Hsiao smiled and said he couldn't.

"Look, I'd like to call home. I haven't been able to reach my wife since we got here."

"No."

"No?"

"No."

He thought about this for a while, then got up. He was halfway to the booth when the agent caught up with him. "I told you, no calls," he muttered angrily, glancing around at the passing crowd: Pakistanis, Koreans, Europeans, all the hired faces and hands the oil wealth of the Gulf had bought.

"Get in the booth."

"What?"

"Get in here with me. So you can hear what I say. Otherwise, you got a fight on your hands, mister."

Hsiao grimaced.

It was a friction fit for two men, and passersby looked quizzically at them as Gordon wedged the door shut. He listened to the buzz, calculating the time at home. Six hours difference—that would be about four in the morning—

"Hello." A sleepy voice. Ola.

"Hi. It's me."

"John?"

"Yeah."

"Where are you?"

"Kuwait. Look, I don't have much time. Got to catch a plane. But I haven't heard from you for a while." He thought about it for a moment. Then added, "Is everything okay?"

"Yes."

"Are you getting the money?"

"Yes." She sounded more awake now. "Yes . . . and Mike's all right, and I've been . . . thinking about us."

Gordon took a fresh grip on the receiver. For some reason it was wet. "So have I."

"I'm sorry I didn't write, John. I was angry. But I'm over it now. We'll make out. Somehow. And I'll be waiting when you come home."

He smiled and closed his eyes. He could hear his voice shake as he said, "I'm real glad to hear that, Ola."

"And Mike, I think he understands a little more now. He's been reading the paper. Everything they have in there about the Gulf, and what you're doing. There was an article about your unit. He took it to school with him. He's proud of you, John."

"That's good," he said. "I'm glad to hear that, too. He's a good boy, Ola. He'll do okay."

"All right?"

"Okay."

"Good night, then, John. I love you."

"I love you, too, Ola. G'night."

He hung up, to find Hsiao looking at him strangely. "What?" he said.

"You don't waste any time on sentiment, do you?" Hsiao said. "If I talked to my wife that way, she'd think I was drugged."

"Mine understands," said Gordon. He smiled slowly.

He opened the door and looked for his men. They were already standing, picking up their gear.

"Let's go," he said, and shut his mind off from everything but the mission.

IV

THE STRIKE

32

U.S.S. *Turner Van Zandt*

S TANDING by the copier in Radio central, the first stapled-
together sheaf hot in his hand, Dan suddenly had to perch
himself on a stool. The shock, the numbness in the backs of his
thighs, was that great.

They weren't being relieved, sent back to the States, as he'd
expected when Commodore Ritchie handed him the buff envelope. And inside it, sealed, the red one.

His mouth twitched humorlessly as he recalled the rumors.
The exec didn't hear scuttlebutt directly, but one of Nolan's
jobs was keeping him abreast of the mess decks. All the officers
were being relieved; they were getting a new CO; a new XO;
and the most imaginative, they were going to Colombo, Sri
Lanka, to help victims of the recent earthquake rebuild the city.

Imaginative or not, they all fell short of reality.

Van Zandt was going to penetrate and destroy the most
dangerous Pasdaran stronghold in the southern Gulf.

He turned the pages slowly, bemusement easing off into disbelief. Then that, too, was scoured away by sharp black print.

Suddenly everything that had happened that day made sense.

Hart had been waiting on the pier when they pulled in. He'd
come aboard as soon as the brow was over, followed by a string
of staffies and technicians. Dan had had a short private talk
with him, basically a repetition of the interview with Sturgis.

He'd thought there'd be some decision then, some kind of
summary judgment. When it was over, though, when Hart
stood with somber courtesy to dismiss him, he couldn't tell what
sort of impression he'd made.

Nor did he know what, if anything, the techies had found in
the missile mag. But when he'd gone out after seeing Phelan,
an unmarked truck was pulling into position by number-two
line. A line of tan-uniformed Bahraini troops was sealing the

jetty off. And eight U.S. Air Force military police were holding
their weapons ready, facing out in an alert circle, as two gray
warhead containers were swung off the forecastle by a vehic-
ular crane.

Van Zandt had gotten under way shortly afterward, anchoring in the southern neck of Sitra Bay. And just now, the operations deputy had come by in Hart's barge.

Now, looking at what he held, Dan understood. Operation
NIMBLE DANCER. Good title. They'd have to be damn nimble
to pull this one off.

Situation, mission, execution. Concept of operations . . . chart,
see enclosure. Their route was a shaded corridor through a
crosshatching that he immediately saw spelled mine field. On
the heights of the island were symbols for missile batteries and
guns.

Good Christ, he thought. For a moment, he considered the
possibility that Hart was sending them in to get rid of them, to
moot the whole question of his accusations and Shaker's trust-
worthiness. But no, there were better explanations. If this was
a retaliation for Hayes and Schweinberg, for the LNG tanker
attack, it would have to be carried out right away. *Van Zandt*
just happened to be available. This was a little late in the twentieth century for a suicide mission. The wrong navy, too.

The chief banged in the last staple. "Here's the other copies
you wanted, XO."

"Thanks. One goes to Lieutenant Wise—" Dan stopped himself; they were marked Top Secret. "Never mind, I'll take them
around myself."

"Aye, sir." The radioman lingered, obviously longing to read
what he'd just copied. Dan shook his head fractionally. The
chief shrugged and disappeared into the transmitter room.

Besides, *Adams* was going in with them. And he'd seen
something about an air strike, mine clearance, electronic countermeasures. He flipped back and forth, already imprinting
data on his brain. Once the raid began, he'd have no time to look
things up.

And there wasn't much time to get ready. The execution date
time group translated into early morning, the day after tomorrow. Thirty hours from now.

He stood up at last and stretched, looking at the overhead.
Letting himself out of Radio, he made his way to the bridge.

Topside it was night. *Van Zandt*, anchored at short stay,
swung gently in a wind soft as veiled lips. And now he caught,
to his right, Shaker's top-heavy silhouette against the city glit-

ter. He was leaning out over the splinter shield. From alongside came the clatter of buckets, the rattle of tools, faint cursing. Dan moved up beside him. They hadn't talked since the magazine. After a moment, he cleared his throat.

Shaker didn't turn, just grunted. "Yeah?"

"XO, Captain. Got the op order copied."

"Give it here."

Shaker didn't look at him. Dan felt the tension like a thin steel diaphragm between them as the captain crossed to the chart table, flicked on the light, and scanned the first few pages. He stopped at the concept of operations, studied it in silence, then, as Dan had, flipped to the chart.

"Have we got this graphic they refer to here? JOG NG forty dash nine?"

"Yessir. Let me get by you there . . . here it is."

He unrolled it and taped the edges to hold it down. Together, they stared down at Abu Musa. Irregularly triangular, like an arrowhead pointed northeast. Surveyed in peacetime, it showed nothing on the island except a hill, on the northeast point, and a lighthouse.

Dan went into the chart room and returned with the *Sailing Directions*. They studied the two pages on Jazirat Abu Musa. Mostly low, numerous hummocks, dark brown due to iron oxide . . . a ridge of hills on the west . . . west side fronted by rocks and reefs, not to be approached closer than one mile.

"Rough piece of territory," grunted Shaker. "Can we get in where they show the base?"

Dan considered it. There was only one entrance. That was bad; it would be covered in advance by overlapping arcs of fire. The western side of the island was unapproachable and the south had drying flats extending out three-quarters of a mile. A *shamal*-proof anchorage lay off the southeastern tip. This was where the IRG base had been established. The Boghammers and other craft would be moored there, or alongside a small pier.

"I think so. If the channel's cleared."

"How will we know if it is?"

"I haven't read the whole thing yet. But according to Annex Y, there'll be an EOD team inserted just after dark. They'll clear a Q-channel along here, leading in through the anchorage to the piers. As we approach, they'll mark the lane with infrared flashlights."

Shaker grunted doubtfully. He was studying the "execution" section now. "Then, let's see. We come in, make a pass at the pier, do a minimum-diameter Williamson turn, another pass, then steam out through the same channel." He walked his fingers across the chart, then showed his teeth. "What about navigation? Going in silent, we won't have radar till the shooting starts. And this light on Jabal Halwa, that's going to be out, unless they have some very stupid guys in charge. How we going to know where we are?"

"That shouldn't be a problem. Not with satellite fixes."

"We only got one receiver, Dan. What's our backup if that craps out as we go in?"

"Oh. Yeah. Well ... DECCA, but ..." He stared at the chart, realizing that mines and Iranians weren't the only dangers. It wasn't overprinted for the old British electronic-navigation system. If they were off track going in, they'd run onto the shoal to the south of the anchorage. He could see that all too vividly, *Van Zandt* perched high and dry in the dawn. And if they didn't navigate carefully once past the mine field, they'd wander into it again. "We'll have to keep an accurate dead-reckoning trace."

"*Real* accurate. What about tides?"

"Six feet. Slack water, high tide will be at two." Dan paused. "I wonder ... didn't Commodore Ritchie discuss this with you, sir? When he left these?"

"He did, yeah, but not in detail. I sort of thought there'd be a bigger force. Not just two ships."

"There's no room for more."

"I see that now," said Shaker. "We'll have to go in column astern, as it is. But I want to do our own navigating, not just follow *Adams* in blind."

"Right."

"And then when we get in close enough, if we do get in, I guess we're supposed to blast the shit out of them with the guns."

"I don't see any restrictions, Captain. It just says 'take under fire and destroy boats and shore facilities.' " Dan paused. "I'd let them have everything we've got. Standards as we come in, aimed at the Silkworm batteries, then guns, right down to .50s when we're off the piers."

"I like the sound of that," said Shaker. "What about our torpedoes?"

"On the small boats?"

"No, no, on the piers."

"I don't see why not."

When Shaker spoke again, he somehow sounded more cheerful. "This is awful close range. World War Two stuff. Will our

missiles work this close in? And our torpedoes are for antisubmarine work. Will they run straight? And detonate on contact?"

"I'll find out, sir. I'll check with Pensker and the leading TM."

Shaker lifted his head. In the light reflected from the chart
his face was a mountainous terrain, his eyes the empty pits of
volcanoes. He said, "We ought to talk about this thing between
us, XO."

Dan leaned both hands on the chart table. Making his voice
neutral, he said, "I'm ready."

"You were wrong to turn me in. Someday you'll understand
how wrong. But I don't hold it against you personally. I understand why you did it."

Dan wanted to ask, Then why don't you confess; wanted to
ask him why he'd lied; why if he couldn't admit it, he didn't just
resign. But something stopped him. In the face of an attack on
Abu Musa, it seemed inconsequential. Twenty-nine hours from
now, they both could be dead.

If they weren't, then either he or Benjamin Shaker had to
destroy the other. There was no other way.

"Anyway, maybe we shook something loose. Look. We got to
work together on this raid. After that, we'll see what happens."

He swallowed. Anger, betrayal, and a remnant of his old
admiration struggled in him for speech. He had to admit that
in one respect at least, Hart's planning was dead on. For a
mission like this, there was no better choice than Ben Shaker.

At last, he managed, "I guess we can leave it at that for
now."

"Okay." Shaker's voice went brisk. "Now listen. We got to
hustle butt in the next twenty-four, XO. Get this around to the
department heads. I want it memorized tonight. But nobody
else sees it till we get under way, understand? I'll talk to the
crew on the 1MC after we're clear of land. Hart wants us out
before dawn; we'll weigh at oh-four-hundred. We got to have
the sides done before then."

"Right."

"Send Pensker and Lewis up to see me. I want to meet with
the missilemen, torpedomen, and gunners' mates separately
tomorrow. Let's see. . . . Break out and test all our night-vision
equipment. Fresh batteries, the works."

Dan was jotting in his notebook. "Test fire," he suggested.

"Yes, damn it, yes. We'll fire a calibration as soon as we get
clear of land. We'll have the pre-action brief, officers and chiefs,
at eleven. Can you have a blowup of the island ready by then?"

"I'll put Mac on it."

A muffled splash came from outside. They glanced toward it, but neither moved. "Think of anything else?" said the captain.

"That'll get us started."

He felt Shaker's hand on his shoulder, just for a moment. "We'll have to think smart and move fast to come through on this one, XO. That reminds me. How are the personnelmen doing? You got them started yet?"

"On what?"

Shaker said quietly, "We're going to lose some people on this one, Dan. Maybe a lot. Especially if they don't get that mine field cleared. I want the next-of-kin forms updated and sent ashore. Check on the Doc, too; make sure the battle dressing stations and sick bay are rigged for casualties."

He paused, looking out at the gulf of darkness to seaward. "And there's something else, too."

Dan waited.

"If anything happens to me, I want you to take charge. Immediately. And fight the ship the way I'd fight it. That means to the fucking end. Understood?"

"Yes, sir."

"Get hot, XO."

"Aye, sir."

He gave McQueen the navigator's copy and moved out to the wing. Looking down, he saw by the light of strung bulbs twenty men alongside, bobbing on Turani's paint floats. They were working like madmen with long-handled paint rollers, brushes, and from aft came the clatter of a sprayer. "Hey!" he shouted. "Alongside!"

"Yo!"

"Who's that? Stanko?"

"Yo!"

"Boats, is Mr. Charaler down there?"

"He's back aft, sir, just a minute and I'll get him."

"Tell him to meet me on the flight deck."

"I'll pass that, sir."

The first lieutenant was waiting by the deck-edge lights when he got back aft. His trou and T-shirt were smeared with paint, and he had more on his forehead, where he must have wiped away sweat.

"How's it going?"

"Uh, we got problems." Charaler wiped his forehead then, laying a fresh deposit. "We don't have near enough black. So I'm stretching it with deck gray. Won't be dead black like the captain wanted, but it'll be pretty close."

"What's estimated completion, Steve? We want to get under
way by oh-four-hundred."

"By *when?* Shit . . . shit . . . we'll get it done by then."

"You sure? Will more men help?"

"No, sir, I can't put any more weight on these fucking camels
or they'll roll over. I've got a man for every paint tool aboard
now. Tell you what, though, if you give me twenty fresh bodies
at one A.M., I'll knock first division off, let them get a little
sleep."

"Okay, I'll take care of it."

They got under way from Sitra at 0420 and headed east at flank
speed. Off Qatar, *Charles Adams* joined up. In the growing
light of that last day, the two ships altered course together,
heading out into the empty heart of the Gulf.

Dan stood on the forecastle, blinking in the yellow-white
glare of a just-launched sun. He'd come up to check the muster
on the forward life rafts, but stopped when he saw the other
ship.

He looked now across the rushing water to the old destroyer
that paralleled their course a thousand yards off. She, too,
was black, but a grin warped his mouth as he saw that part
of her sheer had been left gray. Gray, in the low rakish silhouette of a Boghammer. Typical Jakkel, he thought. Shaker
had been so proud of his own idea about black paint. He'd
have a fit when he saw that, and realized he'd been done one
better.

The bow wave came up with a steady, sullen crash, green at
its root, then shattering into foam the color of a sea gull's
breast. Despite their speed, the racing ships seemed unmoving,
enchanted, sealed magically into an immense waiting stillness.
The *shamal* was coming from astern, blowing at the same
speed they moved.

"This is the Captain speaking," came the hollow stentorian
clamor of the 1MC. A glitter of color caught Dan's eye, and he
leaned forward, only half-listening, forgetting for a moment
what he'd come up there for, where he was, and where he was
going.

"This is Captain Shaker. We are now on our way to Abu Musa
Island to carry out a night attack on the Iranian base there. We
will go to general quarters shortly to zero the guns and test
communications."

They were moving in the midst of a miracle. Spray leapt from
the cutwater, tossed high by the impact of four thousand tons
of ship propelled by fifty thousand horsepower; and out of it,

traveling with them as if welded to the bullnose, the rising sun
cut a brilliant rainbow.

"I've had only a short time to sharpen your battle skills. But
I'm satisfied that you're prepared to take on the enemy tonight
and win."

He'd seen it before, not on *Van Zandt,* but on other ships,
in other seas. But not often. And never before so brilliant, so
clear, and so perfect.

"I'll be briefing the chiefs and officers at eleven hundred.
They'll brief you this afternoon on the plan. We will be fighting
at close quarters, with no margin for error, and every man
aboard will have to do his best if he expects to come out of Abu
Musa in one piece."

A blessing? A warning? An omen? Or just the random inter-
play of light and matter, water and air? He looked beyond and
through it to the ship to starboard. *Adams* had moved slightly
ahead, and now around her as she rose to a sea the same
unearthly halo glowed: red, orange, yellow, down past indigo
into regions where no man saw. Beneath his feet, the deck
trembled with speed. The water roared and the sonar whistled
its shrill, lonely cry. Rising from the sea before them, flying fish
streaked away in graceful wandering terror.

"We have a powerful and battle-ready ship under us. We've
taken shit off these ragheads for too long. But at last we've got
our orders. Close with the enemy, and put the bastards out of
business for good."

He could hear the cheer even through the roar of the cutwater, even through the steel behind him. The whole crew must
be shouting. Cheering Shaker. Cheering the chance at last to
fight those they had feared and watched against so long. Above
it, the brazen voice lifted, grim, inspiring, pealing the kind of
call to arms that he had sometimes feared, sometimes hoped,
belonged only and forever to the past.

"We will hit them and hit them hard. I want every weapon
ready. I want every man to know that we will kill Iranians
tonight until there are no more of them left in range."

Into battle, Dan thought. He'd been there before. And survived. But there was no guarantee he would this time. All men
are mortal; Socrates is a man; therefore Socrates is mortal. The
most basic syllogism of all. How well would their own logic
work? The logic of their plans, and the expensive and complex
electronic logic built into their ship and their weapons? How
many aboard the two black destroyers would make it through
the coming night? Would he?

"That is all. Bo's'n, sound general quarters."

As he turned, already running, he knew that the answer to that question no longer made any difference. He wore the uniform. Not of compulsion. Of his own free will. And with the coin of Caesar came the obligation to die, if he had to, facing the enemy.

Whether he was alive a day from now no longer mattered. The real question was, Would he do his duty.

He had the feeling that he would. And he heard, with terror and at the same time an ancient joy, his own voice lifting to join the paean.

33

U.S.S. *Charles F. Adams,* DDG-2

PHELAN moaned and struggled, hauling the five-gallon bucket, lead-heavy with paint, down the too-steep ladder that led into the sea. Below him the boatswain, the same man who'd taken pity on him on the pier at Mina' Salman, smirked up at his awkward progress, obviously enjoying the sight.

Shit, he was thinking. Screwed again. Screwed bad this time. He shifted the bucket, slopping its contents over his good shoes, and whimpered aloud. In its inky darkness, for one moment a perfect mirror, he knew his tortured and sweating face.

He'd been working now for hours. How many he couldn't tell—there were no watches on the float—but it was almost dark. So that was at least six hours straight down here in the heat, on the pitching balks of wood.

He'd stepped aboard *Adams* from the whaleboat jaunty, composed, his story polished bright as tourist-trap silver. How he'd forgotten the envelope with his orders on the seat of the plane, and how when he went back, they were gone. But he didn't think now *Adams*'s exec had really been listening. "That's too bad," he'd said at last, breaking into Phelan's explanation. "But we're full up with corpsmen. And with no I.D. and no orders, I don't want you working there, anyway. You can stay till we find your ship, but you're going to first division. That's where we need hands now. Get into your dungarees and report to the chief boats."

So now here he was. One of the peons, one of the apes. And not liking it one damn bit.

He got to the bottom at last and grunted the can down on splintered wood that looked like a giant had used it as a palette. He was instantly surrounded by dirty, tattooed, cursing sailors. They elbowed him aside without looking at him, fighting around the dark reservoir like bears around a honey pot. He backed away, almost fell into the water as his foot skidded over the edge of the float. He scrambled back up and lifted his eyes.

Charles Adams rode motionless in the falling darkness in the lee of a small cape. Alongside her were lashed several narrow balks of wood. From them, and from two dented jonboats, thirty men were rapidly slapping rollers and brushes along the looming sides. All but amidships, where they'd left an irregular patch of sea-faded gray. The paint had been a perfect mirror in his bucket. He noticed now that it was drying to dead black.

"Hey, Geronimo! This ain't no time for rubbernecking! Get us some more rollers, the big ones. Chop chop! *Pedal ass*, fuckface!"

"He's thinking," said one of the stained men, his teeth yellow in a black face. "Thinkin' about tonight. Little bastard's scared shitless. Look at him."

"Don't think, asshole, work."

Phelan didn't answer. He didn't belong with these people. And he was feeling bad. The uneasy jostling of the float, the turpentine stink made him want to barf. He wanted another Dilaudid. But they were history now. *Jesu*, he was in bad shape. Could he report sick? It'd be easy to slip going up that ladder. He could sprain an ankle. That was painful and they might give him—

He yelped as a hard and sticky hand slammed him into the hull. "I said move your ass, you little prick," growled a voice in his ear. "The fucking khaki can't see us down here. You want to lose teeth, just keep doping off on us, hear me?"

He found himself loping up the ladder like a scared rabbit.

Topside was covered with men, all of them painting. He did a double take as he saw chiefs, too, with brushes in their hands. He strolled forward, then ducked into an open hatch.

Sick bay. The caduceus on the door, the comforting smells of disinfectant, wax, and medicines. He gazed in yearningly through the open half of the dutch door. "What's the trouble, Jack?" said the second-class on duty.

"I don't feel good."

"Name?"

"Phelan. Bernard."

"Division?"

"Uh, none, I'm here TAD."

"Rate?"

"Hospitalman."

"Oh, *wait* a minute, I heard about you," said the corpsman. "*Phelan.* Yeah. You as fucked up as they say?"

Bernard stared at him, trembling and sweating. "What do you mean by that, fatass?"

"Nothin', only the chief said he heard about you. He knows some guys off the *Long Beach.* What's the complaint today, Phelan?"

"I don't know. I got cramps and all my muscles are sore. I think I got the flu. Or gastroenteritis. It hurts real bad." He moved closer and lowered his voice. "I need something special. You got to help me, man. I'd help you out if you needed it."

"I bet it does," said the corpsman, grinning. "Here you go, Phelan, don't say I never give you nothing."

He stared down at two aspirin in his dirty palm.

Before he could think, he cursed the man and threw the tablets in his face. He was sorry an instant later. He had to make friends, not enemies. But the door had already slammed shut. And a warrant officer, coming down the passageway with his arms full of canvas, was shouting "What are you doing down here, sailor? We got an all-hands working party going. Get your ass up on the weather decks!"

Topside again, his teeth chattering with a sudden chill, he joined a line in front of the paint locker. It moved fast. He said to the man behind him, "Jesus, what's the big hurry?"

"Didn't you listen to the captain? We're going to sink some ragheads tonight, buddy. Going to put some hurts on those little brown fuckers."

"Tonight? What, what are we doing?"

"Going to do some shooting," said the seaman in the paint locker, handing him five rollers. "Going to go in and take some people out. Get moving, pal, we got to finish up tonight."

He couldn't help groaning as he reapproached the ladder. His stomach was cramping so badly it was hard to walk. He didn't want to go down there again. But there didn't seem to be much alternative. He was afraid of the boatswain with the hard fists.

And what was this they were saying, about going in and . . . he didn't like the sound of that at all.

"Hey, you!"

He flinched. This time it was a man he didn't recognize, smeared black like all the rest on this floating Earl Scheib's, but in shorts and T-shirt instead of uniform. Phelan stared at him. "I'm the master-at-arms," he said rapidly, glancing back to where other chiefs were hastily wire-brushing out a paint sprayer. "Wanted to let you know, when we go to general quarters for the attack tonight, you'll be in Repair Two. That's up forward, main deck. You can ask somebody how to get there. You had damage-control training on your ship, right?"

"No, not much, I'm a corpsman. I'm supposed to be assigned to sick bay. Can't you get me put in sick bay, I'm—"

"Repair Two. Don't forget. Be there; I put you on their muster list." The chief ran forward.

Phelan became aware at that moment of threatening voices raised below him. He started, almost tripped over the coaming, but caught himself on the lifeline at the last moment. He hurt. He was scared. But he was more scared of what would happen down there if he didn't turn to.

Praying in Zuni behind his closed teeth, he hurried down the ladder, taking care not to slip.

34

2100 Hours: Off Abu Musa Island, Southern Gulf

THERE was one short but endless moment in his fall when Gordon lost himself. His ears were crammed with the pulse of rotors, but his eyes, dark-adapted, still met nothing but blackness. Then, still falling, he glimpsed a wheeling myriad of stars. They seethed like bubbles around him as he tumbled out of the sky. He couldn't see the water at all. Only sparkling below him, too, the distant golden suns—

He hit so hard his breath drove into the mouthpiece with an explosive grunt. A hundred and thirty pounds of dive gear, tools, and weights instantly dragged him under. Into void, oblivion, now tangible as well as visible.

For a moment, he fought fear. Then drill took charge. His left hand slapped the inflation valve. Gas hissed, and a few seconds later he felt the sea slipping past him, yielding him up reluctantly and only for a time.

His mask broke the surface. At first, he didn't realize it. Then he shook his head, spat out the mouthpiece, and screamed as loudly as he could into the departing engines.

"Over here!" came Terger's voice, hoarse with stress. Gordon shouted again, wondering whether his voice was giving him away, too. Then he began swimming, toward the shape that suddenly appeared a few yards away, taking on form as he closed it.

"Tony!" he shouted.

"Là." Maudit, on the far side of the raft.

"Burgee!"

"Yo."

"Everett here."

"Join up on me," he shouted. Yes, he could hear tension. He swallowed, trying to relax his throat.

The Z-bird was rocking cheerfully on the chop when he

reached it. Already inflated, it was rigged to fall bottom-first
and land upright. He was pleased to see it had done just that.
He cut at the cargo net over it, heard the snore of other knives
helping; it came away and he pushed it into the water. Attached
weights sank it silently from sight. He unslung his gear and
tossed it in, got a leg up and rolled over the gunwale. He
slammed into bags, hard shapes, the lashed-down motor. Lem
Everett rolled in at the same moment on the other side.

Gordon kept low, pulling the others aboard. The raft rode
lower with each body. When the team was in, he grunted a
command and they moved apart, each taking his assigned position, checking and unlashing equipment. He heard a click as
Burgee attached the gas tank. Then the electrician's anxious
mutter: "I think she took some water. Do it, baby, come on, you
whore—"

The muffled Evinrude caught on the first pull. Gordon eased
breath out, then looked around.

Three hours before midnight, the sky soared above them like
the loft of a huge and ancient barn. The Milky Way was a winter
snowfall caught on the points of the stars. To the north—ahead,
as Clint angled the throttle—the horizon flickered orange to
distant flame. Against it, he could make out the island, low to
their left, rising gradually to starboard. A few cold-looking blue
and yellow lights glittered minutely along its flank. He watched
them for two or three minutes but saw no movement.

That was good. . . , He stood up for a moment, bracing himself
on Lem Everett's rubber-covered shoulder. As far as he could
tell, they'd dropped on target. It was hard to judge distance, but
they should be just over ten miles out.

"Lem."

"Yeah, John?"

"Got a fix yet?"

"Working on it." Everett raised the bearing compass to his
eye and sighted on the peak. A moment later, he shifted to the
left tangent of the island, then to a distant red planet that
marked the Mubarek oil field. With three points, they could fix
their position.

"Got it?" he muttered again, unable to wait.

"Five more degrees. Clint, come a little left."

Gordon glanced over his shoulder. He'd thought he might see
the helicopter, the glow of the turbines, but nothing moved
against the constellations.

The trip had been low and fast, terrifyingly low and incredibly fast. After the lift-off, they'd huddled dressed out on the

bench seats of the H-53, not speaking, just waiting. Then at last the green light had come on, and they'd shoved the raft out the rear ramp and followed it silently and without hesitation into the roaring night.

He'd wondered then, as he stepped into space, how many of them would see the dawn again.

He shoved that thought into a hole in his brain and tamped as much of his anxiety as he could down after it. Then he concentrated again on the island. It was closer now, but still there was no sign of movement. He became conscious at the same time that the boat was riding easier, that the seas that had been popping against the port side had dropped. The motor sounded louder. The wind, light before, had fallen away almost to nothing.

He ran over the plan again, then groped about on the floorboards. They'd brought all the standard gear, the standard tools—just in case. But the most important . . . He breathed out as his fingers felt corners through nylon net. The gadgets. God, if they'd lost those . . .

He took three deep breaths, visualizing a blue-green hillside, the straggling forms of grazing beasts. It helped. But instead of grass and earth, he smelled kerosene and rubber and dead fish. His hands moved automatically over the Mark 16, tightening straps jolted by the drop, checking the oxygen bypass valve, the bottle valve handwheel, clamping the display tighter to his mask. In between, they bumped an unfamiliar object and he touched it again, puzzled for a moment before he recognized it.

He hoped he didn't have to use the flare pen. A red star as the destroyers approached was the signal he'd failed to clear the channel, that the attack had to be aborted. Of course by then, the air would already be working the island over, and they could expect irate Iranians galore. How they'd escape then, he didn't know. Except for their knives, and his automatic, they weren't armed. EOD divers seldom used rifles. Nor was there room for them, with all the gear they had in the boat.

"Mark," said Everett suddenly.

"What?"

"Mark, outer boundary. We're here."

They were at the edge of the mine field. Below them somewhere . . . He stopped thinking about that, too. "Cut it, Clint."

The motor stopped suddenly. It hadn't been loud, but now the silence became vast. He eased the hood from his ear and heard the sigh of wind, the splash of waves. Then the rumble of a heavy motor, a boat or truck, from the island. They were only two miles off the beach. He could hear dogs, too. He felt exposed. He wanted to pull the sea over his head like a child's blanket.

"What?" whispered Terger. "What'd you say?"

"Nothing." He was whispering, too. "Lem, you're sure this is it?"

"Just did another round. Good fix. Grab it while you got it."

"Okay. Tony, drop the master."

He saw the paramedic lift it in the rear of the boat, a lumpy shadow by starlight. The master reference buoy, a lead mushroom with two sandbags lashed to it. Lead and sand were nonmagnetic. Their search would be plotted from it in through the mine field to clear water.

A muffled splash and the slither of uncoiling line. "It is down."

"Okay, good. Tending line?"

"Hundred yards."

"Pay out as soon as we're in the water." He knew he didn't have to say all this, but he wanted to be sure everyone understood. "Let her drift off out of the area. Then wait. Stay low in the boat. If anybody comes out to investigate, pop the valves and let it sink. But stay with it; you're our ticket out of here."

"Comprends, moi. But—"

"But what?"

"Don't stay too long." He could hear the grin.

"You leave us here, Frenchy, and I'll come back and ha'nt you and Regine and both your ugly kids. Everybody else! Grab your gear and in the water. By the numbers." He'd made each man memorize what he carried, as Everett had memorized the anchor bearings. But he didn't dare let them forget anything, so he checked it all, hurrying now: jackstays, lift bags, buoys, each man's equipment. As he was satisfied, he slapped each diver's shoulder. One by one, they slid to the side, became humped shadows in the starlight, were gone.

His turn. He wished he wasn't so tense, but it couldn't be helped. He sprayed and fitted his mask and checked that the display was in view. Then cracked the supply valve.

"John? *Bonne chance."* Said very quietly, under the watching stars.

He nodded, and dissolved into the warm sea.

He recalled now, sinking, the sketch they'd studied aboard *Iwo Jima.* Nothing clever, no computer graphics. This had been a pencil diagram on lined paper, just as it had come from the hands of the defector.

Gordon hoped the man was right. And that whoever had debriefed him spoke good Farsi.

He turned his mask from side to side, looking for Burgee. A few feet away, an outstretched arm glowed nightmare green. He remembered his own chem light, and snapped and shook the plastic tube. It began to burn, cold and eerie in the endless night.

The mine field, a kidney-shaped area bent around the anchorage, was said to be eight hundred yards deep. The destroyers would need a marked lane at least a hundred yards wide. That defined the Q-channel they had to clear. He and Burgee were taking the port side, working by compass bearings from the reference buoy. Everett and Terger, meanwhile, would work into the mine field to starboard. He'd overlapped their lanes to ensure they didn't miss anything.

Now, sinking, he ran through the memorized bearings again, then twisted his wrist toward him. The numerals and needle of the compass glowed tritium luminescent, unnoticeable in daylight, but so complete was the darkness through which they fell, it seemed bright.

The depth pressed its thumbs into his ears. He worked his jaw and swallowed, felt the wheeze and pop as they equalized. Passing 33. The sea was quieter here than in the Narrows. Only an occasional distant whistle, and the Rice Krispies crackle of bottom dwellers. The 16 vented no bubbles, so that familiar rumble was absent. Gas sighed through his breathing tubes, and rubber creaked as he finned downward.

When the needle reached 40, he stopped, gripping the line in his glove. The anchor and sandbags should be thirty feet farther down. He pressed the button on his hand light, pointed it at his hand, aimed a finger down.

Burgee nodded and continued his descent. Gordon floated weightless and without motion, waiting as below him the number-two diver's light came on. It fanned slowly around. The visibility was excellent tonight, easily fifty feet, possibly more; it was hard to tell in the gloom.

The light angled up and blinked twice, then went out.

On the bottom, Gordon turned his on again. The mushroom lay quietly on a sandy bottom grooved with innumerable tiny ripples. It reminded him of the desert they'd flown over on the way to Kenya. The sandbags were splayed out from it, leaning inward like a tent.

Burgee had the jackstay out. He clipped it to the fitting on the anchor, then paid out line. Gordon snapped the end to his belt, then fumbled around his body. Where the devil . . . His hand recognized it then dangling on its line: an AN/PQS-2A, a hand-held mine-detection sonar the size of a calf's head.

He took a few deep breaths, appreciating the steady flow of purified, oxygen-enriched air. Then he clipped on the water-proof earphones and turned up the volume.

A steady hissing beat came through them, sounding like the screw of a passing freighter. He steadied the sonar in front of him, chest high, and with his knees in the sand, pivoted slowly, closing his eyes to concentrate on what came through his ears.

The rhythmic sibilance continued without change. When the transducer bumped the buoy line, he unlocked his lids, clicked on his light, tapped the compass, and pointed to the left.

Burgee moved away, swimming slowly just above the bottom. Gordon couldn't see him, but he knew the number-two diver was following 240 magnetic. He paid out line till it ended, then moved out following it. When they collided, they switched off, and Gordon swam while the other stayed.

Doing this three times put them 120 feet to the left of the reference, in position now to turn ninety degrees right and begin the long sweep. He marked the position with a buoy from his vest, cracking the tube of a chem light like a king crab leg before sending it up. Putting lights on the surface added risk, but they had to have orientation in this immense blackness. He didn't think they could be seen from shore.

But if the Pasdaran patrolled the mine field . . .

He swept the sonar through another circle, but the throbbing hiss was unaltered. He signaled Burgee out on 330.

They'd done this twice, stopping to sweep each time they reached the line's end, when he heard a thud. He fanned the sonar back and forth before him. Whooshes to either side, a metallic thud like a heartbeat out to their left. He grabbed Burgee, who was already starting away, and clicked on his light to match compasses.

The green meteor bobbed outward, grew faint, and disappeared. Gordon glanced at his watch as he waited. 2145. This was going about as he'd expected. Slowly. Except for the danger, clearing a mine field was a deliberate, rather boring process. He'd figured it would take them till 1 A.M. That gave them an extra hour, just in case. He hoped they wouldn't need it.

The line tugged twice. He clicked the sonar off and let it dangle, then finned ahead, gathering line in a loose coil as he moved. Burgee's chem light reappeared, then the dazzling beam of his flashlight, probing about in the gloom.

Gordon valved air, the bubbles loud in his ears, and sank till his knees grated on the bottom.

The mine was the size of two 55-gallon drums welded end to end. The nose was half-buried in white sand. Scabrous brown paint discovered olive drab beneath. A rusty cage of angle iron was bolted around it. He recognized it as the shipping frame. It was removed for an airdrop, but more convenient to just leave on if it was laid from the deck of a ship.

Not moving, breathing deep to keep the vise from clamping his throat, he studied it from twelve feet away.

There were two bomb lugs on top, about a yard apart. It had stubby fins at the exposed end. The tail.

His mind brought back the clipped voice of the instructor at Fort Story. Use the logic tree. Take acoustic, magnetic, and pressure precautions. Limit stay time on the site. Don't hurry; always move slowly around a live device, but do what you have to do and then get out.

His hand waved the other back. Burgee nodded and retreated another ten feet. He kept his light on, though, gilding the waiting weapon with a tremulous radiance.

Gordon moved left a little—they'd happened on it at the nose—and began working his way in. You always approached a bottom mine from the side. Since lines of magnetic flux converged at the nose and tail, its sensitivity was greatest there. Six feet away, he stopped again, sinking back to the sand, examining it more closely.

It was a Mark 36, all right. He sipped air cautiously, going over again what he wore and was carrying. Everything was nonmagnetic, recertified monthly to be sure it picked up no stray fields. He hoped Maudit, who'd done the checking, had been thorough.

Usual procedure was to stop here and sketch the mine, in case someone else had to finish the job. But if he didn't, there was no one else. And they had a lot of ground to cover.

He decided to move in.

Slow approach. Avoid the nose. Drift aft, toward the fins. Gradually rising silt was dimming Burgee's beam. Gordon had his finger on the button of his own light before he remembered: No current flow near a detonator, gentlemen, bad for your health. He took his finger off it slowly and exhaled.

He had enough light. He moved closer, close enough to touch the fin. Though he didn't. His glove drifted down to the net bag, found the hard rectangularity of one of the gadgets, and drew it out.

He circled slowly toward the tail. Over the smallest rear access plate. Align the long axis with fin number three. As he reached it, he sculled downward, letting his legs rise.

The tail plate came into view. His eyes searched it, his hand already coming forward with the box, a finger poised against the switch.

And stopped.

The tail plate covered the butt end of the mine. It was two feet across, steel, with a solid brass access plate. Bolted on. With quarter-inch holes hand-drilled through it.

Suddenly he couldn't breathe.

His eye went automatically to the corner of his mask, but the readout was green. Then he realized it was his throat. He reached up and massaged it through the rubber. After a couple seconds, he got a breath. Then another.

He stared at the brassy gleam, rummaging his mind for the characteristics of the mods. The tail cover was how you told them apart. One through three, solid blank cover, magnetic. Mod four was straight pressure sensing. Mods five through eight had three openings, with acoustic and/or magnetic combinations. Eight and up were the latest types, turned over to the Shah just before he fell, and they had the three-plate combination, too.

None of them had a bolted-on brass access with hand-drilled holes.

He balanced there, one fin trailing to the bottom, as thoughts jumbled through his head. There was no way to tell what was inside this thing. Pressure, acoustic, magnetic, it could even be rigged to explode when touched. Tailored for whoever tried to disarm it.

Just like a pineapple bomb, years before, deep in the green hell of the Mekong Delta.

He backed away slowly, following what he figured would be the lines of force emanating from the tail. His fins dug up little gouts of sand that whirled like snow devils across the tail plate.

When he was six feet away, still staring at it, he let his hand drift upward. The marker buoy came out in a flat pack. The weight chunked into the sand. He popped it, wincing at the noise, broke the chem light and released it. It soared upward, dwindling and trailing line till it was out of sight.

Now what, Senior? Four hours left, and seven hundred yards of corridor to clear. But he couldn't touch this thing. The gadgets were useless weight. He thought for a moment of ditching them, then rejected that for two reasons: one, they still might find some off-the-shelf mod elevens. And two, Rothman had made it clear they were secret as hell.

But what was he going to do? There'd be two destroyers tearing through here at 0200. Unless he came up with something, either the raid was already a failure or four, five hundred men would be steaming straight into a live mine field.

He bumped something and flinched around. It was Burgee. His eyebrows were puzzled behind tempered glass. Gordon made abrupt signals: Abort. Surface.

When the sea rolled off their masks, he unseated his and shoved it back on his forehead. After the blackness at seventy feet the stars were a million searchlights focused on him. He picked out a faraway firefly and swam toward it.

Maudit was lying flat in the boat. "What is wrong?" he whispered when he recognized them.

"We found one."

"And?"

"The Iranians modified it."

"*A bordel.* So what are we going to do?"

"Blow it," said Gordon.

He heard Burgee suck air through his teeth. "John, we can't do that! There'll be Pasdaran all over out here!"

"Not *now,* we won't blow it now. We'll rig it and mark the fuze float with a chem light. Then go back just before H-hour and pull the primers. Etienne, how many M133s we got, how many haversacks?"

"Two, three—we have five of them, Senior."

"I hope that's enough. Give me three. Two for Lem's team. They'll be back if they hit one of these bastards. Tell 'em what we're going to do."

Maudit nodded. Gordon looped the straps over his head and checked to be sure a detonator was included with each. "Any last words?" he muttered to Burgee's raised mask.

"I'm glad we went to Nyali Beach."

"Why?"

"I got a lifetime's worth of pussy, anyway."

Despite his fear, Gordon had to laugh. He let go the buoy, turned on his back, and began to swim.

On the bottom again, again in the silent waiting presence of his mechanical enemy, he slowly peeled free the silver Mylar over the charge. They hadn't made them up in advance; hadn't expected to use them. Now he blessed his insistence that they not trust blindly in their orders, that they take along all their regular gear.

The problem was that now their escape plan was shot. According to the operation order, after safing the mines in the corridor, they were supposed to return to the raft, beacon the channel, then leave before the first shot was fired. For pickup, they'd rendezvous with the destroyers again fifteen miles out, after the action was over—again, a good safe distance away.

Now they'd have to stay here. Triggering the destruct charges early would alert the IRG and wreck the whole raid. So at least one diver would have to stay, waiting till the last moment, till the ships were practically in sight, before pulling the fuzes.

Gordon already knew who that last man would be.

Moving with drugged slowness, he scooped out a shallow hole in the sand under the mine casing. He worked the haversack, a twenty-pound slab of explosive, into it. Despite his total attention, his fingers brushed the mine. The paint came off in crackling, drifting flakes.

He paused there, unable to breathe, waiting for his destruction.

It didn't come. Not yet.

He recovered himself and slowly backed away, unreeling the primacord. It floated upward slowly in the side glow of Burgee's light, settling back into coils until he tugged at it.

He looked at his watch. 2322. They'd have to move faster. A lot faster. There wasn't much time left.

He signaled to his shadow, and they began to rise.

He and Burgee finished their lane two hours later. He was groggy from fatigue, cold, and nitrogen when at last they came up at the inner boundary of the mine field.

They found three more bottom mines. Two of them were the modified 36s. The other was a standard mod eleven. A gadget went on the latter as planned, the sticky-tape gluing it against the access plate. He'd held his breath as he eased the switch over. If the spectacled engineer had miscalculated, would he ever know? But it seemed to work. At least the little red light came on. Only a ship passing over would constitute a real test.

Back on the surface, he paused at the center of the lane and sighted over his wrist compass back at the green pinpoint of the master reference. At eight hundred yards, he could only see it occasionally, and kept getting it confused with the fuze float markers. As near as he could tell, though, they were in line.

Three-three-zero. The course in, as planned.

It was a long swim back to where they'd started. Almost half a mile. He was exhausted when they got there.

The raft was nowhere around.

He clung to the float with Burgee, neither of them saying anything. If Maudit had left . . . but that was impossible. They'd been with him through seven years of monthly drills and annual active duty. Once, Gordon remembered, they'd been trapped under the ice at Lake Memphremagog. He'd been steady then, circle-searching and tapping on the translucent ceiling as their air ebbed away till they found a place to break through. No, Tony couldn't have . . .

The night purred. He heard muffled voices, and ducked till only the upper half of his mask emerged between waves.

It was the Z-bird. It purred up to them and a light flashed. Burgee had his up and returned it. Briefly, because at this angle it was aimed toward the island that had brooded over them all night.

"Senior Chief!"

"Where the hell were you?"

"Lem signaled me to pick him up."

"Everett, damn it"—Ola didn't like him to swear, but this one just slipped out—"couldn't you swim back?"

"That's not the problem, John." Everett's voice was sober. Gordon had an instant feeling of danger. Not now, he prayed. Not when they were all but done.

"What is it?" he said quietly.

"We found four in our lane. One was a mod eleven. We safed it with a gadget. One was an old U.S. Mark Six, a contact mine. We put a haversack charge on that one. But the last two were these garage-workshop lashups."

"So? You had—"

"We started with two haversacks, John. So we got one live mine left."

Gordon closed his eyes. He hadn't expected this dense a barrier. And the mix of types made it even more dangerous. Not all would be live at the same time. Not all would explode at the first pass. But any of them, old or new, would break a frigate's back like a steel-toed boot on a hen's egg.

"Where's the last one?" he asked, still hoping somehow it would be at the edge of the channel.

"To the right, but in the area."

"We got to get that bastard out of there, John," said Terger, who'd been silent up to then.

"You're right, but how?"

Against his will, his eyes were drawn to his watch: 0109. The ships would be here soon. Were already on their way. Yet the channel wasn't cleared. That last goddamn mine . . .

It occurred to him then. He knew immediately it would be dangerous. But anything was better than firing that flare. He'd already decided John Gordon wasn't going to do that.

"Lift bags," he said tersely. "Tony, we brought bags in the kit, didn't we?"

"Yeah, but—"

"Lem." He turned instinctively to the older man. "Us two, we'll take the raft in after it. The rest of you pile out, stay here. If it goes off, it'll be far enough away, you won't be hurt."

"John, you can't—"

"No discussion time left, Leroy, sorry. Lem, you marked this last one, didn't you?"

"Chem light. Yes."

"Senior Chief—"

"No goddamn arguments!" He tried to steady his voice. What he had to tell them now was vital. "Listen! If we make it, Lem and I'll pop the fuzes on the way back. That'll give us five or ten minutes to get you guys in the raft and get clear, out to sea."

Maudit: "And if you don't?"

"If you hear an explosion, it's up to you. That mine'll be taken care of. You'll have to go back and pull the primers on the others yourselves." He paused to think it through. A man in full gear swam at a knot and a half; fifteen minutes on the fuzes, they'd be seven hundred yards away . . . it should be enough. If they weren't too exhausted. But then how would they get back? How would they be picked up?

He struggled with this for a moment, then added softly, "Or you can stay here. Leroy, you're next senior. Here's the flare pen. Signal the ships with it. They'll abort the raid, pick you up, and leave. I won't order anyone to go. Volunteers?"

There was a pause, during which he hoisted himself into the raft. The men in it moved back. He felt drained; he had barely energy to pull off his mask. "So. Who'll go in? If we don't make it back?"

"Me," said Terger.

"I'll go, too," said Burgee, sounding gloomy. "I knew something would happen to fuck this party up."

"*Ah, moi aussi, bordel, j'y vais . . .* me, too, I guess," muttered Maudit, his accent somehow more pronounced. "Sure, let's go for it."

Gordon felt sudden pride. They were good men, these reservists. Only half military, more than half civilian. Yet he realized now that they were the best team he'd ever served with. He hoped they all made it out of this. But regardless, he was glad to be here with them tonight.

Aloud he only said, "Good. Okay, into the water."

"Wait a minute, John. Let's save them a swim. We'll drop one guy off at each float, now, as we go in. Then pick them up as we come back out. If we don't make it back, they can each pop one, scatter, then beat feet for the pickup."

Maybe they could, Gordon thought. He looked at the black cutouts around him. He didn't doubt that the same thought was in every other mind, too. It was possible. But not likely. Most of them wouldn't make it. Not in the dark, exhausted, battered by shock waves from tons of explosive and probably with men out hunting them afterward.

But they'd all volunteered. Once again, he felt that electric surge of pride.

"Good idea, Lem. But damn it, we got to hurry. Everybody in. Clint, crank it, let's go!"

He was looking at Burgee at the moment he said it, and never caught the movement ashore. One of the lights had detached itself. Separated from the island. And then, just as he turned his head back, winked out.

His watch read 0120. Facing front with his men, he wiped stinging spray from his eyes as they closed, once again, on the stronghold of their enemy.

35

0000 Hours:
U.S.S. *Turner Van Zandt*

THE digital clock in CIC hummed, clicked, and turned over
six figures at once.

Dan dug his fingers into the cold leather of the TAO chair.
Midnight.

Adams and *Van Zandt* prowled the dark water off Dhubai,
fuse blocks pulled on radars and radios. Sidelights burning red
and green, masthead and range white, to all appearances just
two more of the steady river of tankers bound for Hormuz and
all the ports of the earth.

In two hours, they would be entering the mine field.

He jumped down and pushed through the blackout curtain
into Sonar. The coffee was ready and he freshened his cup. The
watch standers hunched over their displays—no longer did a
sonarman depend on his ears—like bingo fans lacking one
square for the grand prize. He glanced over the shoulder of the
SQS-56 operator. The shallow, turbulent water broke up the
impulses; the display was a shatter of green, like thrown divin-
ing sticks.

He brushed out through the curtains again. The bent backs
over the EW display, the weapons consoles, told the same story.
Even at the shut-down radars the operators sat before blank
screens with the same absorption.

There'd been no official general quarters. Shaker had told the
chiefs and officers to have the crew on station at 2330. They'd
reported manned and ready well before. Now he sipped the hot
brew, considered, then nodded to Wise. It was time. "Al, we set
up?"

"Yessir. Except that Mark 92's still in antiair mode. I'll shift
to shore bombardment when we get in sight of the island."

"Sounds good. Puffball had those kittens yet?"

"Who? Oh. No, not yet." The ops officer grinned like a skull.
"It's been a long day."

Dan smiled back, then went serious again. "Okay, like the captain said, you're going to be handling things down here. I'll be on the bridge backing him up. Keep us posted once the shooting starts. And don't be afraid to take action yourself if you don't get a response from us."

Wise nodded somberly. Dan hung around the space for a few minutes longer, knowing that once he went to the bridge he'd be there for the duration, and then went up.

Charaler had the deck, Ekdahl the conn. McQueen and Stanko were in their usual nooks, the chief by the chart table, the boatswain near the 1MC panel, where he could answer phones, pass word, and still keep a critical eye on the helmsman. The bridge was even darker than usual. All the pilot lights had been taped over and dials and gauges turned down to where they could barely be read with adapted eyes. The windows were lit, though, by the wavering yellow glow of distant separation flares, and through them Dan could make out a coruscating pyramid of light to starboard.

"Engines ahead full, indicate twenty knots. Left ten degrees rudder, come to new course three-one-zero," Ekdahl muttered.

Dan moved up beside Charaler. "What the hell is—oh. The baa-baa express."

"Yeah, that's him." They watched as the glittering mountain crossed astern, headed up the Gulf. It was an Australian freighter that went to Kuwait once a month. For days afterward, they would find the bloated bodies, the sheep who wouldn't make it to Saudi tables, floating in her wake.

"Where's *Adams?*"

Charaler pointed into the dark. "She's shut down her nav lights already. Dead ahead, about two thousand yards."

"Is the captain up here?"

"He went aft for a leak. He'll be right back."

The wind-borne stink of the livestock carrier hit them then, making the bridge team groan. Dan bent over the chart with McQueen, checking their track. There would be no long transit to the objective for NIMBLE DANCER. Nothing in the Gulf was very far from anything else. That was why the Pasdaran were so dangerous at Abu Musa. Even with short-range boats, they could find dozens of targets.

At the new speed they looked solid for a 0200 ETA. He made a very careful check of the loran position against the satellite fix. It was off three-quarters of a mile. Beside him, McQueen sucked a tooth.

Shaker came forward from the bridge urinal, cigarette glow-

ing like a running light. He stood behind Charaler for a time.
Then his chair creaked as he swung himself up.

A faint red circle flickered into existence ahead, brightened
and dimmed, then began occulting rapidly. "Flashing light from
Adams, sir," said Charaler, at the same time fingering the
intercom. "Sigs, Bridge: Message coming in from dead ahead."

"Sigs aye, we're on it."

Dan had his binoculars up, but the letters came too fast for
him to follow. It was a long one. The signalman brought it down
a few minutes after the light transmitted *PP* and went out.
Lenson moved to the captain's side and held the faint rose beam
of his flashlight on it for Shaker.

> *VAN ZANDT* DE *ADAMS* BT ATTACK PLAN FOLLOWS X PRIMARY
> OBJECTIVE ENEMY CRAFT SECONDARY SHORE INSTALLATIONS X I
> WILL LEAD AT 500 YDS INTERVAL X MAINTAIN ELECTRONIC SI-
> LENCE UNTIL CLEAR OF MINE FIELD X *ADAMS* WILL OPEN PARTY
> WITH MIXED ILLUMINATION AND POINT DETONATING X *VAN ZANDT*
> THEN OPEN FIRE AT WILL X WILL ILLUMINATE FOR YOU FROM
> MOUNT 52 DURING YOUR PASS X CONFORM TO MY MOVEMENTS
> UNTIL PAST PIER COMMA THEN TURN INSIDE ME WITH RIGHT RUD-
> DER AND TAKE LEAD X KEEP SHOALS IN MIND X *VAN ZANDT* WILL
> LEAD GOING OUT X COMMUNICATIONS DURING ACTION ON FLEET
> TACTICAL X RETIREMENT COURSE ONE SIX ZERO X SPEED THREE
> ZERO X GOOD LUCK FROM THE JACKAL BT

"There a response, sir?"

"Yeah." The click of a ball pen was followed by rapid scratching. Shaker handed it to Dan.

> *Adams* de *Van Zandt* BT Plan acknowledged X Upon your
> open fire will lay spread of five standards on batteries in heights
> behind pier X Then carry out attack as per your message X
> Except may open slightly for torpedo firing X Good hunting X
> Whoever bags most boats buys drinks Regency Manama Friday
> BT

"Looks good, sir."

"Okay, send it. Let's go to battle dress. Pass the word on the
phones."

In the darkness shadows donned life jackets, crouched to roll
socks over trousers, buttoned their shirts to the throat. Dan
pulled one of the makeshift flash hoods over his head, then
fitted the steel helmet McQueen handed him over it. It smelled

like an old gym shoe. He licked his lips. The heat was oppressive. Where had he left his coffee? He found it wedged behind
a cable run and finished it off.

Pensker came up and he and Shaker held a short confab. The
weapons officer had figured out a way to slave the Phalanx to
the TDT and shoot in surface mode. Shaker seemed happy at
that.

Time went by very slowly.

With the radars shut down, only the sinking lights of the
tankers astern gave them a sense of movement. Ahead was
only blackness. Dan watched the penciled triangles of his fixes
creep closer to the island.

Finally, when he couldn't stand it any longer, he went out to
the port wing and propped his elbows on the coaming. He was
lifting his binoculars when he realized he didn't need them.

They couldn't see the planes, long-range bombers and electronic suppression birds off *Forrestal,* hundreds of miles to the
southeast. Not at this distance. Only the glowing meteor trails
of missiles. A ripple of flashes, then a subterranean, earthquake rumble reached them across the choppy dark. Then a
distant tapping of guns.

The air attack had begun.

Dan hoped the Intruders' radar-homing missiles worked. And
that their jamming was blanking out the enemy's remaining
radars. The display was spectacular. There were flashes all
along the eastern shore now. Unfortunately, the aircraft, unless they got down nose to nose with the shoulder-fired missiles,
wouldn't accomplish much against the real targets: the small,
fast boats that used the island to refuel and rearm between
attacks.

But that, of course, was why the surface Navy was here.

Dan dropped the glasses. He flicked the switch on the night-
vision goggles that hung around his neck, and fitted them to his
eyes.

Through the eyepieces the world became two scintillating
circles of green. Electronically amplified, the device showed him
the island, and at the same moment, in the foreground, the
still-distant silhouettes of three boats stern to them—moored,
and swinging to the tidal current. . . . He tracked his gaze
around till it was cut off by the corner of the pilothouse. The
fires and gun flashes from shore made the goggles strobe erratically, hurting his eyes.

He moved back inside the pilothouse. "Targets on the port
bow, three gunboats, anchored," he reported. The captain's
face loomed huge and distorted, limned in sparkling green fire.

Dan heard his words repeated by the phone talker to the guns.

He shoved the goggles up. It was beginning, the slowed-down sense of time he always had in action. Yet they still had miles to get through. Miles and minutes. He wished they could go in faster, but that would be insane. They had to negotiate the mine field. He thought for a moment of the EOD divers, somewhere ahead. That took guts, to deal with a mine hand to hand. Salty water trickled down from under the helmet and he licked at it without noticing it. The ruby circle flickered again from *Adams*, otherwise invisible, black as the moonless sea itself, and Shaker dropped their speed to fifteen.

At 0150, the forward lookout reported small boats ahead.

Adams's silhouette kept growing. Shaker said angrily, "Where the fuck's he going? Come right, damn it, come right! Slow to ten knots. Helmsman, follow that blue light on her stern!"

"I'll follow it into hell, sir."

Dan crawled back into the eyepieces, staring ahead. The lightless water sparkled pallidly as electrons fired at random. Where in God's name was their lane? If they didn't see it soon, they'd have to abort. But would Shaker admit defeat like that? Would he turn back, this close to the enemy?

Suddenly, for the first time that night, he remembered to be scared.

0130 HOURS: ABU MUSA ANCHORAGE

Gordon sank almost lifelessly into the dark. Into the gulf of night . . . He was exhausted, confused, shuddering with cold. He'd been in the water for four and a half hours now, most of it at seventy feet, breathing mixed nitrogen and oxygen.

He still had air. Not much, but enough for one more dive. But he wasn't sure he had the strength.

The trailing line tugged at his waist. Ahead of him, Everett's light wavered like a lone firefly on the last night of summer. The chemical solution was almost exhausted. Gordon tried to swim, but he could barely move. He clung to the buoy line, letting it slip through his numb fingers. Sinking . . .

As they'd left the Z-bird, he'd seen the flash of bombs ashore. Invisible as a Yankee God above the hell they created, the planes had arrived. The sea squeezed his chest and eyeballs. Detonations shuddered through the water. He hoped they kept their drops out of the anchorage. A diver didn't have to be close to an explosion to be stunned or killed.

But there was no reason they should. By now, according to

the schedule, he and his team should be miles to seaward, motoring to safety.

The job wasn't over, though. There was one more mine to clear.

He was thinking this when he struck mud. Softer, more yielding than the sand farther out. He uncrimped his fingers from the line and shook his head, trying to discipline his thoughts through the drunken fatigue. Everett's beacon flared thirty feet away. He fumbled for his flashlight, aimed it, and punched the button.

The weak glow from the dying batteries showed him the mine. Showed him, too, the gargoyle figure of a diver already almost on it.

Gordon shoved himself forward, mumbling into his mouthpiece. Lem knew not to rush in. But the banker, older than he, had been in the water just as long. He must be tired too, gas-intoxicated too. But this was no time to make a mistake.

Not with two ships due through minutes from now.

The mine lay on its side, nearly covered by the muck. Velvety brown silt was drifted up its flanks, current-carried. He angled without conscious thought into the proper approach. He had to check himself. He wanted to rush in, get it over with. But disoriented as he was, tired as he was, he still knew that haste and carelessness were their deadliest enemies.

Everett lifted his gloves and moved back. Gordon saw the bulky yellow cover of the bag flutter free. The other chief had bent it to the shipping frame. He was paying out the lanyard that would inflate it.

Gordon held up a fist. He waited till Everett was clear—no use tempting whatever infernal detonator this thing contained—and then finned forward with exquisite, tired caution to focus his flashlight.

This one had been down longer than the others. The black paint was almost gone. The steel frame was rustier. On impulse, knowing he shouldn't, he reached out to touch it. A few flakes of sea-corroded metal came free and drifted slowly to the mud.

He reversed his grip and pulled, and a section bent outward.

Hauling himself up and over it, Gordon yanked savagely at the knot Everett had just tied. It resisted him and he had to take his glove off. No feeling in his swollen fingers, immersed for so many hours. He fought a sudden crazy desire to attack it with his teeth.

The knot came apart at last. He slipped it off the frame and swam over the mine. Yes, the lugs. He got the line through one at the fourth try and put three half-hitches on and then a keeper figure eight.

Now for his own bag. He fought it out of his belt, stripped the cover free, and found the line. He started to fasten it and realized no, that was the trip line. He found the right one and put four half-hitches on. Then breathed out and backed slowly away, looking it over.

The mine lay like a piece of rusted, discarded pipe. For a moment he wondered whether it, if all of them, were dummies. Inert. No, that was stupid. He was in bad shape.

Now, when they tripped the flasks, a ton of lift would tug the weapon out of the mud. He hoped. And he hoped the inevitable jarring wouldn't wake whatever slept beneath that brass plate. But even if it did, if in fifteen seconds or thirty he and Lem Everett no longer existed, at least the lane would be clear.

He realized suddenly that he wanted very much for this mine not to explode. He wanted to go home again. Why had he come here, eight thousand miles from Crevecoeur Farm, Stonefield, Vermont? Just then he couldn't remember. But he was here, and he'd at least finish this goddamn job.

Sorry, Ola. Have to watch that goddamn swearing.

He remembered the towline then. He went back, tied it with elephant fingers to the after lug, and retreated again. Without further thought, he gave the lanyard a smooth, hard yank. Beside him he glimpsed Everett's arm coming back at the same moment.

There was a bubbling hiss and the bags began to bulge. The two divers watched them. There was no point in trying to escape. They could barely swim. With this much explosive, the kill radius would be hundreds of yards. So they just watched.

The bags unfolded. Little pops and cracks snapped through the water as air sought out the crannies and folds. The hissing continued, louder now, and the heavy canvas surged and quivered like soap bubbles as the trapped air yearned for the surface. He tried to calculate how much lift they'd get, forty cubic feet of air at four thousand pounds pressure, corrected for seventy feet of depth. But the arithmetic was too complex for his novocained mind.

The tail of the mine jerked upward. Containing fins and sensors, it was lighter than the explosive-packed forward section. The mud burst suddenly apart like a small bomb, swirling out to diffuse and then obliterate the fading beams of their lights. Gordon backed a few more feet away.

The bags strained silently now. The last air hissed and then trickled to a stop.

They hung there. He could feel their pull in his bones. But though the tail swayed free, the nose was still buried.

Shit, he thought.

He moved forward then, and gripped the rusty rails; braced his knees and shoved. The mine grated, metal screeching on gravel or coarse sand. It swung away from him, and then, suddenly, freed itself from the mud and began to rise, penduluming gently.

At the same moment, there came to his ears, through the distant rumble that had never stopped, the mosquito whine of a propeller.

It was time to leave. He signaled Everett and they valved gas into their vests. They began to rise, slowly at first, then more rapidly. The sea rushed past their faces. Gordon breathed steadily, in, out, in, feeling the residual air grow in his lungs. As they ascended the whine came now louder, now softer, as they passed through layers of different temperatures.

They broke surface to a continuous thunder from the island. There were many fires there now, he saw. Then he turned his eyes away.

The mine was free of the bottom. But it was still live, still dangerous, and still in the channel.

Now they had to tow it out.

The raft bobbed where they'd left it, lashed to the float. Lurid gleams played over wet rubber as Gordon pulled himself over the gunwale. He scrambled forward awkwardly to cast off. Behind him Everett's fins thudded into the floorboards. The starter putted, putted again, and then caught and roared out. He flinched, then realized it didn't matter. They could run it as loud as they wanted now.

He glanced at his watch and his throat closed. Only ten minutes before the ships would be here. "Move it, Lem, move it *now!*"

The throttle came open. The line came dripping out of the sea. Everett aimed the bow left, into the unswept portion of the mine field. As good a place as any, Gordon thought, pulling off his mask, then tripping his weight belt and gear and Mark 16, dumping them all pell-mell. If there were more contact mines, what they towed might bump one. But he had no more time for safety. Only just time to haul it clear, drop it, pick up his men, fire the charges, and clear out.

He saw the boat then. A sharp shadow between him and the

fires. He heard shouting, distant but clear, and for a moment didn't realize what it meant. Then he did.

"Down, Lem! Get low!"

Flashes from the dark, a stutter of automatic fire. He sprawled into wet wood and rubber. The little raft, burdened deep with the drag of mine and bags, made way with agonizing slowness across the flame-lit sea.

Another flash and stutter. This time, the Z-bird flinched as humming things plucked their way through rubber and air. One clanked and sparked by his feet, and Gordon started. How could they see to aim? The boat was black, both divers were dressed in black.

Then he saw how. Behind them, aft of the prop, glowed a phosphorescent arrow. Pointing right to them.

If only they'd brought rifles. Anything to keep them off for a few more minutes.

He blinked then, and clawed beneath the floorboards. He came up with Tupperware. He popped the lid, and the Browning dropped into his hand.

Looking back, he saw the silhouette shorten, swing bow on to them. Then it was obliterated in the muzzle flash.

Gordon pumped out fourteen rounds as fast as he could pull the trigger, hardly bothering to aim. No chance of a hit at this range. All he wanted to do was persuade them they were facing rifles, or a machine gun. When the automatic was empty he dropped it, ducking again as a fresh fusillade came in.

They did seem to be lagging back now, though. Two minutes later, he judged that this was far enough. "Cut it!" he shouted to Everett.

But he didn't seem to hear. Gordon flung himself back down, pulling his knife free of the calf sheath, and hacked desperately at the line. It separated with a snap, and they leapt forward.

The acceleration tumbled Everett back, and Gordon saw the gleam of blood across his chest. He shoved him aside and grabbed the throttle. The motor yammered as he shoved it hard over.

The lightened boat swapped ends like a squirrel on a branch and headed back for the channel. Behind him he saw the pursuers hesitate, then turn to follow. They were close, no more than a hundred yards behind, but freed now of its burden the Z-bird romped, throwing luminous curving sheets of spray. He was thinking he might outrun them when he noticed that the raft was sagging in the middle. And that there was water in the bottom now, too.

So that was that.

He froze as suddenly and simultaneously the howl of a powerful engine burst over him, a new stick of bombs tore the shoreline apart, and over it all rose the terrifying clatter of automatic rifles.

Gasping as something seared the back of his thigh, he went over the side as the raft slid downward, pulled under by the still-running Evinrude.

Then he was in the water, enfolded by warm darkness through which bullets slid like frying bacon and propellers whined like a sawmill at full blast.

He wondered then, burrowing for the depths like a wounded mole, whether the rest of the team had seen the boat. Or guessed, from the firing, that he and Everett weren't going to be back to pick them up.

Burgee and Maudit and Terger. They were good men. He'd done his best. As had Lem. As they all had. Now, at the end, it was in God's hands.

He hoped God had read the plan.

0206 HOURS: U.S.S. *TURNER VAN ZANDT*

At that moment, Lenson, sweeping the night sea with the low-light goggles, saw it come on ahead. Low in the water, bobbing up and down and being waved back and forth. He searched to the left, but couldn't see any in that direction. Nor was there one to starboard. Which side was the cleared lane on?

"Light in the water!" he yelled, then lowered his voice instinctively. "Light in the water. Off to port. Only one."

The 21MC said: "Bridge, Sigs: infrared light, one point off starboard bow."

Dan saw it at the same moment, dimmer than the first, but indisputably there. It didn't look like a hundred yards between them. "Christ," muttered Shaker, beside him, "I hope Jakkal picks those up. Steve!"

"Ahead two-thirds, indicate ten knots, come right, steer three-two-five."

"Coming right, new course three-two-five," said the helmsman.

"Farther right," said Shaker. "Farther! I don't like the heading Jakkal's on."

Dan pushed up the goggles, leaning over the chart as McQueen plotted the lights. *Van Zandt* was headed fair for the channel, but he couldn't tell where *Adams* was going. By his chart, they were thirty, forty yards too far to port.

They couldn't both be right. But he trusted McQueen. He straightened now and put his hand on the older man's shoulder. "Okay, Mac, I'm gonna be with the captain from now on. Keep a good track. Yell loud if there're any problems."

"Got it, Commander."

Standing beside Shaker now, gripping his binoculars and sweating under the long-sleeved jacket and canvas hood, Dan recast his mind into taking responsibility for it all: the whole dark length of her, and all her men. For this was how a captain thought, not of the part, but of the whole ship.

He'd felt it before, understudying Bell. He hoped he wouldn't have to take over tonight. But if he did, there'd be no time for hesitation, confusion, or fear.

The whole ship . . . he knew that throughout her now men were leaning into their sights. The target-designation transmitters, atop the pilothouse, where the 76mm was laid from. The .50 machine guns. The Phalanx. The men on the torpedo tubes, ready to fire by hand in case power failed. And the small-arms party aft. He hoped they maintained discipline. Held their fire, held their talk, showed no lights.

The bobbing light slipped down the port side. Through the binoculars he caught for a second the black blur of a head beneath it, an arm.

He turned, to see McQueen lay a tiny triangle just inside the crosshatched boundary.

Suddenly the night split apart. Huge detonations shook the ship like a puppy, rolling her hard to starboard. The men on the bridge cried out. Dimly through the thunder, the shouting, cut Shaker's voice, angry and at the same time cold. "I don't know what it is. And it's too late now. Fuck the mines! All ahead flank!"

It had begun already, he thought, crouching behind the splinter shield. The utter confusion of battle.

The sea leapt up around them in huge columns, wiping out the island, the stars, the very darkness, like a new Deluge. *Van Zandt* plunged through them, still accelerating, as they toppled and roared down like a dozen waterfalls.

The distant whine and howl of jet engines dwindled. Across two miles of water came the frying crackle of small arms and the occasional deeper note of heavier guns. Dan leaned against steel, sweating, waiting for the first flash of a shot aimed their way, the first glowing ball of missile exhaust.

With naked eyes, he could see lights moving on the shore now, trucks or possibly flashlights. They were close enough for that. The island lay behind and above them, a darker darkness,

more menacing by the second. He remembered a passage from
an old story; the looming island to leeward, the deserter's hat
drifting past, telling the new captain when he had steerageway.
He yanked his mind back. Against the flickering sky, he could
make out the double crest of Jabal Halwa.

"Halfway through," came the chief quartermaster's quiet
voice. No one on the bridge said anything for a moment; then
Charaler, also quietly, gave the official response: "Very well."

Something had changed. It was suddenly quieter, like a theater before curtain. The pop and clatter came clear and distant.
Then he knew what it was. The endless whistle of the *shamal*
was gone. They were in the lee of the island. The enemy was
only seconds away now. Yet still his lights searched skyward,
still his tracers blinked upward in fiery streams; here and there
a rocket kindled and rose in its fiery arc, detonating long seconds later over the water as its warhead self-destructed. He
was still firing at the departed aircraft.

There was a bump under the hull, and Dan caught his breath.
Other gasps came from around him. But no explosion followed.
He had no idea what it was.

"Bridge, Sigs: Challenge from the island."

He swung instantly, lifting his glasses, getting them tangled
with the goggle straps, yanking them apart with a curse. The
blue light glinted across the water from the spit, laying a fan-
shaped glisten on the waves. It tapped out slowly P Q P.

Shaker: "Don't answer. Maintain course. Pass the word to
pick out your targets."

Charaler: "Aye, sir."

McQueen: "Sir, navigator holds us passing the inner boundary of the mine field."

Shaker, calmly: "Very well."

Ahead of them, at that moment, the profile of a destroyer
leapt suddenly from blackness, outlined by two balls of bril-
liant-hot gas. Dan could see the dwindling red dots of the shells.
Seconds later, two novas ignited over the island, painful bright-
nesses suspended from streams of smoke. They swung, then
steadied beneath parachutes. They stripped night from the
shore, the hummocks, the tortured rocky crags, the sand spit
to port.

And directly ahead, frighteningly close, showed them a huddle of prefabricated huts and tents, and two piers outstretched.
One long, one short. Several boats—he couldn't tell how
many—were near the short one, not tied up but standing a few
yards off, as if just getting under way. A shapeless dark mass,

probably more craft moored in a nest, occupied the southern side of the long pier. And the harsh light showed him more, five or seven more, scattered between him and the beach.

"Illuminate! Radars on!"

Wise, from CIC: "CWI in radiate. All radars coming up."

"Weapons free," he heard Shaker shout into the intercom.

"Cover your eyes!" Dan shouted. He ducked below the level of the windows, and squeezed his own shut.

The world lit red even behind his covering hand. The bellow rattled the deck plates and windows like a beast shaking a cage. One after another, five missiles flung themselves off the forecastle, filling the pilothouse with unbearable sound, glare, heat, and an incredible density of bitter, choking smoke.

When he straightened, cracking one eye to check, he caught the last at the apex of its trajectory. A moment later, it nosed over and curved down, a ball of lucent fire that was still burning fiercely when it merged with one of the hillocks in a blinding flash.

He thought, They've got to know we're here now. In the guttering light of the falling star shells, the huge fluffy cotton trails of solid-fuel boosters led directly to *Van Zandt*.

"Gun action port, target small boats, batteries released," shouted Shaker. "Torpedo action port, fire when you bear. All hands commence fire!"

Dan was looking aft, standing by for it, but still the first gun flash caught him with his eyes unshielded. The sphere of white-orange fire was big as a house and the blast, with the gun trained forward, blew him back into the bulkhead. He pulled himself back inside the bridge, blinking. But salvo flash destroyed only the central portion of vision. He looked to the side as the 76 fired again.

Adams was firing, too, had been whanging away steadily, the old five-inchers crashing out a broadside every three seconds. Her shells threw up huge spouts of white water. One hit a moored Boghammer, seventy pounds of steel and explosive traveling at three thousand feet a second, and the graceful hull ballooned weirdly for an instant before it disintegrated in a blast of orange flame.

Dan was staring at the pier when he realized suddenly he could see men running along it. They were that close. According to the chart, there was twenty feet of water at the end of that pier. *Van Zandt* drew twenty-six. He jumped to the radar. "Four hundred yards to turn!" he shouted. Ahead, *Adams* was already swinging her stern left, sheering off from the shore.

"Hold your course, Steve," said Shaker, his voice iron. "How far to the pier, XO?"

"Five hundred yards!"

"Torpedoes away. I said that to you, phone talker, pass it and quit gawking around! XO, keep feeding me ranges. Officer of the deck, slow to five!"

"Ahead one third, indicate five knots."

"Four hundred yards."

"Fifties, commence fire."

A hollow whump came from aft: high-pressure air kicking the torpedoes out of the tubes. At the same instant, the machine guns cut in above their heads. The noise was incredible. Yet it still increased, the clatter building to a roar. They had six of them firing, four .50s from above, two M60s from aft on the flight deck.

Dan lifted his face from the scope hood, called "Three hundred yards," and looked to port for the torpedo wakes. He couldn't see them, but he'd heard them go out. The port tubes were now empty.

"Gunboat to port, incoming, firing!"

He saw the red wink from the boat's bow. The sound was lost in the clamor *Van Zandt* was putting out. Then suddenly bullets were whacking through thin metal around him. Someone screamed above him, on the flying bridge.

"Get some guns on that boat! Designate to Phalanx," said Shaker.

Lewis must have had his finger on the button. A deep note like a bass viol, and Dan saw the shadow pause as spray splashes leapt up around it. The splashes tracked it for a second, then stopped. Their attacker looked undamaged for a moment. Then it disappeared. Sunk, he realized. And no wonder, with fifty or sixty inch-wide holes through it from one side to the other.

"Two hundred yards to the pier! Captain, we've got to turn or we'll ground!"

"Hold your course, Steve," said Shaker.

Dan lifted his head from the scope hood to a scene that no one in the U.S. Navy had seen since World War II: a shore installation taking the concentrated bombardment of two warships at close range. White, red, orange bursts flickered fast as the finale of a fireworks display. *Adams* had shifted fire from the boats and her shells were landing ashore now, a little long, but even as he thought this, the next salvo laddered down a hundred yards into the middle of the compound. Buildings blew

apart in mushroom columns of flame. A truck cartwheeled
through the sky. The crash and thud of the heavy shells echoed
back from the mountain like the sky falling in.

It was a destroyerman's dream, the enemy illuminated, dis-
tracted, and confused. They still think they're being bombed, he
thought. Then the fact that they were close enough to spit on
the beach registered with utter horror. "Captain! *One hundred*
yards to pier!"

"Very well."

"Bridge, Main control."

"You can't tie up here, Captain. Not enough water!"

Shaker chuckled calmly. It sounded mad in the clamor.
"Don't worry so much, XO. Okay, Stever, come right and parallel the shore. Kick her up to fifteen."

"Bridge, Main control."

"What, damn it, Rick?"

"Cap'n, something just whanged into us on the port side."

"Damage?"

"No damage, just a hell of a big clang."

Meanwhile Charaler rapped out orders. They swept past the
pier and it dropped behind. Their tracers reached toward it and
dropped into the shadows alongside. The 76 clanged steadily
from aft, its shells going home in crashing white blasts amid
the buildings and boats. Several of them were sinking, listing
over. A bow poked upward; there were men on it, scrambling
about like ants on a sinking leaf. Tracers arched into them. The
Iranians were firing on their own boats.

Dan bent his face again into the radar hood. To his horror,
he saw that one of the Intruders had found their frequency. An
angry seethe of jamming covered the screen. He jerked his
head up and shifted to the alidade. "Mark! Jabal Halwa, south
ridge, bearing two-nine-nine. What's the bearing when we're
out of the anchorage, Chief?"

"Wait one . . . two-nine-oh, say again two-nine-oh."

"Depth," said Shaker calmly.

"Five feet under the keel, shoaling fast."

"Steady, Stever, *Adams* draws more than we do. Stand by
. . . okay. Right hard rudder, *now.*"

The helmsman spun the wheel and the deck leaned under
their feet. Dan grabbed for the chart table. Empty brass from
the .50s rolled above their heads.

She came around fast, faster than *Adams*, and Charaler
steadied her up on the reciprocal. The piers and buildings grew
ahead of them again.

They know we're here now, Dan thought. Now it's our turn to play target.

As if to confirm it, a shell splash leapt up directly ahead. The spray rained down on the forecastle as *Van Zandt* tore into it. Tracers sailed out from the shore, fell short, then lifted. They stitched along the water and began clanging into the hull. "Shore battery, counterfire, to the right of the small pier," someone screamed. He ignored it and took another bearing on the mountain. "Range to the piers, keep 'em coming," Shaker shouted.

"No radar, estimate four hundred yards and closing."

"Starboard tubes, fire when you bear!"

Thuds aft.

"Torpedoes away. All torpedoes expended."

"Mount thirty-one out of ammo, sir!"

The ready magazine held seventy rounds. The loaders below would be sweating now, but for the moment their main gun was out of commission. The .50s resumed their clatter as the range closed.

The ship jerked under his feet, and he heard a crunch like two Cadillacs colliding. "Hit aft," shouted one of the talkers.

"Increase to twenty knots," said Shaker. "Damage control, Bridge: Get me data on the hits! Dan, did you plot those Q markers when we came in?"

"Yessir. Plotting a course out now."

There was a sudden jolt, not loud, but hard. It came through the water. Dan saw a plume of spray leap up from the short pier. Then another jolt, and the pier disintegrated, the little house disappeared, the boats disappeared, geysering upward on three huge underwater explosions.

"Okay, let's get the fuck out of here! Give me a course."

"One-seven-zero looks good."

"Left hard rudder, come to one-seven-zero," said Charaler.

"Mr. Charaler, did I direct you to come to that course?"

"You said to get the fuck out of here, Captain."

"Okay, just checking."

"Bridge, DC central: Loamer here."

"Talk to us, Percy."

"Sir, we took three hits a couple minutes ago. Shell hit in Auxiliary Machinery Room number three. Fragment damage. Number-four diesel generator and number-five fire pump off the line. Hit in starboard helo hangar, class bravo fire. Fire boundaries set. Initiating foam flooding. Hit in chiefs' berthing, class alfa fire, Repair Two's providing."

"Percy, we're gonna need the AMR back, give that priority unless the fires spread."

"Aye, sir. Uh, how's it look up there, sir?"

"Hell, I forgot all about the guys below," said Shaker. "We're doin' good, kicking ass, on our way out now, I'll talk on the 1MC after—"

The flash and crack came simultaneously. Fragments clanged against the starboard wing. Before they could react, another shell exploded a few feet aft, on the signal bridge, another back by the 76. Dan caught muzzle flashes and grabbed the radio handset. "Lariat, this is Apache. Taking fire from shore. Gun battery on flat-topped hummock to the right of the pier."

"Apache, Lariat, roger, out."

"Ahead full," shouted Shaker, his voice distant. Dan reached up to rub his ears. No, not distant, he'd been deafened. Good thing those hadn't been armor-piercing. From the rate of fire, it must have been an AA gun, depressed to a horizontal trajectory.

He checked the radar—it was still flickering like heat lightning, hopelessly jammed—and then the chart. McQueen's track showed them headed fair for the lane out.

He was taking a deep breath, ready to accept a strategic retreat, when he saw a piece of the burning pier, the one their torpedoes hadn't hit, slide away from the rest. He stared at it in disbelief, then remembered his binoculars. He stepped out onto the wing, lifting them, and sensed something soft underfoot. "Who the hell's lying down out here?"

"He's wounded, sir."

Dan caught the shape then in the twin circle of the night glasses. For an endless second, his mind refused to accept it. Then it did.

"Submarine to starboard!" he screamed.

Every man on the bridge spun around. Shaker swore. "What? Where?"

"The long pier, alongside! Getting under way now!"

Shaker's binoculars came up for the first time during the action. After a long moment, he muttered "It's him, all right. Camouflaged. He's been sitting right here in Abu Musa. Good eye, Dan. Okay, call Lewis. Get the Phalanx on him."

"CIWS out of ammo!"

"Shit! Get the 76—"

"Still reloading, sir."

"Let *Adams* take her, sir," said Dan. "Five-inch'll crack the pressure hull—"

"Jakkal's headed out! He doesn't see it—or doesn't want to!" The massive head steadied on the shape that now accelerated, driving silently out from shore. Orange flames, parts of the pier, still flickered on its decks.

"Let's stand by outside the anchorage—" But even as he said it, Dan stopped. As soon as the sub cleared the island, it would submerge. And with sonar conditions as bad as they were, they'd never see it again. Till its fish slammed into another tanker.

"Hard right rudder!" shouted Shaker. The helmsman responded instantly, repeating the command as he twisted the wheel.

"There's a shoal over there, sir!"

"I think we can turn inside it—Lewis! Get that motherfucking gun reloaded! *Now!*"

Van Zandt came around fast and tight at full speed, almost in her own length.

They were halfway around when there was an ungodly noise from the wing. Dan stared out for a three-second-long year as *Adams* screamed by not fifty feet away, her blowers and turbines whining like a battalion of banshees. The steady flashes from her guns lit the smoke and spray of her passage. They lit startled faces on her bridge. They showed the old destroyer's bow twisted and mangled as if she'd hit a wall. There were answering flashes, redder, from ashore.

Shaker shouted, "Is the gun ready?"

"Not yet, sir!"

"Okay, fuck it! Ahead flank emergency. Let's ruin this bastard's paint job!"

"Engines ahead flank emergency, steady as she goes!"

A low black shape ahead, perhaps a hundred meters off the burning pier, its deadly bow swinging toward them . . . no other choice now, unless they wanted a torpedo up the ass . . . *Van Zandt* gathered speed fast as she steadied.

He saw then what Shaker was going to do. There was nothing to say. No time to do anything but jump for the collision alarm, yank it over. Then grab a cable and brace himself.

They hit with a long, grinding crash that threw every man on the bridge to his knees.

0212 HOURS: U.S.S. *CHARLES ADAMS*

Phelan was looking at the clock when the steel he was leaning against whip-cracked into his back. The fluorescents flickered, went out, flickered again, blue, then came on again full force.

He half-scrambled up, but he was one of ten men sprawled and squatting on the deck, and gear covered the rest of it; he found no room to stand. With a hopeless moan, he sank back, feeling his bladder loosen suddenly, a warmth crawl down one leg.

The repair-team leader yanked open the watertight door and stood in it, looking out. Bernard saw men running in the passageway outside. Like him, they wore dungarees, leather gloves, miner-style hard hats with lights on top. His bell-bottoms were tucked into his socks and his feet felt heavy and strange in the cracked old steel-toes they'd issued him for GQ.

"Repair Two! Repair-team leader!" came a hoarse, scared voice somewhere forward.

"Repair Two leader aye!"

"Hit forward, suspected mine, vicinity frame ten, investigate and report."

The team leader yelled it back, grabbed his clipboard, and disappeared. The rest of the team waited, not talking, their faces varnished with sweat. The ventilation had been secured for GQ and the air was as close as if they were waiting in a stalled elevator.

More boots thudded by outside and there were clangs and thuds from above. The lights flickered again. Phelan sat without looking, his brain empty of thought. His face was screwed closed like a jar, and he hugged his knees, rocking slightly in the cocoon of web belts, cables, fire axes, hoses, and line.

They'd pushed him around when he reported to the locker. Laughed at him, thrown his gear at him. They didn't care how he felt. Along with hurting like a rattler-bit dog, he was lonely and scared. Here in the repair locker, no one knew what was happening topside. Like coal miners buried by a cave-in, they knew of the world above only through sounds. There'd been a lot of noise, guns firing just above their heads. Noise over the 1MC, a voice shouting something about Iranians.

But he didn't care if they got hit. He didn't care if they stayed afloat. He'd be better off dead. At least he wouldn't need anything then.

The team leader was back at the door, shouting. Vaguely he thought, Everyone's shouting tonight. "Flooding forward. Mine hit. No fire, leave the OBAs here. Shoring and tools. Let's go!"

Before he could puzzle it, someone was shouting "Move, goddamn it," in his ear, and yanking him to his feet. He grasped feebly at a heavy long chunk of wood someone thrust into his arms. A line clacked onto his belt. Like the last man in a chain gang, he was dragged out the door after the others.

The passageway went dim a few yards forward. Somewhere ahead battle lanterns flickered like heat lightning over the mesas. He was dragged toward them, the tail end of a snake of men. He blinked, suddenly understanding that the waviness under his feet was steel, rippled upward, deformed by some incredible force.

All light ended. Blind now, the snake blundered through doors, into bulkheads, then crawled down a ladderway. His timber caught on the hatch cover and he almost fell.

At the bottom his boots splashed into a foot of water. Helmet lamps and hand lamps flashed and dimmed ahead. He was lost. He didn't know this ship or where he was. He didn't have a light and only the line on his belt told him where to go. He tripped over things, sprawled, got up, reshouldering the heavy splintered beam like a driven Christ.

The rapid clatter of hammers ahead, the whine of saws. Word came back for shoring and he pawed for the line, unsnapped it, shoved forward.

The lights showed him men working frantically, some measuring, others cutting beams to fit, hammering in wedges, laying wires, patching broken pipes. The dark smelled of explosives, seawater, sawdust, shit, and fear. A door gaped open, a well of blackness, and from the far side came cries and screams.

He pushed forward with his load. Somebody grabbed it, measured, and started sawing. In thirty seconds, it was part of a brace. He staggered back and leaned into a locker, gasping with fear, withdrawal, and exertion. What was he doing here? He didn't know what was going on.

His ear caught, then, one of the screams. "Corpsman! For the love of God, get a corpsman up here!"

There was a battle lantern by his feet. On, but it didn't seem to belong to anybody. There was also an olive-drab pack with a red cross on it. He hesitated, glancing around with his head down. Nobody was watching him. They were all busy, sawing, cursing, stringing lines.

He grabbed the light and the kit and hobbled through the door.

The space was, or had been, some kind of sonar room. The gear was wrecked. Glass all over, water up to his knees. The air was thick with a burnt heavy smell that made him think of firing ranges. He saw a hand sticking up out of the water. It didn't move. The voice was farther ahead.

Bernard saw him then, lying on top of a workbench.

His eyes were closed but his face was warm. No shock yet, then. Blood all over him. Black man. Phelan tore open the med kit and began ripping off clothes.

He found leg wounds and glass cuts. He was tourniqueting the legs when the man's eyes opened and he screamed, right in his ear. Bernard said angrily, "Knock it off, *way* too loud. How you doing, buddy?"

"Fuck. Fuck, ah, *Jesus!*"

"Just hold on, now, you got the best medicine man in the Zuni Nation in charge, you gonna be all right now, hear?"

He finished the bandaging, then searched through the kit. There they were. He tore open the little box, broke off the tip, and had the needle in the guy's thigh before he thought, No, man, you just tourniqueted his legs. He shifted to an arm and squeezed the syrette empty like a toothpaste tube. "You gonna be all right, man," he whispered over the clatter of hammers, the distant shouts.

"Thanks, pal. Hey—" the eyes opened for a moment before the drug congealed them—"there oughta be another sonar tech up forward. See if you can find him, huh?"

"I'll get him. You take it easy." Phelan patted him, then took out a ball-point and wrote across his forehead *M 0220*. He didn't have a watch, but that was close enough for a dose time.

So far, he hadn't seen any litters. But the guy'd been moving his legs; probably his back was all right. He swung him up in a fireman's carry, staggered through the water to the hatch, and screamed for help. Two seaman ran to grab him. He told them to get him some litters, he was going back in. As he turned, they shouted something at him, something about a door, but he didn't wait for a repeat.

The water was deeper now. Through the compartment, past the dead hand, into the next. He almost walked through the hole before he realized there was no more ship in front of him. Just a black gap where there'd been shell plating, and a waterfall roar outside.

The moans he'd heard while he was taking care of the black guy had stopped. He flashed the lantern around the compartment, then around the hole, fascinated by it. Half-inch steel had been bent inward and upward. The sea bulged in every time the ship dipped her bow. It sucked in the light, gleaming blackly. He shuddered, and returned to the search.

He found the second guy by stepping on him. Bernard hauled him up out of the water. He turned him over and pumped his arms. He'd done it a million times on the dummy. He got a weak cough and some retching. He turned him over and started work.

When he was breathing again, Bernard realized this one probably wasn't going to make it. He didn't have much left of his guts. He gave him the shot anyway. Then stood up, trying to remember what it was he'd been about to do.

Then he remembered.

There were five more syrettes in the kit. And no more wounded up here. He picked one up and started to open it. Then he realized he didn't seem to need it as badly as he had a half hour before.

He felt weird and light-headed, he was shaking, but he didn't seem to need a fix. He also realized then that the black man had been much bigger than he was, but he'd carried him out alone.

Tuh, he thought. Maybe this was that natural high you were supposed to get in danger. It was a primo rush, all right.

The bow dipped, the sea gurgled at his waist, and he started, suddenly realizing he had to get the guy out of here. He might die on the way, but for sure he'd drown here. They both would.

He got him up on his shoulders and began wading aft. Through the sonar compartment, the water deeper here, too. Dark ahead, he couldn't see the team's lights. He came to the door. It was closed and dogged, solid as a safe.

"Holy shit," he muttered. He slammed at it with the lantern. The bulb broke with sparks and a fizzing pop. Now he was in the dark. He could hear them hammering faintly on the far side, and realized the last pieces of shoring were going into place. "Holy shit," he said again, to the darkness, and the man on his back.

The light on his helmet. He fumbled around the weight pressing him down and got it on. It was dim but he could see enough to navigate by.

Phelan slogged his way forward again, through water to his chest, looking up at the overhead. Hoping for a scuttle, a ladder, any way to get out. There wasn't any.

"We got problems, man," he muttered to his burden.

When he reached the bow again, the gurgle was louder. Water streamed in, frothy-glowing, pulsing with weird green light. He shifted the body, hoping he wouldn't have to do what he was thinking about doing. But the sea was still rising. He had no way of knowing when it would stop.

He thought again of the morphine and knew that was impossible. He couldn't use now. Or he could, but it would be the last hit he ever took. He stuffed it into his pockets instead and threw the rest of the kit away.

The guy on his back had his Mae West on, like you were supposed to for GQ, but it wasn't inflated. Phelan rolled him off into the water and slapped his face. He moaned.

So he was still breathing. He unsnapped the life vest, pulled the collar over the guy's head, and popped the inflator.

Unfortunately, he didn't have one for himself. He was in excess, and there hadn't been any spares in the repair locker.

The ship seemed to be picking up speed now that the shoring was completed. The water coming in was swift and strong. Phelan bent into it. It ripped at his chest and tried to tear the life jacket from his hand. He held on grimly, fighting his way, till he lost his footing. The current punched him backward and he felt jagged steel slice his flesh.

He got up again and bulled forward once more, maddened now, screaming into the roar of the sea, and suddenly he was out, tumbling, sucked down helpless into a roaring void. His right hand struck out; his left cramped closed on his companion's heel. He wasn't going to let go. If they got separated, the poor bastard didn't have a prayer.

Too late, just before they were sucked into them, Phelan remembered the screws.

0225 HOURS: U.S.S. *TURNER VAN ZANDT*

Eight hundred yards away, *Van Zandt* staggered slowly away from her collision with the submarine.

At thirty knots her bow had bitten deep, but the damage went both ways. The impact sent her upward, over the pressure hull, crushing it down into the mud and sand. And then, backed by the incredible momentum of four thousand tons of steel, had kept going. The whole ship had groaned and shuddered, then pounded as the propeller chewed itself into junk against the sub's conning tower.

Now, as she drifted free, Dan felt her agony, her mortality, in the sluggish way she responded to Shaker's shouted orders.

The machine guns were still clattering from shore. And *Van Zandt*'s were still answering. There was no more heavy fire, though. Orange pyres soared upward from buildings and fuel dumps. They could see it all very clearly, see the tiny figures running about. Between bursts, they could hear shouts and screaming from the shore.

"Cease fire!" Shaker shouted, and voices repeated it. The .50s hammered a last burst and fell silent.

Shaker crossed to the intercom. He hesitated, then pressed the switch. "Main control, Bridge. Rick, are you there?"

"Main aye. What the hell's going on, Captain? Are we aground?"

"No. We rammed a submarine. I didn't mean to ride over it, but it was smaller than I thought. What's the status?"

"Well, I don't think we have a prop anymore, Captain. The shaft ran away and I just shut it down."

"You don't think we have power back there?"

The intercom hissed, but the chief engineer said nothing. In the background Dan heard the crazy seesaw whine of electronic alarms.

Shaker tried again. "Rick, we got to get out of here. See if you can deploy the bow thrusters."

"Stand by." Guerra was back in a moment: "Starboard unit's deploying. Port doesn't respond."

"Steve, take control of starboard APU. Give it all the power she'll take. Train it to zero-nine-zero and try to get us turned around," the captain snapped to Charaler.

Dan, meanwhile, had been punching buttons to get Loamer. The damage control assistant had bad news. The fire in chiefs' quarters was out of control. The AMR was still taking water. And his petty officers were reporting heavy damage and flooding from forward to midships.

Van Zandt drifted helplessly a mile offshore. They still had electrical power. They still had weapons, nearly a full magazine of sophisticated missiles. But they couldn't move. Dan faded back toward McQueen. The last fix showed them two hundred yards away from the mine field, and moving closer, set by the making tide and the slight wind that still came over the island.

"APU responds," said Charaler. "I'm coming right."

"Use the rudder, too," said Dan. "We're getting close to the mine field."

"Rudder's fucked, XO. Think it went the same place our prop did."

Pushed around by the bow thruster, an electrically driven auxiliary motor usually employed only for docking, the bow drifted right with agonizing slowness. They all stood silent, watching it. From back aft came a continuous low sound. It hardly seemed human. Dan remembered the shell that had hit the signal bridge. But there wasn't anything he could do. Other than try to get them all out of here.

He noticed then how the deck was gradually sloping under their feet.

What could they do? The alternatives were terrifyingly simple. With maybe two knots available from the APU, they might be able to beach her. If they could make way against the wind and tide. That would save the crew . . . but for captivity in Iran, if not execution in the heat of revenge. And the ship and all her weapons and electronics, codes and operating procedures, would fall into their hands, too.

The silence from shore could not continue. Disoriented by the attack, and probably still being jammed, they obviously thought both American ships had left. For a moment, he wondered whether Jakkal, missing them, might come back. Rig a tow. Then he remembered the smashed-in bow. *Adams* was damaged, too. She'd have her hands full getting out of range before daylight revealed her to Iranian aircraft.

He glanced at the silent silhouette of the captain, and knew he was pondering the same dilemma. "We got to get out of here, Ben," he muttered.

"No shit, XO, but how? This tide's picking up by the minute. It's all I can do to hold her where she is."

Dan took a deep breath and glanced again at the chart. Making sure it was the only choice left. It was.

"Captain, I recommend we go through the mine field."

There was nothing else. He didn't know how thick the mines were here. But at the speed they were making—creeping through, with no bow wave and very little noise—they just might make it. If they were lucky.

"Steady on—what do you recommend, Dan? Shortest path through."

"One-one-oh ought to do it, sir."

"Steady on one-one-zero," said Shaker. It sounded very loud. "Quartermaster, log that I have the conn for that last order and from now on."

"Aye aye, sir."

Dan went out to the wing for a quick look around. Behind them, a slowly distancing flicker now, the base burned on. The last firing had ceased. They didn't realize *Van Zandt* was still in the harbor. The paint job was working. As his eyes opened fully, he made out things in the water, and stiffened before he realized what they were. Debris from the anchorage, broken hulls, bodies, too, no doubt. He turned his face upward and shouted angrily, "Lookout!"

"Sir!"

"Have you reported this stuff? Report everything in the water!"

"Hell, sir, what difference does it make? We can't maneuver."

News traveled fast, Dan thought. "Report it anyway! You hear me?"

The voice turned fatalistic and persecuted. "Aye, XO."

"You've been doing a good job up there," he called. "Don't slack off now. Keep it up and we'll get home okay."

As he went inside, he heard the anonymous voice mutter, "Did you hear that? The fucking XO said I done a good job. Give me a break!"

He had to smile. Sailors would never change.

"There you are," said Shaker. "I'm passing the word for all hands not involved in damage control to get topside. I want them all up on deck. I need you to go down and see what kind of shape we're in."

"Okay."

"Check the bottom damage and see what progress we're making on the fires. You know what to do. Call me back soon as you can."

He saluted and went below. The hatches were opening and men were coming up. Quietly, in their battle dress and life jackets, not saying much. He noted that beside each DC fitting, sealing off each compartment from its neighbors, a petty officer stood, ready to close it instantly.

In DC central, Loamer sat at a table with four phone talkers. He looked much older than twenty-two tonight. The compartmentation diagrams were tacked up beside him, and he was drawing on them with a grease pencil. "How's she look, Percy?" Dan asked him.

"I think we're making headway. Repair Two's getting the fire in chief's quarters under control. They lost three men to smoke."

"Dead?"

"No, collapsed. They're back aft now; Doc's taking care of them along with the other wounded."

"How about the AMR?"

"That's not so good. We're flooding in five places and that's one of them. It's full to the access hatch. Unfortunately, that loses us a third of our bilge-pumping capacity." Loamer pointed to a diagram of the tanks and voids that lined the hull. "We're tore up bad, XO. Repair Three and Five are down there rigging eductors. It's not shell holes. I think it's split seams. I've got flooding boundaries set. What worries me"— he paused to scan a fresh message—"is the weight. That imposes a hogging stress. If the keel's been weakened, it may break her back."

Dan studied the diagram. Loamer was right. Hundreds of tons of water forward . . . "How about the other damage? Helo hangar, the hits to starboard?"

"Hangar fire's out. We got personnel casualties but the hull's sound there."

"Sounds like you're doing all you can. You know we're going through the mine field now. Knock off everybody you can to get topside."

"Okay, XO, but most of us snipes are gonna have to stay on station."

Guerra was one compartment aft, in main control. The engineering officer was glum. The engines were fine, but when he turned the shaft, there was no thrust. He could supply just enough power, with three generators running on battle short, for the fire pumps, interior lighting, and the APU. Dan told him the same thing, to get everybody out of the spaces who didn't have to be there, and left.

He came out in the central passageway to find himself in a makeshift aid station. The men lay on litters, moaning and some of them crying. There was blood on the deck, real blood, slick and glistening, and a first-class DK he bent over did not respond to his touch. He went out on the flight deck, saw Fitch and Golden at work, and didn't interrupt. Farther aft, sitting and lying about, the crew was silent, looking back toward the island. There was the flare of a lighter, but before he could say anything, three men near the would-be smoker had their hands over it.

He was turning, ready to head back to the bridge, when the forward half of the ship jumped. A gush of fire came out of the stack, momentarily lighting the entire flight deck. The blast shot flame a hundred feet out of the intake louvers.

He hoped, as he ran forward, that Guerra had acted swiftly. Whoever had been in the engine room would stay there, now, for good.

As he came past the midships area, he heard a cracking groan. Settling fast now, the frigate was breaking up. The superstructure was buckling as beneath it the hull folded like a jackknife. The men on the boat deck fell back, reaching for him, asking him what to do.

Dan told them to stand by, word would be passed.

Climbing the last ladder, he thought for just a moment of another time he'd run like this through a dying ship. On the

Reynolds Ryan. But *Ryan* had gone down in the midst of a task force. Friendly boats had been alongside minutes after she went down. While *Van Zandt* was sinking in hostile waters. Hours might go by before help could arrive.

A dull sound reverberated from the darkness, and he caught the ghostly glow of falling water. The column of flame had attracted attention from shore.

The bridge was dark. No power now. Shaker was standing by the steering console, looking down at the bow. Dan saw that the sea was licking around the bullnose.

"Captain, I'm back. Did we get a message off before we lost power?"

"Yes. I sent it out fleet broadcast and followed it up with an HF call."

"Do you think they'll understand? When we don't answer anymore?"

The captain looked wordlessly at him, and Dan thought, How blank his face is. The same look he'd seen on James John Packer's face that long-ago night: the look of the man who has lost everything.

Shaker was still thinking, though, because the next thing he said was "Did we get everybody up from below?"

"Not everybody, but I estimate three-quarters of the crew was topside when the mine went off. They're at their life-raft stations. I think we should start getting them clear."

"Mr. Charaler, pass that word on all the sound-powered circuits. Complete the muster, then abandon ship. Nearest friendly land—"

McQueen said quickly, "Fifty miles southeast, sir, coast of Dhubai."

"Pass it, Stever. Make sure Radio gets the word. It's not real deep here. That means emergency destruction charges on the crypto gear before they vacate. The rest of you in the pilot-house"—Shaker raised his voice, though everyone was still—"get the hell down on deck. Get aft. Help the wounded. Stick together. And good luck."

He turned away, and Dan saw him hesitate for a long moment. Then he went to the chart table. He took a position report form, scribbled on it for what seemed an interminable length of time. Finally, he held it out.

"Sir?"

"This is for you."

There were things he ought to be doing. He had to coordinate the muster, then get down on deck. . . . He stiffened as he realized what he was reading.

Admiral Hart: Lenson's testimony was the truth. Mine was not. I intended to fire a nuclear weapon against Iran. I have fought the ship hard and the men all did well. Please consider the matter closed. Very respectfully, Benjamin Shaker, Commanding, U.S.S. *Turner Van Zandt.*

He raised his eyes to Shaker's. The captain looked tired. Or maybe just resigned. "Thanks . . . Ben. But what does this mean? You're not leaving her?"

"All things considered, Dan, maybe it's best I stay."

"I hope you'll reconsider."

"Thanks, XO. Now cut the chatter and get hot."

"Aye, sir."

Buttoning the note into his pocket, Dan turned to go. He paused once, at the top of the ladder, looking back up into the darkened bridge. But Shaker, one shadow among the others now, had already vanished from his sight.

0210 HOURS: ABU MUSA ANCHORAGE

Lift a hand, dip it in the inky sea.

Drive a fin downward, then up, biting his bloody lip, stinging with salt, to keep from crying aloud.

Foot by foot, more slowly with each stroke, John Gordon fought his way toward the open sea.

His eyes were open but he could not be said to see. Loss of blood and a nearby shell burst had turned him from a man into a smashed, struggling insect, jerking across a darkened floor toward a hole to die in.

He'd stayed below after leaving the raft till the screaming hunger for air drove him up again to the flashes and detonations. The shadow that had tracked them, killed Everett, and wounded him was waiting thirty yards off, engines idling. Between them was the nose of the raft, bobbing weakly, like a dying seal. A light came on, swept across it, and reached out toward him.

He dived again. Finned away, angry at himself for ditching his gear. Now he was alone, hunted, and his only weapon was a knife.

He was down there when a sudden concussion squeezed him like a mouse in a cat's jaws. It shook him, then went on and on, an endless throbbing crush. It could only be the mines going off. He tried to count them, but somewhere in there his mind went black as the sea.

He came up again into the whine of props. The boat was on

him. The light came around. He ducked his head in reflex but was too exhausted to dive again.

This then was the end. He thought that dully, without much regret. At least he'd done his job.

He heard shouting from the boat, excited screams. For a moment, he was confused. No shooting? Capture? Then he raised his head.

To something terrifying and huge looming out of the night. To the whine of turbines and singing throb of huge props at maximum speed. To a destroyer, head-on, a huge black shadow above a phosphorescent roar.

It was almost on him when it heeled, showing him black length, and then the air above him exploded as her guns went off. Deafened, blinded, he tumbled helplessly in the bow wave, choking and fighting to stay on the surface. Sucked down, the screws would shred him with the pitiless efficiency of a garbage grinder.

He came up, whooping air in and out, and tried to inflate his vest. He had his hand on the stem when a second ship solidified from the night. As it roared by, he dove, driving himself down in weak panic, and stayed in the warm, dark womb of the sea for as long as he could. His ears throbbed to the hammering pulse of a single screw.

He came up and surged again in its wake. After a while, still unable to see for the flash-blindness, he got his vest inflated.

He turned on his back and began swimming again, weakly, away from the shore. Behind him the ships were outlined against the fires.

They were firing almost continuously. The great orange balls of flame lit up the island like flashbulbs.

And now he stopped swimming. His arms no longer moved. He was surprised he'd been able to for so long. He'd felt the wound through torn rubber after the ships passed. Half his buttock was blown away. No way to tourniquet or bandage it.

So that was that. He floated without thought. His leg no longer hurt. Had just stopped, almost magically, gone numb like his water-swollen fingers and feet.

He was no longer afraid. His mind was serene now. He was grateful for that. Blurry white sparks chased themselves across his eyeballs. Tracers, he thought dimly, then realized they existed only in his retinas.

He began to slip downward. There wasn't enough air in the vest to hold him up. He should inflate it, but the cartridge was exhausted, and he found he couldn't get the oral inflation valve to his lips. His head slipped under, and the sea closed over his open eyes.

Something animal in him fought him upward, and he floated exhausted at full length. But he knew he couldn't do that again. Where was he? Somewhere in the mine field. The tide . . . the tide would set him out through the length of it. The mines didn't worry him. A body wouldn't trigger them. But he was going the wrong way for the pickup. Drifting out, into the empty Gulf.

He knew then he would die out there.

Some time later, he heard a splash. Not far away. He opened his eyes again. He couldn't see anything there. Nor could he see the stars, nor the flames, though he knew they must exist. Loss of blood, he thought slowly. Optic nerve goes just before you lose consciousness.

Someone bumped into him. Arms struck him; there was a muffled grunt of surprise. "Hey," said a voice, guarded, suspicious.

"Hey," whispered Gordon.

"Hey, who're you? You from the *Adams*?"

The voice sounded young. Some sort of accent, not southern, definitely not New England. "No. EOD," Gordon said after a while.

The voice was silent for a time. Something exploded, back on the island, and he heard screams and dying groans from far off.

Gordon had an idea then. He gasped as a wave came over his face, coughed, then got it out. "You got a life jacket?"

"No."

"I do. Take it," he whispered.

"What? Hey, man, you might need it."

"Wounded. Can't swim anymore. Don't argue."

"Does it work?"

"Just blow it up . . . the valve."

Then he couldn't get any more words out, even whispering. The sea heaved warm under him, warm and dark and waiting.

Gordon felt the hands move over him. Velcro ripped as the waist strap came free. The hands supported him as they slipped it off. The plasticized nylon dragged cold over his face.

The mutter again, from miles away: "You really sure you don't need it?"

Gordon didn't answer. He heard the voice say something. "Thanks," he thought it was, but he couldn't be sure.

His strength had all vanished, leached away by the sea. But he held on for a moment, hoping he'd done well enough.

He hoped he'd been a good enough husband to Ola; a good

enough foster dad to Mike. For a moment, he worried about the herd. Then thought, They'll be all right. They'll be taken care of.

Then the last strength left him, and he felt himself slipping away.

John Gordon's last feeling, as his body dropped away, was regret. He wouldn't be buried in the earth. He regretted that. He'd loved it.

The golden glow behind his eyes was the same, he thought wonderingly, as a Vermont sunrise.

He smiled, ten feet down, watching the dawn.

36

The Southern Gulf

THE water was warmer than he'd expected. Stepping off the
stern had been like stepping into a Japanese bath. Hot, and
dark, and all but calm, roughened just a bit by the cat's-paws
of returning wind.

Dan sculled his hands gently beneath the blurry stars, looking back toward where they'd left the ship. He couldn't see her
anymore. The night was impenetrable, save for the vague
luminosities of the sky and sea, the amber quivering behind
them.

Back there, clearly visible, the island was still burning.

He floated comfortably, buoyed up by his half-inflated vest.
Behind him in the water were rafts, men, but they too were
engulfed by night.

He'd warned the petty officer at each abandon-ship station
not to show lights after they went over the side. Some had
already broken their wands, and in the cold luminescence their
faces were pallid and frightened. He told them to throw them
inside, and dog the hatches.

For a while then, the night was filled with stealthy sound. The
hollow crackle of inflating plastic, the plash and suck of waves,
and along the lifelines the crowding, the hesitation, and then
the plunge. There was confusion but no panic. He'd gone from
station to station explaining the plan. It was simple. Stay together, lashing the rafts, and make as much distance to seaward as they could before daybreak.

Unfortunately, some of the crew had left in advance of the
word. He was in search of them now, breaststroking along
downwind of the rest.

Now, alone, he stopped swimming and rested. No sense tiring
himself. The fever of battle had passed, leaving him prey to a
crumbling lassitude. As he drifted, tossing gently about, he
heard a rumble and looked up.

Two jets, so low he could see the flare of the exhaust, but darkened. No lights at all. They continued on over him, going south.

He gave himself two minutes, fighting back the craving for unconsciousness that came whenever he stopped moving. Then he began swimming again.

Some time later, a shape jelled from the sea darkness. He made up on it with a cautious, silent reach-kick-and-glide. There were probably Iranians out here, too, survivors of the boats they'd sunk. At last, he sensed himself face-to-face with it. He hesitated, then reached out.

His fingers sank into rubber, and within it, air. "Who's that?" he muttered.

"Crockett. And there's a couple storecreatures hanging off the other side. Who're you?"

"XO. Lenson."

"Hey, Commander."

"Evenin', sir. Come to join us by the pool?"

His lips twitched. He hoped they could keep that careless lilt in their voices. "Yeah. Don't drink up all the beer, okay? You guys get the word about lights?"

"No, what was it, sir? We didn't figure we ought to show any—"

"That's right. And stay quiet." Quickly, he explained, made sure they had an operating flashlight and compass, and pointed them back toward the main group. They told him they'd heard voices downwind, and after a few words of encouragement, he shoved off again. Behind him he heard the splash of paddles and hands as they began to move.

How warm the sea was . . . and bitter as aloes when a wave slapped his face. Salinity was high in the Gulf. That was good, the denser water would make it easier for the poor swimmers.

He thought, We're not doing too bad so far. He'd gotten all the wounded into rafts. And the warmth was a blessing. He remembered the North Atlantic, when *Ryan* went down. How after ten minutes in that liquid ice men's hearts simply stopped beating. They could last for hours in water like this. Till the sun came up.

Then their chances would start to drop. Slowly at first, then faster with every hour of exposure.

Mutter of voices ahead. They grew slowly louder as he swam, rested, swam. He was up on it before the rapid murmur made sense. ". . . full of grace, the Lord is with thee—"

"Don't let me interrupt, son. But who are you? Anybody else with you?"

"Hello, XO." They identified themselves: two firemen from "A" gang. They were both in life jackets. They'd relieved on a hose when Repair Five took smoke casualties, then gone topside after the mine blast. They didn't say why they hadn't waited for a raft and Dan didn't ask. He told them which star to head for to reach the others. One said, his voice like a sleepy child's, "Sir, we really socked it to 'em, didn't we? You think we'll get medals for this?"

"You will if I have anything to say about it."

"Commander, how soon ya think our guys will be out looking for us?" said the other. He sounded older, and more practical.

"I figure soon. The captain told me he got a message off that we were in trouble. And *Adams* will send one after they miss us at the join-up. I expect them at dawn. But for sure sometime tomorrow."

This was all true, but Dan didn't add what he feared: that the planes he'd heard overhead were Iranian. That a full-scale counterstrike was in progress, and the rest of the Middle East Force might be busier defending itself than rescuing survivors. There was no use burdening them with his apprehensions. "Anyway, they'll be here. As long as we stick together, we'll come out of this all right."

"Thanks, sir."

"Get going, now. Remember, the big blue star. I'm going to check over this way."

"So long, sir. Be careful."

He swam east. His arms were tiring and he switched to a clumsy crawl. The vest kept getting in his way. But he didn't want to deflate it. Every so often, he called out into the dark. His voice sounded harsh and desperate.

Finally he felt there must be no more men ahead. He stopped swimming and floated there, feeling the sting of some other drifting creature burning on his bare hands. The sea bobbed him like a fishing float, and the speechless wind cooled the sweat on his face.

Yeah, a hell of a lot better than the last time. Then he'd been cut and burned as well as freezing. He'd made it all right. But then he'd been responsible only for himself.

He hadn't seen Shaker since he left the bridge. And although he'd asked, no one else had seen him since the word to abandon went down. So he was in charge.

Thinking this, that he had some 150 human beings to bring through, he decided to turn back. Stop looking for stragglers and concentrate on welding together the remainder. He had to get them organized. Get the rafts lashed together. Appoint leaders. Put out rules on water. The little pop-up rafts didn't carry much, five gallons apiece, and they could be out here for a long time.

He pirouetted sluggishly around, and had taken his first stroke when he heard a sob. He lingered, holding his breath to hear better.

A cough, then a sob.

"Hey! Anybody there?"

"Yeah. Yeah! Over here. Help. Help!"

"Keep calling. Swim toward me."

Some minutes later, the man toppled off a wave into his arms. Lenson grabbed him, his fingers slipping on plasticized fabric. "Who is it?" he muttered. But the man was blubbering, about losing someone, then about a man who gave him something.

Dan dug into his shoulders and felt the wince. "Hey! Take it easy, fella. Just calm down. Who are you?"

The other had to try several times. Then he said, more clearly, "Phelan."

"Okay—*What?* What the hell are you doing here?"

"Who are you?"

"Lenson."

"Jesus. *Van Zandt.* I was swimming for you, then I couldn't see the ship anymore. But I'm sorry—I lost the guy—he didn't come up with me—and then the other guy, I was getting ready to steal his life jacket, and instead he gave it to me—"

Phelan started sobbing again. Dan floated beside him, holding him, wondering which of them was going mad. He didn't have any idea how the hospitalman had gotten here, or what he was raving about. But he was another man, and he needed help.

Dan got him calmed down and aimed back toward the group. He waited for a few minutes more, calling out, then decided that was it.

He turned again, and began swimming back to his men.

He was back in Philly, in the old house, and he'd discovered a secret room in the basement. Everything from his childhood was there. He stared astonished at his old books, his old toys, the model battleships he'd painted so lovingly and, he saw now, so clumsily. The house was still and he knew peace, knew somehow his father would never be drunk again, would never beat them or threaten them. Bill Lenson was never coming back.

He was recalled to reality by a clatter. He turned on his back, floating, and looked ahead. The group wouldn't be far away now.

Fireworks blazed cheerfully over the water, floating upward, then drifting down in a pyrotechnic rainbow. He stared at the falling stars, his face dreamy and empty. Then, suddenly, he blinked.

Simultaneously came the hum of a motor. It wasn't loud, but over the sigh of the *shamal*, increasing in strength as they left the island's lee, it was chillingly clear. It was the familiar drone of bass boats on lazy August afternoons. He couldn't see lights. Probably they weren't showing any. Then, just for a moment, they did. A searchlight glinted out. It moved here and there, then steadied on a patch of sea.

The gun clattered again, three short bursts and then a longer one.

Dan began swimming again, feeling now a sudden acceleration of the heart, a sudden dryness in his mouth that wasn't from thirst. Not away from the light. But toward it.

It had moved off by the time he reached them. For one horrible moment, seeing no one in the rafts, he thought they were all dead. He began to shake as he came close enough to hear. Their groans and screams made it all too plain what had happened.

They were in the water. They'd abandoned the life rafts. When one drifted by and he felt it, he understood. It was soggy, deflating. His stomach cramped with nausea and rage.

When he called out several voices answered at once. "XO here," he called. "Cluster up here with me. Did they try to get you to come aboard? Ask you to surrender? Or just start firing?"

"Just started shooting soon's the light hit us, sir."

"Don't let the rafts go!" he shouted. "Keep them even if they're damaged. Bring them over here."

Gradually, the group recoalesced, sailors on the outskirts calling in those who'd swum off. They had only two fully inflated rafts left. Dan ordered their occupants into the water and got the wounded hoisted into them. Some of them were unconscious and it was a struggle to get them up.

He called out for corpsmen then, but only one voice answered. After a moment's thought, he told Phelan okay, to get in the raft with the wounded, find the medical supplies, and get to work.

He was hanging panting on the hand line after hoisting the last man up when doubt hit him. Was he doing the right thing? The Pasdaran were still out here. He couldn't hear engines, but they might be shut down. Listening. Wouldn't it be better to split up? Scatter the survivors and trust to luck?

Then he thought, Either way, we'll lose some. If we split up, the weak, the wounded won't make it. Let's just do the best we can together.

"Commander, hey, it's Stanko."

"Hi, Boats."

"Huxley here."

"Hi, Chief Warrant."

Jimson, Dorgan, Charaler, and Proginelli made their way gradually to him. He couldn't make out features, but their voices, though roughened by smoke and salt water, were reassuring. He asked about the department heads. Al Wise was in the water on the far side of the group. Rick Guerra had made it out of Main Control but was badly burned. No one had seen Pensker and Brocket.

He raised his voice over a growing mutter. "Listen up! How many people we got? Count off, starting nearest me."

There seemed to be between 100 and 110, but some didn't answer. He wished he could show a light. There must be more beyond the range of their voices. They'd gone over the side mustering 142. Where were the rest?

It was shortly after that the engines started up again. "Uh oh," said a voice near him. He sculled around, fearing the worst.

The searchlight was on again. It skated slowly over the water, probing in their direction.

A man swam up to him, bumped him. "Commander," he said, gasping, as if he didn't swim very well.

"Who is it?" Dan whispered.

For answer, something hard was shoved into his stomach. His hands moved downward to take it. "It's Lewis. I brought one of the M-14s, sir. We can get one or two of them, anyway."

His fingers examined the rifle beneath the water. His thumb caressed the stock. For a moment he was tempted. Then reality supervened. He opened his hands, bobbing up as the weight fell away. "No good, Frank. If we fire back, they'll kill all of us. Let's just play to survive."

A hundred yards away, the light flickered off the waves. The engine rumbled, creeping toward them. He lifted his voice cautiously. "Keep your heads down. Play dead. Pass it on."

The muttered warning moved away in a widening circle and was lost in the growing burble. Over it, he could hear voices in Farsi. And the clank of a breech block feeding rounds.

The waves turned from blackness to a glittering cobalt. The wavering circle of light moved toward him, and he felt it on his neck like a blade as he put his face down, willing his body to stillness. For twenty or thirty seconds, he undulated limply,

counting his heartbeats as the round green brilliance, like a
huge all-seeing eye, hovered above him. But he couldn't stand
it, waiting for the firing to begin.

He turned his head, putting one eye above the water, to
watch death bear down on him in a thirty-foot boat. It grew at
the edge of his sight, then suddenly became not a shadow but
a hull, a curved nothingness blocking out the heavens. The
waves knocked hollowly against fiberglass. In his submerged
ear, the propeller whined a high note with a metallic edge, like
a wire poked into an electric fan.

"Kasy as anha mebeny?"

"Faghat mordha."

There was a sodden thud as the bow struck flesh. Dan heard
it gasp; the Iranians apparently didn't. The motionless bundle
slid along the hull and in the backwash from the light, he saw
it spinning in the wake.

The propeller increased its tempo. The boat moved past them.
The light lifted and moved ahead. He raised his nose for a
breath, and heard the same sigh around him.

The boat moved over the curve of sea and out of sight. They
were alone again under the stars.

He sculled gently, trying to master the terror that had
purged his bowels. Deep breaths, three, four. There were other
things to think about now. So let's think about them, Lenson.
Such as what? Such as Shaker. And Pensker.

No. He grabbed his mind like the wheel of a truck and turned
it into a different road. All that was past. Benjamin Shaker had
paid his forfeit. He was beyond punishment or revenge. Nor
had the black lieutenant answered up to their verbal muster.
For the rest of the night, he had only one thing to think about.
And that was, how to save as many of the men around him as
he could.

"Chief McQueen," he called.

"Here, sir."

"Swim over here, Mac, we got to talk."

It took the older man a while. Dan worried: Was he failing
already? But his voice sounded strong when he got to him.
"Yessir."

They went over the situation. High-tide slack had been at
0130. That meant—he lifted his arm, 0347—they were into the
ebb now.

Like any body connected to the sea, the Gulf went through
the tidal cycle. It had peaked early that morning and now it was
going out, a billion tons of water walking sluggishly out into

the Indian Ocean through Hormuz. The chief quartermaster remembered max ebb around Abu Musa at two knots, bearing east by northeast. Dan liked the direction but thought three knots was more accurate. They compromised at two and a half.

A wave hit them and he sputtered, grasping the back of McQueen's life jacket. It felt like one of the kapok models, great for the first few hours, but with a bad rep for waterlogging. He hoped there weren't too many of those out here. "Okay, but isn't there a counterclockwise current, too? I think I saw something like that in the *Sailing Directions*. That'd swing us left, toward Iran—"

"Nosir. Wrong month."

"Okay." He tried to picture it; realized too late he should have brought a chart down from the bridge with him. Well, paper wasn't much good after a couple hours in the water. But still he felt guilty. He closed his eyes and concentrated.

Fifty miles off Dhubai, but the tide was setting them parallel to, rather than toward, the coast. The Gulf looked crowded on an NTDS display, twenty miles to the inch. To men in the water it took on a different scale. It was at least seventy-five miles to the Strait. At two and a half knots, that'd be what, thirty hours.

No, damn it, his mind wasn't working. They wouldn't drift that way for thirty hours, or even ten. The tide would just slide them northeast for six hours, then start sliding back. Except for whatever component the wind introduced to their motion vector, ten hours from now they'd find themselves back in the Abu Musa anchorage. At one in the afternoon.

McQueen had reasoned to the same conclusions. They agreed that the best strategy was to get the group moving south. The Mubarek oil terminal lay in that direction, as did the Dhubai merchant traffic. The wind would help, too. If they could make five or six miles by noon, then they'd be out of view of the island.

Dan didn't like it. The wounded couldn't swim. They had to be towed. That would slow the group down. The only other thing to do was leave them. And he wouldn't do that. Should he sink the last rafts, make them harder to see? That would mean putting wounded, bleeding men in the water. He decided to wait till dawn before making that decision.

Dan looked up at the stars for a while.

Then he passed the word to start swimming.

The first peach tint of day showed him heads around him. To the west they were lost in darkness. It was still night back there. But where the oily, gently heaving surface absorbed the first light, he could see black dots, like drifting coconuts.

Like them all, he was swimming, counting dully in his head. His arms moved mechanically, grabbing water and shoving it behind him, like a tiredly digging dog. And like the rest, he made very little way.

They'd tied themselves together around the rafts. They had five left, two inflated, the others with only a breath or bubble remaining. These the men simply towed, using their lashings, keeping them for the water and supplies; there was no one in them.

He'd looked forward for weary hours to the sun. For one thing, it would make it easier to swim in the right direction. The unwieldy organism around him had a hundred legs, a hundred arms, and when he got tired or confused among the stars, it drifted off course and then, when he tried to reorient it, stopped dead.

But when the bloody ball heaved itself into view he realized he'd been wrong. Even the first red paring, suddenly popping over the curved edge of sea, burned his salt-tenderized skin. Above it, he noted the wispy lines of contrails. Aircraft or missiles.

It was going to be another hot one.

"XO."

Proginelli. The familiar face was puffy and the eyes reddened. Dan slacked a little to let him catch up, and also to rest.

"Sir, the corpsman, he asked me to tell you three of the wounded died during the night. One of them was Rick Guerra."

Lenson grunted wordlessly. He'd miss the stocky, close-mouthed engineer.

"What are we doing, sir?"

"Swimming, Tad, just swimming south."

"What's down that way? Shouldn't we go for the strait? Where are our ships? We ought to head for our ships."

Patiently, Dan explained it to him. Raising his voice, knowing the others would swim better if they knew. The men weren't talking much. Just an occasional word. They all looked worn.

He called a halt at 0600. They gathered around the rafts and the corpsman shared out water, crackers, and a piece of chewing gum to each man.

Dan pulled himself up and stood briefly, his feet sinking into the soft unsteady floor. Some of the wounded cried softly, like pigeons. Others lay unmoving. They all had bandages and some had writing on their foreheads. Apparently Phelan was doing

his job. Dan glanced at him; he was tipping water into the little
cup, frowning over it as if it were liquid silver. His hands were
shaking but he didn't spill any.

The scene reminded him suddenly, incongruously, of a painting he'd seen once. Naked men on a wooden raft, and in the
distance, a ship.

There was no ship here, though. He shaded his eyes and
recalled himself. To the west, sure enough, the island. Maybe
twelve miles away. Through the morning shimmer, he could
make out Jabal Halwa, its outline changed from the night
before. To north, east, south . . . he searched long and carefully
but found only weird garbled mirages, shimmering and running
together like dark mercury. Too bad; he'd hoped to see something over toward Mubarek, if only the tops of the flare-off
towers.

He squatted then, and waited till they had their gum unwrapped and in their mouths. Then he lifted his hand, and they
quieted, looking up at him, a gently jostling seethe of inflamed
conjunctiva, stubbled cheeks, twitching or chewing lips. There
was something like hatred in a few of those eyes. Here was
disbelief, there emptiness, there delirium. Most of them,
though, held only suffering and a trust that made it hard for
him not to turn away.

Was it worth it, this pain, this madness? Men destroyed and
were destroyed, for . . . for what? Oil, religion, patriotism
. . . but no one who died won anything. He raised his eyes to the
empty sky, blurry and vague but immensely far and high. Suddenly it all seemed insane, purposeless, and absurd.

But when he looked down again their eyes were still on him.

"Okay guys, *Van Zandt*'s still together, and we're still alive.
I'd hoped by now there'd be people out looking for us. But it
looks like we'll have to wait a while yet for that."

The corners of his mouth were cracked. Each word hurt. But
he made himself go on. They needed to hear him. Especially this
next. "It's a little past max ebb now, but we'll be going east
with the current for another couple hours yet. Then it'll start
moving us back toward Abu Musa."

Several voices exclaimed. He went on, raising his: "That's
right, right back where we started. So you see why we got to
keep swimming. As soon as we see a plane or a friendly ship,
we'll fire a flare. But there's one place on earth we don't want
to go back to. So we got to swim like hell for the next few
hours."

Nobody disagreed. Dan asked them to join him in the Lord's

Prayer. When it trailed off into the disagreement of Protestant and Catholic he stood up again, looked around, and then swung himself back down into the water. This time it felt cool, after the quickly heating air.

The sun lit the inside of his skull even through closed eyelids. The heat grew steadily as it rose. The sea heaved and around him he heard men being sick. From time to time, someone would lose control, and wailing or despairing, weak curses would live for a moment in the heated air before it too ebbed back into silence and the slow splash of many hands.

His arms felt like wet wool, and he could barely pull himself from group to group. The membranes of his nose and throat burned and his tongue was swelling. The bitter water submerged his head every so often as he swam, stinging like iodine. His skin was raw where his clothes rubbed. He'd given McQueen his ball cap. The older man's bare scalp was already blistering.

The swells were heavier now. The wind had come up with dawn. That was good. What he feared was a calm. They'd be broiled alive. The more wind, the more southing. If they weren't so close to the island, he'd hoist a sail on the raft.

Once again, for the hundredth time, he searched horizon and sky. Where were the ships? The planes? The helicopters?

Had *Van Zandt* and her crew been forgotten?

Was the United States Navy still in the Gulf?

Around eleven the wind veered, slackened, then died entirely. When the sun was at its height he called a halt. The crawling mass of men, barely inching for hours now, drifted to a stop. They rolled on their backs. Few spoke, and those only in dry, harsh notes like ravens.

Dan waited till last for his drink. It made no impression on the desert in his throat. He tried to think of something else. How long should they rest? They needed rest. He decided twenty minutes would be okay.

Leaning his head back on the vest, he fell into a doze. The swell jostled him gently up and down and bumped him from time to time against other bobbing bodies. Only his head, covered now by his skivvy shirt, protruded above the water. The tropical sun blazed above the ocean, but by dousing the cloth occasionally, someone had discovered you could stay cool.

Some time later, he was awakened by a voice not yet too tired to be terrified. "Shark. Shark!"

He jerked the cloth from his sight, heart battering suddenly into his first real terror. He'd feared a bullet, the tearing shock of a machine-gun slug. But somehow this seemed more horrible.

"Where away?" he shouted. Extended hands showed him nothing. He hoped for a moment they were imagining it.

Then he, too, saw it, rising between two crests. Not in the curving dive of a porpoise. This fin simply rose, glided along atop an indigo darkness, and then sank again.

He saw a second fin and felt his bones freeze. He remembered what had happened to the crew of the *Indianapolis*. "Close up," he shouted. Other voices, McQueen's, Stanko's, were shouting it already. The men, who had drifted apart during the rest period, grouped again, splashing and yelling hoarsely.

"Stay together . . . link your arms, face out . . . kick at 'em when they get close."

The rafts rocked lazily on a glutinous sea. The sun glittered from a million waves, shimmered and sparkled. Far to the west, the black mass of the island seemed to draw them back toward it, like an immense magnet.

The dorsals slipped sinuously through the chop, drawing rapid glittering wakes behind them. In the waiting silence he could hear the ripple. Beyond them, a single cloud gleamed like spun fiberglass.

A man cried out at the edge of the group. The linked line bucked. "Kick it!" "Kick his fuckin' head in, Tony!"

"What we going to do, sir? Just let them eat us?"

Dan knew what he wanted. He moved back to the raft, every cell of his frightened flesh wanting to get out of the water. God, how safe he'd feel up there! But he had to dangle his legs like bait, waiting for teeth in them, and croak, "Doc, get the bodies ready to go over."

"You sure about that, sir?"

Suddenly he was so angry he could barely choke out words. He wanted to murder whatever had created a world so cruel and stupid. "No fucking back talk, Phelan! You want them to eat live men or dead ones?"

"Aye, sir."

The corpses slid into the sea with a sullen splash. Then fell behind as the group, pursed tight around the rafts, began swimming again. Dan tore his eyes from the humped backs, facedown in the water. He knew them both.

To his surprise, the sharks left, staying with the bodies. He was glad to lose sight of them before the feeding began. The island hung on the horizon. The sun hung in the sky as if it was nailed there.

He looked at his watch. Thirty minutes. He squinted around, sealing and then ripping his eyelids apart, and got them all headed south again.

He was crawling blindly when excited voices woke him. He did not see immediately the transparent bladder floating toward him. It was almost on him before he understood, and jerked away. His first thought, as always, was of a plastic sandwich bag scudding over the waves. They spent an hour picking their way through the fleet of drifting, deadly men-of-war.

When they were clear, he called another halt. He turned over and floated, his breath a rusty hacksaw in his throat, gradually freeing him from the prison of his body.

Abu Musa was visible every time a swell lifted him. But thank God, they'd made southing. Better than he'd expected; or else the current had taken mercy on them. It was at least six miles away. From this low in the water, he couldn't see the beach or the roadstead, so he couldn't tell what the Pasdaran were doing. There was still smoke rising from the southern end. Behind him the men clustered around the rafts. Once voices rose to a gabble, and he understood dully that Phelan had spilled a cupful of water.

He was debating whether to go on. The brine flamed steadily in his face and hands. He touched his eyes; they were swollen, tender as wounds. There seemed to be pus left on his fingers, but he couldn't see them well enough in the glare to be certain.

Losing so many rafts put them in a bad position. They could survive without food for many days, but not more than two, he judged, without water. Their existence was dependent hour by hour on luck.

He'd never have believed men could drift through nearly a day in the southern Gulf and not see a tanker. Where were they when you needed one? The sharks wouldn't stay away forever.

Then he remembered the contrails. The last time there'd been a big U.S.–Iran mix-up, all traffic had stopped.

Now, that was a depressing thought.

For the first time in his life, he was confronted with the question each man must face one day: whether it was worth the effort to keep on. His whole body either stung from salt or sunburn or was numb from immersion and hours of swimming. His swollen hands were splitting. The heat was deadly, and there was no shade. They were sweating away more water than they were drinking.

He thought briefly of increasing the allowance. But he didn't know whether he should. His swollen tongue, his parched esophagus said yes. The rules said no. They advised going without for the first day. But that couldn't have been written for the Gulf. If Phelan hadn't been doling out water every couple of hours, the men would be delirious.

Was it worth the pain? What did he have to live for? He thought of Blair. But it had been all too short. Good while it lasted, but the memory failed to move him much. To see Nan grow up, that meant more.

It meant . . . but then he remembered she was all but grown now. She wasn't a baby he had to protect anymore. He only saw her two, three times a year as it was. Her foster father would be happy to occupy whatever foothold in her heart still belonged to him.

No, she'd grow up fine without him. Fine and beautiful and happy.

He didn't have to stay for her.

In the end, all he came up with was the men around him. Dan Lenson didn't matter. There were billions of others as worthy of life as he was. There were thousands of lieutenant commanders in the Navy. He probably wasn't the best for this job. He could think of several who'd be better.

At the moment, though, he seemed to be the only one on the scene. The only one here, and in command.

So, let's think . . . just keep going south, that still seemed to be the best plan. By the next cycle of tide, if the sharks stayed away, they might be far enough out to risk raising a sail. They'd move a lot faster then.

Around him the men prayed in guttural murmurs, their blistering lips unable to grasp the words.

He must have passed out, or gone to sleep, for a while. When he woke Phelan was leaning over him from the raft. His stubbled face was copper-dark, dripping with sweat. "Your turn, man," he whispered.

"What?"

The aluminum cup came over the turgid curve and made for his lips. He tilted his head and let it, God, let it come cool and fresh down his tongue and throat. He squeezed his eyes shut, almost crying when he realized that was all.

"You're doing a good job, Hospitalman," he whispered.

"Thanks, sir." Phelan stared down; Lenson saw something strange in his eyes. "Sir?"

"What?"

"I haven't used any of it. I gave it all to the wounded. It's all gone now."

Dan didn't know what he was talking about, but he nodded anyway. "That's good," he whispered. "Keep it up."

"What's next, sir?" muttered someone behind him.

"Let's get swimming again," he said.

They swam till four. Some of the men reported sea snakes. Dan saw two. Vermilion and gold in a lapis sea. A couple of feet long, they were deadlier than cobras, but if you were alert, you could fend them off before they got their teeth into you.

They lost Dorgan. He was drowsing when one bit him on the web of his thumb. The chief storekeeper took several hours to die. But for most of that he was paralyzed and said nothing, just stared blindly up from the raft.

Some of the men were raving now. Dan could no longer force himself to move. His arms were dead. And it seemed that no one else could do better.

He knew now how Shaker had felt, there at the end.

He should have turned them around, brought them ashore, and surrendered.

He didn't pass an order to, but they all stopped, anyway.

He floated there, eyes fixed and staring. After a while, he saw a silver train rolling along the horizon. He knew it wasn't there. But still he could see every detail. Why wasn't it real? How could you tell?

They drifted on the sea. The wind had stopped again and now every breath was like drawing in melted metal or superheated steam. They had no more moisture in their bodies. The island floated shimmering in the western sky, a magic land no one could reach. In silence now, together but each man alone, they waited motionless for death.

Out of the dream, out of the delirium, he peered into a hell of light.

The sun was drowning in a sea of blood. Red sparkled from the sea and stained the clouds. The star that had tortured them since dawn hung just above the horizon, its rays flogging them to the last. And to the north, a black mass cutting the sea in two, the brooding, distant double peak.

The sea was filled with dying and nothing he did could change it. It was immense and never ending. For a while, the waves would toss these bundles of flesh. Then they would die one by one, and slip away, back into the eternal recurring of the tide.

And become part of it again. Part of the gulf that sucked into itself all life, and gave forth all life, over and over again unto infinite time.

Here at the end, he did not find he really minded.

His eyes were sinking closed when he saw something move, out in the dying glow.

It was dark at first against the bloody and hurtful light. Later he saw that it was neither black nor red. Its ends rose to absurd points. There was a stick on top of it. There were men on it, bent peacefully over what looked like animal cages.

Dan blinked sleepily at it. Its bow shattered the sea into a million glowing drops of blood. It moved across the face of the dying sun, and its shadow reached out across the darkling sea. Around him no one moved; perhaps no one else saw it.

And he wondered for a time, between sleep and death, whether he was imagining it. It was the kind of thing one might imagine, adrift, facing another night. But the funny thing was he could hear it, too. The hollow faint *pung-pung-pung* of an old-fashioned single-cylinder engine. It heeled gradually as it went by them, sea creaming under the prow, headed southeast, toward Dhubai.

He pulled himself very slowly, as if in a dream, to the raft. A bare foot stuck over, rose-colored by the declining sun, reflected in the still indigo beneath.

Phelan was asleep or unconscious. He didn't move when Dan shook him. Nor could he get words around his swollen tongue. He thrust his arm over the inflatable's side and groped in the bottom.

It took a long time to find it and he cursed in his head, squeezing his eyes shut in weakness and anger and fear. But at last his sea-softened fingers closed on plastic. He thrust an arm through the netting, turned, and raised his hand.

The flare departed with a hollow crack, igniting as it left the barrel. The cherry-red ball of flame arched upward, brighter than the sinking sun, over the foredeck of the dhow, and disappeared.

For a moment nothing happened. Then the figures straightened, calling out in high, excited voices. One whirled, stretched up to tiptoe, pointing. The others turned, too, and looked out toward him with comically open mouths. One wore what looked like a white nightshirt.

Then, to his tired horror, Dan saw that they were arguing. One pointed ahead; others gesticulated. At last, an old man with the beard of a Sistine God appeared from inside the wheel-

house. Shading his eyes, he looked down for what seemed like
eternity. Then turned his head toward the helmsman.

The bow dipped, and the boat slowed, then foreshortened.

It was coming toward them.

He felt his men pushing him, hitting him, expressing with
weak blows what their swollen tongues could no longer utter.
He couldn't respond, either. He was glad they were happy. His
eyes were too dry for tears. They felt as if they were bleeding.

It was all he could do, when the rough splintered wood rose
above them in the final light, and the sinewy brown arms
reached down, to wave, weakly, for the others to go first.

V

THE AFTERIMAGE

Manama Airport, Bahrain

B LAIR sat curled in the royal lounge, flipping through the summer issue of *Global Affairs*. The staid blue-bound pages, once so penetrating in their strategic and economic analysis, their subtle explications of the issues beneath the headlines, now seemed abstract, pretentious, even callous.

They hadn't changed. She had. And she wasn't sure, yet, what she was becoming.

She sighed, and set it aside. Glanced at her watch. Stretched, lifting clenched fists, and then unfolded herself.

The hostess came over, offering tea, coffee, Perrier with a twist. She declined.

Standing at the window, she looked out and down.

Below her was the flat expanse of tarmac, inked with the black cryptographs of each arriving flight. And beyond it, the Gulf, blue and smooth today as the ribbon a mother twists around a little girl's braids. Silver aircraft trundled along feeder strips. A 747 bulged into view, Air India bound east for Delhi or Bombay. It gathered speed with ponderous slowness, then lifted its nose and drifted upward, folding its wheels delicately as it dwindled to a receding spark.

She was waiting for Bankey Talmadge's charter. Four of the most powerful men in the country would be with him, coming to review the conduct of the Gulf-wide battle that had followed the strike at Abu Musa. Three-quarters of the remaining Iranian navy and air force had sortied from their ports and airstrips, attacked, and been wiped from the sea and sky by the missiles, guns, and aircraft of the Middle East Force, the Indian Ocean Battle Group, and the French and British task forces. Two U.S. ships had been damaged, and one Tomcat from *Forrestal* hit; the crew had ejected into the Gulf of Oman and been picked up by helicopter.

She stared out, her mind turning analytical. An exhausted and isolated dictatorship had lost its final gamble to prevail. Now peace had to be made. But not just any peace. She wanted no cease-fire, no temporary armistice, but a fair and durable settlement that would benefit the region and the West alike. It would not be a quick process, nor a simple one. The military had made it possible. Now diplomacy had to make it real.

And then, without warning, she was thinking of herself.

She was still standing there when she saw a drab-green military transport taxiing in. She leaned into the glass. Below her men in whites and khakis leaned or squatted in the building's shade. Three of them stood apart. One was tall, brown-haired, very thin.

She turned suddenly. The attendant jumped to her feet, looking startled. She said, "I'll be right back, please watch my things," and her heels clicked briskly on marble.

Dan was standing a few feet from the chiefs and officers, sweating in the baking heat of buildings and asphalt, when the C-130 swung into view. McQueen was briefing him on the wounded; he'd just come back from the hospital. "They think they'll all pull through," the quartermaster concluded. "Rest, that's all they need now. The docs said they'll be ready to follow us in a few more days."

"Good," he said. He had to feign interest. Since they'd been picked up, he'd felt an immense apathy. He didn't understand why. Maybe it was just fatigue.

The chief left. Jack Byrne, beside Dan, tilted his head back, peering at him. His eyes were invisible behind the sunglasses. "Well, friend," he said. "I'd say you did all right. In spite of your unlucky choice of commanding officers."

"How can you say that, Jack? He got your sub for you, didn't he?"

"Could be we needed you both, then. A hundred and ten survivors, after two days in the water . . . there wouldn't have been near that many without leadership. And some fast thinking, too, I understand."

"The men did it themselves, mostly. But thanks."

"Well, gotta go. People to meet. Flesh to press. Good luck back in the States. Maybe we'll run into each other again." The intel officer hesitated. "That is, if you're planning on staying in, after this."

"I guess I'll ride it out, Jack. If they still want me." He grinned faintly. "Luck's got to change one of these days."

Byrne smiled. He nudged Dan's shoulder with his fist. Then turned quickly away.

He heaved a sigh and glanced around. "Al. Steve—"

Wise and Charaler stood up. The ops officer looked weak, but fit. The redheaded first lieutenant looked rumpled as ever, despite new uniform shoes in place of scuffed combat boots.

"Have the men fall in, please, and get them mustered. We'll be boarding as soon as they refuel. Do it manifest-style. Names, rates, and socials."

He was searching his mind for anything else he ought to do when he saw her. She was standing by the door to the terminal, shading her eyes against the sun.

"Keep an eye on things," he said. "I'll be back in a minute."

"Yessir." The officers glanced at each other and then turned for the tarmac. A moment later, Stanko was shouting, "Getcher meat on your feet, barf bags! Next stop, U.S. of A.! Get those duffels in the cart! Those who can, help those who can't. Fall in for muster!"

Blair felt her legs begin to tremble as he came toward her, out of the heat and light and sound of engines. His face and arms were coated with white ointment. His left hand was bandaged. He walked cautiously, as if he'd just returned from a long time in space.

"Hello, Dan."

"Blair." He came to a stop a few feet away, then moved sideways to find the shade. He took off his cap and rubbed his hand over his forehead, smearing the paste. "You're looking well."

"Thanks. Is that your plane?"

He glanced back. The fat green body was fitting itself cautiously into the loading area, like a ship into a dry dock. "Yeah."

"You're going home?"

"Bethesda, for recuperation. Then there'll be some kind of inquiry, I imagine. Depending on how that comes out . . . either civilian life, or else the next duty station." He smiled faintly.

"I'm glad you came through," she said.

"I lost a lot of men."

"I know. Hart worried about you. But he just couldn't divert anybody to search during the attack." She paused. "The strike, and sinking that submarine . . . your captain was very brave."

"He was a good man," said Dan. He considered saying more, but he didn't.

"And I think it was worth it."

"Was it?"

"I think so. The remaining Boghammers have been with-drawn from Farsi Island. We have a report through Syria that Rafsanjani is going to ask for a cease-fire tomorrow in the UN."

"Good," he said. But the way he said it bothered her. He looked away from her, toward the men. They were forming straggling ranks, handicapped by canes and crutches. She lis-tened for a moment to the gut-deep, ancient martial chant as the names snapped out, the "Present," "Yo," or "Here" as each individual answered for himself.

He turned back to her. "Are you going back with us?"

"No. I'm here to meet the senator. We've got to review our policy in the light of our—" She stopped herself; she'd almost said "victory." "Of changed circumstances. It looks like now we'll be able to reduce our commitment honorably. We'll be here for a few days, I imagine, and then it'll be back to the Hill."

"Will I see you again?" he said, shading his eyes, and she caught her breath.

Suddenly his arms were around her. She held lightly, trying not to hurt him, trying not to cry.

"Do you want to?"

"Yes."

"Then you can. I want you to. I've learned something here. In the Gulf."

"What's that?"

"I'm not sure how to say it yet. Maybe just that people mat-ter. More than anything else."

He held her for a moment longer, his arms tightening till she could hardly breathe. There were howls and wolf whistles from the battered crew of *Turner Van Zandt.* He turned his head toward them, and the tumult died; they shuffled their feet and examined their shoelaces. But Blair saw his eyes crinkle be-neath the frown, softening, changing to something that looked, if you saw it this close, not far from love.

"What happened to your hand?" she said into his ear.

"Your fingers swell, when you're in the water too long," he said. "Remember my Academy ring? They had to saw it off."

And then the whistles started again, and kept on and on.

When she was gone, he turned suddenly and walked back to-ward the formation.

He stood by the ladder, watching his men board. So many faces he missed, faces he'd never see again. Ben Shaker. Terry Pensker. Doc Fitch. Rick Guerra. Chief Dorgan. And so many others. Enginemen, electronic repairmen, boatswains, mess specialists, yeomen, seamen, firemen. He nodded back at Phelan, whose dark face was burned swarthier than ever, his cheeks drawn. The hospitalman had refused medication. He was still facing charges. Now, though, Dan felt he had something to go to bat for him with.

Behind the Indian, a stocky dark man nodded to him. Dan searched his memory for a moment before he recognized him, the graying older fellow, and the mustached blond. Maudit, Terger, Burgee. The divers had joined them during the long night, fought off sharks and sun and snakes with them, until they had come through. He smiled back. They weren't *Van Zandt*, but without them, they'd never have made it in.

He was proud of them all.

Along with Schweinberg and Hayes and Kane. With those who'd died in the water to get them into Abu Musa. With all those who had died for a people who were no longer sure, in their hearts, that their defense was necessary or even moral.

But it looked like—if what Blair said was true—this time they'd held the line.

Not that it was anything grand, any crusade or redemption. It had been just a little war in a far place and it would soon be forgotten. Except for those who'd been there, and the families of the dead.

In the land of their enemies, in their souks and places of council, they would shrug and say, It is the will of Allah.

But it wasn't.

Suddenly his apathy gave way to a vast anger against those who sent men to make wars, whatever their names or cultures, whatever piece of cloth they wore. It was the final obscenity. To send others out to kill for you, and necessarily to die.

For over both sides, above all arched the same sky. Limitless, sweltering, crowded with the thunder of the silver birds.

"Commander! You comin'?" said McQueen, his bandaged head hanging out of the door. Behind him two flight attendants, uniformed Army women, stood waiting, half-smiles curving their lips.

He started climbing, but had to turn again for a last look back. This time, he saw a small jet beside the terminal, portly men in suits descending, the glitter of brass and gold from a reception committee. His eye picked out a short figure—Stansfield Hart, lifting his hand in salute.

And then as Dan watched, he pivoted, his eyes flicking across the heat-shimmer, but still holding the salute, facing them now, his face grim and warlike and his back straight. And the men with him turned, too, their faces going sober and noble.

Dan started to return it. Halfway up, his arm stopped. His fingers trembled.

He gave them another, quite different gesture. He held it for a long moment, looking across at the silent group of old men. Then turned away.

"Commander?"

"I'm coming," he said. Settling his cap firmly, he hauled himself up the last steps toward home.